On the
Hillwilla Road

On the
Hillwilla Road

Melanie Forde

Mountain Lake Press
Mountain Lake Park, Maryland

On the Hillwilla Road
By Melanie Forde

Published by Mountain Lake Press

Library of Congress Control Number 2015910476
ISBN 978-0-9908089-3-0
Printed in the United States of America

Design by Michael Hentges

Cover photo by the author

This is a work of fiction. Any resemblance of
the characters to real persons living or dead is
unintentional and purely coincidental.

*To Lawrie, the archetype of resourcefulness,
who preferred the road less traveled*

AUTHOR'S NOTE

With the exception of White Sulphur Springs, Beaver, and Charleston, all of the West Virginia localities mentioned in this book are fictitious. Although "Seneca" figures in many place names in West Virginia, the state has no "Seneca County," but that mythical locale has much in common, for good and ill, with many a deeply wooded, seriously mountainous, and amazingly isolated county in southeastern West Virginia.

Contents

PROLOGUE

The golden eagle coasting on the updrafts rising from Beatrice Desmond's forty mostly wooded acres surveys a landscape little influenced by man. No, the black walnuts and maples and sycamores far below did not coexist with the indigenous people who occasionally hunted and trapped but established no permanent settlements in this deeply crenellated section of the Allegheny Mountains. Nonetheless, the trees are old. Although logging is an ongoing industry in other parts of Seneca County, these particular hardwoods in southeastern West Virginia have stood undisturbed for many decades.

In spring, shade-loving morels and pungent wild leeks flourish beneath the trees. In summer, bear cubs exercise their claws on the bark. In fall, randy bucks leave traces of antler velvet on the trunks. In winter, legions of dark-eyed juncos hunker down on the low branches, just at the edge of the deep wood, to wait out the snow squalls before carbo-loading anew on dried seeds. The woods teem with life. Little of it is human.

The satellites that orbit far, far above the trees can spot all sorts of earth-based minutiae in exacting detail. But even their sharp eyes cannot penetrate the dense hardwoods — not even in winter — to say nothing of the full canopy months from May to early October. Google Earth is able to zero in, however, on the pasture lying in the lowest section of the Desmond farm. The eye-in-the-sky can make out the red barn at the pasture's southwestern corner and, upslope, the small white farmhouse. Google Earth can identify the even smaller cabin, standing about one thousand feet south of the main house and serving as Beatrice's office. And where the creek cuts through open land, it shows up on overhead photographs, as does the small pond fed by springs and mountain runoff.

But more than thirty acres of Desmond woodland remain inscrutable, blending seamlessly with hundreds and hundreds of surrounding forest acres. So many of the daily struggles that play out beneath the trees — competitions for sunlight, water, food, shelter, territory, and mates — are hidden from both the golden eagle and the orbiting satellites, much as the daily struggles of Seneca County residents remain invisible to the culture that prevails in the rest of America.

Not surprising, most of the humans occupying this remote, rugged landscape were born here, like their parents and grandparents before them. Beatrice Desmond, born and raised in Boston, is an exception.

ONE

The Thrill of the Hunt

IT WAS AN IDEAL MORNING FOR DEER HUNTING. Two inches of powdery snow made for easy tracking, and the already rising temperature promised some comfort for the hunter, especially after the wisps of fog evaporated.

On this day after Thanksgiving, entire businesses had been shut down so workers could indulge their passion for buck season. Throughout Seneca County, pickups were tucked just off the road. Their owners had long since disappeared into the brush.

Rodney Madsen was among them. Before first light, he was already ensconced in his chosen tree stand. He had spotted the structure several weeks earlier on a five-hundred-acre, heavily wooded property. Its owner, Abel Sharp, was now too old to police the land.

Like most West Virginia males, Rodney had been exposed to hunting at an early age. Although competent enough, he had never understood the thrill that stirred the blood of so many of his counterparts. But as a well-respected businessman, the owner of a tractor dealership in nearby Marlboro County, he had to project the correct persona. Because most of his employees and most of his clients were avid deer hunters, Rodney feigned similar enthusiasm.

This Friday morning, however, he had other prey in mind.

Always aware of his image, Rodney had brought along the appropriate gear. If any passersby happened to spot him walking into the woods, they would have seen a middle-aged man in camo, with a .444 lever-action Marlin slung over his shoulder and a four-inch Gerber knife sheathed at his belt. Observers would have taken him for a typical hunter, prepared to shoot and field-dress a buck. He even carried a valid hunting license in his wallet.

For Rodney, however, the most important gear was a pair of Orion binoculars he wore around his neck. They had exceptional light-gathering capabilities, essential for a dim morning like this. And they covered a good range, with a minimum of image-wobble.

It was now just a matter of patience. Rodney had a boatload of patience.

He was waiting for Clara to stir. The only good thing about his stepdaughter living with that annoying Desmond woman was the location of her property. It was just across the road from the neglected Sharp acreage. The old tree stand currently housing Rodney was oriented away from the road and away from the Desmond farm. But Rodney had only to remove one of the back slats to get a decent view of Beatrice's house. His tinkering made the stand only a tad less stable.

From his earlier reconnaissance trips, Rodney knew the woman kept late hours. Witch hours. Her lights were often on until two in the morning. Rodney was grateful Clara had not been corrupted by such wayward habits. The early-rising teenager still had a chance of growing up a proper Christian. She would have a better chance, of course, with the right paternal guidance, Rodney thought, wishing yet again he could fill that role.

He reflected briefly on the disappointment some months back when his wife had miscarried his child. He had so hoped for a daughter. The pregnancy was the main reason for marrying Charyce Trask, Clara's mother, in the first place. He would compensate now by keeping an eye on his stepdaughter, even if Charyce no longer had charge of the girl, even if a court had declared Mike Buckhalter the sole custodial parent.

And the good Lord knows, that father of Clara's ain't worth a bucket of warm spit.

Finally, the light switched on in the bathroom. Rodney had figured out there was only one bathroom in the tiny upstairs. Clara and Beatrice apparently shared it.

Good, the light is staying on.

That meant the occupant of the bathroom was almost certainly Clara. The woman might get up at this early hour for a pit stop but was unlikely to linger. The window was clouding up, a sure sign someone was in the shower.

Little Clara is cleansing herself, God bless her!

Rodney prayed the bathroom was equipped with a fan to clear the steam. Otherwise, his carefully planned mission to check on his little girl would be for naught. He just needed to make sure she was all right. He needed to make sure she was still pure.

Rodney's prayer was answered. The bathroom mist dissipated. He could see someone moving toward the sink, just within his line of sight. At this distance, the binoculars' focus was shaky but manageable. He could make out the back of a towel-wrapped head. But nothing covered the body.

Rodney's excitement grew. Sooner or later, Clara would turn around to reach for a towel, to search for her robe — and show her stepdaddy just how much she was blooming.

All Rodney had to do was wait. And then it happened. She turned. Rodney ogled two small breasts.

Two small, perfect breasts.

He wished he were positioned higher in the sycamore, so his angle of vision could take in Clara's lower torso. But he would not be greedy. He would savor the lovely sight he now had before him.

He was so focused on those breasts that he paid little attention to his prey's face. Facial identification would be tricky at this distance, of course, even with fine binoculars. Rodney stroked his erection and sighed.

And then the worst thing imaginable happened. The lovely creature in the bathroom pulled the towel from her head. Rodney could see the hair was short and quite dark. It was not the long tumble of reddish hair that crowned Clara.

Oh, my God! It's not Clara!

When he realized he was spying on Beatrice, Rodney's manhood shriveled. He could not believe a fifty-something woman would parade around in the nude like that. Café curtains shrouded the lower windowpane, leaving the upper pane uncovered. At just the right elevation, anyone could see her nakedness.

The brazen witch! And my little Clara is being exposed to that!

Rodney realized he needed to insert himself into Clara's life, to rescue her from damnation. But how?

In his indignation, Rodney forgot how precarious his perch was. One vigorous shake of his head—to expel the image of the naked Beatrice from his brain—unbalanced him. Flailing an arm in search of the stand's partially dismantled backboard, and not finding sufficient support, he pitched forward.

It was not a free-fall but a series of falls. After his feet lurched off the stand, Rodney managed to grab a branch. But the branch was slippery with snow, and he soon lost his grip. That scene played out repeatedly, with some branches breaking under his weight.

By the time Rodney hit the ground, his velocity had slowed. Because the snow and leaf duff were deep enough to reduce the impact even further, there would be no broken bones. But the sycamore had beaten him up. He would have many bruises to explain to his intrusive wife. Worse, his slip from that first branch had wrenched his left shoulder. Rodney groaned as he inched his way upward, bracing himself against the trunk of the same sycamore that had been his undoing.

Once vertical, he tried to remember the technique his coach had used years ago, when the young Rodney dislocated the same shoulder in a wrestling match. He remembered something about slowly rolling it up and back.

"Sweet Jesus!" Rodney couldn't stifle the outburst when his first attempt sent a jagged shard of pain into his scapula. Panting, he bent forward, holding his drooping left side with his good arm. As he righted himself for another try, the injured shoulder voiced a loud pop, and the arm ratcheted back into place.

With that problem eased, Rodney surveyed the damage and noticed a dull throb in his chin. He saw the reason why: His expensive binoculars were twisted out of alignment, one eyepiece smeared with blood. The binoculars had obviously suffered multiple collisions, at least one of them with Rodney's chin.

He searched for other gear. His knife had somehow stayed strapped to his belt. His steel thermos lay dented on the ground. Where was the rifle?

Scanning the ground, Rodney saw no gun. He looked up. The Marlin's shoulder strap had snagged on a branch, only somewhat lower than the tree stand.

Noooooo!

There was no alternative but to climb back up the sycamore's crude ladder made of nailed slats leading to the stand. Rodney stood a little straighter, squared his shoulders—and gasped in pain. He began a one-armed ascent, whimpering all the way up and all the way down

TWO

Handling the Holidays

BEATRICE DESMOND COULD HANDLE LONELINESS. At least that's what she told herself this Saturday after Thanksgiving. Hadn't she spent most of the past sixteen years alone since her husband died? Hadn't she even felt some initial relief at the solitude that followed his death? In the last few years of his life, Bill hardly qualified as convivial company, to say nothing of behaving like a supportive partner. He spent much of his time railing against the world for plotting his persecution. Or, he would retreat into a Vicodin fog where work deadlines, regular meals, showers, and normal sleeping rhythms had no relevance.

So why on earth was Beatrice feeling sorry for herself *now*? Just because she was alone on a holiday weekend? Just because she missed the funny, expressive teenager who had been thrust upon her almost ten months earlier? Yes. She did indeed miss Clara Buckhalter, who was currently spending the weekend with her father, Mike.

What irony!

The previous winter, Beatrice was a relative stranger to Clara — and to the intricacies of West Virginia family ties. Nevertheless, she became a last-ditch solution when the girl, then thirteen, needed to escape from an abusive domestic situation, involving her mother, Charyce, and her stepfather, Rodney.

At the time, job obligations, space problems, geographic distance, and legal concerns prevented other Buckhalters from taking in the child. Always wary of letting new people into her world, Beatrice had to be tricked into providing safe haven for Clara. The clumsy tricksters were Eltie Davis and Ben Buckhalter.

Eltie, a Buckhalter cousin, was the veterinarian for Beatrice's small herd of llamas. Ben was both Clara's uncle and godfather, as well as builder of Beatrice's barn. He was uncomfortable with his younger brother Mike's neglect of Clara and, childless himself, tried to act as her father without criticizing Mike.

Clara's temporary shelter at the Desmond farm had become more or less permanent, even if Beatrice lacked legal authority as a foster mother. Mike Buckhalter, a master carpenter, eventually extricated himself from job obligations in Virginia's Shenandoah Valley. After returning to West Virginia, he won full custody of his daughter. To his surprise, however, she insisted on staying with Beatrice, ostensibly because the Desmond farm was fairly close to the private school where Clara had recently won a full scholarship. In reality, the girl resented the tardiness of the paternal rescue and wasn't sure she could depend on her father for more than the occasional overnight visit during school vacations.

Beatrice's review of the dizzying events of the past year now focused on the embarrassing scene in her kitchen on Thanksgiving morning. Ben and Eltie had arrived to escort Clara to a local Thanksgiving Day parade before ferrying her to her father's house, where she would stay for the long weekend. Later that afternoon, the extended family (minus Clara's mother and stepfather) would gather at that small cabin to enjoy the traditional turkey feast, prepared by Eltie's partner, Vaughn, a culinary wizard. Ben and Eltie had assumed Beatrice would follow later in her truck and join them for dinner. But then they learned Mike had not invited her.

That news infuriated Eltie, who stamped her large foot on Beatrice's tile floor. "That baby brother of yours has puppy poop for brains," she groused at Ben, who nodded his head in weary agreement.

Eltie continued her rant. "You know dang well that Vaughn wanted Beatrice included. As chief cook and bottle washer, she should be able to invite whoever she wants! Right? But no, Vaughn felt it was Mike's place to invite his guests. And you know Mike would forget his way home without a trail of breadcrumbs! So why didn't you do it for him, Ben?"

Clara pleaded with Beatrice to come along anyway, maybe even stay over to avoid the long drive home alone in the dark over twisting mountain roads. Ben argued unpersuasively that Mike was surely figuring on Beatrice's presence.

Too proud to accept the last-minute invitation and wary of Mike's actual mindset, Beatrice declined politely, made light of the snafu, and wished them all a happy celebration. Then she cited her own difficult schedule as another reason to stay home. Because of an appointment with a knee specialist on Friday morning, three hours away in Charlottesville, she needed to tuck into bed early the night before. Unfortunately, that argument did not prove sufficient to quell the uncomfortable discussion. She tried another tack.

"Besides," Beatrice said, "from what Clara tells me, Mike's cabin might burst at the seams if I imposed on his hospitality."

Of course it was the wrong thing to say. Beatrice realized this almost as soon as the words left her mouth. The memory of the collective reaction still made her squirm two days later. She envisioned how Ben had begun chewing on the inside of one cheek, how Clara had dropped her head to her chest, how Eltie had stiffened her shoulders.

Way to go, Beatrice! You did it again. You offended that feral West Virginia pride.

Eventually, she had managed to shoo everyone out the door without further loss of face. Eltie promised to save Beatrice a slice of Vaughn's famed pecan pie. Clara grabbed Beatrice in a fierce hug. And Ben said the gathering of the clan would be diminished without her. "You're kind of an honorary Buckhalter after all you've done for Clara," he added.

Now sitting at her kitchen table on Saturday afternoon, Beatrice groaned as she recalled the scene. The noise awoke Ralph, whose flews were splayed over her right sneaker. A polka-dotted, furry eyebrow twitched in her direction. Slowly the English setter sat up, arching his head backward for a thorough spinal stretch before focusing his full attention on his human. She laughed. He thumped his well-feathered tail on the floor then laid his head in Beatrice's lap. She absentmindedly stroked his blue-Belton bangs as she returned to her queasy woolgathering.

She did not doubt Ben would have enjoyed her company. He was one of the few West Virginians with whom Beatrice had developed some rapport since her move to Seneca County six years earlier. He was less guarded than most, had a kind spirit, shared Beatrice's ironic take on the world, and had a real gift of gab.

That last trait was not unusual for mountain folk, for whom storytelling, gossip, and philosophizing were primary sources of entertainment.

There was no local TV. Satellite television and Internet connectivity were relatively recent arrivals in the Southern highlands. Someone of Ben's age, in his early forties, would have spent his childhood without electronic babysitters. His conversational skill benefited from their absence.

What was unusual about Ben was his willingness to share his skill with an outlander. For most of the other Thanksgiving celebrants, however, Beatrice's presence would have inhibited conversation.

Vaughn was an exception. Although she had earned her way to the festivities by cooking for the extended family, the petite woman would have been grateful for another come-here at the table, but her status was only one reason why she might feel misplaced in a cabin packed with mountaineers. Mike's guests numbered among the few locals who knew of Vaughn's and Eltie's relationship. At best, the kinfolk didn't understand. At worst, they actively disapproved. But they were fond of Eltie — and fearful of incurring her smart-mouthed wrath. So they were always polite, albeit distant, toward the Thanksgiving chef.

Beatrice would have encountered little friendliness from other guests. Ben's wife, Amanda, was standoffish toward almost everyone — except "Uncle" Virgil, her steadfast godfather. Virgil often worked handyman jobs on Beatrice's farm yet was always ill at ease around her. And his comfort level would have been low to begin with because he would worry about table etiquette and perhaps splashing gravy on his go-to-meeting clothes.

Beatrice knew that Clara's father, Mike, had almost certainly not forgotten to invite her. In fact, he seemed to blame her for the rift between him and his daughter. Apparently, that was easier than blaming himself. He really had wanted to drop everything to come to Clara's aid the previous year, but perhaps he had seen her problems as a threat to his own ambition. The specialized carpentry gig in Virginia was lucrative. It was supposed to fund Mike's new career of crafting acoustic guitars for the glitterati of Nashville and Branson. Because of Clara, he left the job before acquiring a sufficient grubstake to launch his dream business.

Beatrice didn't comprehend all of Mike's frustrations. But she did suspect that Clara's attending The Marlboro Academy for Girls was a problem for him. A fancy prep school in the next county was a stretch for a Seneca County girl and might fill her head with lofty notions.

Still, Beatrice felt grateful that Mike grudgingly permitted Clara to continue living with her and commute to the academy.

Beatrice sighed. It would not have been much fun to break bread with the resentful Mike Buckhalter. Nevertheless, it might have been nice to share some sense of family on Thanksgiving Day, to feel like she was part of something bigger than herself—however ephemerally.

Ralph nudged Beatrice's right hand to animate it into stroking his head once again. She complied briefly but stopped as she turned to look at the clock on the kitchen wall. It read four. Glancing at the counter beneath the clock, she stared hungrily at the pristine fifth of Jack Daniel's standing there.

Too early, dammit!

She exhaled loudly between pursed lips, whistling discordantly. Ralph jerked his head upward, yodeled a cheerful response, mimicking the pitch of the human whistle but ending in a questioning tone. He dashed to the adjacent utility room and aimed his long nose at the shelf holding a large canister of dog food. He stared at Beatrice then whipped his head back in the direction of the canister.

Laughing, Beatrice rose and walked toward the setter. "You'll give yourself vertigo, Ralph. Okay, you can have an early dinner and maybe a treat afterward, huh?"

Ralph panted in enthusiastic agreement.

"For me, too, I think," she mumbled, as she scooped kibble into Ralph's bowl.

THREE
Not Exactly Norman Rockwell

ONCE RALPH WAS FED, NINETY MINUTES OF DAYLIGHT REMAINED. Yet the sun had long been tucked behind the mountain. Since mid-afternoon, the Desmond homestead had been veiled in crepuscular light. Eyeing the bourbon bottle yet again, Beatrice recalled Emily Dickinson's apt observation about the oppressive heaviness of "a certain slant of light on winter afternoons."

The oppression stemmed from the rainforest factor as much as the sun's low angle. This was not the Western mountains, where dry air gives ski resorts myriad photo opportunities featuring smiling, buff tourists sporting stylish shades to protect against the twin dazzle of sun and snow. Here the moist air conspired with the dense hardwood canopy to shroud the landscape in perpetual mist, low clouds, and fog. In certain pockets of the southern highlands, anyone wearing sunglasses on a typical January day would bump into a tree. Color perception was skewed enough without the shades. In winter's dim light, the color scheme boiled down to grays, dull blues, and necrotic browns. Even the snow often had a bluish tinge.

Noting the ghostly, insubstantial shadows cast by the dim light outdoors, Beatrice began turning on lamps. She didn't fear the arrival of Jacob Marley rattling his chains in warning. She feared the hobgoblins of her own making, phantasms that surfaced more readily in the gloom of winter than the glare of summer. With a forceful flick of an index finger, she turned on the kitchen's overhead fluorescents. It was a childishly defiant gesture, as if she could thereby banish all things that go bump in the night. As if she could ensure that the coming cold, dark season would not reprise the fugue state of the previous winter.

Last winter was her first without Kate, her closest friend. Kate Stuart had figured in Beatrice's move to Seneca County. Beatrice could not afford the real estate in her friend's neck of the woods—Augusta County,

Virginia—but she could manage the acreage price here in southeastern West Virginia. For a while she had enjoyed the best of both worlds—the peace and privacy of her little Appalachian farm and the knowledge that, when the isolation became overwhelming, her best friend was just two hours away. A day with Kate and Kate's llamas always put her in a sunny mood.

Since freshman year in college, Kate had been a constant in Beatrice's life. No stranger to abandonment, Beatrice treasured that constancy. Despite differing life paths, the connection never wavered.

The archetypal sun-kissed Florida girl, Kate looked a decade younger than her years and lived a disciplined, healthy lifestyle. Logically, she should have been around forever, long after Beatrice dissolved into a pile of bone meal. Except one day she wasn't around. The aneurysm that blew out Kate's brain also sent Beatrice into a quietly morose tailspin.

Unwilling to surrender anew to that downward spiral, Beatrice willed away the depressing thoughts. She headed for the llama barn to seek an infusion of young camelid energy. She grabbed her jacket and cane. Even though her leg had healed from last winter's fracture, she didn't want to take any chances with the snow.

Stabbing at the slippery slope with her blackthorn stick (a scarred but venerable legacy from her Connaught grandfather) Beatrice grinned as the llamas crowded the fence line closest to the house. Their irrepressible curiosity always made her smile.

She still felt like a greenhorn around them. But the arrival of two healthy babies in the past year boosted her confidence. Now weanlings yearning for their mothers on the other side of the weaning fence, the pair romped toward her as she entered their paddock. Buck puffed a short burst of melon-scented air into Beatrice's nose then levitated skyward before tucking his head down and zipping away. Dip—for Serendipity—hung back at the last minute then gave Beatrice a thorough, if shy, sniffing. Satisfied that nothing was amiss, Dip leaned in for a brisk neck rub, while Buck pranced around the human-camelid pair.

Buck's friskiness reminded Beatrice that very soon, once the weaning was complete, she must subdivide the herd along gender lines to keep the intact boy away from all the open girls. Later she would schedule

Buck's gelding. Days earlier, when she had shared that plan with Clara, the teenager protested. Clara had developed a special affinity with Buck, whose full name was Buckhalter.

"Why don't we breed him instead? Maybe with Dip, when they're old enough?"

Beatrice instantly nixed the idea. "I can barely take care of the eight I have."

"You could always sell a couple of the older ones."

That idea appalled Beatrice. She had not taken on the llamas for profit. In fact, she had never wanted any animal larger than Ralph. But fate, as usual, had other plans.

When Kate Stuart learned about the time bomb ticking inside her brain, she drafted a codicil to her will. Knowing her husband, Arthur, would have enough on his hands without dealing with his late wife's time-consuming hobby, she bequeathed her llamas to Beatrice.

For Beatrice, the llamas were a mixed blessing. She had felt incompetent and overwhelmed for months after Arthur Stuart trailered the small herd to West Virginia. It didn't help that one of the llamas was pregnant and none too happy about the little cria inside her belly. Unbeknownst to Beatrice, another, older llama was also pregnant. And so Kate's six remaining llamas became Beatrice's eight llamas.

Eight was enough. But that didn't mean Beatrice could part with any of them. They were all she had left of her best friend.

Visiting the llamas did indeed lighten Beatrice's mood on this Saturday after Thanksgiving. By the time she finished putting out new flakes of hay, graining the babies, and double-checking the weaning fence, she was humming to herself. She continued humming as she hiked back up the hill to the house. Ralph followed, joyfully tossing up the occasional fluff of snow with his long black nose.

Back in the kitchen, Beatrice noticed the blinking red light, signaling a phone message. The caller was Clara, still at her father's cabin. Sounding casual, the girl said she just wanted to chat. But then, right before hanging up, she added pensively, "Are you okay, Beatrice? I can come home if you need me."

Beatrice wondered if Clara was uncomfortable in the bosom of her family. Or, after being uprooted from several homes in the past year, was the girl worried about losing her current nest?

Beatrice promptly phoned the cabin's land line to assure her young charge that all was well. Although she sounded a bit subdued, Clara relayed some silly knock-knock jokes Virgil had shared on Thanksgiving. She described the river otter fishing in the creek parallel to her father's road. She asked whether Ralph had missed her. After reporting that the dog dutifully checked Clara's bed every morning, Beatrice described the afternoon's happy scene in the llama barn. The chat ended on that light note.

Beatrice deposited the phone in its wall cradle and turned her attention to Jack Daniel. With a practiced hand, she poured out three fingers of bourbon, tossed in six ice cubes, stirred the bronze liquid with her index finger, and inhaled deeply. She postponed her first warming sip until she relocated to her recliner in the den.

Halfway into the drink, she could almost hear her body unlock. All tension drifted away, along with morose thoughts about being alone on the long weekend. Enjoying the contentment, she allowed her mind to travel back to earlier holidays.

She recalled her elation when her brother, Bart, would arrive home from college for Thanksgiving vacation. Unable to afford wheels of his own, he usually bummed a ride to Boston from a fellow Yalie. His ETA was unpredictable, which made his eventual arrival all the sweeter. Ten years older than his little sister, Bart alternated between paternal protectiveness and fraternal teasing. In either mode, her brother was a sunny presence.

By Bart's senior year, Beatrice had figured out the basics of Thanksgiving dinner and could turn out a respectable turkey breast, boil some frozen veggies, and heat a can of prefab gravy. Bart would carve the turkey on the kitchen table, while Beatrice sorted out the place settings. She would talk and laugh so long with her brother that the turkey got cold.

That was the best part of Thanksgiving. Later they would rouse their widowed father from his alcoholic stupor in the living room. And all three Desmonds would gather, subdued, around the table. If not exactly Norman Rockwell, it nonetheless held bonding moments.

For this Thanksgiving, Bart had invited Beatrice to join him and Evie

Rudner—his fiancée and Beatrice's old friend—in his Massachusetts home. Beatrice declined, citing the misery of holiday flying and her reluctance to kennel Ralph. She did not mention her dread of yet another awkward encounter with Bart's grasping daughter, Martha.

Downing the last of her bourbon, Beatrice contemplated the holiday activities of other friends and relatives. Inevitably, her thoughts turned to Tanner Fordyce, another entry into her life during the past year. Tanner, that maddening man, lived part-time atop a Seneca County mountain with commanding views of lower altitudes. A steep, twisting, rutted road was his only connection with the hoi polloi beneath him. Beatrice wondered where he was spending his holiday. And with whom. The possible answers made her crave a second bourbon.

Before the usual internal debate began, pitting the wisdom of temperance against the need for liquid solace, the sound of two shotgun blasts boomed through Beatrice's little hollow. She chided herself for starting at the noise once she realized the source: a deer camp about a mile down the road. The hunter, who apparently enjoyed holing up in that crumbling plywood structure four or five times a year, must have claimed his buck. Beatrice hoped the trophy was indeed a deer, bagged just barely before sundown. Although she was a carnivore with no philosophical aversion to hunting, her tolerance of deer season rarely lasted through the first day. All too often, buck fever took its toll on property rights, innocent phone and electric lines, and livestock.

Although these shots had disrupted the stillness in the opposite direction from the llama barn, Beatrice peered out one window to check on her herd nonetheless. The llamas she could see were kushed and tranquil. All was well. But she couldn't resist grousing, "Damn fool hunters!"

FOUR

Hunting for a Game Plan

THE BIG RED TRUCK GROWLED TO A STOP about fifty feet short of the Gurney Mountain homestead. Ben unfolded his lanky frame from the pickup, stretched his back, and surveyed the legacy of the Buckhalter clan. He paid particular attention to his latest extension off the kitchen. A mid-October snowstorm had overtaken that project. At this elevation, above four thousand feet, winter often arrived early, and his hasty weatherproofing left something to be desired. Satisfied that the exterior was holding up, Ben entered the house and inhaled deeply. All he smelled was a slight mustiness. He listened for drips and looked for stains on ceilings or walls. The only thing amiss was a large limb, thicker than his thigh and angling skyward, just outside a kitchen window. Still holding its leaves, the blow-down had been vulnerable to that first heavy snow. Ben spotted it during an earlier visit but decided to let it age in place for a few weeks before chain-sawing it into firewood.

Ben was hard-pressed to find the time — away from his regular job or the well-maintained doublewide he shared with Amanda and Virgil. Restoring the homestead was all about Ben's hopes for his family's future. The old house would be large enough to accommodate any loved ones in need — both Virgil, so often down on his luck, and young Clara. Never again would the girl want for a safe haven among kinfolk. What's more, the renovated homestead might also spark new life into Ben's marriage. And so the Gurney Mountain legacy was a labor of love. Of course, it was also a fathomless guilt pit. Something always needed caulking, painting, or shoring up.

But there would be none of that today — not merely because of the snowy weather. Ben just didn't have the energy. That was one reason why he caved in to his crew's pleas to extend the Thanksgiving weekend for one more day of hunting. As a contractor who specialized in agricultural projects, Ben was entering his slow season anyway.

He had shrugged and told his crew he might just stalk some bucks, too. That's what he told Amanda as well. She knew otherwise. Never had Ben's hunting trips yielded venison. Amanda sensed his periodic need to be alone. Even at her most paranoid, she was never threatened by Ben's occasional turns inward, which sometimes took him from home. The survivor of a violent first marriage, she chose reliability and an even temperament in her second husband. Nor was Amanda saddened by Ben's unwillingness to share his troubled feelings with her. Wrestling with her own demons was exhausting enough without taking on her husband's.

Ben took along a minimum of appropriate gear. A multipurpose shotgun rode with him, and a blaze-orange visor cap squatted low on his brow. For Ben, however, the most important piece of equipment was the pair of beaten-up Bushnell binoculars.

They had belonged to his mother, Mary Moriarty Buckhalter. He inherited them, along with her interest in birding. For Ben, watching birds was guilt-free relaxation. Ostensibly, he had a job to do this Monday morning: to watch for any late migrants he might add to his life list and monitor the usual crowd of year-round residents. His spirits always lifted from witnessing the perseverance of the plucky chickadees, squabbling over coneflower seedpods. At the same time, his observational tasks left ample opportunity for pondering.

Only his kid brother, Mike, knew of the peace Ben derived from watching birds. Mike had shared in the childhood expeditions and appreciated the beauty of their songs in spring. But as an adult, Mike had about the same interest in bird watching as in deer hunting.

Mike and Ben had both been schooled in hunting lore. Their teacher was their father, Carl. And that was the problem. He was not a harsh taskmaster, but unlike his energetic, irreverent wife, he wasn't much fun. Carl was determined his boys would know how to put food on the table. They would understand there were no free dinners. For them to eat, something had to die.

Ben once shot a squirrel that had been raiding their mother's bird feeder. Proud of the clean shot, he and Mike brought the trophy home to show their father. Seeing the boys carelessly swinging the dead animal,

Carl chided them for their disrespect. He handed Ben and Mike a folding knife and ordered them to dress the squirrel. The rest of that weekend afternoon was spent over a stewpot, as the boys slowly simmered the chopped squirrel meat. Then, after dredging the few shriveled pieces in flour, the brothers—under Carl's solemn supervision—fried the meat and ate it.

Ben later realized it was a valuable lesson. But it left him with little desire to procure his food from anywhere but a sanitized supermarket. He and Mike were grateful the squirrel yielded so little meat, with so little taste.

Now perched in the bed of his F-250, Ben raised the binoculars to identify the vortex of scavengers circling high above. He shuddered when he spotted the gray head that distinguished a black vulture from the larger, more common turkey vulture, whose head displayed a spectacularly ugly—but harmless—accordion of reddish skin pleats. There was something sinister about that quietly gray head with its dark eyes sharp enough to spot carrion at great distances. Even the way black vultures wheeled together was sinister. While the often solitary turkey vulture, relying on exquisitely tuned olfactory senses, served as Nature's sanitation engineer, gangs of the other species occasionally spiced up their diet with the living. They had a fondness for newborn lambs.

Ben turned his binoculars toward the meadow, where dead vegetation protruded well above the snow. Clusters of drab passerines snatched seeds from the stalks. For all the fussing, the little birds shared the bounty—until two large blue jays swooped in. Chased off to the sidelines, the finches and nuthatches and chickadees indignantly scolded the larger birds, but for now the field belonged to the jays.

Suddenly depressed by the warring for seeds and survival, Ben rested his binoculars on his lap. The birds he loved could sometimes prove as disappointing as the people he loved.

The person Ben had in mind was his brother. Mike had tried to be a good host for the Thanksgiving celebration. There was no shortage of food and drink. An adept storyteller, Mike shared anecdotes from the months spent working in Virginia. He cracked everyone up with his tale of the wealthy homeowner, newly ensconced in one of the estates Mike had helped build.

When a cell of thunderstorms scoured the central Shenandoah Valley, the irate homeowner called the builder. At great volume, he complained that his new well had gone dry. The perplexed builder asked if the homeowner's lights were on. "Of course not. The storm knocked out the power!" For the next ten minutes, the builder patiently explained how the well pump and pressure tank required electricity to send water to the tap.

There's nothing a born-here likes quite so much as confirmation of the utter helplessness of a come-here.

But Mike's party was eclipsed by a little surprise: a five-foot-two, eyes of blue, curvaceous blonde. Mike had chosen this family dinner to introduce Loretta Lowther, his new live-in girlfriend, who bore an unsettling resemblance to his ex-wife, Charyce.

Loretta's shy demeanor had little in common with Charyce's brashness. But her social awkwardness wasn't much of an improvement. She kept confusing her guests' names. At one point, she called Amanda "Charyce."

Ben's cousin Eltie, never one for diplomacy, responded by hooting, "No, honey, this here is the lady of the Buckhalter clan. She's the *real* Mrs. Buckhalter."

"Why thank you, Eltie," Amanda said, sharing a rare bonding moment with the tall vet. Then Amanda turned to her husband, placed a territorial hand on his forearm and added, "It's just that I married the *right* Buckhalter brother."

The two siblings promptly engaged in clumsy banter, trying to calm the troubled waters. The tension did not ease until Vaughn got Mike talking about the history of his cabin. Nevertheless, a few more eye rolls would pass among the female relatives—with the exception of Clara, who kept her eyes down while she picked at her turkey.

Only recently had the girl signaled any willingness to forgive her father. She was still angry with him for failing to come promptly to her rescue last winter. Her stepfather, Rodney, at his deviant worst, had been spying on her while she slept. Her mother, Charyce, had become furious and blamed her—even struck Clara. That's when the girl had grabbed at the chance to live with Beatrice and her animals. Even after Mike's return to Seneca County, Clara didn't spend much time with him. As her godfather, Ben was both gladdened and worried about her willingness to stay at her father's cabin through the long holiday weekend.

He hoped for a happy rapprochement, but he was also a realist about Mike. Ben didn't need a psychology degree to recognize that Clara would feel displaced yet again by Mike's engagement to Loretta. He doubted she would leap at the chance to spend Christmas with those two.

Now focused on *that* holiday, Ben leaned against the cab's rear window and hatched plans. Amanda was unlikely to reconsider taking in Clara on a long-term basis, what with Virgil being a permanent resident. But Virgil's back surgery six months earlier had been a success, and he was able to resume working part-time. Surely his back could handle sleeping on the living room couch for a few days, so Clara could have the only other bedroom. Amanda might just agree to that, in view of her icily hostile reaction to Mike and Loretta.

Happy to have figured out a game plan, if not a comprehensive solution, Ben raised his binoculars once again to locate a tail-twitching Carolina wren. Smiling, he listened to the little bird's raucously cheerful "teakettle, teakettle, teakettle" refrain.

FIVE

Bonding over Bimbos

KATE ONCE ASKED IF BEATRICE ACTUALLY HAD DOUBLE-X chromosomes in view of her intense dislike of shopping. But here Beatrice was, one week after Thanksgiving, helping Clara find new clothes. Well, sort of. Beatrice minimized the disagreeable task by combining it with her almost equally unpleasant weekly grocery run to the Marlboro Walmart. While she dragged herself up and down the food aisles, she sent Clara off to the Juniors apparel section. Beatrice wasn't sure Walmart's selection of clothing was adequate, but there were precious few brick-and-mortar alternatives locally.

The shopping expedition traced back to Thanksgiving dinner, when Vaughn had noticed Clara's wrists protruding from her sweater cuffs. Vaughn took Mike aside and suggested the need for a wardrobe update. A quick scan of his daughter revealed that the fourteen-year-old had shot up more than an inch in the past half year. The jeans that once scuffed along the floor now dusted her anklebones. The next day, Mike produced a compressed wad of twenty dollar bills and told Clara to pick up a few new jeans and tops — with Beatrice playing chauffeur.

Once again, Beatrice found herself resenting the parental duties thrust upon her. But she reminded herself Clara was a good kid and acknowledged that Clara's relatives often shuttled the girl to various appointments. Still, on this late afternoon, Beatrice couldn't keep her mind off the chores left undone in her office. An editing deadline loomed. And two translations needed dispatching sooner rather than later.

Beatrice had earned abundant goodwill from Wolfgang Pohl, director of the Washington, D.C., think tank where she had worked, telecommuting for more than two decades. Starting as a lowly translator, she became Wolfgang's jack-of-all-trades, supporting every phase involved in publishing his foreign-policy quarterly and his weekly blog. Even though he would give her slack if she needed it, Beatrice had never missed a deadline and was loath to start now.

Despite the mess on her desk, the institute was experiencing a slow spell. The holidays didn't help. Fewer submissions to review, edit, or translate meant a smaller paycheck for a contract worker like Beatrice. A reduced paycheck sowed a pip of panic in her stomach lining. A childhood of economic hardship kept her mindful of financial peril. Her panic was not rational; her native frugality had created a decent nest egg. But her long experience with the Cosmic Chuckle taught her to be alert for disaster lurking around any given corner.

Freed from the checkout lane and lighter by two hundred dollars, Beatrice anxiously revisited the new expenses in her life. A steep price tag had come with Kate's llama legacy. Building the necessary agricultural infrastructure had made a five-digit dent in Beatrice's savings. The llamas' regular maintenance was not cheap, either.

And now there was Clara. The Buckhalters saw to the cost of her medical care, her school needs, her clothing, etc. But keeping a refrigerator stocked for two instead of one added up, as did the extra gas mileage. Beatrice bit back a new surge of resentment.

Leaning against her full grocery cart, she glanced at her watch again. *C'mon, Clara!* Only an hour had passed since their arrival at Walmart, but that didn't soothe Beatrice's deadline jitters. After another twenty minutes, she spotted the girl going through checkout. Clara lifted a limp hand, waggled her fingers, and squeezed her eyes in exasperation. She was stuck behind a large woman with a huge assortment of junk food on the conveyor belt and a huge problem locating the wallet inside her cavernous purse.

Finally, Clara emerged, two bulging plastic bags bobbling against both hips. "Sorry, sorry, sorry! I hate Walmart!"

The stern expression on Beatrice's face evaporated. Guilt now replaced resentment. She flashed on all the ways Clara helped with the llamas, with housework, with Ralph — especially during the months when Beatrice had been less than ambulatory.

She feigned interest in Clara's purchases, but the teenager evinced little enthusiasm for show and tell. Undeterred, Beatrice pressed on, in the belated realization that a halfway decent foster mother should have some input about her charge's wardrobe. She often took Clara's sense of responsibility for granted, so another stab of guilt poked her. Beatrice recalled her own childhood, when she was forced to mature at an early age. At times, that had made her feel special. At other times, she questioned whether she had really earned her father's trust or was merely invisible to him.

Recognizing that Clara deserved better, Beatrice peered into the bags, as the bored teenager lifted various apparel items for inspection. The cursory check proved Clara would not be parading around like a hooker. The tags identified the jeans as sitting slightly below the waist. No ridiculous low-riders for Clara! The sizes were one level above what Clara had been wearing, so inappropriate tightness was unlikely. The tops were sweatshirts or long-sleeved tees devoid of any graphics.

"Looks like you'll be well stocked for a while, unless you have another growth spurt."

"I guess," Clara replied with a shrug.

"You don't sound very enthused about your purchases," Beatrice prodded.

"Oh, they're okay. I just hate shopping." She stuck out her tongue in disgust and shuddered.

"You, too?" Beatrice exclaimed with delight. "I thought I was the only female who felt that way. With me, it's about having to wade through all the people, wait for a dressing room then wait in the checkout line." She stopped herself from sharing another peeve: her perennial discomfort over the cost of any goods she bought.

No need to dump that on the kid.

Instead, she said, "Shopping online is a lot easier. Of course, you're never sure about the fit."

"I guess."

Clara's newfound parsimony with words set off a klaxon inside Beatrice's brain. She sorted through the possible explanations: Lousy body image? Depression? Worry about not dressing like the more affluent girls at Marlboro Academy?

That close call with Rodney the Pervert could possibly make Clara uncomfortable with her body—right at the age when the typical girl is bombarded with disturbing developments like cramps and bleeding every month, zits, breasts that refuse to grow, or breasts that grow at a far greater rate than her sexual IQ.

The pair walked through the parking lot in silence. Beatrice searched her memory for earlier warning signs. Clara had occasionally gone nearly silent for a day or so after some family crisis, like the last time her mother raised a hand to her. The week since Thanksgiving was marked by another quiet spell. Normally eager to share her observations, often with admirable powers of articulation, Clara had given only a meager account of the holiday weekend. Several times she expressed discomfort over Beatrice's exclusion. Did Clara think it would be ill-mannered to inform Beatrice about the food and conversation she had missed? Maybe. Maybe not.

As she got behind the wheel of her pickup, Beatrice conjured one likely sore spot. Once her passenger was strapped in, she asked, "So, you didn't say much about this Loretta person. Is she nice?"

Clara snapped her head to the left and stared, disbelieving, at Beatrice. After a heartbeat, she said, "Define nice."

"Was she decent toward you?"

"She called me 'Pudding' and offered to fix my 'pretty wittle braid.'"

"Ugh," Beatrice groaned. "Extremely annoying but hardly criminal."

"Annoying? You think? She talks like a baby! Probably because she has a baby-sized brain. A tiny brain and big boobs!" Clara folded her arms and slumped down in her seat.

"I take it you're not going to be painting each other's toenails any time soon?"

"Oh, gross, Beatrice! She's just so... What's that old-timey word I've heard you use? What is it you call a woman who's dumb and slutty and embarrassing?"

"Bimbo?"

"That's it!" Clara shouted. "She's a bimbo! My father is living with a bimbo! It's mortifying!"

Beatrice couldn't help it. She erupted in laughter. Feeling Clara's indignant glare, she attempted an explanation. "Women with brains, we have a real thing about bimbos. And there are just so, so many of them.

Bimbos to the left of us, bimbos to the right of us…"

Beatrice risked moving her eyes from the road to read Clara's face. The glare morphed into a curious stare, then a smile. Then a laugh.

"I hate people," Clara said, shaking her head but smiling.

"Me, too," Beatrice agreed, reaching over to squeeze Clara's arm.

SIX

Quirk Management

No fashion model, no dancer, no physical therapist had
keener body awareness than Charyce Trask Buckhalter Trask Madsen. As
she sidled up to her husband, scrolling through the inventory management
display on his QuickBooks software, she knew the precise angle to curve
her lower back as she leaned in to examine all those five-digit tractor
prices. The optimal angle would showcase her high, firm rump. At the
same time, she clasped her hands between her knees, so her upper arms
would squeeze her breasts just enough to amplify her cleavage, but not too
much to generate the unattractive chest wrinkles that suggested middle
age. The posture was intended to simulate unintended lasciviousness.

Charyce had deduced from the men in her life that, although they
expected access to their women whenever and wherever, they wanted the
fiction of being the sole initiators of sex. It was folly to appear sexually
assertive. So she postured, accessible rump in air, as the helpless victim
of hormonal urges triggered by the mere presence of a virile man. That
ploy had proven hugely successful for Charyce, enabling her to extract all
sorts of benefits.

Usually. Charyce's kohled eyes shifted from the computer screen to
the left side of Rodney's face. His gaze had not strayed from the monitor.
Fuck!

Affecting befuddlement over the numbers on the screen, she placed
her left palm on the desk, while her right hand rested on the back of
Rodney's chair and her breasts "accidentally" grazed his left shoulder.
"Dang, lover-man, I don't know how you keep all them squiggly columns
straight. Income. Expenses. What have you. All that stuff would make
my brain explode. I'm glad I married me such a smarty pants." With her
right index finger, she traced a line up Rodney's neck into his thinning
hair and twirled a stray lock.

"C'mon, Charyce, I gotta finish going over this new inventory before tomorrow."

Charyce combed her fingers up the back of Rodney's head and sighed. "I just worry about you working so hard. All day at the dealership. And here it is bedtime and you're still hard at it. A man needs his rest. And a girl can get awful lonely up in that big ol' bed." She tugged playfully on a hank of hair.

Rodney jerked his head away — and gasped, grabbing for his injured shoulder.

"Aw, sugar, is that still hurting?" Charyce patted the shoulder lightly. "How about I run a nice hot bath for my wounded hunter? Think that might help the boo-boo go bye-bye?"

Rodney grunted, "Maybe later. Gotta finish this first."

"Whatever you want," Charyce said dully, no longer able to maintain the sweet tone of wifely concern.

She retreated in mincing steps, her three-inch sling-backs tapping on the tile floor like a toy poodle's overgrown toenails. After closing the door to her husband's home office, she pulled off her shoes and plodded flatfootedly up the carpeted stairs. A litany of curses scrolled through her brain. She surprised herself when she heard "goddamned prick" come from her mouth. She paused to gauge the audio level of that slip. No, there was no way Rodney could have heard her.

Once upstairs, Charyce muttered, "Hunter, my ass! That boy couldn't catch hisself a deer if it fell off a cliff and landed in his pickup bed." Charyce had no love for venison. She certainly had no interest in cooking deer meat. But a freezer full of venison could significantly reduce her supermarket bills. Rodney, ever the businessman, allotted five hundred dollars every month to the food budget. The money covered her expenses at Food Festival but afforded little leeway for diverting part of the grocery funds into her secret savings account. She had to rely on other household expenses for skimming opportunities.

"Ain't like he's short on cash," she continued, as she entered the bathroom. "Not if he can order up all them big balers." In her seemingly casual perusal of Rodney's accounting data, Charyce — who had no problem multiplying multi-digit figures, as long as they were preceded by a dollar sign — concluded her husband's tractor dealership was thriving.

What wasn't thriving was their sex life. And that was problematic. Sex was the glue that kept Rodney by her side. Theirs was not a marriage of kindred spirits. Their evenings and weekends did not sparkle with witty repartee. Apart from a shared appreciation of material comforts, they had few goals in common. It wasn't as though they were planning on starting a new family. Charyce had undergone a tubal ligation not long after Clara was born. The last thing she wanted was more stretch marks.

She did not share her aversion to motherhood with her husband any more than she clued him in about the sterilization procedure over a decade earlier. But then, hadn't Rodney outfoxed her as well? Given her past experience, Charyce naturally assumed that regular booty calls would be enough to secure half of Rodney's assets. Not too long after his first overnight stay at her apartment, however, she realized his libido had some quirks. Her first clue came one night when, as he approached climax, Rodney moaned, "Oh, Clara!" into Charyce's ear.

But that was a quirk she could work with. Until Clara spoiled everything. When the teenager realized she was the focus of Rodney's interest, she ran off to other relatives — and promptly spilled her guts. Charyce tried to reason with the girl. Didn't Clara owe her mother for bringing her into this world? Couldn't she put up with Rodney's idiosyncrasies to be on easy street?

The girl didn't appreciate her mother's logic. Charyce lost patience. And that awful Desmond woman witnessed the meltdown. Then everything unraveled. With Clara removed from her mother's custody, Rodney started backing out of the engagement.

"But I always got me a Plan B," Charyce said to herself, winking at her reflection in the bathroom mirror.

Slowly, she stripped off her clothes and coolly appraised every inch of exposed flesh. Frowning at the pooched-out upper abdominal ridge, she reached for the diet pills in the medicine cabinet. The fifteen pounds she had deliberately gained to fake a pregnancy — and thereby coerce Rodney into recommitting to the engagement — might have enhanced her bosom, but other portions of her anatomy jiggled less attractively. She was having difficulty losing the weight. Months after the alleged miscarriage, she was still ten pounds too heavy.

Nevertheless, her reflection told her she was still one fine piece of ass. She looked younger than most of her contemporaries. Men, normal men, would sprout a hard-on if she so much as crooked an index finger at them. But Rodney's quirk posed a challenge.

She leaned in to scrutinize her face more closely. She liked what she saw. The skin was still firm. The only wrinkles could be explained away as laugh lines. And her makeup job made her lips pouty and her eyes sultry. She looked like one foxy woman. A delectably experienced woman.

"Shit!" she exclaimed, blinking from a sudden insight. Charyce opened the medicine cabinet again and pulled out a bottle of makeup remover. She passed the oily pad over her eyes repeatedly until the smears of mascara, eyeliner, and shadow faded. She rubbed cold cream into her lips. Sniffing her wrists, she wrinkled her nose at the heady fragrance of Womanessence, a cheap Chanel No.5 wannabe. Then she ran the shower. As the bathroom filled with steam, Charyce stepped into the tub and scrubbed.

When she emerged, she pouted at the sight of her wet blonde hair. The wrong color. The wrong length. But with the help of her hair dryer, mousse, and styling brush, she could come close to the right texture: full and curly and slightly wild. When her hair was dry and poufy, she gathered it into loose, short ponytails on either side of her head. Smiling, Charyce thought she had dropped a decade. She enhanced the effect with pale pink lipstick.

Still naked, she walked to the bedroom to inspect her wardrobe options. She briefly considered donning her Naughty Nurse costume—worn on Halloween, the last time she and Rodney had sex. She wore the outfit while greeting the little trick-or-treaters at the front door. Several mothers accompanying the youngsters turned tail and dragged their daughters and wide-eyed sons away without collecting their candy. When Rodney came home from work, he was excited to see his wife sexually overwhelming a cluster of children. He relished the symmetry of her spilling out of her costume as she spilled candy into little Jack-o'-Lanterns. Within fifteen minutes the front porch lights went out, and Rodney bounded up the stairs, two at a time, as he looked up Naughty Nurse's short skirt.

"Naw, that ain't gonna cut the mustard this time," Charyce said, casting the outfit aside. Then she remembered an alternative she had purchased years earlier but never deployed because it hid too much of her charm. She regarded the frilly, white Victorian-style nightgown, a crafty smile spreading across her lips. The top buttoned nearly up to her chin. The sleeves were long. But the full skirt was short. Very short.

Now appraising herself in the full-length bedroom mirror, Charyce stroked her smooth crotch and congratulated herself for investing in the most extreme waxing option during her recent visit to Marlboro Old Town's nail salon — a one-stop center for female grooming and tanning needs. Before donning the nightie, without benefit of panties underneath, she thought of one more detail. She padded to the hall closet and fished around for the bottle of Jean Naté after-bath lotion. Clara was crazy for that crisp, lightly acidic smell and often used it for special occasions.

Charyce splashed the lotion on her inner arms and inner thighs. Then she walked to the window and opened the curtains. All she saw outside was formless darkness, but she hoped a car might pass by. Before going downstairs to arouse Rodney, she badly needed to feel aroused herself. Fantasizing about being coveted by some dark and dangerous man on the street below, she stood by the window, poured more Jean Naté into a palm, dipped a middle finger into the liquid and languidly spread it around one nipple, then the other, until both hardened.

Charyce set her jaw, closed the curtains and dropped the deceptively chaste nightgown over her head. Looking into the mirror, she twirled lightly to see how much the hem would lift — and reveal. More than enough to catch Rodney's eye, she felt sure. Then she slipped downstairs and called out in a girlish tremolo, "Rodney? You there? Baby had a bad nightmare and needs her daddy!"

SEVEN

You Gotta Love Karma

NIGHT OWL THOUGH SHE WAS, Beatrice usually dragged herself out of bed before Clara headed down the road to rendezvous with her ride to school. The Buckhalters had an arrangement with a neighbor lady who worked at a medical supply shop near the Marlboro Academy. In exchange, Ben and Virgil would make occasional repairs for her, for material costs only, in return for her playing chauffeur. The scheduling wasn't perfect. Clara had to wait two hours after her last class before catching the ride home. She usually filled the gap with homework.

The schedule left Beatrice without much face time to keep her charge on track. Of course, she wouldn't really know what to do if Clara did slip off that metaphoric track. She supposed she could seek Mike's intervention but doubted it would be productive. Ben was a likelier alternative, but being an uncle he had limited authority.

For now, Beatrice resolved merely to encourage conversation and listen. Before nine in the morning, however, her conversational skills left something to be desired. On this particular morning, she and Clara exchanged trivial observations about Ralph's bangs and Dip's luxurious lashes. Then Beatrice asked the teen to set aside some evening time to help install a new hay rack in the barn, a task that needed four hands. Clara cheerfully agreed. That was expected; Clara liked feeling useful. Beatrice shamelessly concocted the odd chore to boost the girl's self-worth. She didn't have much more in her meager bag of parental tricks.

"It's the blind leading the blind," she mumbled to herself, as she stood by the kitchen window and watched Clara trudge down the driveway. Shaking off a shiver of inadequacy, Beatrice warmed her palms on her teacup and willed her mind to focus on business.

She needed to call Evie for an update on Tanner Fordyce's autobiography. Two years earlier, a small Boston publisher had accepted Tanner's manuscript. Evie Rudner, a Northern Virginia publicist, got into the act to hype the book, which was on a fast track to bookstores until Beatrice stumbled across some inconvenient facts.

The manuscript abounded in lies, even by autobiographical standards. For one thing, Tanner Fordyce wasn't really Tanner Fordyce. The dashing venture capitalist and philanthropist had come into the world with the more ethnic name of William Francis Berrigan. He had not grown up with a silver spoon clenched between perfectly straight, white teeth. His up-from-bootstraps rise, launched from a gritty Boston suburb, was much more interesting — and potentially embarrassing if actively concealed. Publisher and publicist alike insisted on a rewrite, and Evie dragooned her old friend Beatrice for the task. Given her research and editing background, Beatrice was certainly competent. Her proximity to Tanner's West Virginia retreat facilitated regular working sessions. And a novice like Beatrice cost much less than a professional ghostwriter.

The collaboration had begun with mutual aversion. But as Beatrice unearthed the human being beneath the persona, she liked what she saw. She didn't always like the feelings Tanner stirred up, however. Her romantic history nurtured no faith in a happily-ever-after ending. And she was far too serious — and cautious — to enjoy a casual romp with anyone.

Beatrice had already received payment for her six months of collaboration. And the credit she would earn on publication could open some new doors professionally, if she wanted to test her wings beyond Wolfgang's aerie.

At last report, the book might hit the market before year's end. Her direct collaboration with Tanner had concluded months earlier, but the publisher roped Beatrice into several editing sessions — often because Tanner himself was unavailable. She had seen him last in October. Evie's Virginia office was the venue that brought together the author, his de facto ghostwriter, the Boston publisher, and the publishing house's chief editor to hammer out the final details.

On that occasion, the Fordyce persona was working overtime. He arrived with a case of ridiculously expensive champagne, popped corks without spilling a drop, and regaled everyone with anecdotes about his latest trip to Afghanistan, where he had arranged yet another supply convoy for Doctors Without Borders, his favorite charity.

Beatrice wanted to fade into Evie's bleached cedar woodwork. She had always felt awkward around strangers. And the focal point of this gathering, Tanner, was acting more like a stranger than the man she had come to like and admire.

Nearly two hours into that meeting, Beatrice ascertained that the editing stage was indeed over, and an approximate release date was set. With those two meager facts in her brain, she looked for a corner where she might retreat. She found a likely spot, sat down, and pretended to sip from her champagne flute, as she scanned a handout from the publisher.

In reality, she was making a mental list of the errands she needed to run on the long drive back to West Virginia. When country folk stray into civilization, they take advantage of opportunities to stock up on hard-to-find items—like a new dog bed for Ralph, new halters for the growing weanlings, real French bread, Chinese chili paste, and something else.

Before she could remember the fifth item, someone had stolen the glass from her hand, seized that hand, and pulled her out of her chair. Of course, it was Tanner.

Moving her back into the midst of celebrants, he began lobbying for Beatrice to receive more prominent credit for her contribution to the autobiography. With a hand on her shoulder, he extolled her editing, research, and writing chops and insisted that the book would have been impossible "without my Boswell."

Beatrice reflexively shrugged away from Tanner's touch then realized she looked like a petulant child. She relented. There was no escaping. Conflicted emotions flooded her.

Seeing her discomfort, Tanner winked at Beatrice with malicious glee and continued with his inflated praise. It took another two minutes before he brought his promotional monologue to a close.

As the group drifted toward the exit, Beatrice caught Tanner's eye and raised her middle finger to her lower eyelid, ostensibly to flick a speck from her eyelashes. She let the finger rest there long enough, however, to send a defiant message that would be unmistakable to a fellow blue-collar Bostonian. Then she smiled beatifically. Tanner burst out laughing. He covered by pretending to find one of his colleague's comments uniquely amusing.

Smiling over that memory, Beatrice punched in Evie's number. The early hour of the call increased the likelihood of catching her workaholic friend.

"Son of a bitch, I was just about to call you."

"You lie."

"You suck," Evie quipped nonchalantly. "No, really, I have news about the autobiography."

"That's what I was hoping," Beatrice said. "Any further word on the date?"

"Now it looks like mid-January. Too bad. We were hoping to cash in on holiday sales. But this gives me time to plant more seeds. Pity you were an upfront payment. I'm optimistic about the buzz."

"Damn. I was hoping for earlier."

"Hey, if you need a ghosting recommendation before then, I'm sure Edward would have no problem with that," Evie said, referring to the publisher.

"That would be helpful. But I guess I was also looking for closure."

"You sound like my old psych professor," Evie groaned. "Everything was about closure. But why do you need it? Oh wait! I bet I know. For some reason, you think you need to wash a certain man out of your hair."

"Oh, shut up."

"Struck a nerve, did I?" Evie snorted triumphantly. "What's been going on with you two? You guys looked downright conspiratorial as we were leaving that last meeting."

"Not a thing has been going on, thank you very much. That was the last time I laid eyes on him."

"Aw, damn. I knew he was off to one of his favorite dirt-bag countries. Has he at least emailed you?"

"Not a word," Beatrice answered, unable to stifle a sigh. "Probably just as well."

"Just as well, my ass! I'll see what info I can dig up. And by the way, publication will not mean closure. It could be very useful to include you in a few interviews about the book. You know—some nonsense about a Southie Mick being the perfect choice to bring to life Fordyce's gritty roots in Boston's North Shore."

"I am not from Southie."

"Yeah, yeah, but right next door. And now you're right next door to him in the wilds of West Virginia. Ya gotta love karma. Hey, there might be an angle in that, too!" Evie chuckled.

"Not if you want to keep those expensively capped teeth!"

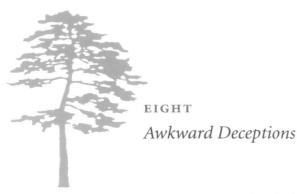

EIGHT

Awkward Deceptions

SETTLED INTO THE SOFA, Amanda split her focus between the laptop on her knees and a folder balanced on an adjacent pillow. Meanwhile, the television featured contestants vying for prize money on *Jeopardy!* Virgil, devoted to game shows, periodically prodded his goddaughter to join in the competition.

"C'mon, Amanda, I bet you know this one."

Without looking up from her accounting chores, Amanda complied. "What's Sherlock Holmes's address?"

"Dang, if you ain't right! You always was the smartest little thing! I bet you're smarter than that Alex Trebek."

From the kitchen, Ben shouted, "Do I know how to pick 'em or what?"

Although Amanda continued keying data into her spreadsheet, a tiny smile softened her lips.

Ben dried the last dinner pan, popped a can of beer, and headed for the living room. He refrained from offering beer to Virgil, who had just downed a pill to quiet a back spasm, or to Amanda, who considered beer low class. Since her first marriage, she also feared hard liquor. Whiskey had done nothing to improve her former husband's perpetual ill humor.

Ben collapsed into the sofa beside his wife, gave her shoulder an affectionate squeeze, and took a long swallow. "So can I go ahead and invite Clara for all of Christmas vacation? I know we agreed on the 24th and 25th, but I was hoping for the full ten days."

"Ben! I've got to enter these figures. I think the co-op overcharged you for that T1-11 siding."

"I don't envy Lester when you call him on it tomorrow. But can't you spare just a minute? I'd like to start the ball rolling this evening."

Amanda exhaled dramatically and closed her laptop. "All right. I don't really see her staying with her father and that Loretta for any length of time. Goodness, I don't think it's proper for a teenager to be exposed to cohabitation."

Ben grinned at Amanda's predictably prissy choice of words. He found Loretta a bit dim but likable enough—certainly an improvement over Charyce. He didn't think Clara would be morally scarred from knowing her father was having premarital sex. The knowledge that a new girlfriend had priority over a daughter was another matter, albeit one that would carry little weight with Amanda. So Ben opted to play up the moral issue instead. Amanda would have loathed the poorly educated Loretta regardless, but she needed to justify her bitchy reaction. The evils of "cohabitation" were as good a justification as any.

A few days earlier, Ben had mentioned the small size of Mike's cabin and rhetorically wondered how much Clara would overhear. Then he watched that casual observation register with Amanda. It was manipulative of him, for sure. But a certain degree of manipulation figured in the best of marriages. As long as it worked both ways, Ben's Catholic conscience was clear.

"Great!" he said. "Then we'll have her over here for the entire Christmas vacation. We could invite Mike and Loretta for Christmas dinner. S'ppose we could have Charyce drop by the night before? Yeah, I know. I'd just as soon never see her again, myself. But she's still family because of Clara. And I think the kid needs some kind of connection with her mother. A supervised holiday visit would fit the bill, dontcha think?"

Virgil clapped his hands and said, "It'll be a real Christmas with Clara in the house! Maybe I can rig up that old sleigh on the roof. Clara used to love that."

"You'll do no such thing, Uncle Virgil!" Amanda said. "I won't have you up on any ladder with your back only just healing. Besides, Clara is much too old for silly Santa decorations. As for Christmas Eve, Ben, two big dinners in a row? Really? If we have to invite Charyce, can't it just be for dessert?"

Ben mentally blessed Virgil for lending his enthusiasm to the plans. "Sure, that'll work. Now, what about Beatrice?"

"What about her?" Amanda asked dully.

"Well, she got overlooked on Thanksgiving. It would only be polite to ask her for Christmas dinner. I hate to think of anyone being alone on Christmas."

"I'm sure she has plans of her own," Amanda insisted.

"If she does, she can always say no. But with her around, I imagine Mike and Loretta would mind their Ps and Qs. They can get awfully lovey-dovey."

Ben's ploy worked.

"I saw quite enough of Loretta's fawning on Thanksgiving," Amanda said with a shudder. "I suppose I can handle another person at the table, if I get a big turkey." She sighed in resignation.

"You're a keeper!" Ben gushed, leaning over to kiss her cheek. Before she could add further objections, he bolted for the kitchen to make the call.

"Hey, godkid!" Ben boomed into the phone as Clara picked up.

"Oh. Hi, Ben."

"I take it you were expecting someone else?"

"My friend Leslie. We were gonna talk about a book report for *The Scarlet Letter*."

Ben dimly remembered reading that novel but was sure he was a high school senior before he did. "Heavy stuff for fourteen-year-olds. Good for you for being able to tackle it."

And good for Marlboro Academy for challenging the kids.

"I guess."

"I won't keep you long, but I wanted to firm up plans for Christmas. Haul out the big suitcase. We're gonna put you to work here for your whole vacation. Uncle Virgil got one of those darn jigsaw puzzles. A snow scene, so he won't get to square one without your help. And Amanda needs your expertise putting sprinkles on the Christmas cookies. And me, I need company for Mass. Your aunt won't set foot in a Catholic church, and Uncle Virgil worries about the roof caving in if he trots his sinful self into any house of God. So it's you and me."

"Only if I can finally go to Midnight Mass."

"I reckon you're old enough."

"Will there be lots of carols and candles?" Clara asked.

"Candles and carols and hemlock garlands all over the place. And if we're lucky, Leroy Baumgartner will play his trumpet solo of 'Silent Night.' He'll send chills up your spine."

"A trumpet? In church?"

"If trumpets are good enough for the angels, I expect they're good enough for us mortals."

"Oh, right," Clara said. "I forgot about all those paintings of Christmas angels with long golden horns."

"And if you play your cards right, I'll make eggnog when we get back. The real stuff, to warm the tummy on a snowy Christmas Eve."

"You make it sound like a movie scene."

"It'll be better than a movie scene," Ben insisted. "As long as you're part of it."

"And maybe we can all watch *It's a Wonderful Life* together? Unless you think Uncle Virgil will get too teary-eyed?"

"Like you won't?"

"Not me!" Clara protested. "I only cry in Bad Spit movies."

"How's that?"

"Brad Pitt. I can't stand him. He's a crying shame."

"He does mumble a lot," Ben chuckled.

"I know! I can hardly understand anything he says."

Ben laughed, relieved that his niece was in good spirits. Absorbed in happy thoughts, he ended the call without remembering to extend a Christmas dinner invitation to Beatrice.

Clara smiled as she hung up the phone. The smile faded as she, too, remembered Beatrice, who had just entered the kitchen. In an instant, Clara decided to prevent a repetition of the Thanksgiving gaffe. She would invite Beatrice herself. She would worry about clearing it with Ben later.

"That was Ben and he wants me to spend Christmas vacation at his place. And, umm, he wants you, too. To come to dinner, I mean. With us. On Christmas Day. Can I tell him yes?"

Recognizing Clara's artless, well-intended shuffle, Beatrice tugged on the girl's pony tail. "Damn if I didn't just make other plans! My brother Bart wants to drive down to visit Evie for the holidays. They'll drive together out here. Suddenly, he's become the king of road trips."

It was a lie, of course. But considering the weather in late December,

Beatrice could cite slippery road conditions somewhere along the route as the reason for a last-minute cancellation. She had little desire to be the fifth wheel at the Buckhalters but was touched by Clara's sensitivity. Scarred or not, Clara had all the makings of an upstanding adult.

Like many too-forthright West Virginians, however, she needed to work on her powers of deception.

NINE

Fitting In, Sticking Out

Dear Diary,

It's been a long time since I wrote. So hold tight. There's a lot to catch up on.

Christmas is coming up and I'm not sure what I should do. I feel bad about not being with Beatrice and, the more I think of it, wonder if her brother really will be visiting her for the holidays. Maybe she lied because she realized Ben never got around to inviting her to join all of us at his place. Or maybe she doesn't want me for Christmas. I don't even know whether she celebrates Christmas. She never goes to church.

Originally I was thinking about staying with Daddy. He SAYS he wants me to spend Christmas with him. But I wasn't all that thrilled about seeing dumb Loretta too. If I had to watch her and Daddy slobber all over each other I'd probably hurl. She's such a pasty-faced hillbilly. She can't speak right. "Was you always such a pretty little thaing?" Like I'm supposed to be all flattered that she called me pretty. And she's always pushing those big boobs in everyone's face.

And you won't believe this but a while back Momma called to talk about the holidays. That was the first time I heard from her in weeks! She says she misses me so much. Hah! If she misses me so much how come she doesn't visit me? She could have come to the maple festival Ben took me to in October. I asked her to. She was too busy, she says. Hah!

She says Rodney misses me too. Yuck! So then she gets pouty about not having me "to home" for Christmas. Yup, Dear Diary, that's how she said it. I overheard Ben and Amanda talking about Momma one day and Amanda called her "flat-faced trailer trash." Amanda can be a real pain, but Momma sometimes DOES talk like trailer trash. It's so embarrassing.

Anyways, Momma claims Rodney wants a real family Christmas. It wouldn't be a Christian day without the family all together, he says. Can you believe she told me that? He's not MY family. I don't care if Momma did marry him. She acts like he never did anything wrong!

It will be weird to have Christmas without Momma. I'm still mad at her for how she reacted to the whole Rodney mess. But she's still my Momma, the only one I'll ever have. I'd like to visit with her, but I'm not gonna get anywhere near that gross old man if I can help it.

So I guess Ben's plan makes sense. He wants me to stay with him and Amanda and Uncle Virgil over Christmas. Ben is great. Uncle Virgil is a cutie, a little dumb, but sweet. But Amanda? I know she doesn't like me. And I'm not all that sweet on her either. She always acts like someone just cut a stinky one or something. It's like being around Mrs. Fuller, the principal. Her nose wrinkles up whenever she comes into the classroom, like we smell bad. Who would want to spend Christmas with Old Lady Fuller? Well, that's what my vacation at Ben's might be like.

Ben said he'd ask Momma to come over one of those days. That might make Christmas feel more normal. When he mentioned inviting Momma, though, I must have looked nervous. So then Ben says it would be JUST Momma, not Rodney. I'm pretty sure Ben knows all about Rodney, because his face gets dark as soon as he hears Rodney's name. Ben must know it wasn't my fault. All I was doing was sleeping! And I was wearing PJs and everything. Honest, Dear Diary! The only thing creepy old Rodney would have seen was my head sticking out from the blanket. Why would he get all weird just seeing my head?

Maybe Amanda thinks it WAS my fault, Rodney acting like a pervert. That's probably why she wouldn't let me stay with her and Ben afterward. She's always talking about how important it is to behave like a lady. I guess I'm not very ladylike. Sometimes I get the feeling she thinks I'm trailer trash—just like Momma. Huh? Maybe Momma isn't all ladylike the way Amanda is. But Amanda's the one who lives in a trailer. Not me. Not Momma.

I wish I was grown up. Maybe 25. By then I'll have figured out what I want to do. Maybe by then I'll have my own family to celebrate Christmas with. Or maybe I'll have a good job and money and can spend the holidays wherever I choose and with anyone I choose—instead of being a kid no one really wants stuck in "the sticks."

That's what Leslie Dubois calls Seneca County. She's in my class at the academy. She's spent most of her life in New York City. On Sutton Place, which is where the really rich people live. Her daddy runs some huge international business and travels all the time. I guess that's why Leslie couldn't stay in New York City when her parents got divorced last year. Her momma came to West Virginia to live. She has family in Marlboro County. They own a big cattle farm. They're pretty rich themselves, but not like Leslie's daddy.

Leslie seems to like me, even though she teases me about being an old Seneca County hillbilly. I don't think she's happy living on a farm. She can't even remember visiting her West Virginia grandparents when she was little, and she misses Sutton Place something awful. The other girls at Marlboro Academy treat her kinda mean, because they think she's a snob. SHE'S a snob? You should see some of those Marlboro County girls, how they look down their noses at Seneca County. At me. That little skank Randy Carver had the nerve to ask me how I got into the Academy. She didn't think anyone in Seneca knew how to read and write.

Well, I showed her. Randy the Bitch just got a C in English. I got an A. Leslie got an A, too. We hate Randy Carver. So I guess we have something in common. That and both our parents are divorced. And we don't come from Marlboro County.

Anyways, Leslie and her momma are gonna spend Christmas at this fancy place in Virginia called the Homestead. It's a big hotel. But it's more than that because you can ride horses there and ski and play tennis and golf. Leslie knows how to do all that. Well, I guess they won't be doing all that in December. But she said they'll dress up like "princesses" when they go to Christmas dinner. And they'll have fun seeing what everyone else is wearing. You can sit by this big balcony, Leslie says, and spend a whole afternoon just watching people parade on by. Sounds boring to me, but Leslie claims "people watching" is fun. Also, she really loves fashion.

Leslie has beautiful clothes and I haven't even seen any of her fancy stuff. Everything she wears to school fits perfect and shows off her best features. And she not only wears makeup but knows how to wear it. She doesn't have raccoon eyes like Randy Carver with that greasy eyeliner. Leslie looks classy, pretty.

Leslie said maybe I could come visit her at that hotel. It's only about an hour away. Her momma would take us all to lunch there. And I could order anything I wanted.

I haven't mentioned anything to Beatrice yet. I don't know whether I want to go. Maybe I'd stick out like a hick in a place like that. I sure don't have any princess dresses.

I hope I have nice clothes by the time I'm 25. I hope I'll know how to act in fancy restaurants.

Maybe I should think about going to a college like Beatrice went to. She says she was poor as a kid. She doesn't look or act poor, but maybe that's because of that fancy college. So should I apply there in a few years? But I'd be sooo far away from home. I live less than an hour away from the Marlboro Academy and almost everyone there acts like I'm from Mars. How would the girls treat me at a fancy school way up in Massachusetts?

But if I DON'T go to a really good college, what will I look like when I'm 25? Will I be fat and dumpy and need to buy my groceries with food stamps, like Joanie Boggs's mother, just down the road from Beatrice? Will I have a bunch of sticky, whining babies by then? What kind of job will I have if I stay in Seneca County? What am I supposed to do, slice meat at the deli counter at Food Festival? While wearing a hair net mooshed down over my forehead? I'd rather choke!

There are so many things I want to see. I read all the time about these great places. Wouldn't it be wonderful to walk down the Champs-Elysees in Paris? To ride on the Tube in London? Even better, to live in a place that's totally different. Like Tokyo! Just think how awesome it would be if I could speak Japanese like a native! I'd love to eat with chopsticks (without dropping anything, lol). Maybe I'd even try raw fish. Sushi? And imagine what it would feel like to wear one of those gorgeous silk kimonos!

It could even be exciting to visit some of those dangerous places Tanner goes, like the mountains of Afghanistan or the jungles of South America or the African bush. (On second thought, I'll just stick to the African bush. I don't think there are any wars there. And I'd get to see lions and elephants.)

I don't think I'm ever gonna see any of those places if I stay in West Virginia. And that scares me. Almost as much as the idea of leaving West Virginia scares me.

TEN

Sounds of a Winter Night

THE DISHWASHER WAS HUMMING AS CLARA DRIED THE LAST POT and Beatrice mopped up the stove and counter. Ralph lay *au couchant* just barely out of the way, on watch for any crumbs he might vacuum off the kitchen floor. Or, perhaps another plate would need the kind of scouring only a large pink dog tongue could accomplish.

"There's nothing worth watching on TV tonight, and I've already finished my homework," Clara said, flipping the dishtowel over her left shoulder. "S'ppose you could lend me some of those CDs you were talking about? I'd like to listen to them tonight, if that's okay."

"Sure. Just let me pour a drink first."

Ralph sighed, stretched his front legs, then his hind legs, and exited the kitchen. The clink of ice in a glass signaled the end of the eating part of the evening. The best he could hope for now was a little playtime with a squeaky toy. The girl was usually good for a few tosses. He scuffed into the den to await further developments.

Unfortunately for Ralph, Clara wasn't in play mode this evening. She was bent on a music-appreciation lesson. Days earlier, after sneering at the latest Grammy-winning adolescent heartthrob, Clara's new friend Leslie had intoned solemnly that jazz was the only music worth listening to. Only the truly sophisticated could understand jazz.

Just one month ago, on one of those rare occasions when Clara intruded on Beatrice's inner sanctum, the teenager had sniggered over the music Beatrice played while working in her office. Jazz figured prominently among the selections. Hearing the "corny" lyrics of "A-Tisket, a-Tasket," Beatrice agreed the nursery rhyme lyrics were silly but suggested that Ella Fitzgerald could sing The Yellow Pages into a work of art. "Just listen to how she teases the tempo, stays dead true to every note, even the ones she scats."

Clara, happy to remain ignorant of the meaning of "scat," rolled her eyes. Beatrice snapped childishly, "Ella could sing circles around a squeaky little toad like Justin Bieber."

"Oh, Beatrice! He is so yesterday."

Beatrice would have enjoyed tweaking Clara over her sudden turn-around, but she didn't want to sour the girl's newfound interest in exploring different music styles, even if the motivation was spurious. As Beatrice assembled likely CDs for Clara, she sadly excluded Ella and most other jazz vocalists but slipped in a few younger artists, like Kat Edmonson. Most of the selections were instrumentals, with the focus evenly split between tenor sax and guitar.

Beatrice settled into her easy chair with the latest Dean Koontz thriller. Clara collapsed into a bean-bag pillow on the floor. Ralph stretched out beside her.

Looking up from her book, Beatrice said, as casually as she could manage, "You can play the music on the big disc player and skip the earbuds if you like."

For the next hour, all three shared a comfortable camaraderie, with barely one word exchanged. The air was rich with music and the fragrance of cherry burning in the wood stove. Beatrice wasn't making much progress with her book. Her focus was on discreetly monitoring Clara's reactions to various artists. Clara made no comments. She furrowed her brow and scrunched her lips together through most of the selections. Her facial expression suggested not disapproval but intense concentration.

Enigmatically, she said at last, "Interesting." She turned off the player and stacked the CDs in her hands. "Okay if I keep these a bit longer?"

"Sure. I've got plenty more in my office."

Score one for jazz. Thank you, Leslie.

"Okay. I'm gonna play crossword online for a while." Clara headed upstairs. Ralph relocated and flopped down beside Beatrice's chair.

Beatrice contemplated another drink but was loath to leave the cozy den. She figured she'd stay there reading until the fire died and then, for once, tuck into bed early.

Fifty pages later, the air felt stuffy, so she risked opening a window. Although it was early December, the night was remarkably mild, barely below freezing. Faced with months of isolation from the outside world for much of every day, Beatrice seized the opportunity to invite fresh air inside. Along with the sounds of the night.

In winter, those sounds were subtle. If you listened carefully, you could hear the naked hardwoods creaking. Fallen leaves made an arid scudding noise as they swirled from one patch of earth to the next. And tonight Beatrice was treated to the sepulchral booming of a great horned owl and the penetrating tremolo of a screech owl.

Continuing intermittently for the next half hour, the eerie duet transported Beatrice back to the tiny bedroom of her childhood home in Massachusetts. When the family's ever-fluctuating finances failed to cover winter fuel needs, Beatrice would entertain herself by chipping ice flakes off the interior window panes. In fatter times, however, the radiator in that small room would crank the temperature to ridiculous heights. On such nights, she would commit the taboo of raising the window an inch and lie on her side and breathe in the dark air, redolent of saltwater and exhaust fumes. And she would listen to the sounds: the bass rumble of trucks on the Southeast Expressway, the muffled arguments of neighbors inside their three-deckers, the occasional bark from a neighborhood mutt. But on a good night, Beatrice would thrill to the screams of a screech owl. Even there, Mother Nature was not completely trumped.

The eerie duet ended abruptly. Snapped back from her childhood memories, Beatrice strained to hear whether the owls had merely relocated. She heard nothing. As she rose to close the window, Ralph harrumphed and, skidding across the kitchen floor, raced out the dog panel in the back storm door. Once outside, he barked with real authority.

Then Beatrice heard the llamas shriek. It was their alarm call, an unsettling cross between the braying of a deranged donkey and the crowing of a hyperactive rooster.

Maybe the bear was back, the one who was a semi-regular visitor. The temperate weather could have delayed its hibernation. Although black bears posed some threat to llamas, especially young ones, the resident ursa had always proven wary of humans, dogs, and llamas. But that didn't mean it wasn't trouble. Occasionally, instead of walking around the pasture that separated upland hidey-holes from the creek, the bear clambered over the llama fencing. That not only sent the llamas into a trumpeting tizzy but also did a number on the woven wire, even on the heavy locust cross-stiles.

Coyotes were another possibility. So far, Beatrice had experienced no trouble with them. Often deployed as guardians for sheep herds, llamas usually intimidated coyotes, especially a singleton. A pack of the wily canines was another story, all the more so with weanlings in the pasture.

In the seconds it took to consider these possibilities, Beatrice knew she had to go outside into the once enchanting but now threatening night. She was glad of the gibbous moon but grabbed for her big LED flashlight and then hurried upstairs to retrieve the revolver from her bedside table. She cursed herself again for not yet buying a shotgun. Nevertheless, a revolver, fired into the ground, had the potential of scaring off both bear and coyote.

Before she went back downstairs, she asked Clara to suit up and go out on the deck to await any instructions.

The llamas were clustered in two groups, on either side of the weaning fence. They glared at the hillside in back of the house. The two mothers periodically issued forth with their vibrato shrieks. Each time they did, Beatrice jumped, and Ralph began a new round of barking. His attention was similarly focused on the hillside.

Beatrice moved the flashlight in a grid pattern, working from the barn up the hill. One hundred feet upslope, she spotted a dark mass, obscured by brush, which was still dense despite the lack of leaves. In the white LED beam, the object looked very black.

Must be a bear. "Hah! Git!" Beatrice yelled. This was a bolder bear than usual. Or, it wasn't a bear at all. The black mass moved slightly but held its ground.

Switching the flashlight to her left hand, Beatrice dipped her right hand into her jacket pocket. She found the comforting, hashed grip of the Smith & Wesson. Looking for a likely spot, free of boulders that could cause a ricochet, she squeezed off two rounds into the ground.

At the first report, the brush around the black mass quivered. The llamas jumped back ten feet. Ralph barked. At the second shot, the black mass scuttled up the hill. Beatrice trained the flashlight on its escape route. At one point, she spotted the creature beside a familiar tree, offering enough perspective for a crude estimate of size. It was about the height of an adult bear, standing erect. Its height remained disconcertingly constant, however. The typical bear would shrug down on all fours to make a speedier getaway. But maybe the steepness of the slope only made the creature appear to be running on just two legs.

Or maybe it was a man dressed in a black hoodie?

Stop it Beatrice! Your imagination is working overtime.

She waved the "okay" signal to Clara on the deck and shouted at the girl to go back inside. But Beatrice kept the revolver in her hand with the hammer pulled back. She stood vigil for a good fifteen minutes after the llamas stopped trumpeting and Ralph stopped barking.

ELEVEN

Sparks—or Static?

EVIE RUDNER PUFFED TO KEEP UP with her secretary as they exited the conference room.

"Chrissake, Shirley! I don't know how you can walk on those stiletto heels, let alone canter!"

"I'm not partial to equine comparisons, Boss."

Evie grabbed her companion's elbow, forced her to stop and then breathlessly fired off tasks that needed doing before the close of business. Shirley jotted them down on her ubiquitous notepad, one of her old-school legacies. Then, somewhat inconsistently, she fielded an incoming call via a wireless earbud, half hidden by artful layers of her champagne-colored hair.

Evie tapped a foot impatiently as Shirley finished telling the voice in her auricular canal that Miss Rudner would be unavailable for the rest of the day.

"But before you do all that, get me Beatrice on the phone," Evie said. "I have some hot information to relay, and I'm really interested in her reaction."

"Are you still trying to figure out whether that charming young Mr. Fordyce is her beau?"

"Young?"

"He's a decade younger than I am," Shirley explained patiently. "And I, as you well know, am in the prime of life. So, yes, Mr. Fordyce is young. And quite a stallion by the look of him."

"I'm too tired to argue the point. But the stallion has been trotting around a mare, and I wonder how that will sit with Beatrice."

"You seem tired a lot lately, Boss. You nearly nodded off over Miss Perkins's presentation at the meeting. That young lady does lack for vigor, but her ideas were not entirely boring. Normally, she would have triggered that despotically maternal urge you have to bring up the newbies in your own graven image."

"Sue me. Big fucking deal. I'm tired of this conversation, among other things."

"I only have your best interest at heart. Which is why I've taken the liberty of making an appointment for you at Mitzi's day spa. She hired herself a buff new masseur. That boy's well-muscled hands will knead your stress away." Shirley handed Evie an appointment card. "It's for late tomorrow afternoon. I know you're free. You can leave early, go to Mitzi's, and then straight home. And get to bed early for a change, you hear?"

"Yes, Mother. I'll think about it." She headed for her office.

From halfway down the hall, Shirley shouted back, "Miss Desmond on line two. And you'll do more than think about it, or Mother will tan your sorry hide."

Settling into her executive chair and easing off her low-heeled pumps, Evie picked up the phone. "Beatrice?"

"So your poor little fingers are too tired to punch in my number?" Beatrice groused. "I have to listen to one of those annoying requests to hold for the actual caller?"

"Gimme a break! I don't do it that often. Besides, with that Georgia drawl, Shirley can make a hold request sound like she's doing you a favor."

"It's a good thing I like Shirley. What's up? You don't sound so hot."

"Christ, I'm getting it from all sides! Just tired. A good night's sleep and I'll be my usual dynamic executive self."

"Gag," Beatrice teased.

"Be nice. You sounded like you wanted information about Tanner's whereabouts. So I found out he finished his do-gooding tour of Third World dust bowls and ended up in Germany. Bremen, to be precise, where he just put some big bucks into an alternative-energy company. They're into windmills. Talk about reinventing the wheel! Anyway, he returned to his D.C. condo last week. So maybe he'll show up in your neck of the woods soon."

"Does that mean he'll handle the interviews promoting the book? Am I off the hook?"

"We'll see. But here's the interesting part…" Evie paused for dramatic effect. "While in Bremen, he was photographed with some Aryan princess hanging off his arm, the daughter of the windmill king."

"Let me guess — a buxom blonde in her twenties?"

"Well, you're right about the hair color. As for the cleavage, Shirley has her beat."

"Shirley has everyone beat."

"And no, he's not robbing the cradle. I'd guess Fräulein Ilse is around forty. A very well-tended forty. And she's not just daddy's little darling, either, but one of the engineers who developed some newfangled wind turbine."

"Tanner's arm candy is getting more refined. Glad he has someone halfway decent to squire around to all those boring German business parties."

"Not just the German ones," Evie said. "A few days ago, the style section of The Washington Post ran a photo of Tanner and Ilse attending a Kennedy Center event honoring some do-gooder who gives pots of money to the arts. So did she follow him there, I wonder?"

"How the hell would I know? And why would I care?" Beatrice protested.

"Oh, gee, I dunno. Maybe because the two of you spent a huge chunk of the past year closeted together to work on his book. And whenever I saw you guys together, I saw sparks."

"Static electricity."

"Bullshit!" Evie said with exasperation. "So what are you gonna do about this? Isn't it high time you called him? Surely you can come up with some pretext about the book? I have his D.C. number."

"I'm not doing squat. What would be the point?"

"Defending your territory would be the point."

"Not my style. Not interested."

"You're hopeless," Evie groaned. "But I'll send you the number and the photo links anyway. We'll see how interested you are then. Tanner may need rescuing from that Nazi."

Beatrice ignored the suggestion. "I'm far more interested in finding out what's going on between you and my big brother. You and Bart got engaged after that preposterous road trip to Miami. The fact that you could drive all that distance — with a dog yet — without killing each other was nothing short of miraculous. So you clearly passed the compatibility test. But that was in July. Since then, I've heard zero planning. From you or from Bart. Do you even have a wedding date?"

"He'd like May, when his irises will be in bloom. He wants to get hitched at his house."

"He certainly has gorgeous gardens and a yard big enough to hold everyone. But I can't envision you barefoot with flowers in your hair."

"Like that would ever happen," Evie laughed. "I dunno about the date. May can be a busy month here."

"Huh? I thought you were going to retire and live the life of leisure up in Massachusetts."

"I can't just go cold turkey. I'll need to do it in stages. And Christ, Beatrice, the thought of living through a Massachusetts winter makes me cross-eyed."

"So keep your McLean townhouse and spend the winter there."

Evie shot back, "If I'm gonna head south for the winter, I can do a lot better than Northern Virginia. But I'm not sure I see Bart doing seasonal relocations."

"You've already busted him out of Massachusetts once. And that went great. Sounds like he's more open to new experiences than he used to be."

"Maybe," Evie said thoughtfully. "But will he be open to my giving his Dover house a major overhaul? He loves that stodgy old place. And he probably wouldn't want me messing with the homey design touches of his late wife. Betty Crocker, wasn't that her name?"

"Don't be bitchy," Beatrice chided. "Just Betty. And she's been dead for decades. The house has undergone two renovations since then, courtesy of my niece, the interior designer."

"Martha?" Evie gasped. "No wonder the girl is having trouble keeping her business afloat. She's got the artistic eye of a trout."

Beatrice sniggered in appreciation. Having little tolerance for the pretentions of her only niece, she speculated, "I doubt Bart has any great attachment to Martha's décor. He probably just went along with her ideas to please her—as long as she didn't mess with his recliner. You'd be doing him a favor changing things up. But I can't imagine interior design is what's got your knickers in such a twist. Are you getting cold feet?"

"Oh, shit, Beatrice, I dunno. Truth be told, I may be the one who's too set in my ways."

"The Evie I know has always embraced change."

"When I'm the one engineering the change. But after the vows, change will be a team effort."

"Yeah, I dimly recall that theory."

"Christ, don't bring your marriage into it. If you had waited for Bill to take any action about anything, you'd still be living in that shitty Reston townhouse, putting kitchen pots beneath the leaking ceiling. You and Bill hardly inspired optimism about the institution of marriage. Best gift that man ever gave you was to drive his car into a tree."

"Happy birthday to me," Beatrice said dully.

"Jesus, I forgot. He died on your birthday, didn't he? Look, I'm sorry. I know that was an awful time, and I didn't mean to put you back there. I'm just glad it's over, but I'm also glad you're free of Bill. Sorry again.

"Oh, damn. This is a horrible place to leave off, but Shirley's telling me to skedaddle to my next meeting. Look at the pictures or don't look at them. Call Tanner or not. Just take care of yourself."

"You take care of yourself, too. And remember, I may be Bart's sister, but I'm here if you need to talk."

TWELVE
Revisitations

NOW THAT DECEMBER WAS LIVING DOWN TO APPALACHIAN expectations, the temperature was no longer conducive to schmoozing with the llamas. Beatrice needed their calming influence nonetheless. Shortly after the pale sun dropped below the mountain, she trekked down to the barn to set out the hay flakes that would fuel furry furnaces through the single-digit cold that lay ahead.

As usual, the dominant herd members muscled the lesser camelids from certain troughs and racks, but Beatrice smiled at a sociable pair of geldings, amicably sharing the same flake, each keeping politely to his chosen side of the wall rack.

As the carbo-loading died down, Beatrice parked on an old bench inside the barn. A few llamas wandered her way, snuffled her hair, puffed friendly greetings into her face, and then kushed nearby.

The rhythmic gurgles from their elegant necks were magically soothing, as boluses of hay moved back and forth between stomachs and molars. She marveled at the ease with which the llamas synchronized those esophageal waves with equally rhythmic, deep breathing. The cud-chewers half closed their long-lashed eyelids. Each square inch of face was steeped in tranquility. It was infectious.

Beatrice shrugged more deeply into her down parka and reflected on the reasons why she needed this inoculation of camelid calmness. One day after Ben's call inviting Clara for Christmas vacation, Beatrice experienced a surge of loneliness, even though joining the Buckhalters did not register high on her wish list. It didn't help that her birthday came a few days after Christmas. So she would face not only Jesus's birthday but her own alone. Again. That reality made her feel unloved, unworthy. Then she felt whiny. Then she felt guilty for feeling whiny.

Being alone at the Yuletide was not necessarily a curse. In her early widowhood, her solo status was actually a source of relief in late December. That time of year had always deepened her late husband's depression, and she would undertake pitiful efforts to jolly Bill up. In vain. He spent his last Christmas — and the entire last week of his life — in the spare bedroom.

But Beatrice could also recall happy holidays and birthdays spent with Kate and her family. Beatrice never felt like a fifth wheel there.

A few of her childhood Christmases were worthy of remembrance, especially when her father made an effort to moderate his alcohol intake. By the time she was in college, Walt Desmond had had his last drink. But those sober holidays nonetheless felt hollow. They lacked the cheerful presence of her brother, who by then had his own family. Adjusting to a competent father wasn't as easy as it should have been. On the first day of Christmas vacation, she would come home to find the fixings for a turkey dinner already in the refrigerator. For so many years, that had been her job. She was no longer sure of her role.

Then she tried to visualize the holidays before her mother took that nap inside the gas oven. Beatrice dimly remembered eating turkey as a small child. She wondered who cooked it.

Truth be told, the Christmas/birthday blues were only a small factor in the funk that required llama therapy in the barn. Evie's recent phone call still reverberated. Tanner had been seen repeatedly with the same woman. Worse, the woman could not readily be dismissed as fluff. Why should it matter? Beatrice had made it clear Tanner's romantic interest was unwelcome. She had essentially told him nothing would ever happen between them.

Certainly, the prospect of being involved with another man terrified her. Beatrice's track record offered little reason for optimism. Before her bleak marriage, there was a brief affair with a Lothario motivated by the challenge she posed. But once he proved he could finally bed her, he quickly lost interest. After her marriage, there was a lengthy involvement, never consummated, with a genuinely nice man, amicably divorced for several years. He was so nice he couldn't get his former wife out of his heart. Less than a year after he and Beatrice parted ways, he remarried his ex.

Then there was that little matter of sex. After years of celibacy. After menopause. Would everything still work? The feelings were still there. But acting on them might prove problematic.

So Beatrice chose pride and safety over romance and risk. It was the right thing to do.

Then why do I feel so crappy?

Unwilling to revisit her decision and fearful of returning to the morose fog that had enveloped her for so much of the preceding winter, Beatrice forced herself to focus on the here and now. She rose from the bench, scrabbled Graf's neck, and headed for the house. Ralph, patiently sitting in the snow while his mistress communed with the llamas, yodeled a greeting, jumped up, turned a half-circle in mid-air, scooped up a tablespoon of snow with his nose when he landed, and trotted ahead of Beatrice with preposterously purposeful dignity.

She was relieved to find Clara already home and in cheerful disposition. The teenager's moods had become less predictable in recent weeks. Although rarely snappish and never petulant, she was often withdrawn. But not tonight. Clara bubbled with anecdotes about an obnoxious classmate who got her comeuppance from a sharp, smart-mouthed teacher; about Leslie's insight into male communication skills; and about the extra-credit humanities project Clara landed on the subject of Japan's love affair with the dragonfly.

By the time Clara went upstairs to bed, Beatrice's mood was light. And two more pleasures lay ahead: a nightcap and a return to the Dean Koontz thriller, at a point that promised some delectable payback for the villain.

Beatrice settled into her recliner, a full, frosty bourbon glass on one side of her and Ralph recumbent on the other. She soon became so engrossed in the coming confrontation between Good and Evil that she barely touched the drink. But she did feel the need to ground herself by reaching down occasionally to stroke Ralph's head. He sleepily sucked his tongue in and out in a long-distance kiss of gratitude.

Suddenly, Beatrice heard Ralph's flews snap wetly, as he spun his head toward the back door. Seconds later, he was out the dog panel and broadcasting bass notes of warning.

"Shit!" Recognizing the seriousness in Ralph's barks and worried that the pushy bear of a few nights earlier might be back, Beatrice headed for the kitchen. After the last bear encounter, she had left her revolver on the table with the intention of replacing the two expended bullets. She had promptly forgotten. The next day, she tucked the gun into a nearby drawer and made another mental note to reload and return the weapon to her nightstand. Once again, she forgot. Right now, however, she was glad it was so handy. She hoped three bullets would be enough to scare the bear away. If it was a bear. She grabbed a jacket hanging near the back door and tucked the gun into the right-hand pocket.

She looked toward the hillside where the bear was last spotted, but Ralph was focused on the driveway. And then Beatrice heard what had set him off: a baritone voice, singing in the darkness. She heard the minor chords of a vaguely familiar lament — whether of Irish, Scottish, or Appalachian vintage she could not tell. The song was getting louder. Her closed front gate lay a thousand feet from her house, but the singer was much nearer and moving up the driveway.

Hearing the jingle of keys in her jacket pocket, Beatrice had an inspiration. She opened her truck door, put the key in the ignition, moved it clockwise, and turned on the headlights. Because she always parked facing away from the house, the headlights would improve her view while destroying the intruder's night vision.

The truck lights showed a man, all right. He was carrying something about a foot long in one hand. A small bag was in the other. Beatrice wedged herself in the V formed by the truck door and the cab, pointed the revolver through the opening, just above the top hinge, and bellowed, "Stop right there! I'm armed. A gun is pointed at your chest. Drop whatever you're carrying and put your hands up!"

She didn't know whether her handgun would have much effect at the current distance. But being more sure of her aim would presuppose an unsettling proximity to the trespasser.

"Jesus!" said the intruder. "Okay, okay! Easy does it! I'm stopping."

The figure gingerly lowered to the ground what he was carrying. He raised his hands to his shoulders, naked palms facing forward. He dropped to his knees.

Even in her wired state, Beatrice recognized the significance of that move. The intruder was making himself smaller, less of a threat, even vulnerable. Ralph apparently inferred the reduced threat, too. He stopped barking and began wagging his tail.

"I come in peace, Hillwilla," called the stranger.

Hillwilla? Only one person called her that name, an invention denoting her halfway status between full-blown hillbilly and snooty come-here. Hillwilla was shorthand for "Hill Wilhelmina."

Tanner's shorthand.

THIRTEEN

Hallooing the House

"WHAT THE HELL?" Beatrice shouted after recognizing Tanner's voice. She tucked the gun into her pocket, ran at him, and slammed her palms against his chest just as he was rising from his knees. He staggered but managed to remain upright.

"It's midnight!" Beatrice exclaimed incredulously. "I could have shot you! What did you think you were doing, you bozo?"

"I was hallooing the house, of course," Tanner responded innocently.

In the country, especially in the South, an unexpected visitor doesn't just march up to the front door and knock. Not unless he wants a chest full of buckshot. By the time he reaches that door, he has intruded deeply into the homeowner's property. So the prudent individual—whether tax assessor, traveling salesman, or neighbor from down the road—announces his unexpected approach. Some tap their car horn a few times. Some wait in their vehicle until the resident comes out to investigate. Others shout a "halloo" of some kind. The hallooers may call out the homeowner's name. They are far less likely to sing stanzas from an Appalachian folksong about death and desertion. They usually choose a more propitious time than midnight.

"Where's your car?" Beatrice asked.

"By the front gate. Umm, I couldn't figure out the latch. So I climbed over the gate to see you."

Beatrice heard the slur in Tanner's diction and smelled alcohol. She had never seen him drunk before.

"Give me your car keys," she commanded, sticking out her right hand. "You've got no business driving."

"I only had two drinks before I left. Funny. They really hit me. No food, I guess. I don't want to go anywhere else, anyway." He handed her the keys.

"Two drinks? And you're this hammered?"

"I realize legions of hollow-legged Berrigan ancestors are sniggering in their graves," he said, referring to the name he was born with, two decades before he created the persona of Tanner Fordyce. "But you needn't make it sound like my manhood is in question."

"Get inside," Beatrice said, unable to resist a small laugh despite her anger.

As they neared the rear entrance, they saw Clara standing just outside, a flashlight in her left hand and a baseball bat in her right.

"Jesus! I've entered the land of the Amazons. Ease up on the bat, please, I bring a peace offering." Tanner handed Clara a small bag. The teenager splayed out her encumbered hands in confusion and after some juggling accepted it.

"Someday, Clara, we'll have a talk about what to do in an emergency. Better you should call 911 than come out here with a baseball bat. But I admire your instincts," Beatrice lectured.

"Hello? This is Seneca County. He could have chopped us up for fish bait by the time any deputy showed up."

As the quartet entered the house, Tanner placed a hand on Clara's shoulder and said, "I'm sorry if I scared you. Stupid of me. And she'd make poor fish bait. Even sharks would swim away in terror."

Clara snorted in amusement and shook her head.

Beatrice signaled for Tanner to sit at the kitchen table, as she busied herself at the sink. Clara plunked down beside him and opened the bag. Inside was a pair of ornate chopsticks. Carved into each head was a delicate dragonfly.

"Get out!" Clara squealed.

"Well, all right, if you insist," Tanner said, rising from his chair.

"Very funny. It's just that I have to write a paper for school on dragonfly symbols in Japan. You couldn't have known that. Weird coincidence."

"I remembered you expressing interest in Japanese culture. So when I transited Narita a few weeks back, I thought I'd look for something appropriate in the duty-free shop. And since you're too young to drink sake…"

"Here," Beatrice interrupted, as she placed a glass of water in front of

Tanner. "For the dehydration."

"No, thank you. Perhaps Clara would like it. In fact, we should all have a drink, so we can make a proper toast." With that he produced, from the floor, the other item he was carrying up the driveway: an unopened bottle of Glenfiddich.

"More booze?" asked Beatrice.

"More booze," Tanner replied. "All will become apparent once you fetch two more glasses. Besides, as you insisted, I won't be doing any more driving tonight."

Beatrice shrugged, went into the den to retrieve her now-watery bourbon and, on the way back, pulled out another glass for Tanner.

After pouring one finger of Scotch, Tanner said, "Raise your drinks, ladies, to honor the passing of a noble spirit. Gertrude is with the angels."

Tanner drained his glass. Beatrice and Clara exchanged alarmed looks.

"Oh, Tanner, I'm so sorry," Beatrice said as she slumped into a chair. "To Gertrude," she added, and took a swallow of bourbon.

"Aw, gee, she was such a great dog. To Gertrude," Clara said, raising her glass of water.

"The arthritis had been a problem for quite a while. When I left for my travels, she seemed no more troubled than usual. But when I returned, she was so much worse. The vet told me she had bone cancer. Jesus, she must have been suffering while I was away. I had the vet come out for a farm call this afternoon. I cradled her as he put her down. And then I hacked through the frozen ground to dig her grave, near the iris garden. And buried her." Tanner recited the history without audible emotion, but his eyes looked off into the distance. When he finished, he poured out a more generous drink, took a sip, and kept his eyes on his glass.

Beatrice placed a hand on his forearm. He covered it with his other hand and nodded. Looking uncomfortable, Clara motioned to Beatrice that she was going back to bed. She got up to leave but turned back and gave Tanner's shoulders an awkward hug. "Thank you for the chopsticks."

Beatrice and Tanner said nothing for a while after Clara left. Finally, Beatrice said, "It's miserable to lose a dog. Never gets any easier."

"No, it doesn't," Tanner said into his glass. "But in an awful way, it's like losing Tim all over again," he added, referring to his late son.

He explained how Tim, whose company trained various kinds of therapy dogs, had not only presented Gertrude as a gift but personally trained her.

"I didn't realize she wasn't from your own breeding stock."

"Nope, she was something special. In more ways than one. As a pup, she must have absorbed Tim's nobility—and sense of humor. And now they're both gone. And I didn't do right by either of them."

At that, tears came to Beatrice's eyes. "I never had the chance to meet Tim, but Gertrude was a happy dog. She adored you. And dogs are excellent judges of character."

Tanner's eyes met Beatrice's. "Thank you for that," he said softly.

They sat together silently for a while. Then Beatrice rose. "I'll get a blanket so you can sleep on the sofa."

By the time she returned, Tanner was already sprawled on the couch, one elbow over his eyes. The other hand dangled over Ralph, lying on the floor.

Beatrice draped the blanket over Tanner. As she bent down to secure it between seat and back, Tanner grabbed her forearm and pulled her toward him. Losing balance, she fell forward. He caught her shoulder with one hand and eased her onto her side as his other hand circled the back of her waist. And then he kissed her.

It was a kiss she would remember. Tender. Lingering. Deep. Hungry. Her whole body responded—heedless of the circumstances, of Clara's presence upstairs, the taste of Scotch on Tanner's tongue. As they kissed, his hands began exploring her curves.

With more willpower than she knew she had, Beatrice braced a palm against Tanner's chest. "Not like this," she whispered, shaking her head. "Not with Clara in the house."

Tanner exhaled through pursed lips, rubbed his eyes, and said, "You're right." Smiling, he added, "But a guy can't help wondering about the possibilities if Clara were at her dad's house."

Beatrice began pushing herself upward, but Tanner restrained her gently. "Stay just a while longer. I promise I'll behave. Honest." He crossed his chest with his thumbnail.

Beatrice nestled into his armpit. He kissed the top of her head and stroked her shoulder. Within minutes, he slept.

She lay there, breathing him in. How long had it been since she had experienced that musky, male scent, detectable only with intimate contact? Her fingertips tested the muscle cover on his ribcage. She marveled at the sensation of being enveloped by someone so much stronger. She felt … safe. And terrified.

Gradually, the rhythmic rise and fall of his chest worked magic. She joined him in sleep.

An hour later she awoke, wondering if it had all been a dream. No, she could feel the warm weight of a hand on her hip. Reluctantly, she eased herself from Tanner's embrace. He stirred briefly, rolled to one side, and continued sleeping.

Beatrice quietly extinguished all the lights and crept upstairs, Ralph padding silently behind her.

FOURTEEN

Just a Seneca County Saturday

SATURDAY MORNING MEANT CLARA SLEPT LATE — all the way to seven. She had already set out hay for the llamas, tossed a cup of kibble into Ralph's bowl, and wolfed down cereal by the time Beatrice got up an hour later. By nine, the teenager was utterly frustrated that the visitor lightly snoring on the sofa had yet to stir. It wasn't merely because she wanted to turn on the television or talk in a normal tone of voice. She was intensely curious.

How would Tanner react after the previous night's drama?

As Beatrice, sitting at the kitchen table, tapped a translation into her laptop, Clara crept into the living room. She knelt behind the sofa, splayed her elbows atop the back cushions, rested her chin on her overlapped hands, and peered intently down at the sleeping Tanner, as if he were a dissection specimen for Biology 101. Happening to look up, Beatrice noticed Clara's vigil. The Clara radiating beady-eyed impatience was an improvement over the withdrawn Clara. Nevertheless, Beatrice vigorously waved the girl back into the kitchen.

"Is he ever going to get up?" Clara whispered, as she sat down beside Beatrice.

"Sleep will help a hangover and maybe ease the grief."

Clara exhaled exasperation and then darted to the sink. She turned on both taps full force and looked toward the living room.

"What are you doing?" Beatrice asked in a low voice.

"He's gotta pee, doesn't he? The running water should give his bladder ideas."

"How do you know he didn't visit the john before you got up?"

"I checked the downstairs bathroom," Clara explained. "The lid's down. Guys always leave the lid up."

"You ever think of becoming a detective? Turn off the faucets!"

As Clara complied, a cough sounded from the living room. A very rumpled Tanner sat up, rubbed a palm over his face, and suddenly noticed the audience in the kitchen. He rolled his right hand from forehead to chest in a deferential Arab greeting. "I'd kill for a cup of coffee, ladies," he called out. "But first things first." He headed for the half bath near the back door.

Clara nudged Beatrice. "Told ya."

Beatrice measured out coffee grounds, while Clara wheedled for a cup of her own.

"Oh, all right," Beatrice said, adding more grounds to the basket. "But just one."

The coffee maker beeped its readiness by the time Tanner entered the kitchen in his socks. Despite the facial stubble, the wrinkled jeans and shirt, he looked remarkably together. He had combed his thick white mane. His eyes were clear. He showed no signs of a headache or wobbly stomach.

"I don't suppose you have an extra toothbrush lying around? A bat's curled up and died inside my mouth."

"As a matter of fact, I do," Beatrice replied. "I have a backlog of freebies the dentist hands out. Drink up. I'll go get one."

Grabbing a mug of coffee, Tanner settled, just a bit gingerly, into a seat beside Clara. Noting the innovative way her hair was piled atop her head, he said, "Fetchingly creative use for the chopsticks."

"You like? They're so pretty, they shouldn't get all gunked up with food. I thought I'd try them as hairpins. Work good." She shook her head to prove the do's sturdiness.

"You may just set a new fashion trend."

"Hey, let me show you the stuff I downloaded about dragonflies. Did you know they're a sign of courage in Japan?"

"No, I didn't. How appropriate. With that baseball bat last night, you looked commendably fierce."

Beatrice returned with toothbrush and paste. Tanner headed off to scour his teeth, while Clara dashed upstairs to look for her dragonfly material.

Beatrice went to the kitchen window to look for Ralph. She spotted him sitting alertly, head pointed away from the house toward one notorious deer copse. As she opened the freezer door to retrieve chicken breasts for dinner, something inside the house, near the back door, registered in her peripheral vision. She assumed it was Tanner returning from the bathroom. But the blur was too low. When she turned to look directly, she gasped. A short man was heading silently but briskly toward the stairs.

Incongruously, she took in the details of his clothing: baggy khakis, a plaid flannel shirt, and a stupendously ugly cap with ear flaps.

Where have I seen that outfit?

"Hey! Where do you think you're going?"

The intruder paused briefly then continued toward the stairs leading to the bedrooms. Only after grabbing the back of his shirt did Beatrice deduce who was in her house: Rodney Madsen!

He spun around. His eyes were wild. "Gotta save Clara," he mumbled. He wrenched his shirt from Beatrice's grip and reached the bottom stair. "Gotta save Clara," he repeated.

Beatrice yelled at full volume, "Rodney, stop!" She grabbed his upper arm. He wheeled and slammed her to the floor. She lunged for his ankle and caught it briefly, but he kicked her off. As she struggled to rise, he pushed her down with his left hand while he wound up his right. Before he could deliver the blow, he was yanked backward, his flannel collar in Tanner's fist.

Just then, Ralph thundered inside, barking frenetically and skidding on the kitchen floor before locating the source of the chaos. Growling, he got between the two men and his mistress.

Ignoring the dog but unable to shrug off Tanner, Rodney whipped around to face the taller man. He jabbed at Tanner's stomach. Tanner dodged but caught a kick to one shin. He grabbed the front of Rodney's shirt with his left hand. His right arm retracted then shot forward in a long arc, his fist landing on Rodney's jaw. Blood spattered from the impact. Rodney reeled but went down only long enough to miss a second blow. Seeing an opening under Tanner's arm, he ran for the back door, Ralph speeding after him. Tanner turned to check on Beatrice, who was struggling to her feet while rubbing her right knee.

"Clara, call 911!" Tanner shouted.

She had beaten him to it. Minutes earlier, Clara was at the top of the stairs checking on the noise. She instantly recognized Rodney, heard his weird refrain about saving her, and retreated to the bedroom. She locked the door behind her and punched in 911. Her second surprise of the morning came when the dispatcher announced that deputies were already at the scene. She ran downstairs to relay the news. By then, Tanner had helped Beatrice to her feet and gone outside to pursue Rodney.

Beatrice returned to the kitchen table. She was experiencing the drama in fast-forward. Clara seemed to be talking at warp speed beside her. Then she noted Tanner, who had reappeared holding a wad of blood-stained khaki. A heartbeat later, Ralph entered, tongue lolling, hackles still up, and tail frozen in a horizontal position. She remained dimly aware of Clara. The next thing Beatrice knew, one deputy, one state trooper, and one suit were at the front door. She rose to approach them, but a pressure wave inside her ears skewed her balance. She slumped back down abruptly, leaving Tanner to field the visit from law enforcement.

Although the events did not, in reality, play out in the jagged strobes of Beatrice's perception, the police did indeed arrive with spectacular speed. It turned out they had been watching Rodney closely for several days and followed him to Beatrice's farm. They initially hung back to see what Rodney was up to, in the hope of nabbing an accomplice in his lucrative side business of manufacturing and running methamphetamine.

Tanner elicited more information than he provided during his conversation with the small group of strangers now in Beatrice's living room. He learned that Seneca County, Marlboro County, and state authorities had long been investigating Rodney, suspected of using his home and his tractor dealership as staging areas in the meth trade. The actual production plant was in northern Seneca County, in two trailers kept ostensibly as deer hunting camps. Rodney had become so successful at his second career that he developed clientele in six different states. By ascending to the status of drug kingpin, he attracted the interest of both the DEA and the FBI. Rodney might have eluded notice for much longer had he not developed a taste for his own merchandise. Strung-out kingpins often have short careers.

During Tanner's chat with the police, Rodney was already on his way to lockup. At some point, medics would reset his dislocated jaw and administer antibiotics for the gouge Ralph had ripped in his leg.

By the time the uniforms and plainclothes agent left, Beatrice's head had cleared, and Clara's chattering slowed from gerbil to squirrel pace. Using the kitchen phone, Tanner called his lawyer to preempt any nuisance lawsuits that poor, injured Rodney might conjure.

As he joined his shell-shocked companions at the kitchen table, Tanner accidentally brushed his right hand against the back of one chair. "Jesus, Mary, and Joseph!" he howled, cradling the swollen fingers against his chest.

Clara erupted in nervous giggles. Beatrice wordlessly removed the ice bag she was holding on her knee and handed it to Tanner.

"Pardon my outburst. I just hope Elmer Fudd's jaw hurts a lot more than my knuckles."

"Thank you! I've been struggling to remember who Rodney resembled with that stupid hat!" Shaking her head, Beatrice added, "And there's so much more to thank you for." She reached across the table for Tanner's — left — hand.

Accepting her grasp, he asked impishly, "So, what else do you ladies do for excitement on a sleepy Seneca County Saturday?"

FIFTEEN

Dishing the Dirt

As Eltie led the way into her kitchen, Ben looked around the old farmhouse his cousin had inherited from her parents. He marveled at the change. Until recently, none of the residences Eltie occupied as an adult ever looked remotely like a home. For years, her walls were devoid of paintings, photographs, and prints. Her refrigerator had no cutesy magnets. The farmhouse's hardwood floors had no rugs. Its windows had Venetian blinds but no drapes. The kitchen counters were barren, lacking even a salt shaker or coffee maker.

All that changed with Vaughn's arrival. Drapes of Vaughn's making now dressed the windows. But Ben thought the change was about far more than Vaughn's homemaking skills. Many of the new wall hangings were clearly of Eltie's choosing, including a stunning photograph she had taken of a mare and foal gamboling in the mountain fog. Finding Vaughn helped Eltie find herself, with a fully realized personality, one she now considered worth showcasing, at least in her home décor.

Ben once felt uncomfortable visiting his cousin. Now it was pleasant to stop by for a chat.

Eltie returned from the refrigerator with two domestic beers in one hand and a glass of Chardonnay in the other. Vaughn was arranging various cheeses and crackers on a large platter.

Ben had arrived after work to share the latest information about Rodney Madsen. Vaughn insisted on fortifying everyone with food and drink before addressing such a dreary topic.

"Not so dreary, now that the bastard is behind bars," Eltie had countered.

Ben opened with his latest news item. The feds seized not only the hunting camps that were Rodney's production facility but also Rodney's nice middle-class home and his tractor dealership. Both buildings had doubled as meth warehouses. Under counternarcotics forfeiture laws, property suspected of serving the illicit drug trade could be confiscated long before trial or conviction.

"Holy shit! Charyce must be spitting bullets," Eltie chortled.

"If her house has been impounded, where is she living?" Vaughn asked.

"Apparently, she was regularly skimming money off the household budget," Ben replied. "Little did ol' Rodney know, but she kept the crummy apartment she'd been renting before she married him. That woman always has a Plan B. The first thing she did when she learned of Rodney's arrest was withdraw everything from their joint savings account. Man, was he ever surprised when he couldn't raise bail. Looks like he won't be bothering Clara for a good long while. And that's a relief. The deputies found evidence he'd been spying on Beatrice's house."

"That's just dreadful! Poor Clara!" Vaughn said.

"Hope the pervert never sees daylight again," Eltie added. "I hope the feds take every last nickel he has—including the money Charyce lifted. Couldn't they argue it came from drug sales?"

"I dunno. Maybe it's small potatoes for them. From what I heard, most of his money was tied up in his business—the legitimate one."

Vaughn shook her head. "I sort of feel sorry for Charyce."

Eltie gasped. "Oh, puhleeze!"

Ben nodded. "She's got a place to live, her own car, and her waitress job at the karaoke bar. She's better off than a lot of folks around here. Besides, she's probably angling to reel in the next fat cat who walks into that saloon."

"How many fat cats frequent karaoke bars?" Vaughn asked skeptically.

"Not many, I guess. But I have the feeling Charyce Trask will land on her feet."

"On the platform soles of her hooker high heels, you mean," Eltie added.

"Is Beatrice all right?" Vaughn interjected. "I heard Rodney struck her."

"Her knee got banged up when he slammed her to the floor. Good thing Tanner Fordyce was around, or she could have been hurt a whole lot worse."

Eltie whistled. "What I'd like to know is just what Fordyce was doing in her house at that time in the morning."

"Clara said he showed up unexpectedly the night before," Ben offered. "He was pretty drunk, apparently all cracked up over having to put down his favorite dog."

"So he shows up at Beatrice's?" Eltie snarled. "I sure hope she's not sleeping around while Clara's under her roof."

"Buzz — you know, the guy who does all my fencing jobs? — has a brother in the sheriff's office. The deputies said someone had been bedding down on the living room sofa. Tanner must have slept it off there."

"But was he the *only* one on that sofa?" Eltie asked.

"Oh, for heaven's sake, Eltie!" Vaughn chided. "I would imagine if Beatrice was going to be intimate with Mr. Fordyce, she would have chosen a more comfortable, private venue, like her bedroom. Besides, dear, what would be so awful if she and Mr. Fordyce *did* get together?"

"And what kind of message would that send to Clara?"

"Isn't that the kind of logic Charyce used against us a while back?" Vaughn asked. "Our relationship would somehow corrupt the girl? And that's why Clara ended up staying with Beatrice in the first place."

Eltie slumped defeated in her chair. Like most Seneca County natives, she enjoyed a good dishing of gossip but now felt thwarted. Entertainment options in such an isolated, rural area were limited, so swapping stories — good and bad — about local events was a welcome diversion.

Gossip was even more delicious if the subject was a come-here like Beatrice. Many born-heres nursed grudges against anyone who was not a native or had no blood ties in West Virginia. It saddened Ben that Eltie seemed to number among them.

Her judgmental streak toward Beatrice also traced back to some shared vulnerabilities. Eltie had often commented on Beatrice's fondness for hard liquor and gleefully reported evidence of hangovers. When visiting Clara in the evening, Eltie was quick to sniff out alcohol on Beatrice's breath.

Ben could remember not so long ago when the extended Buckhalter family was swapping similar stories about Eltie. In her thirties, before she enrolled in vet school and while she was working as a vet tech, caroming from one man to the next, Eltie drank enough vodka and gin to displace a PT boat. No one knew exactly what turned her around. But things started coming together for her about seven years ago, when she had the gumption to apply to vet schools, when she swore off men, and when she sharply reduced her alcohol intake. That change anteceded Vaughn. But Vaughn deserved some credit for Eltie's continued interest in taking better care of herself.

"Well, Tanner strikes me as a decent guy, once you get to know him," Ben said. "He was easy to work with when I set up his kennels a while back. He always paid me upfront and never acted uppity. For all the bucks he has now, I heard he started out working in places like a tannery and the docks of Boston. That's probably where he learned to use his fists. I reckon Rodney was a mite surprised that a rich fifty-something Yankee could pack such a punch."

"Mr. Fordyce used to be poor?" Vaughn asked. "That's something he has in common with Beatrice. She came from meager beginnings, too."

"Oh, come on!" Eltie said, skeptical that anyone born in Massachusetts could have known the hard times so common in Seneca County.

"Yes, indeed. When I've visited Clara, Beatrice and I have chatted some about childhood experiences. Hers sounded bleak, even though she wasn't complaining. It's a big world out there, Eltie, dear. West Virginia doesn't have the lock on hardship."

Eltie was about to make a snotty comment about outlanders when she remembered that Vaughn was a come-here, too, by way of Maryland's Eastern Shore. And Vaughn was a very nice come-here.

"Wouldn't it be lovely if Beatrice and Mr. Fordyce got together?" Vaughn mused.

Even Ben looked skeptical. "I'm not sure Tanner's the marrying kind. And Beatrice doesn't strike me as someone who'd be comfortable rubbing elbows with high-society types."

"You never know. Stranger things have happened. I think they'd make quite a match."

Eltie and Ben exchanged glances.

SIXTEEN

Misalignment

SITTING ON THE FRONT STOOP OF HIS GURNEY MOUNTAIN homestead, Ben massaged the inside of his right ear with his middle finger. As usual, his ears had closed up as he passed three thousand feet of elevation during the steep drive to the old farmhouse. Sinus problems, a concomitant of the perpetually damp climate, often made it difficult to adjust to even minor changes in air pressure. Ben tried yawning again. The third time worked. His auditory fog eased.

Without the distraction of congested ears, Ben's impatience intensified. He checked his watch. "Half an hour late," he grumbled.

Winter's icy fangs had yet to sink deeply into Seneca County. So far, the snowstorms had been unimpressive and alternated with temperatures more typical of late October. Even here, at nearly four thousand feet, the snow cover had melted. Ben seized the opportunity afforded by the mellow weather. One of the day's chores was to replace the crown molding damaged by a roof leak, long since repaired. The original molding was spectacularly ornate and, as a special order, would have cost a small fortune. But when one has a master carpenter for a brother, the price becomes manageable.

Naturally, his brother took forever to turn out the molding. Three months after the promised delivery date, Mike was finally ready. Although Ben was perfectly capable of doing the mitering himself, he would need a lot more time than Mike would to do the job. So he asked for help. After two cancellations, Mike assured him he would show up on Gurney Mountain at nine o'clock sharp.

Ben had already pulled the generator out of the barn and plugged it into the house's transfer box, in case Mike needed more power than his cordless tools could provide. The permanent hookup to the public power grid wasn't scheduled until spring. Ben had also fired up the woodstove and planned to flip on the circuit breaker governing the well pump and pressure tank, even though he'd need to drain the pipes all over again before he left. In order to tackle multiple jobs after Mike's work was done, Ben planned to stay at the homestead for the entire weekend. They might as well be comfortable.

If Mike ever showed up, that is.

Resisting the urge to check his watch again, Ben poured more coffee from his thermos. As he drank, he heard a familiar rattle. He picked up his binoculars and trained them on the creek just east of the kitchen. Sure enough, a kingfisher was the source of the noise. Ben admired the little bird's low, undulating flight over the cold water. The kingfisher swooped down, shouting its rattle of a call, and retrieved some tasty morsel, most likely a tiny crawfish.

Distracted by the avian hunt, Ben failed to note the crunch of gravel, as Mike's black Ram 1500 pulled into the parking area on the other side of the farmhouse.

"I swear, Ben, you should just glue those binoculars to your eye sockets," Mike called from the driveway. "Wanna give me a hand with my gear?"

Knees popping, Ben rose from the stoop. He rubbed the stiffness out of his lower back and walked toward his brother.

"You got old man's disease already, bro?" Mike teased, smiling affably.

"At least I still got me a full head of hair," Ben replied, tugging on the visor of Mike's cap.

The two men, weighted down with tools and materials, entered the old house. Mike whistled appreciatively, "Shoot! You've done a boatload of work on this mausoleum! It dang near looks livable. Though why you'd want to live all the way up here is beyond me."

Later, as they got into the rhythm of working together, Ben felt a stab of remorse. He regretted all the times in the past year he had criticized Mike. Watching those quick, sure hands at work, Ben realized anew his brother was the kind of artisan he himself could never aspire to be. Mike deserved to earn a bundle from crafting world-class acoustic guitars for the country's best musicians. Who could blame him for making that dream a top priority, occasionally outranking the needs of his own daughter?

Life is short—and hard. If Mike can do something big with the time he's got here on Earth, then why not go for it?

When they broke for lunch, Ben eased into Mike's guitar-making dream. He brought up last year's high-paying gig in Virginia. During that assignment, Mike basically had no life. He cut costs by sleeping in the contractor's trailer and occasionally in one of the houses he was detailing. He scarfed down the free donuts and coffee the contractor would lay out for his crew every morning. On his own dime, Mike rarely ate more than a peanut butter sandwich and soda for lunch and a can of soup for dinner. He was determined to build the grubstake he needed to launch his new business.

Then Clara's troubles got in the way. Mike's return to West Virginia came months after Clara first needed rescuing from Rodney and her abusive mother but months before the Virginia job was finished.

"So how much more would you need to really get the guitar business off the ground?" Ben asked, as the two men unwrapped their sandwiches. "Maybe I could help."

"Nice of you to offer, big brother, but I think that ship has sailed."

"Is the shortfall that bad?"

"It's not that. I'm gonna need the money for other things now," Mike said between gulps of coffee.

"What other things?"

"Loretta. I'm gonna be a daddy again."

Ben was dumbstruck. He jammed the last of his tuna fish sandwich into his mouth, so he wouldn't be capable of immediate comment.

"Swallow, Ben. And then congratulate me. And tell me you'll be my best man again. Loretta and me figure on getting hitched in late January."

"Congratulations," Ben said dully. "But what about Clara?"

"Well, I stopped paying Charyce for phony child support after Clara moved in with that Desmond woman," Mike replied, completely missing the point of his brother's query.

Ben tried to clear the cobwebs out of his head as Mike continued, "You know, Charyce actually had the nerve to drop by the other day? She claims she's so lonely since Rodney got his ass locked up that she wants custody of Clara."

"What?" Ben gasped.

"I figure she wants custody so she can get me to cough up more child support, now that she's lost her meal ticket."

"Please tell me you stomped all over that idea."

"Well, duh! One smart thing that Desmond woman did was to record Charyce admitting she knew about Rodney jacking off in front of Clara. So I threatened—again—to use that recording to make dang sure no judge ever lets Charyce get ahold of Clara again."

"Good. How'd Charyce react?"

"She cried crocodile tears. Saying how she was too scared of Rodney to stand up for Clara. Next thing I know, she's resting her lying, crying head on my shoulder."

"You … didn't fall for that, did you?"

"Do I look stupid? I'm not going down that crooked road again. I told her me and Loretta were getting married. That sure got Charyce off my trail."

"I hope it gets her off Clara's trail, too."

"What can Charyce do? I've got formal custody now and that ain't gonna change. Besides, the kid seems happy to keep living with Desmond. Maybe that's for the best, with a new baby on the way and all. Which reminds me, Loretta's got a prescription that needs picking up. Something to help with the morning sickness. So if I want any peace tonight, I'll need to leave in an hour to make it to the pharmacy. Closes early on Saturdays." After balling up his sandwich wrappings, Mike rose, hitched up his jeans, and pulled on his work gloves.

The next hour was spent in trivial conversation. Mike chattered away, with his older brother interjecting "uh-huh" or the occasional "I heard that." Ben's brain was far too cluttered for more sophisticated comments.

As the sickly sweet diesel fumes dissipated from Mike's departure, troubling emotions intruded into Ben's consciousness. Desperate for a new distraction, he struggled to remember the next chore on his list. He wandered into the room he'd designated as the office and almost stumbled over the stack of four-by-eight drywall panels before he remembered. Moving slowly, he hefted one sheet more or less into place against two studs. His biceps were shaking by the time he shot a temporary tack into the panel. He had planned to enlist his brother's help for this job, best accomplished with two pairs of hands. Mike's unexpected early departure scotched that hope. "Reliable as all hell, aren't you Mikey?" Ben grumbled as he more closely aligned the drywall sheet.

While recalling how many times his brother had let him down, how many times Mike had ignored or trivialized his own daughter's needs, Ben positioned the second sheet. He spotted a small misalignment but screwed the panel into the next stud, nonetheless. Molding would conceal the gap between top edge and ceiling, he told himself.

Things don't have to be perfect to work out. Mike doesn't have to be an ideal father for Clara to turn out okay. I don't have to fix everything.

Sweat stung Ben's eyes as he struggled with the third panel of sheetrock. After butting it up against its neighbor, he realized the misalignment between top edge and ceiling was getting worse. Staring up at the gap, he pondered easy fixes, just as he contemplated how he might fix Clara's childhood and how he could knock sense into his brother's head.

Ben squeezed his eyes shut and dropped his chin to his chest. When he raised his head again, he took a huge gulp of air and drove his right fist into the drywall.

"Goddamn you, Mike!"

He pulled his hand from the ragged hole. Looking up at the telltale gap, he roared in frustration—and punched a hole in the second sheet. "You miserable son of a bitch!" he bellowed, moving to the first sheet and assailing it again, first with his right fist, then with his left.

Ben folded down onto his haunches then rocked back onto his butt with palms pressing into the gypsum rubble around him. Panting, he took in the damage. Eventually, he would rinse the blood off his hands and start picking up the mess. But for now, he savored the quiet in his brain, cleansed—at least temporarily—of the rage and disappointment triggered by his beloved baby brother.

SEVENTEEN

Text and Subtext

NOW THAT CLARA WAS ENROLLED AT THE MARLBORO ACADEMY, her homework requirements were challenging and took more time. Occasionally, they even absorbed her interest, as in the case of her present English assignment: an essay describing a winter scene.

Inspiration struck shortly after Clara arrived home from school and noticed the inch of fluffy powder covering the grassy areas. Although the driveway surface was too warm to allow any accumulation, the llama pasture was completely white. As Clara headed toward the barn to set out hay, she experienced a moment of panic. She counted only six llamas. Tess and Barrie were missing.

Or so she thought. Now running toward the gate leading into the front paddock, Clara startled the little herd. Several llamas that had been approaching her in anticipation of dinner danced a few steps backward. A rustling attracted her attention on the left. The source was Tess and Barrie, shaking off the snow that had concealed them as they slept, kushed with their heads stretched out on the grass. Their heavy wool minimized the escape of body heat, which would otherwise have melted whatever snow fell upon them. As they rose, each left behind a negative image in the grass: an ovoid blob with a "tail" etched by a long neck.

Clara was glad she had taken the advice of the teacher who doubled as adviser to the school newspaper, where she recently had begun working. The adviser urged the girls to have paper and pen with them at all times, because no good reporter should ever be without the "tools of her trade." Clara dug into the deep pocket of her parka to extract a small notepad and pen. She sat on the edge of one metal trough and furiously scribbled her llama-inspired essay. One by one, the herd members wandered by to sniff the top of her head. Barrie, out of playfulness or hunger, did more than sniff. She nibbled at the fuzzy ball atop Clara's black knit cap and jerked it up and off the girl's head.

"Hey, pushy llama!" Clara exclaimed, snatching the hat from the ground where Barrie promptly dropped it. Her annoyance over the disrupted word flow quickly gave way to amusement at the llama's pluck.

Clara pocketed her notepad and began peeling off flakes of hay for the many feeders, realizing gratefully her mood had lightened. The llamas had a way of doing that. But she suspected writing was a factor, too. She was discovering she was good with words, something that provided a badly needed boost to her self-image.

She wasn't getting many boosts from her family these days. Clara's face darkened anew, as she thought back to the phone call from her father a few days earlier. He was so excited to share his "good news." He and Loretta were getting married in a month, and Clara would have a baby brother or sister sometime next summer.

Clara knew she was supposed to be happy. But all she could think of was how summer was to be her time with her father. Once school was out, Clara had planned to relocate from Beatrice's farm to Mike Buckhalter's cabin in the northern part of the county. Angry with him for not coming to her rescue earlier, Clara had dreaded the approach of the previous summer. But her father proved attentive and entertaining, more like a big brother than a dad. Although she was often alone when he was off working, he sometimes took her along on a job. And he chipped away at her resentment, at least occasionally, with fishing trips, blueberry- and blackberry-picking expeditions; cookouts including Ben, Amanda, Uncle Virgil, Eltie, and Vaughn; plus some lazy, hot afternoons spent tubing in a nearby creek.

Her father even shared one of his favorite childhood experiences: bird watching. He gave Clara his old binoculars and beat-up identification guide. He praised her when she correctly recognized not just the easy targets like cardinals and titmice but also challenging characters like the small, nervously flitting yellow-rumped warbler.

What chance would there be to identify a warbler with a screaming baby around? Next summer was unlikely to offer Clara any solo time with her father. Even worse, she resented the possibility of being press-ganged into babysitting.

Absorbed by her gloomy thoughts, Clara took a while to notice that the llamas were no longer engaged in their complicated ballet, as they competed for the best feeding positions. The new focus of camelid attention was waving to her at the paddock gate.

"Permission to enter, Captain?" Tanner shouted.

Clara waved him inside. As he came into the barn, she asked, "Since when am I a captain?"

"You looked like you were firmly in charge of this furry crew while making sure the barn was shipshape. So Captain Clara it is. Need any help, ma'am?"

Clara pursed her lips in annoyance. This was not the first time Tanner had gone overboard with his attempts at flattery, she thought, even if she was pleased to be perceived as competent. But all she said was "nope."

She topped up the last hay rack, aware of being watched. When Tanner observed someone, it was as if he could read his or her mind. Clara had witnessed him doing that to Beatrice a few times, and Beatrice looked rattled on those occasions. Now Clara understood why. She didn't particularly feel like sharing her thoughts.

On the contrary, she hoped her unsociable manner would make *him* uncomfortable. She didn't necessarily want him to leave. She just wanted to avoid explaining why she was in a bad mood. Her behavior didn't appear to ruffle him. But at least he wasn't asking any nosy questions. He merely waited calmly for her to finish her barn chores.

When she did, he opened the gate for her. Wordlessly. Her attempt to give him the silent treatment was backfiring. Frustrated, she broke the silence before they had moved very far from the gate. "Beatrice isn't at her office."

"So I gathered. I was hoping I could wait for her at the house, if you're expecting her soon."

"I suppose," Clara shrugged.

Ralph greeted the two humans as they hiked up the hill to the house. Wagging his tail happily, he wiggled from one to the other. Clara realized he had never barked to alert her to Tanner's presence. Clearly, Ralph considered Tanner no threat. Clara wasn't so sure.

Tanner never used to show up unexpectedly. His arrivals were always scheduled and connected to the work on his autobiography. Casually dropping by suggested something more than work was on his mind. Clara was pretty sure that "something" was Beatrice, even if Beatrice herself appeared clueless about Tanner's interest.

She wondered if she would lose Beatrice to Tanner, just as she was losing her father to Loretta and the new baby.

When they entered the house, Clara briefly considered excusing herself to do her homework upstairs. But she wanted to monitor Beatrice's reaction to Tanner's presence. So she sat down at the kitchen table to copy her notepad essay onto proper paper, while they both waited for Beatrice to return home.

"May I?" Tanner asked, motioning to one of the kitchen chairs. His face was impossible to read.

"Sure," Clara said. In spite of herself, she was embarrassed by her own bad manners. But she persevered with her scribbling.

Tanner, sitting beside her, retrieved an ebook reader from his pocket and began scanning. Clara couldn't resist letting her eyes wander to the device, still quite a novelty in Seneca County. The Internet was filled with ads for them, but she had never actually seen one.

"Is that a Kindle?" she asked.

"Nope."

"A Nook?"

"Nope." Tanner scrolled a page ahead. At least Clara assumed that's what he was doing.

"But it is an ebook reader, right?"

"That it is," Tanner murmured, engrossed in the text.

"I thought Kindle and Nook were the only brands."

"Depends where you are. I picked up this txtr when I was in Germany."

Clara fidgeted in her seat and craned her neck for a better look at the device.

Then Tanner turned to her and said, his face a mask of innocence, "Oh, I'm sorry. Did you want to look at it?"

He passed it to Clara, who scrunched up her eyes as she tried to parse the reader's controls.

By the time Beatrice's truck rolled into its parking place near the back door, man and girl were deep in conversation about the txtr's functions, as well as beloved books and favorite authors.

EIGHTEEN

Worrisome Relationships

SEEING BEATRICE LIMP INTO THE KITCHEN with her arms full of groceries, Tanner jumped up to help her unload her truck. Before he headed outside, he turned to Clara, who had resumed her scribbling at the table. He whistled sharply and jerked his thumb toward the door. A startled Clara rose and traipsed behind him.

Once outside, Tanner asked Beatrice, *sotto voce*, "Does the kid always sit on her ass while you do the heavy lifting?"

"She's pretty good. Sometimes she just gets preoccupied."

"Not a habit I'd be inclined to indulge."

Beatrice paused over the carryall in her truck bed and faced Tanner squarely. Hands on her hips, she asked, "What's got your knickers in a twist?"

"There it is: the territorial stare-down. All right, I'll back off," Tanner said, shaking his head. "I just don't like the idea of anyone taking advantage of you."

Clara, who had caught up to the two adults, heard the last comment. Her eyes widened.

Tanner reacted to her shocked expression by thrusting a loaded paper bag into her arms. "Close your mouth or you'll swallow a fly." He picked up his own armful and, whistling cheerfully, headed for the house.

Wounded, Clara looked to Beatrice for backup. Beatrice merely smiled, briefly cupped the girl's chin, picked up the final bag, and closed the lid on the carryall.

Tanner retreated to the far corner of the kitchen and observed the unloading process, with Beatrice and Clara working in tandem, wordlessly and efficiently opening and closing cabinet, fridge, and freezer doors.

"What's so funny?" Beatrice asked, conscious of Tanner's amused gaze.

"You two look like you've been sharing a household your entire lives.

It's quite the charming domestic tableau."

Clara turned warily to Beatrice, who shrugged. "Relax. I think it's a compliment."

"From that lurch in your step, I gather your knee hasn't recovered?" Tanner asked, no longer smirking.

"It's better. How's your hand doing?"

"Tip-top. Good enough to pummel the bastard's pudgy little chin all over again. In fact, after seeing you still among the walking wounded, I'd quite like to have another go at him." Tanner's face darkened.

"I don't imagine you're here to discuss Madsen. I need to sit. And then you can tell me what's up," Beatrice said, motioning toward the living room.

Clara decided against joining them and returned to the table. But she chose a different chair, so she could keep an eye on the other room.

Tanner was pleased that Beatrice nestled into the sofa instead of her easy chair. Before joining her, he shoved the nearby ottoman toward her. "Shouldn't you elevate that leg?"

"Thanks."

"The holidays are what's up," he continued. "From the grapevine, I hear your young charge will be at her uncle's. Which leaves you footloose and fancy-free. Alas, I'm tied up for Christmas—playing the extra male at a Richmond dinner party. But I'm having my own New Year's Eve celebration at the lodge. A small gathering. I'd very much like to have you at my side."

"Since when are you plugged into the Seneca County grapevine?"

"Are you stalling for time to ponder my invitation? If you must know, the grapevine is Ben. He was doing some new work on the kennels yesterday. Holiday plans came up in the course of our conversation. Satisfied? Now, care to give me an answer? Or do I need to send an engraved invitation?"

"I guess I was stalling, but only because I was worried about my pitiful wardrobe, not because I didn't want to accept. I'd really like to spend New Year's Eve with you, Tanner." Suddenly feeling like an awkward teenager, Beatrice was unable to meet his eyes.

"*Alhamdulillah!* For a moment there, I was propelled back to my acned teen years at St. Mary's High School where rejection lurked around every corner."

"Like you ever had acne!" Beatrice japed.

"All right. I exaggerate. Yes, I was stunningly attractive—for someone who stood six-feet-four and weighed one hundred forty pounds, soaking wet."

"I'll bet you were adorable."

"That isn't the adjective the average sixteen-year-old boy pines to hear."

"Maybe not, but 'adorable' goes a long way with sixteen-year-old girls."

"You mean my adorable sixteen-year-old self would have gotten lucky with your sixteen-year-old self?"

"You forget. I would've been an eighteen-year-old college girl."

"Effervescing with sophistication, no doubt." Tanner winked.

"Oh yeah, that was me. When I didn't have my nose firmly planted inside some book, I was doing perfectly silly stuff."

"Do tell. I'd love to hear about your romantic escapades."

"Who said anything about romance? No, college was where I met Kate. Because of her, I suddenly had lots of friends. And our escapades amounted to skating the whip on Lake Waban, gorging on pizza, or laughing ourselves stupid over a Laurel and Hardy marathon. College was hard work. But it was a lot of fun, too."

"Wish I'd known you then."

"Nah, you wouldn't have looked at me twice."

"I don't know whether your dearth of feminine confidence is endearing or tedious. But I suspect a little dress-up on New Year's Eve would do you a world of good."

"How dressed up?" Beatrice groaned.

"Black tie for men, which would translate into an instantly recognizable dress code for most ladies—present company excluded. You probably do need to go shopping. Splurge a little. Dazzle me! And leave the brogans at home." Tanner pointed to her footwear.

From the kitchen, Clara was unable to hear much of the living room conversation, but she noted the smiles and laughs and the frequency with which Tanner or Beatrice leaned in toward the other.

Suddenly, Clara felt excluded—and worried. She had often fretted about her mother's relationships. Rodney was the first boyfriend to pose a direct physical threat. But Clara had felt uncomfortable about most of the men in her mother's life. Many had resented her.

There was George, who expected Charyce to follow him on short notice wherever his gambling mania took him. Once, Charyce had abandoned Clara for a whole weekend to hare off to a casino in southwestern Pennsylvania. Clara was ten. Her father, knowing Charyce had custody that weekend, was in Tennessee to deliver a custom-made guitar. After spending one scary night alone in her mother's apartment, Clara called Ben, who brought her home with him and Amanda. When Mike learned what happened, he threatened to sue for full custody and withdraw child support. The latter threat clipped Charyce's wanderlust with George. His resulting resentment eventually transferred from Clara to Charyce, and the romance withered.

There was J.D., whose ideal weekend was spent in bed with Charyce, a half-gallon of vodka, and a bowl of weed. He did not take kindly to interruptions from an eight-year-old whining about loneliness, boredom, or hunger.

After moving in with Beatrice, Clara assumed a woman of that age would never have any interest in men — nor they in her. That was a major plus, even if Beatrice was short on maternal warmth and even if she would occasionally drift into a bourbon-scented fog. Scarier still were the times when she would fall eerily silent, absorbed by worries or melancholy. But even at her worst, Beatrice was a solid presence. She might not always anticipate Clara's needs, but if Clara reached out for her, she was reliably there.

Now someone else was reaching out for Beatrice.

Limping slightly, Beatrice walked Tanner to the back door. As he passed the kitchen table, he squeezed Clara's shoulder in farewell. The girl grunted "bye" without looking up from her essay. But she shifted in her seat so she could discreetly monitor Tanner's departure.

She saw him finger one of the side belt loops of Beatrice's jeans. He and Beatrice chatted in low voices for several minutes. Then he kissed her cheek and left.

From her sideways perspective, Clara watched Beatrice stand by the door for a heartbeat after it closed. The woman's eyes focused on some distant point. Her lips parted slightly as she exhaled. With astonishment, Clara thought Beatrice, in that single moment, looked almost beautiful.

NINETEEN

Teen Trinity

DURING CLARA'S MONTHS WITH BEATRICE, the girl had never brought friends over. For a long time, she didn't feel sufficiently "at home" to extend invitations to the Desmond farm. In addition, she was inclined to keep schoolmates at arm's length to prevent them from learning about her family crisis.

The teenager's privacy concerns eased after her enrollment at the academy, where the Seneca County grapevine did not thrive. Dismissed as a rural oddity, Clara attracted relatively little attention from classmates. They were far more interested in the newcomer from New York. Leslie Dubois's alien credentials were the focus of hostility and envy. It was perhaps inevitable that the two outsiders, for all their differences, would bond.

On several occasions, Beatrice had made it clear that Leslie would be a welcome guest. Clara responded with apparent interest, while fretting that the transplanted New Yorker lived an hour away. Logistical problems were not the main reason for Clara's inertia, however.

Leslie eventually wangled her own invitation to the wilds of Seneca County, after Clara let slip some interesting details of life with Beatrice Desmond. A central aspect of that life was the llama herd. Though Leslie might have learned to ride horses as a small child, she was at heart a city girl, repulsed by her grandparents' smelly livestock. But llamas—with their long eyelashes, elegant necks, and Andean cachet—were an intriguing alternative, one Leslie was eager to inspect up close.

Clara stalled the initial requests to see Beatrice's exotic animals. So Leslie played the guilt card by referring to the upcoming luncheon treat at The Homestead. Even a Seneca County girl knew that accepting someone's hospitality incurred an obligation to reciprocate.

Leslie suggested she could piggyback on Clara's carpool arrangement after school. Her mother could retrieve her around nine after an evening computer class at Marlboro Community College, only twenty minutes south of the Desmond farm.

Deprived of her pretext of logistical impediments, Clara finally asked Beatrice to add a guest to the dinner table—just twenty-six hours before the appointed date. Annoyed by the relatively short notice, Beatrice nevertheless didn't want to quash the girl's newfound sociability.

Annoyance flashed anew, however, when Clara, after laying out the details, asked nervously, "Are you gonna wear those jeans tomorrow?"

"No, I thought I'd wear my coveralls. You know, the ones that got all those white spots after the llamas spat out their tapeworm paste?"

Beatrice's tone was nonchalant, but her eyes had all the warmth of the waters off Inishmore. In mid-January. In mid-blizzard. Clara gave up all curiosity about the next day's wardrobe choices and retreated to her room to finish her homework.

The next afternoon, Beatrice's eyes frosted over anew when her labors were interrupted by a frazzled Clara, intruding into the office/cabin after an unexpectedly early homecoming. There had been a last-minute carpool change.

"For Christ's sake, Clara, I've got a deadline! Is your friend here already?"

"Umm, yeah, she and Lane are at the house. I'm really sorry. I didn't know Mrs. Leach would need to leave work early today. But we don't have to eat dinner any earlier. I just thought I'd check with you and maybe I could chop veggies or turn on the oven or something?"

Clara was close to tears and wringing her hands. So Beatrice's anger subsided—until she focused on Clara's first sentence.

"Lane? Who the hell is Lane?"

"Umm. Lane Utterback. He's a friend of Leslie's. They're working together on the Christmas concert the academy holds with the Marlboro High School choir. Lane's the tenor in a duet with Leslie. They were rehearsing after school when I got Mrs. Leach's message about leaving early. So I ran to get Leslie. Since Lane was there, she invited him along. I couldn't un-invite him, could I? Oh jeez! I didn't think. Do we have enough food?"

"Dammit, Clara, you sure didn't think!" Beatrice sputtered. "It's not like there's a supermarket a mile down the road. Jesus, why do you think I put so much time and planning into every goddamned grocery expedition? It's a seventy-mile round trip over switchbacks, with every bloody meal figured out ahead of time for every bloody day of the week. And that's providing winter weather doesn't screw with the game plan. So, yeah, last-minute guests mess with my schedule big time."

As Clara sniffled quietly, Beatrice pressed the heels of her hands into her temples, squeezed her eyes shut and counted to ten. When she reopened her eyes, she said, "All right. Wipe your nose. We can punt. But next time, give the cook a proper heads-up, will ya?"

Grateful she had chosen spaghetti for the entrée, she told Clara to pull another baguette and another tub of homemade marinara sauce from the freezer and turn the oven on to WARM. Beatrice added, "I've got another half hour of work here. So be a good little hostess until I can join you."

Amused by the dread freezing Clara's face, Beatrice suggested, "Show 'em the llamas, if you need to fill the time."

"Oh, okay. That would work," Clara said gratefully.

"Now shoo, so I can finish."

✳   ✳   ✳

Completing her translation proved more challenging than Beatrice anticipated, because thoughts of her young guests kept intruding. The addition of a teenage boy raised all sorts of questions. Clara had yet to show any interest in the opposite sex. Was Lane a potential boyfriend? Was Beatrice supposed to add a sex education lecture to her list of imminent chores? At least she had heard something about Leslie. Lane was a complete unknown. For all she knew, he was a meth-head, snooping through her medicine chest and jewelry box even now. Shaking the permutations and commutations out of her brain, she forced herself to focus on the deadline.

✳   ✳   ✳

When Beatrice and Ralph arrived at the house, it was empty, apart from books and backpacks littering the utility room. After sniffing the school gear, Ralph dashed through the dog panel and barked in the direction of the barn.

Beatrice poked her head out the back door to listen for sounds of trouble. Once Ralph stopped yodeling, she heard youthful chatter and soft laughter. She couldn't see much in the twilight, but two of the llamas — illuminated by the barn lights—appeared relatively relaxed, neither threatened nor threatening. Concluding all was well, she went back inside and began preparing dinner.

Minutes later, Ralph happily led the trio of humans into the house. He sniffed knees and crotches and wiggled around denim-clad shins, while Clara stammered out introductions. Smiling broadly, Leslie extended her hand toward Beatrice. The girl's grasp was solid, but she avoided eye contact and retracted her hand quickly.

Lane, who had been slouching awkwardly against a wall, straightened up, grinned, and waved a greeting. He met Beatrice's curious gaze with alert, puppy-dog eyes.

"What a cozy place you have here, Ms. Desmond," Leslie commented, eyes darting around the small house. "The llamas are absolutely gorgeous. Such soulful expressions."

For all her ostensible social grace, Leslie fidgeted about the kitchen. Lane's soft brown eyes followed her every move, while Clara's focus jerked from one person to the next. She was painfully obvious in her effort to read everyone's reactions.

Those first five minutes provided Beatrice with a wealth of information. The teens in her kitchen were clearly bright misfits. One day they might merge into a trinity of safe haven in the midst of a hostile world—if they could just minimize the complications they would inflict on one another. Leslie was a gem in the making, but she appeared troubled, uncertain of which values she should embrace. Lane would probably outgrow his painful gangliness, but Beatrice wondered how much bruising his thin skin could endure without permanent damage. He was almost certainly headed for his first heartbreak, courtesy of the lovely Miss Dubois.

Beatrice lacked the objectivity to encapsulate her housemate with equal glibness but doubted she would need to brush up on Sex Ed basics anytime soon.

Suddenly aware of the lapse in conversation, Beatrice assigned tasks to the three teenagers. Leslie reacted with surprise when pointed to the stack of dishes on the kitchen counter, but she dutifully carried them to the dining room table and arranged the napkins with artful flair.

Lane energetically dug into the task of washing, drying, and shredding lettuce and offered to chop the salad vegetables, too. He made little roses of four radishes.

"Cool," Clara said.

"Cook used to make those," Leslie said dismissively as she peered over Lane's shoulder en route to the flatware drawer.

Stifling a sigh, Beatrice felt a wave of gratitude her teenage years were far behind.

TWENTY

Marlboro Impressions

GOOD FOOD, EVEN WITHOUT SPIRITS, has a way of lubricating social interaction. Once the youngsters had full plates in front of them, the conversation flowed more naturally. Beatrice hung back, listening to complaints about obnoxious teachers, arguments over the best composers of Christmas music, and comparisons of the worst school cafeteria dishes.

After cramming a chunk of garlic bread into his mouth, Lane said, "This is soooo much better than the frozen stuff my daddy buys. How do you make it?"

As Beatrice started to list the ingredients, Lane raised an index finger and dived down for the notebook he had placed on the floor by his chair. He began scribbling the recipe. Aware that three pairs of eyes were closely observing him, he looked up sheepishly, flipped an errant black lock away from his eyes, and said, "What? Am I being lame again?"

Clara giggled nervously. Leslie shook her head and smiled. Beatrice said, "No cook ever thinks it's lame when someone praises her food and asks for the recipe."

Twisting his napkin, Lane explained, "It's just my daddy and me at home. He's not the greatest chef. And I really like good food. So I figure the best way to get it is to make it myself. Which wouldn't be all that weird, except I really *like* cooking."

"Well, I certainly like to cook. And I don't think I'm all that weird," Beatrice said.

"Yeah, but you're a girl."

"Some of the world's greatest culinary artists are men."

"I guess." Lane shrugged.

Beatrice suddenly flashed on a personal experience. "Years ago, my husband and I used to frequent this amazing Cuban restaurant owned by an ex-Marine. His wife took care of the business end of things. One of his sons was the maître d'. The one creating all those incredible dishes was the Marine."

"Really?"

"Really."

"We told you not to listen to idiots like Randy Carver," Clara interjected.

"I've heard you speak of her before," Beatrice said. "She's the pushy little snot, right?"

"That's pretty accurate," Leslie observed, stabbing at her pasta.

"She comes up with names for everyone," Clara continued. "I'm 'Sticks,' because I live in Seneca County and, I guess, because I'm skinny."

"Sounds like a charming girl," Beatrice said.

"And I'm 'Lame,'" Lane added. "Now Randy's got the jocks at my school calling me that."

"Yeah, and the little jerk calls Leslie..." Clara stopped abruptly.

"She calls me 'Lesbian Dubois,'" Leslie said, finishing the sentence. "I'm from New York and I'm different, so I guess being a lesbian is about as different as Randy can imagine. It doesn't help that I turned down one of Marlboro High School's football dimwits when he asked me for a date."

"Kids have always called each other mean names," Beatrice said. "Sometimes you just have to suck it up and ignore it. Sometimes you can fight fire with fire." Noting all eyes on her, she continued, "So what are the lovely Randy's defects?"

The teenagers bubbled over with comments about Randy's terrible grades, her whiny voice, her incessant use of the adjective "inneresting," her tight sweaters, and her dull, stringy brown hair.

"And there's something odd about her face," Leslie mused. "Hand me a piece of paper, Lane."

Chin propped on one hand, with his nose buried in his knuckles, Lane was gazing so intently at Leslie that he took a heartbeat before responding with a ripped-off notebook page and pen. Leslie hunched nearsightedly over the paper and after a few bold, sure strokes, penned a caricature of a full-faced girl with a pouty mouth, round eyes, and a remarkably low hairline.

Clara snatched the drawing the instant it was finished. "It's perfect! It looks just like Randy!" She passed the sketch around the table.

When it reached Beatrice, she clucked gleefully. "The kid has no forehead! Does she live in a torch-lit cave and hunt wooly mammoths?"

Lane chortled so hard he sprayed crumbs of garlic bread onto the table. Clara slapped her thigh in appreciation.

A crooked smile formed on Leslie's lips. "Hmmm, Randy *Caver*, perhaps?"

"Randy *Flintstone*?" offered Clara.

"How about *Wilma*? You know, Fred Flintstone's wife?" Lane suggested.

"I like it!" Clara said.

"She may be too dim to catch the reference," Leslie fretted.

"Who cares?" Clara countered. "If we all start calling her that, we'll drive her nuts whether she gets the meaning or not. Eventually, someone will explain it to her and she'll get royally pissed."

Lane nodded rapidly in beady-eyed assent, his bangs bouncing over his long lashes.

Leslie mouthed the name. Then she smiled, first at Clara and then at Lane. "Our very own little Wilma," she said with soft malice.

"My work here is done," Beatrice said, rising to clear dishes from the table. "But when you guys get called into the principal's office for being politically incorrect, just remember: I know nothing."

*   *   *

After serving up ice cream and cookies, Beatrice kept to the kitchen, with an old John Irving novel as her ostensible focus, while the kids watched television in the living room. She kept an ear out for anything that might require her intervention. As a parenting novice, she wasn't sure what that might be. All she heard was energetic chatter, often involving snarky comments about something playing out on the screen. A few times she heard female squawks, chiding Lane for his overuse of the remote.

A few minutes after nine, Ralph harrumphed from his pillow, a moment before a knock sounded from the rarely used front door. Leslie's mother was on schedule to ferry two of the teens back to Marlboro County.

She introduced herself as Mary Beth Vanderlick. Beatrice recognized the name as belonging to a prominent Marlboro County family and thereby deduced that the former Mrs. Dubois had reclaimed her maiden name after the divorce. She also noted that Mary Beth didn't look like the kind of woman who would have declined to take her husband's name in the first place.

Then Beatrice realized she likewise had been "that kind of woman" and wondered what vibes she emanated. Her political beliefs might be well to the right of the stereotypical feminist, but she was certainly independent, preferred jeans and boots to skirts and high heels, and was far more comfortable around puppies than babies. Not for the first time, Beatrice mused that perhaps the Cosmic Chuckle had known what it was doing, two decades earlier, when it unraveled her hard-won pregnancy with a miscarriage.

Realizing the folly of trying to fit anyone into a neat stereotype, she made another discreet scan of her visitor. She noted the Fair Isle sweater, pleated wool slacks, buttery leather flats, and short string of pearls. Mary Beth Vanderlick dressed at least twenty years older than her age. The woman had Leslie's hazel eyes, ash blonde hair, and dimples. But she lacked any of the light that shone from Leslie. The approach of middle age wasn't the reason for the absent aura, Beatrice thought. Someone had extinguished Mary Beth's spirit.

The conversation didn't last long. Mary Beth was pleasant and polite but appeared too tired to speak more than a few sentences. As soon as her mother arrived, Leslie began collecting her school gear, jacket, and gloves. Lane, as always, keeping a close watch on Leslie's movements, followed suit. Within ten minutes of Mary Beth's arrival, the two guests had piled into her Volvo.

Now freed from the possible need to play chauffeur, Beatrice went to the kitchen, grabbed the bourbon bottle, and poured a generous drink. Before the first sip, Clara approached and softly fist-bumped Beatrice's shoulder.

"Thank you," she said. "That was actually fun! You were great! I think they liked you."

"Well, you don't have to sound so surprised. I've never been known to drool over my dinner. But you're welcome, I think. And I like them, too. Invite 'em back, if you want. Just give me some decent notice next time. Okay?"

"I promise," Clara said, raising three fingers in a Girl Scout salute.

TWENTY-ONE

Dreamscape and an Inbox Message

Why is the furnace fan clicking on? I'm in the middle of a freakin' meadow, for Christ's sake!

Forced-air heat wasn't the only thing wrong about the meadow. Struggling for clues, Beatrice slid a palm over the smooth surface beneath her. She felt a cotton sheet but couldn't imagine why fabric would be covering grass. Nor could she fathom why her heart was racing.

Then she realized what the cotton fabric probably concealed: Kate Stuart, lying on the very spot of pasture where she had collapsed after her brain imploded from a ruptured aneurysm. And now Beatrice would have to identify the body. She would have to peel back the sheet and see how Death had contorted the lovely face of her closest friend.

Desperate to pull herself from this nightmare, Beatrice focused more keenly on the susurrations emanating from the bedroom heat vent. She strained to hear Ralph breathing deeply in slumber from his nearby crate. With those guideposts, her consciousness found its way back to her bed.

Now fully awake and hyperventilating, Beatrice reminded herself that nearly two years had passed since Kate's death. Arthur Stuart had been the one to discover the body in the pasture. For Beatrice, the unlovely task of identifying a corpse had played out years earlier—with other loved ones, not with Kate.

Beatrice had long understood that dreams had a merry disregard for logic. They often served up simultaneous memories from disparate decades, while inserting new events—including ones completely alien to a planet governed by the reassuring laws of physics. So why couldn't she shake the feeling that this particular nightmare offered some core truth? Maybe she should have stayed dreambound long enough to peer under that winding sheet.

Unable to recapture sleep, Beatrice got out of bed at the ungodly hour of six. By the time she fed Ralph and poured her first cup of tea, the laws of physics were kicking in, and she was beating back her sense of foreboding.

It was Christmas Eve, and so she decided to get a jump on the coming week's deadlines. Work would distract her from wallowing in holiday loneliness. Clara was already celebrating the Yuletide at Ben's house. Beatrice missed the girl more than she cared to admit.

The phone rang at ten. "Merry Christmas!" said her brother Bart heartily. "I didn't expect to find you in your office. Not on Christmas Eve. And not this early. See? If you had accepted my invitation, you might actually be enjoying the holiday with me right now."

"Merry Christmas yourself! Or did you expect me to do an impression of Scrooge?"

"I just thought you might be a little lonely with the kiddo gone."

The siblings exchanged anecdotes about the weather, their dogs, and a childhood neighbor Bart had encountered recently. As the small talk dragged on, Beatrice deduced something was weighing on her brother, the real reason for the call. She suspected that reason was Evie.

"So why am I not hearing any background noise?" she asked. "Like Evie singing off-key as she whips up plum pudding? Or did you send her off on a last-minute grocery run? I know how much you and Addie-dog treasure your quiet time in the morning."

"You know me too well. Addie and I had our walk in the park a few hours ago. But truth be told, things are a lot quieter than I'd like right now. Evie's not here."

"Not there? Did you guys have a fight?"

"Nope. She canceled her travel plans. I'm surprised she didn't tell you."

"Not me. Jeez, Bart, I'm sorry. Why'd she cancel?"

"She said things were crazy in the office. She said sorting them out would be ten times trickier if she took a week off. She said she was feeling really tired and wasn't up to the craziness of holiday plane travel."

"Well, all of that could be legit," Beatrice said. "And you know she's a workaholic. But I get the feeling you aren't buying it."

"I know the idea of getting married scares the bejeezus out of Evie. So is this a sign of her backing out? Has she confided in you? I don't want you to violate some sacred girlfriend code, BB, but I could use whatever insights you might have."

He paused. Beatrice let the silence hang between them — in the expectation that the next words from Bart's mouth would strike at the heart of his distress.

"The thing is, Beatrice, she sounded just awful. If I have to, I can handle getting dumped. But I'm worried about something far worse. When we talked on the phone, Evie said all the right things. Apologized profusely. Promised to make it up to me. But the way she said everything was so — I dunno — sluggish, dull. Not like her at all."

A shiver contracted Beatrice's kidneys. "Sure, Evie's a little scared about getting married. Hell, Bart, at our age, after all the years of independence, it's daunting to contemplate merging your life with anyone, even a sweetheart like you. But Evie's no coward. If she wanted to back out, she'd tell you up front."

"I wish I could say that made me feel better. But now I'm more worried than ever. Have you noticed anything off about her lately? Could she be ill?"

Beatrice exhaled sharply. "Damn. The last time we were on the phone — a few weeks ago — she sounded really tired. Still her smartass self, but she wasn't talking in her usual machine-gun bursts. When I told her she sounded under the weather, she blew off my concern."

"Crap."

"Look, I may not be able to get a straight answer out of Evie. But I bet I know where I can find some answers. Let me contact Shirley, and I'll get back to you."

*   *   *

After hanging up, Beatrice checked her contacts list to see if it contained the home number for Evie's secretary. She never got that far, because she spotted a new inbox message. In a freakish coincidence, the author was Shirley.

Communications between the two women had been infrequent and always linked to business — involving Evie's role promoting the Fordyce autobiography, for example. But the title of this latest email didn't sound business-like: "Thought You Should Know…"

With thudding heart, Beatrice opened the message.

After weeks of dragging her tail and looking like the Wrath of God visited on His people, the Boss decided to see her doctor. I'll take full credit for that momentous development, Beatrice (I do hope you'll forgive the familiarity, but, goodness, it feels like I've known you forever). I told the Boss to scurry off to her handsome young internist, tout de suite, or else the next visitor to the office would be my first-cousin-once-removed, Lawson (that's DR. Lawson Greeley, member of a fashionable D.C. medical practice). I made it clear that boy would indeed press a call on her if I asked, because he owes me one super-sized favor. The Boss knew better than to call my bluff. So she got an appointment last week.

At the time, I didn't know about the chest pains. Just little ones, she now admits, like the kind you get with indigestion. But on top of profound fatigue, that's probably not the kind of discomfort a girl can simply burp away.

The handsome young internist promptly sicced a cardiologist on the Boss. After hooking her up to this machine and that, the cardiologist (a chic woman who dresses quite smartly underneath that dreary white lab frock) found a blocked coronary artery and ordered an angioplasty. For today.

I drove the patient to Fairfax Hospital before dawn this morning. During the ride in, she was doing a passable imitation of Camille: pale, frail, and even wearing a green dress. But she wasn't so ill or so scared that she could resist flipping the bird at a motorist who cut me off.

By now, her salty vocabulary probably has the interns and residents bleeding from their young ears. They're planning to jettison the Boss late this afternoon. Her sister Darleen will pick her up and keep her for the night, just long enough for some overdue sibling bonding but not long enough to lead to fisticuffs. If all goes well, the Boss will resume her reign of terror at the office immediately after New Year's. And I will make her life miserable if she overdoes it.

She wasn't intentionally keeping anything from you, Beatrice. Events moved so quickly she had no time to process the news, let alone inform good friends like you. (BTW, I'm the one who contacted the amazingly conventional sister. And I'm glad I did, even if it takes quite a leap of imagination to discern any similarities between the boss and Darleen, bless her heart.)

Shirley signed off with "warmest regards" and her home phone number.

Rereading the long email, Beatrice realized her hands were shaking on the computer keyboard. She would call Shirley to thank her for the information and the life-saving intervention. She would share the news with Bart. And she would order flowers, online, for delivery to Evie's townhouse.

But first, Beatrice planned to have a long, noisy cry. "I'll be goddamned if I lose you, too, Evie!" she vowed, already choking on a sob.

TWENTY-TWO

Things Seen and Unseen

MARY BETH VANDERLICK NEEDED THE SUPPORT of the glistening
pedestal sink before she could come face to face with the woman staring
out vacantly from the bathroom mirror. The face was neither wrinkled nor
puffy with years. But it should not belong to a forty-year-old woman, unless
that woman had contracted a serious illness. It radiated pain and fatigue.
Just looking at it made Mary Beth even more tired. She wanted to return to
that deep, white bathtub where she had spent the previous hour. Or maybe
take another nap. But she was not alone in her well-appointed suite at The
Homestead in Hot Springs, Virginia. She shared those accommodations
with her teenage daughter, who reacted to signs of maternal malaise by
caroming between panicky concern and peevish disdain.

*Ah, Leslie. Would you be better off remaining ignorant? Thinking this
stay at a luxury resort marks the seamless continuation of your privileged
life? Instead of a one-time Christmas gift from your quaint West Virginia
grandparents? All is not what it seems, my sweet girl.*

For one full year, Mary Beth had let her daughter remain blissfully
blind to realities.

*Leslie probably blames me for the divorce, for being too ordinary for her
extraordinary father.*

For one full year, Mary Beth had been scrambling to salvage her few
remaining assets, to relocate to West Virginia, and to come up with some
kind of plan for her future. She had begun taking business courses, preparing
to manage her father's cattle farm now that his longtime manager was
retiring. Soon she would earn a real salary, even if she and Leslie would
still be receiving free room and board at her childhood home.

In her more focused moments, Mary Beth thought perhaps she could
expand the Vanderlick farm by adding a horse-breeding operation. An
accomplished rider, she also had some talent for spotting promising

bloodlines. She might eventually increase her parents' Schedule F income and thereby restore some of her own self-worth.

But focused, energetic moments were hard to find these days. All Mary Beth felt like doing was sleeping. Except sleep all too often eluded her. Unless she drank. So she drank, even though she loathed the taste of liquor.

Mary Beth realized she couldn't stay numb forever. But the next step toward her new life was particularly challenging. That next step was telling Leslie. How do you tell a fourteen-year-old girl that the father she adores has not only abandoned her but also looted the family's assets to finance a life on the run? How does a teenager process her father's new status as a criminal, wanted on two continents for turning his grandfather's business empire into a money-laundering hub for the N'drangheta — the mob, the Mafia?

But it was essential for Leslie to know. She needed to understand the new significance of the almighty dollar. She needed to know the authorities might be listening in if Magnus Dubois ever decided to contact his daughter. And so, with the New Year, Leslie would learn some new, hard truths. And maybe Mary Beth could finally move forward.

But her mind kept drifting backward…

*   *   *

That day on Long Island when she met Magnus Dubois, she was visiting a breeding farm in search of a new mount, now that her favorite gelding was too arthritic to ride. She was enjoying a gap year after graduating with respectable but unremarkable grades from Foxcroft School in Middleburg, Virginia. She had picked Foxcroft over her parents' first choice, the Marlboro Academy, because students there could board horses. Mary Beth couldn't handle being separated from her bay gelding with the soft brown eyes.

Magnus, recently graduated from Brown, had driven to the same horse farm from his mother's Newport home to scout for a polo pony. He was charmed by the horse-trading expertise of this young southern girl, with her athletic grace and lovely ash-blonde hair gathered into a haphazard ponytail. Mary Beth was intrigued by his extravagant black eyelashes, angular Mediterranean features, and buttery accent. The chance encounter led to lunch and soon progressed from museum dates and picnics at the beach to romantic dinners and sex.

The relationship would probably have remained a casual fling had it not been for the intercession of Magnus's grandfather. Blessed with an uncommon amount of common sense, Magloire Dubois believed that only the grounding influence of a good woman could save his grandson from useless dilettantism. Five minutes after meeting Mary Beth — happily flushed from a long trail ride — the old man decided she was that woman, despite her youth. He made it worth his grandson's while to marry her.

Flattered to have the old lion's approval, Mary Beth was determined to be the kind of wife worthy of an international business scion. She adopted a more sophisticated look, even though she preferred informal attire. She made all of Magnus's important friends comfortable by showing genuine, innocent interest in their anecdotes, their children's progress, their health concerns, their favorite foods. Mary Beth grew skilled at her job.

She got even better after Leslie was born. Mary Beth was a natural at motherhood. She was also delighted to have a little riding companion on her weekend getaways. Life was good.

"Until it wasn't," Mary Beth muttered, still peering into her hotel bathroom mirror. Had the contentment of the early years blinded her to the changes in Magnus? An equestrian attuned to her ride, she could keep a twelve-hundred-pound, spirited horse on track. Why couldn't she do the same with her husband? If she had known what was going on beneath his polished surface, perhaps she could have set him right before it was too late.

*   *   *

It was certainly too late on that gray November day three years ago, when she received a frantic phone call from Patrick, the groom at her country home in East Hampton. After signing off with Patrick, Mary Beth shed her Sutton Place clothes for baggy jeans. Then she set off for the lengthy drive to Long Island — but not before she retrieved one item from Magnus's closet.

When she arrived at the stable, Mary Beth saw that Myra — the rescue mare she had rehabilitated and trained to be a stellar hunter-jumper — was as bad as Patrick had described. One week earlier, the horse had sprained her right foreleg while romping about the pasture. Although minor and likely to heal completely, the injury caused a temporary limp. Mary Beth had ordered the groom to ice the leg and make sure no one rode Myra.

The limp was improving. Then Magnus, supposedly in Europe on business, appeared unexpectedly at the stable. He told the groom he needed to work off some stress with a long, vigorous ride. When Patrick fetched the usual gelding, Magnus objected, saying he was in the mood for a more biddable mount, Myra. Magnus waved off the groom's recitation of Myra's orthopedic woes and ordered her saddled.

The speed with which rider and mount approached the nearby bridle path worried Patrick. Walking outside for a better look, he winced when he realized Magnus was urging the mare to jump a fallen tree limb instead of walk around it. Normally, Myra would have cleared the obstacle with ease. Still favoring her right foreleg, however, she hesitated before the jump. She nearly made it cleanly to the other side but stumbled at the last minute. From one hundred feet away, Patrick could hear her cannon bone crack.

Myra went down. Magnus went down. Patrick ran to the scene. While Magnus shook off the jolt and stood up, Myra struggled to get her hooves beneath her. Finally, she managed to wobble herself upright, elevating the injured leg.

"I could have fixed her up, most likely," Patrick told Mary Beth later that awful day. Down on her knees, she was trying to soothe Myra, lying on one side, breathing heavily, with foam at the lips.

"Looked to be a clean break," Patrick continued. "But then Mister Magnus, he took to whacking her rump with his crop. She took off. Horrible it was, her nearly tumbling again with every lurching step. Somehow she made it back to the barn. By then, her leg was all tore up. Bone poking through skin. I knew what needed doing. But the Mister, he wouldn't let me. 'Do you know what I could sell that mare for?' sez he. 'Tape her up and let her heal by herself. I won't waste money on a vet visit. A little pain will teach her not to throw her rider ever again.' And then he gets in his car and drives away."

Mary Beth couldn't take her eyes off the suffering mare. All she could do was nod.

"So I done what I could, Missus. Splinted the leg best I could. Gave her something for the pain and then called you. Can I call the vet now?"

"Thank you, Patrick. But I don't want Myra to suffer one minute longer than necessary."

Signaling the groom to step aside, she opened her large shoulder bag. Mary Beth pulled out the Glock 30, which her husband had purchased a year earlier on the recommendation of his security adviser.

*　　　*　　　*

In her Homestead bathroom, Mary Beth recalled how Magnus had brought the Glock to target practice in Newport. He was unprepared for the gun's kick and missed all ten cans lined up on a board. No stranger to target shooting on her family's West Virginia farm, Mary Beth asked if she could try. Her first three shots went wide, too, for the same reason. By the fourth attempt, she adopted a balanced equestrian stance and braced the gun more securely in both hands. Her next three shots demolished the cans in line. Scowling, Magnus retrieved the pistol. After a cleaning, the Glock went into the closet in Manhattan. As far as Mary Beth knew, he never used it again.

But one year later, it had proved terribly useful.

Standing over Myra, Mary Beth prayed she would remember how to brace against the gun's recoil. She took a deep breath, positioned the muzzle over the large white star in the center of Myra's forehead. She exhaled. And fired.

When she returned to Manhattan, she went online immediately to investigate the status of her joint checking and savings accounts with Magnus. The next day, she withdrew one thousand dollars, cash, from each one. Then she used that money to open solitary checking, savings, and safety-deposit accounts in her own name, at a completely different bank. Over the next two years, she made regular cash withdrawals from the joint accounts — never more than she could logically explain, for this purchase and that. Magnus never asked about the withdrawals.

"Thank God I did that," said the bathroom mirror image.

For two years, Mary Beth continued playing socialite wife to respected international businessman. She shared the same bed with Magnus when he was in New York, which was less and less. She officiated at his gatherings of colleagues and VIPs. She continued to hone her equestrian skills on Long Island almost every weekend, albeit with one less mount. And she doted on Leslie. On the surface, everything was as it had been. Beneath the surface, she fantasized about a life free of Magnus.

Mary Beth was not surprised when he disappeared. What did surprise her was how thoroughly he raided their holdings during his final months in the States.

"How foolish I was not to insist on being listed as joint owner," she told the mirror.

Then she told herself to get dressed. If she could play hostess for Magnus in the last two years of their marriage, playing hostess to her daughter's new friend should be a snap. If she could shatter Myra's noble brain, she could shatter Leslie's illusions about family history. Besides, that painful talk was still a few days away. Between now and then, Mary Beth would numb herself with as many baths, as many naps, and as much liquor as she could stand.

TWENTY-THREE

In and Out of Comfort Zones

As soon as Clara laid eyes on the massive exterior of The Homestead, she regretted accepting Leslie's earnest entreaty to stay several days in the grand old Virginia hotel. When Leslie called Ben's house, where Clara was spending the holidays, she had groused, "I'm bored out of my mind here. Mother doesn't want to do anything. Please stay a few nights and keep me from going stir crazy. Please say you'll come. Our suite has tons of space."

As Amanda dropped Clara off in front of the hotel's imposing entrance, the girl paused before exiting the car. She needed to remind herself why Leslie's invitation had seemed providential. Her thoughts wandered back to Christmas Eve.

*   *   *

It had started well enough, with her mother uncharacteristically well-behaved.

"Y'all are right decent to invite me," Charyce said, almost humbly, as she entered the Buckhalter home. Her eyes sparkled flirtatiously at Ben as he took her coat. She smiled sweetly at Amanda, who flinched when Charyce seized her forearm and whimpered, "It's hard for a woman to be alone at Christmas. It's good to have kin."

Then Charyce thrust a store-bought fruitcake tin into her hostess's hands. "Thought you might could use some more dessert."

Recognizing the cheap brand, Clara stifled a groan. She knew her mother was re-gifting the perennial Christmas offering shipped from Florida by an ancient great aunt.

Ben grabbed the fruitcake before Amanda could react and led everyone to the kitchen table, already set with dessert plates. He poured small glasses of sherry, and the celebrants commented on the cold weather and shared predictions about the timing of the next big storm. Though hardly convivial, the conversation was civil. But just as Clara started to drop her guard, Charyce began pressuring her to come "back home." Pressing the side of her middle finger into her lower eyelid, to prevent a mascara bleed from (nonexistent) tears, Charyce continued, "I'm just so durn lonely in that apartment. What with Rodney in jail. So he wouldn't be around to bother you none. Couldn't you keep me company, sugar?"

Ben interrupted the wheedling. "You know the custody arrangement, Charyce," he said sternly. "It's not up for review. This is just a temporary visit. For Christmas. For Clara." He nodded toward his niece while staring coolly at her mother.

Christmas Day offered its share of unease, as well. "Ho, ho, ho!" Clara's daddy bellowed as he entered Ben's house with Loretta in tow. Mike assumed an exaggerated stoop from the package-laden laundry bag on his back. Widening his eyes with the hyper-merriment more appropriate for a toddler, he dug into the sack, pulled out a clumsily wrapped gift, and handed it to Clara.

Despite the hokey presentation, her eyes brightened when she spied a chrome blade poking through the wrapping. Weeks earlier, she had dropped a hint about outgrowing her old ice skates. "Thank you, Daddy!" she said, tearing through the reindeer-festooned paper. Then her face crumpled when she noticed they were too small, by two sizes.

"Try 'em on, honey!" Mike urged.

"Umm, later," Clara said. "Don't want to mark up Amanda's floor."

Mike's heartiness faded, but he gamely pulled other packages from the bag. A small bottle of tasteful cologne for Amanda. "Sweets to the sweet!" Heavy-duty booster cables for Ben. "I know you haven't gotten around to replacing those god-awful corroded battery terminals on your truck, bro'." And a pair of lined work gloves for Virgil. "I expect the seasonal bitching about cold hands has already started, Uncle Virgil?"

Loretta smiled nervously at Amanda and said, "With all them pretty Christmas decorations, you'd never know this was a trailer."

Clara held her breath. Amanda's lips froze into a grimace only somewhat resembling a smile, but said, "Why, thank you, Loretta."

Awkward exchanges continued throughout the evening. The conversation never really flowed. Eventually abandoning all efforts at socializing, Loretta was preoccupied with other concerns at the dinner table. As heaping spoonfuls of squash, stuffing, and mashed potatoes plopped onto each plate, Loretta's face drained of color. Thrall to first-trimester nausea, she could only pick at her food — and thereby attract disapproving glances from her hostess.

The awkwardness persisted the day after Christmas. Ben and Virgil had to attend to some construction project that couldn't wait for the New Year, which meant Clara was alone with Amanda. The two shared no activities, apart from eating meals together. Clara became uncomfortably aware of the ticking of the grandfather clock in the living room. But that was less chilling than the sounds of sucked-in breath — Amanda's default reaction to Clara's dipping a teaspoon into her soup bowl or Clara's overuse of such colloquialisms as "awesome" or "hurl." The teenager wondered if her hostess feared being contaminated by people perceived as riffraff. It was as if mere association with her less-elegant relatives would unravel all of Amanda's hard-won accomplishments — such as getting an education, finally landing a worthy husband, ably managing his business, and turning their doublewide into a tasteful, comfortable home.

There were times Clara felt sorry for her aunt. More often, she just felt ill at ease. So when Leslie called two days after Christmas, another day when Ben and Virgil would be away from home from dawn till dusk, Clara jumped at her invitation to The Homestead.

*   *   *

Now that she was in the central lobby, where a very well-dressed Leslie greeted her, Clara's gumption wobbled. What was a hillbilly like her doing in a place like this? She had never even heard of some of the activities Leslie promptly proposed. To Clara, hot-stone massage sounded more like torture than a treat.

It didn't help that Mrs. Vanderlick was so withdrawn she made Amanda look downright effusive. During that first day, Leslie's mother retreated to the master bedroom in her suite — to nap — rather than join the girls for lunch.

Clara had looked forward to heading to the ice rink that first afternoon. This was a sport she could handle — unlike horseback riding or skiing, alien activities that could quite possibly kill her. But not long after lacing up her sleek rentals, she realized there was a huge difference between skidding around a frozen, bumpy farm pond and cutting figure eights as Leslie did on The Homestead's mirror-smooth rink.

That night, as Clara tucked into her very own double bed, in the big room she shared with Leslie, homesickness set in hard. Leslie could be a lot of fun, but she was not above mocking her friend's awkward moments in the face of the hotel's grandeur. The venue showcased the two girls' differences more than their common bonds. Clara found herself longing for an environment where she didn't feel the need to fake competence or be something other than what she was. With a start, she realized she was homesick for Beatrice's farm.

In the darkness, she whispered toward the other bed, "Leslie, do you suppose Beatrice could come here for lunch tomorrow? I feel bad she's all alone for the holidays."

"Sure. Mother would probably welcome adult company. And I find your great aunt interesting. Odd, perhaps, but interesting."

After thanking Leslie, Clara made a mental note to clue Beatrice in about the lie she had concocted for the benefit of her Marlboro Academy schoolmates. Few mountaineers could conceive of any but the most shameful circumstances causing a child to find shelter with someone unrelated by blood or marriage. So, with a wave of her wand, Clara had made Beatrice kin.

Luck was with Clara early the next morning. She timed her telephone call perfectly, just before her "great aunt" left for a shopping expedition in Roanoke. Worried that her fanciest evening dress was below "black tie" standards, Beatrice decided at the eleventh hour to head for Virginia to hunt down more appropriate attire for Tanner's New Year's Eve party. Since The Homestead was roughly en route to Roanoke, Beatrice agreed to an early lunch with Clara, Leslie, and Mary Beth—with the understanding she wouldn't be able to stay long. She had detected the nervousness in Clara's voice and wanted to make sure the girl was all right. Besides, Beatrice so loathed shopping that even a slight postponement was welcome.

During the brief telephone chat, Clara added in a low voice, "By the way, you're my great aunt. Please go along with that little fib? I'll explain later."

*   *   *

Beatrice was prepared for The Homestead's imposing structure. Looming up from the small town of Hot Springs, the resort did a good job of competing with the Alleghenies for dominance. It was hardly surprising that Clara might feel out of place there.

Beatrice herself felt uncomfortable with the legions of Homestead employees helpfully guiding her to a parking space, the central lobby, and her friends—while at the same time vetting her to make sure she wasn't a grifter targeting the resort's well-heeled guests. Her comfort level shrank even more when Mary Beth, after a tired greeting, discreetly eyed Beatrice's attire and suggested they all head for one of the resort's smaller cafés. Only then did Beatrice remember that certain old-school Virginia venues maintained strict dress codes, even for lunch, at their main dining facilities. The code often extended so far as to ban certain collar styles and certain fabrics—most definitely including denim.

Beatrice was wearing her dress jeans, one of the few pairs never exposed to physical labor. Even though they were set off by gold earrings, a silk blouse, an expensive sweater, and a relatively new leather car coat, they were still taboo.

Her embarrassment gave way to rebellious satisfaction as the quartet passed the main dining room. Eyeing the crisp linens, expensive table settings, and bustling wait staff, Beatrice realized she would be far more comfortable at the lesser café. She had a strong hunch Clara would, too.

TWENTY-FOUR

A Talent for Taking Charge

AS THE FROSTY GIMLET MATERIALIZED in front of Mary Beth, Beatrice felt a pang of envy. The conversation had been stilted ever since her arrival. The prospect of soldiering through lunch without benefit of alcohol was grim. But a lot of driving lay ahead.

Halfway through her drink, Mary Beth relaxed and rose to the occasion. She animated the conversation by expressing genuine interest in Beatrice's llamas. The horsewoman showed none of the snobbishness some horse-lovers exhibited toward camelids. Never once did she pose the annoying question, "But what do you *do* with llamas?" As Mary Beth explained, two of her own horses had become too arthritic to be ridden. She thoroughly enjoyed their company nonetheless.

Suddenly the light in her eyes flickered out. She corrected herself: "I used to love spending time with my horses. My ex got them. Along with almost everything else." She bolted the rest of her sugary drink and signaled the waiter to bring another.

Leslie fidgeted in her chair, and Clara became absorbed by the table's small vase of freesias. Beatrice desperately searched for a safe response and opted for, "We get so attached to our critters, don't we? Every single one of my llamas occupies a unique place in my heart. They're all such individuals. I'd be hard-pressed to name a favorite. Of course, Clara probably has one: Buck. That's because she brought him into the world."

The ploy worked. Clara was eager to talk about helping with Reine's difficult delivery the previous spring. The other two diners were intrigued. Mary Beth was no stranger to newborn calves staggering after their mothers, but she had never seen a cow give birth. Nor had she or her daughter ever been on hand for a foaling.

The spirited conversation didn't flag until the arrival of the entrées.

Figuring she had exhausted her limited social skills with her Introduction to Llamas 101, Beatrice focused on her Allegheny trout.

Let the well-bred set show how charming they can be.

Unfortunately, Mary Beth wasn't likely to charm anytime soon. Having polished off the second gimlet, she was working on a merlot. The mood-enhancing effects of the first cocktail were gone. Alcohol's depressant properties were kicking in.

The well-bred Leslie entered the breach. "I'm glad the llamas came up, because Lane had a question about them. He was too shy to ask you when we were at your farm."

"You know, Lane really can be kinda 'lame' sometimes," Clara commented.

"Don't be mean, Clara," Leslie chided. "It just takes him a while to be comfortable around new people."

"I know how he feels," Beatrice offered, more forcefully than she intended.

"Lane wanted to know if you use the llamas' fiber," Leslie continued.

"Clara and I have made some attempts, but we haven't quite gotten the hang of spinning. That's a shame, because we're developing a backlog of fiber. I inherited a few bags of wool from the llamas' original farm. We did our own shearing last spring. I wasn't fully healed up from a broken leg. So Clara was an indispensable part of that effort. She wields the shears much better than I do. She has good hands, this one."

Beatrice smiled at Clara. The teenager beamed back.

"You and Lane ought to do fiber crafts together," Leslie said, turning to Clara. "He's really good with his hands, too — everything from woodworking to knitting. He spotted your spinning wheel and was dying to try it. Would it be okay if he did, Ms. Desmond?"

Beatrice paused before responding; she needed to dissect Leslie's words. What was the girl's interest in Lane? Earlier, she had defended the boy in a way that was sisterly but not romantic. Now she was fobbing him off on Clara. Beatrice's initial impressions were confirmed. Lane was sweet on Leslie, but the sophisticated Miss Dubois did not return those feelings. She probably felt sorry for him. And she wasn't above using Clara to distract him. Clara, for her part, seemed underwhelmed by the boy but liked him well enough. Beatrice herself had found Lane endearing, if a little goofy.

And the poor bastard knits? As well as cooks? High school's gonna be a bumpy road.

Beatrice decided more exposure to Lane wouldn't pose any threat to Clara. But she wondered whether the same could be said of Leslie, given this little display of manipulation. Still, the girl's father was out of the picture; the mother was currently melting into her chair. Unable to prevent her family life from circling the drain, Leslie might be compensating by taking charge in other areas. Thinking back to her own teen years, with a mother in the grave and a father inside the bottle, Beatrice was no stranger to the comfort of taking charge. So she decided to cut Leslie slack. At least a little.

She became aware of the lag in conversation—and two pairs of youthful eyes scanning her face, awaiting her response.

"Well, sure. You and Lane can give my spinning wheel a whirl—whenever we can all work out a convenient visit," Beatrice said pointedly. She wasn't about to have Lane dumped on their doorstep like some charity case. And there would be no "visit" unless Clara showed interest in socializing with Lane as well as with Leslie.

Leslie blinked. Bright girl that she was, she clearly understood the woman's subtext. "That's very nice of you. I hope the three of us can get together at your place. Of course, whenever it's convenient for you."

"I didn't know Lane could knit," Clara said, with admiration. "I've been thinking of getting into 4-H. Remember, Beatrice? To make me look like I'm 'well-rounded'? The guidance counselor keeps telling us that's the way to get into a good college."

"I'm so sick of that term," Leslie interjected. "Mrs. Ackerman uses it to death. I'm not 'well-rounded' enough. As for you, Clara, Ackerman must think you're hopeless."

"Gee, thanks, Leslie!" Clara said peevishly. "So if we're bad, what about Randy Carver? Is she well-rounded enough for Ackerman?"

"Wilma? Certainly round enough," Leslie said, chuckling.

"You read my mind!" Clara laughed, thumping the table. "But anyways, I couldn't figure out what to do with the llamas for 4-H. We don't have a trailer to take them to fairs. So then I thought about doing something with their wool. Except I suck at spinning. But I'm pretty good at shearing. So maybe I could clip their wool, wash it, and pick it clean. Beatrice, remember that time when we picked out the weeds and bugs? That was sort of fun. And if Lane could spin it into something that really looks like yarn, he could knit a scarf out of it. I bet a llama scarf would be a first for the Marlboro County 4-H. And maybe that would get Ackerman off my back."

"Get real," Leslie commented.

"Well, at least I'd have something decent to write down on a future college application. And it would be a lot more fun than some of those other activities Well-Rounded Ackerman is always pushing us to do."

"You mean you don't want to dump bed pans at the Marlboro Community Hospital?"

"About as much as you want to put on a hair net and serve lunch at the senior center." Clara flattened her bangs over her forehead.

"4-H fiber art sounds like a dandy option," Beatrice said. "I've got some how-to books that might come in handy. But before you launch this project, just make sure Lane wants to go along. He might be too busy with his own stuff, you know."

"Oh, he'll go along," Clara said, cocking her chin at Leslie.

Beatrice noted Leslie might not be the only one with a talent for taking charge. She also included herself and insisted on splitting the lunch tab with Mary Beth.

After ascertaining the other woman planned nothing more risky that afternoon than a post-prandial nap, Beatrice decided it was safe to leave — especially when she learned the two girls were heading for the resort's family-friendly billiard room. Neither teen had any experience with the game. Both thought it would be a "cool" activity to learn.

Mary Beth veered toward the elevators to return to her suite. Beatrice and Clara consulted a site map so the former could figure out where the main exit was and the latter could locate the game room. Leslie, meanwhile, retrieved something from her gigantic over-the-shoulder bag. When Beatrice turned away from the map, the girl handed her a manila envelope.

"This is to thank you for the evening we spent at your farm," Leslie said with uncharacteristic shyness.

Puzzled, Beatrice opened the envelope and extracted a pen-and-ink drawing. It portrayed Reine. Perfectly. Down to the prissy way the llama held her nostrils when she was annoyed.

"When did you do this, Leslie?"

"I did a quick pencil sketch when I was in your barn. When I got home, I worked from that and from memory."

"Oh, Leslie, you have a real gift. You have absolutely captured Reine's soul! If you're this talented at fourteen, you'll be the next Georgia O'Keeffe by the time you're eighteen. Wow!"

The come-here from Sutton Place lost her poise. She blushed magenta and looked down at her expensive boots, while autistically drumming thumb-tip against outer thigh. But Beatrice couldn't miss the hundred-watt smile that lit up the girl's half-hidden face.

TWENTY-FIVE

Blessed Insults

AFTER EVIE'S ANGIOPLASTY, Beatrice followed up the flowers with a get-well card crafted in the worst imaginable taste, replete with crass sexual innuendo and sick humor about mortality. In other words, right up Evie's alley. In a brief email, Evie expressed thanks and complained about the mind-numbing boredom of her recuperation. The griping was reassuring, but the email, lacking a single obscenity, suggested Evie was not yet back in fighting trim.

For several days Beatrice hesitated about phoning her old friend. For one thing, she worried about disturbing Evie's rest. Naps might exacerbate the boredom problem but were probably just what the patient's traumatized body needed.

The second reason was entirely selfish. Beatrice dreaded the prospect of hearing defeated, scared, or lethargic tones on the other end of the phone.

But her sense of obligation, combined with curiosity and her own need to chat, eventually took over. She was curious about both the latest health news and the overnight at Darleen's house. In the decades she had known Evie, Beatrice met the sister just once, at a family funeral. The siblings were not estranged; they just had zero in common apart from DNA. Beatrice couldn't imagine what they would have talked about for a whole day.

The dread dissipated one second after the phone call began.

"About fucking time!" Evie shouted into her smartphone as soon as she spotted the West Virginia number on the touch screen. "Jesus, I needed to talk with someone who isn't overflowing with lugubriousness. My one little brush with the Grim Reaper prompts people to swoon about the infinite mercy of God or to share the details of their own medical emergencies. Do people really think they're cheering me up when they launch into lurid descriptions of their gall bladder surgery?

"Apparently, they thought a personality transplant was part of the angioplasty."

"Goddamned right! I mean, am I someone who cares? And you should see the flowers some people sent!"

"Let me guess. Coffin arrangements?" Beatrice asked, chuckling.

"Damn close. You and Shirley knew to steer clear of the hated glads and lilies. Not so with certain associates. My townhouse smelled like a fucking funeral parlor. I scared the shit out of Jadwiga the other day. Just before she arrived, I lay on the sofa, beneath one of those god-awful bouquets. I'd snatched a white lily and clutched it to my breast. With my eyes closed, of course. The little Polack almost had a seizure!"

"One of these days, your housekeeper is going to march out the door of your McLean digs and keep on trekking till she's back in Cracow. As for your other associates, ya gotta realize people just don't know how to handle an Evangeline Rudner who isn't cooking on all four burners — simultaneously texting a client and dressing down an errant employee. So they aren't necessarily able to tailor their reaction to your unique style."

"Please. I heard enough lectures from Darleen. I don't need more from you. And by the way, it's bad enough Sister Dearest calls me by my dreadful birth name. *Et tu, Brute?* Be careful, or I'll start using Bart's pet name for *you*, BB."

"I gather the sibling bonding didn't leave you with the warm squooshies?" Beatrice asked, laughing.

"Oh, don't get me wrong. It was nice of Darleen to take me in. Maybe it would have been scary to be by myself that first night, listening to my heart beat. I get that she was probably unnerved. The older generation is all gone, and if I pop off, Darleen becomes the oldest surviving family member. But, Jesus, she can be a trial!"

"Was she a source of the religious lectures you referred to?"

"Of course!" Evie exclaimed. "Ever since she became a Unitarian minister, she just overflows with divine love. She kept reminding me how I could have had a stroke or a heart attack if Fairfax Hospital's Dr. Mengele hadn't snaked that giant catheter up my groin. She insisted God was watching over me. I told her if God was really watching over me, he wouldn't have put plaque in my artery in the first place."

"And her comeback?"

"The usual song about God giving us the free will to mess up or pull up our socks. In other words, everything good that happens is God's doing, while everything bad is our own fault."

Beatrice exhaled through pursed lips. "Yeah, that argument has always bugged me, too."

"I'm surprised. You never struck me as any great secularist. Not with that obsession you have with your 'Cosmic Chuckle.' I always thought that was your own twisted take on Catholic guilt."

"Probably is. But at least I don't pretend to be logical. I figure on covering all the bases. Put a little sticky rice in Buddha's belly button. Bead through the occasional rosary. And keep a loaded revolver in the nightstand."

"Jesus, you're such a fascist! But at least you're not boring. Which is why I want to ask a favor of you."

"Shoot. Or is that un-PC?"

"Very funny. With all these people pressing calls on me and putting mirrors under my nostrils, I'm feeling the need to get away. It's not just the stent in my chest. It's the prospect of retirement. And marriage. As much as I hate to ponder my navel, I need to do some thinking. And that won't be easy around here, despite Shirley's best efforts to keep the office humming and insulate me from administrivia. What I really need is one of those sensory-deprivation chambers. Your farm is the next best thing."

"Oh, stop, I can't stand so much flattery!" Beatrice chuckled. "I'd love to have you visit, Evie. When are you thinking?"

"I'll have to scrutinize my schedule when I get back to work. Figure what to postpone and what to delegate. But how about the last week in January or first week in February?"

"Are you sure you can handle this place in winter? You went stir crazy here last year after you got socked in by snow."

"I'm in a different frame of mind right now. I might actually welcome Mother Nature shutting us down for a while. Just make sure your freezer is packed, your liquor cabinet is overflowing, and your woodshed is stacked high. As I recall, electrical service is a whimsical concept in your neck of the woods. Unlike my paternal ancestors, who shrugged off the wintry blasts of Poland's ghettos, I get very cranky when the temperature drops below seventy. Must be my mother's Southern Presbyterian DNA."

"Plenty of firewood. Plenty of booze. Plenty of food. Can do. But there could be one fly in the ointment."

"What's that?"

"I finally got around to scheduling the partial knee replacement. In Charlottesville. If you recall, the doc treating the broken leg last year warned me that my right kneecap was on borrowed time. It actually seemed better for a while, probably because I wasn't using it much for months, as the break healed. So I told myself I could put off the surgery. But I took a fall a few weeks ago. Naturally, right on that knee. And it's been grumpy ever since. So I get sliced and diced the first of February. How about you plan on the week before?"

"I've got a better plan. Why don't I pick you up in Charlottesville after surgery, on my way down to your farm? And then I'll spend the next week with you."

"With both of us convalescing? Post-op, I won't be much of a hostess for you, Evie."

"What do I need you to do for me that I can't do for myself? I don't need a caretaker, just a quiet place for rumination. And with you as a crip, I'll have a captive audience when I want a sounding board for all those deep thoughts. Besides, the doc says I need more exercise. I'll get plenty just walking to and from your office, where I figure I'll be staying, since Clara now occupies that closet of a guest room in the main house. So say yes. You'll just have to find someone to truck you from West Virginia to the hospital beforehand."

"Then, yes! I'll welcome your company. Especially then. As for getting to the hospital, I can probably ask Tanner."

"My, my!" Evie said archly. "Making hospital runs, already? That's one relationship stage beyond picking someone up at the airport. Clearly things have progressed to a new level. Last time we talked, you sounded like you weren't sure you ever wanted to see him again."

Beatrice sighed. "Never say never."

Evie hooted. "The next thing you'll say is you two will be ringing in the New Year together."

"Um, well, as a matter of fact…"

"Damn, girl, you've got game! Reeling in a whopper in your own quiet way."

"Yeah, that's me: the quiet angler."

"You've obviously done something right. I'm impressed. Oh goody! I'll be visiting after the great event. I'm looking forward to hearing all the blow-by-blow details. Wink. Wink."

"Oh shut up."

Evie laughed and said in a sing-song voice, "Beatrice has a boyfriend. Beatrice has a boyfriend."

Beatrice sang back, "Evie is an evil bitch. Evie is an evil bitch."

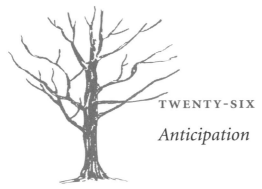

TWENTY-SIX

Anticipation

THE SUDDEN SQUEAL OF A RED-TAILED HAWK startled Beatrice into dropping the empty grain buckets she was carrying up the hill from the barn. Realizing how tightly wound she was, she forced herself to stop and look up at the circling raptor.

Take a breath, Beatrice.

Even in her urban childhood, she recognized the calming potential of the natural world. Back then, there were no hawks screeching outside her Dorchester three-decker. But many a seagull wheeled above the Neponset River. Despite their propensity to relieve themselves with great frequency and even greater volume in mid-air, Beatrice enjoyed watching them. She envied their freedom but also recognized purpose in their movements. They were hunting for food or mates or staking out territory. Yet even with such serious missions, the seagulls—like the hawk now scouting for rodents—were living in the moment.

The hawk was not obsessing, as Beatrice was, about what might take place in a few hours. She acknowledged that a healthier human being would be happily anticipating the imminent New Year's Eve celebration. But half of her mind was focused on the tedious details of putting her farm to rights beforehand.

Yesterday, Tanner had phoned to say his driver, Cal—who also served as kennel master, stable manager, and caretaker—would pick her up and drive her to the dinner party. Snow was in the forecast, and even a small amount could prove treacherous on the switchbacks that snaked up to Tanner's mountaintop lodge. After inviting her to stay over in one of his guest rooms, he explained that he would take her back home the next afternoon. He also invited Ralph to stay in the heated kennels adjoining the house.

Beatrice appreciated Tanner's thoughtfulness. But a full day away from home presupposed some last-minute chores. She had to cram an extra ration of hay into the llamas' wall racks, grain the youngsters, replenish the water troughs, and pray the electricity held so the stock heaters would prevent the water from freezing.

More complex thoughts occupied the other half of Beatrice's brain. Staying overnight—on New Year's Eve, no less—suggested a new and intimidating level of intimacy. Except, why had Tanner made a point of mentioning her own separate accommodations?

Adding to her puzzlement was the detail that two other guests, an elderly couple, would also stay the night at the lodge. Cal would be picking them up, too, from The Homestead where they had spent the previous week. At dawn the next day, he would drive them to the Roanoke airport for their flight home to North Carolina.

A makeshift valet service would spare the other guests the challenges of Tanner's mountain road in the dark, after a champagne-filled party. The guests would park at a lower altitude near the cabin housing Cal's family. The overworked but well-paid caretaker and/or his teenage son would convey them up to the festivities and back in a monstrous SUV accommodating eight passengers. Beatrice was familiar with that behemoth because Tanner had lent her the services of his driver when she was laid up with a broken leg the previous winter.

Shivering over the memories of that dark time, Beatrice retrieved the buckets and plodded on toward the house. A spike of pain from her right kneecap reminded her of the upcoming surgery. She questioned anew the wisdom of scheduling a knee replacement for mid-winter. She remembered how trying it had been to crutch her way around the ice and snow last year. Nevertheless, the February date for the procedure would allow sufficient recuperation time before llama-shearing in the spring. And if Evie and Bart followed through on their plans, Beatrice wanted to be sufficiently ambulatory to dance at their wedding in May.

Besides, she told herself, what better season than winter to be housebound?

When she lived in Virginia, Beatrice had taken winter's vexations in stride. Her New England origins had made her more than a match for January and February on the eastern side of the Alleghenies. There, spring actually arrived in March. But the mountains were a different story. What bothered Beatrice most was not the extra snow or prolonged cold but the gloom of an Appalachian winter. In January, sun shards rarely ricocheted off the snow cover and closed pupils down to pinpoints. Beatrice looked around at her farm on this overcast final day of December and sighed at the prevailing grays, offset only by the dull browns of desiccated ironweed and goldenrod.

On many a dim morning like this, Beatrice would leave her office early, so she could fire up the woodstove—not because she was cold but because her retinas longed for the brilliant oranges of the flames inside.

Aware of how closely she had flirted with full-blown mental illness the previous winter, Beatrice reminded herself of the differences between then and now. As she entered her house, with Ralph bolting in a heartbeat behind her, she willed herself not to wallow in apprehension. The odds were excellent that the recuperation from her upcoming surgery would be speedier and less troublesome than healing from that broken leg. She was also far less isolated today than she had been a year ago. Clara's presence then was a fluke. Now the girl was a permanent member of the household—a welcome companion, not merely a go-for. She was funny and smart and usually cheerful. She was becoming family.

Then there was Tanner. As often as his words or actions made Beatrice want to pull her hair out, she smiled more, laughed more when he was around. There was so much pure, simple pleasure in just observing him. It was not all that different from the joy she took in admiring her llamas' spectacularly long-lashed eyes or in savoring Ralph's balletic sprints after a deer. Beauty was a miracle to be appreciated, whatever the source. Even more miraculous was the realization that Tanner seemed to admire her, too. She couldn't quite trust that perception. But her pulse quickened under his gaze.

Proud of herself for shaking off some of her earlier fears, Beatrice returned to practical matters. She inventoried the items piled up in her utility room, where they awaited loading into Cal's SUV: purse, carryon bag, garment bag containing her evening dress, jacket, Ralph's leash. Then she grabbed a handful of dog treats and stuffed them into her pocket.

She was ready to leave, with twenty minutes to spare. Unfortunately, that was more than sufficient downtime to agitate her inner demons.

One worry promptly lurched to the fore. With all the fuss over the New Year's Eve party, she had yet to arrange for her post-op transportation needs. Clara was too young to drive to the supermarket, and Evie would be on hand for just seven days. When scheduling her surgery, Beatrice had assumed Tanner would be around to help. In yesterday's phone conversation, however, she learned he was heading overseas in late January. He happily shared the news that an old friend had invited him to Connemara to close out the season for woodcock—those elusive, big-eyed upland birds that demanded patience, quick reflexes, and sharp shooting from the hunter.

Hearing Tanner's plans, Beatrice promptly decided to withhold the news of her upcoming surgery, lest she undermine his obvious delight over the Irish junket. The week in Connemara would be his reward in an otherwise taxing schedule. From Ireland, he would fly to Germany to consult with his alternative-energy partners and then to Africa, where local authorities were bullying the directors of two of his foundations rehabilitating former child soldiers. He told her he dreaded the weeks of haggling with Rwandan and South Sudanese bureaucrats, while he cooled his heels in the substandard accommodations of Kigali and Juba. Well-placed bribes would eventually make the obstacles disappear but only after precious time was wasted stroking egos.

As she waited for Cal, Beatrice wondered anew whether Tanner's stopover in Bremen would involve more than boardroom meetings with one of his German business partners. She had yet to ask him about the lovely Ilse. Justifying that omission, Beatrice initially told herself that, as a purely platonic associate, she was hardly entitled to have any say about Tanner's female friends. But that fiction had died weeks ago with the realization that she no longer wanted to resist Tanner's gravitational pull on her heart and body. Now here she was, preparing for a heavy date that would most likely end in bed. She could no longer pretend indifference to Tanner's extracurricular activities.

Beatrice was appalled at the prospect of being just another sexual liaison for him. Aware of his sketchy track record during his marriage to Patty Scanlon, she questioned Tanner's capacity for monogamy. She needed answers—answers she probably should have gathered before now.

It had been decades since having "that talk" with a man. It wasn't easy back then. And Beatrice wondered what new rules had been written in the meantime.

Do potential lovers always feel this confused? Or am I just overthinking everything?

Once again, Beatrice experienced envy for that hawk outside, flying unfettered by cares of what tomorrow would bring. So she was relieved when Ralph harrumphed in response to a short tap on a car horn. Cal's arrival put an end to Beatrice's scab-picking. After slipping the leash on the setter, she opened the back door and beckoned the driver inside to help with her gear. When the last item was tucked into the SUV, she went back to take a final look around the house before locking up. She needed a private moment to beg the Cosmic Chuckle to stay far away for the next twenty-four hours.

TWENTY-SEVEN

The Next Level

BEATRICE CAREFULLY PLACED HER VELVET, empire-waist dress on its hanger. It had been a long time since she had purchased such extravagant apparel. But she had been determined to look attractive — desirable, even — for Tanner. The dress was supposed to boost her confidence as their relationship graduated to the next level.

But here she was, alone again, in the dark, in one of the sumptuous guest bedrooms at Tanner's lodge. The New Year's Eve celebration had not played out as anticipated. Yes, Tanner had swooped by on the stroke of midnight to give her a brief kiss. Yes, he had been attentive about introducing her to fellow dinner guests and making sure a convivial elderly couple, Angus and Elizabeth Whiteside, sat near her. But for Tanner, apparently, New Year's Eve was not a romantic occasion. It was an opportunity to raise money for his pet charities and solidify some business contacts. So he schmoozed and circulated while Beatrice wondered what the hell she was doing there.

She slipped into her ankle-length nightgown — another item she had chosen with great care. It was feminine and elegant and made her look almost willowy. The bodice had lacings. A front button closure extended from bust line to hem. She had looked forward to Tanner untying the laces and unfastening each tiny button.

She shivered — not in anticipation of sexual delights. She was simply cold. She regretted the nightgown's scooped neck and capped sleeves. She longed for one of her trusty flannel nightshirts. Noticing a heavy silk and wool shawl draped over an easy chair, Beatrice slung it around her shoulders and knelt by the bedroom hearth to poke some life into the glowing logs.

She watched the fire for a while until restlessness overcame her. She needed to walk off her frustration but felt trapped, even in the large bedroom. Warmed from the fire, she risked a breath of cold night air. She wrapped the shawl more tightly around her and opened the bedroom's French doors, leading onto a large deck. The temperature was frigid, but the snow had yet to arrive. In the clear, moonless sky the stars were spectacular. Searching for a few familiar constellations provided a welcome diversion. Shivering, she just made out the Northern Crown and its brightest star, Gemma, when a noise startled her.

Unbeknownst to her, the deck extended to other rooms. Someone was opening yet another French door. Knowing that the Whitesides were staying over until Cal shuttled them to the airport at dawn, Beatrice wanted to avoid an encounter in her nightgown. She moved silently toward her door but not quickly enough.

"Beatrice? I didn't realize you were still up. Are you all right?"

It was Tanner's voice. Beatrice briefly considered feigning deafness, slipping back into her room and closing and locking the door behind her. She was tired and hurt and disappointed and didn't feel like sharing those feelings — or making the effort to hide them. She settled for calling back, "I'm fine. Good night, Tanner." And then she entered her room.

Tanner sped after her. He was still dressed in his tux. His tie hung around his neck, and the top two buttons of his shirt were unfastened. He reached for her hand, but she pulled it away.

"You're angry. And you should be. I thought the bloviating congressman and his blue-haired wife would never leave. I dashed upstairs as soon as I could, but your lights were off. You don't know how badly I wanted to wake you, but I didn't know how welcome I'd be. And so … here we are." He fanned out his arms in frustration.

"Oh, Tanner, what am I doing here?" Beatrice slumped onto the large oak settee at the foot of the bed and stared into the fire.

He sat down beside her and placed a hand on her knee, which she jerked away.

"You're here because I couldn't imagine New Year's Eve without you," he said quietly. "And I neglected you. Some suitor I am. I'm so sorry."

"For Christ's sake, don't be sorry!" Beatrice got up and began pacing. "You were doing what you do. You were being a good host. You were entertaining your guests. You were hitting them up for money. You were wheeling and dealing. And if I were a different kind of woman, I'd be circulating right there with you. I'd be hanging on your arm and tossing out bon mots and pretending I knew my way around this log castle of yours. The evening just showed how different we are."

She knelt down to poke the fire, her back to Tanner, who maintained a heavy silence on the settee. Beatrice sat, tailor-style, on the floor before the hearth and wished she could just disappear. But finally the silence became so oppressive she needed to break it.

Still turned away from Tanner, she said, "It's perfectly obvious why I'd be attracted to you. It's not just your looks and money. There's a buoyancy about you that makes my jaw drop. You survived a catastrophically abusive childhood and your share of woes as an adult, but you refuse to let life extinguish that flame that burns so brightly in you. It's just irresistible."

"Apparently not," Tanner said, rising wearily.

Beatrice sprang up and turned toward him. "Oh, don't give me that! You could have your pick of smart, attractive women. I've seen the Style section photos of you with that stunning German businesswoman. What I can't figure out is ... why me?"

He snorted with annoyance. "Are you fishing for compliments now?"

"You damn well know that's not my speed. I just don't get it. What could you possibly see in me?"

"What is this obsession you have with analyzing everything?" He began pacing. "It was bad enough when you tried to dredge up every little detail as we worked on my memoirs. Now you're probing for some ulterior motives for my attraction to you? I will not be dissected, Beatrice. I detest controlling women."

Stung by Tanner's sudden vituperation, Beatrice stammered, "Controlling? No. That's not what I'm trying ... I'm confused. I'm scared. I just need a better fix on what's going on between us."

"Good God, you *are* scared! And more than a little obtuse." He stopped pacing and stared down at her. His expression combined challenge, mirth, and exasperation. "Fine. If you're asking if my intentions are serious, they are. Why? You're one of the realest things in my life, right up there with the hounds and the horses. And you of all people know that's high praise. You have a grounding influence on me. You see through my considerable bullshit and actually seem to like what lies underneath the ordure."

After a pause, Tanner added, in a gentler tone, "But that's only part of it. I can't figure you out. And I can figure *everyone* out, most definitely including that German businesswoman. You can be infuriatingly brittle and achingly vulnerable at the same time. I want to fight with you. I want to laugh with you. I want to protect you. I want to spark some gaiety into those sad, intense gray eyes of yours."

Suddenly tearing up, Beatrice hesitantly reached up to brush his cheek lightly with her fingertips. As her arm dropped back to her side, she sensed she had just received some significant answers. Right now, however, analyzing them—analyzing anything—was the last thing she wanted to do. "Ah, Jesus," she whispered, shaking her head. Then she rose up on her toes to kiss him.

Surprised, Tanner hesitated for a heartbeat before circling her waist with his left arm to pull her tightly toward him. His right arm swooped down behind her knees to pick her up. Unfurling her onto the bed, he kissed her lips and nuzzled her neck. She responded hungrily. After a while, he stood up and began removing his clothes, slowly and confidently, while smiling softly down at her.

Beatrice sat up with the intention of lifting off her nightgown. Tanner thrust a palm in her direction and barked, "Stop! That's my job. You'll not deprive me of one nanosecond of peeling you like a grape."

She laughed and focused instead on opening the covers. He quickly joined her. Lying on his side, he tugged gently on the topmost bodice lacing. As he worked his way down, he paused to nibble an ear or caress a clavicle. With excruciating deliberation, he addressed the buttons next. As he unfastened each tiny sphere, he explored the new square inch of skin thereby exposed. When he finally reached the hemline, he stroked down both sides of her body to part the material fully.

Executing a Marine-worthy push-up over her, Tanner leaned in for a deep kiss. Ever so slowly he entered her. Beatrice exhaled sharply, releasing some of her pent-up excitement. As he moved more deeply inside her, she uttered a small gasp.

"Sometimes, Hillwilla," he purred, "you know just the right thing to say."

Later, as the first glimmer of dawn cast a gray light over the bedroom, Beatrice stirred from a deep slumber. After reassuring herself that Tanner slept beside her, she recapped the events since her arrival at his lodge. She marveled at how the night had shifted from disaster to bliss. She relived the light and shade of Tanner's lovemaking—tender one minute, hard-driving the next, sweet and urgent all at once. She felt like a well-played guitar, with the selections ranging from minuets to Flamenco stand-offs. Smiling, she hugged the covers to her chest, closed her eyes, and curled onto her side.

Tanner shifted his position to spoon her. He slipped an arm around her waist. For some time, they lay that way, as they drifted in and out of slumber. Tanner mused sleepily, "You know all those cogent points I made? This is what they boil down to. We may not always mesh, but when we do, ah, how we mesh."

He pulled her even closer.

TWENTY-EIGHT

On the Hillwilla Road

AN INTENSE WHITE LIGHT DISTURBED BEATRICE'S SLUMBER. Ten o'clock. Late, even by her standards. The sun was at a sixty-degree angle with the horizon, and snowflakes were hurtling against each other, chaotically responding to orographic wind shifts.

Her sleepy fascination with the frosty sun shower ended abruptly when she realized the windows showcasing the dueling snowflakes were unfamiliar. They were without drapes and afforded a nearly floor-to-ceiling view of the wintry landscape. When a house is in splendid isolation atop a mountain, the occupants have little concern about peeping Toms. The windows were Tanner's, of course. He was clearly someone who disliked feeling closed in.

She reached out for him, in vain. The sheets on his side of the bed were cold. He had obviously been gone a while. His absence triggered an irrational fear of abandonment, followed by relief that she had privacy to tend to morning rituals.

Beatrice was almost finished with those rituals when she heard a commotion beyond the din of her hair dryer. She shut it off and left the bathroom to check. She promptly recognized the noise as a dog charging up the stairs. A moment later, Ralph barged through the partially open bedroom door. Reacting to the forward rush of canine energy, she lurched backward, thudding onto the bed. The setter launched his forelegs onto her lap and snuffled her adoringly.

"Oh, yuck, Ralph! Enough!" she laughed, wiping dog slobber from her face.

Tanner appeared, grinning, in the doorway. "Good morning!" he said. "I thought a visit from your familiar would be the proper way to start the New Year. But now it's my turn."

He walked to the bed, tilted Beatrice's chin upward, and kissed her. The kiss would have lasted longer, except Ralph, still halfway on his mistress's lap, bestowed his own greeting to Tanner's cheek.

As both humans groaned, Ralph, now off the bed, wiggled joyously around Tanner's knees. The dance was soon interrupted by an inconsolable wail from downstairs.

"That would be Horatio," Tanner explained. "He's the latest rotation from the kennel. But he's too uncivilized to allow into a lady's boudoir. So I closed the gate to the stairs."

"Rotation?"

"Every week when I'm in residence, I bring one of the hounds into the house—that's in addition to whichever dog lives here permanently, as Gertrude did. It's a great way of socializing the beasts. Horatio's up this week, but he's still a hooligan, I'm afraid. It doesn't help that he smells bacon on the stove just now."

"Ooh, so do I!" Beatrice placed a palm over her stomach to stifle a growl of hunger.

"The lady's worked up an appetite, I see? Excellent. Breakfast awaits. I'm a tolerable cook, but don't expect anything fancy. Scrambled eggs with cheese and chives, bacon, English muffins, coffee for me, tea for you. It's just you and me, in case you were wondering. Cal has already returned from depositing the Whitesides in Roanoke, and he has the next two weeks off. But I made sure his wife stocked up the larder beforehand."

Ralph led the way down the stairs, while the bloodhound yodeled his impatience. "Oh do be quiet, Horatio," Tanner chided. "And don't slam into our guests."

At the bottom of the stairs, he nudged Horatio's substantial brisket with his knee. "Sit!" he commanded. The hound slammed his butt on the floor but couldn't master his impatience for long. Horatio inhaled the new human from feet to chest, while Beatrice thumped his sides and Ralph stuck his nose under the host-dog's tail and tummy.

"Now that everyone's properly introduced, forward march!" Tanner waved toward the kitchen. He had already set that room's giant oak table with a merrily slapdash assortment of linens, silverware, crockery mugs, ironstone plates, and Waterford hocks as juice glasses. A Limoges candy bowl filled with floating hellebores was the centerpiece.

"Sit. Drink your orange juice like a good little girl, while I put the eggs on."

*   *   *

As the two humans attacked breakfast, in the presence of two vigilant canines, the talk turned to training animals. After questioning the merits of treat-training, Tanner sighed, "Of course, my efforts with Horatio here will probably be undone during my upcoming travel. Cal's wonderful with the pack but isn't as consistent as I'd like about discipline."

Suddenly, Beatrice slumped in her seat and blurted out, "This isn't fair!"

"Well, don't keep me in suspense," Tanner prodded with amusement.

"I mean, gee, we only just … got together, and now you're off trotting the globe again."

"'Got together'? Aren't you the demure one! I don't recall you being all that demure last night," he chuckled.

Beatrice snapped her napkin. "Don't ignore the point. I'm going to miss you. A lot."

"No, I'm not ignoring it, *mo mhuirnin*," Tanner said softly. "In here," he patted his chest, "I'm savoring it. You're so bloody independent, I couldn't be sure I would be missed."

Beatrice quietly noted the ancient Irish endearment then squeezed Tanner's hand. "Be sure! And I'll worry about you. The African itinerary doesn't thrill me. Those stops sound dicey."

"More tedious than anything else. I'll need to knock a few bureaucratic heads together. Last night's long-winded congressman may be of some help. Ages ago, he was posted to Rwanda with AID. One of his old friends from that era now holds high office in Kigali. Unfortunately, that official is heading off to his Avignon villa for an extended vacation. If I can find it, I'll pay him a visit before flying on to Africa."

"Will your German appointments leave you enough time to do that?"

Tanner leaned back and cocked his head. "You're awfully interested in my German business dealings. That's the second time you've mentioned them. And watching that blush creep up your throat, I have to wonder if I'm seeing just a hint of jealousy? I'm flattered."

"Well, I'm not!" Beatrice said, simultaneously annoyed and embarrassed.

"Easy, Hillwilla," he purred. "The stunning—I believe that's how you described her?—Fräulein Ilse is no threat. Oh, mind you, she would eagerly use sex to get more capital or a bigger market share. Just another bargaining tool for her. But that sort of sang-froid is off-putting. Besides, I don't require sexual favors to help her make whatever contacts she needs in D.C. or elsewhere. If her business does well, my considerable investment pays off. Win-win. Now do let some of that high color drain from your lovely face while I refresh your tea."

Tanner rose to fetch the kettle. Beatrice swatted his leg as he passed her chair. He leaned over and kissed the top of her head before moving to the stove.

When he handed her the cup and reclaimed his seat, Beatrice mused, "Funny you mentioned Avignon. The other day, when I had lunch with Clara and her new friend Leslie Dubois, the girl said her father lives in Provence. Small world. He's some international business mogul."

"So does the new friendship mean Clara's easing into the school scene okay?"

"I can't be sure," Beatrice said, gently blowing on her tea. "So much has happened to the kid. And my parenting skills leave something to be desired."

"You've been there for her, and that's the most important point. And now maybe she'll have a pal to stand by her, too. Although a girl from a wealthy French family is rather an odd find for a practical lass like Clara."

"Leslie's only half French. Her mother's a Vanderlick. You know, that big cattle farm in Marlboro County? Leslie lives there now, since her parents got divorced. That's a long way from where she grew up, Sutton Place, as Leslie *often* points out."

"I gather Clara's new friend has her nose tipped skyward?"

Beatrice shrugged. "She's a bit of a snob, but her heart's in the right place. I think. I also think she's vulnerable right now."

"Divorce is hard enough on a kid, but she must be reeling from the change in lifestyle. However well-off the Vanderlicks may be, a West Virginia farm is a radical move after Manhattan." Tanner whistled for emphasis.

"Ironically, the Marlboro girls act snobbishly toward her. Just because she's different. Her slight New York accent brands her as a come-here despite her Vanderlick roots. She probably feels every bit as much a fish out of water as Clara does."

"Is the Marlboro Academy a bad fit for Clara?" Tanner asked with concern.

"No, Clara seems to love the academic challenge and is doing quite well. But she chafes at being the lone Seneca County girl at school. The 'hick from the sticks.' She also worries that the Rodney drama will become common knowledge. Shared alienation is probably what brought the two girls together."

"And just maybe," Tanner mused, "Clara is modeling her foster mother, as she rolls along the Hillwilla Road. Like you, she's neither fish nor fowl." Seeing her eyes widen, he added quickly, "No offense intended. There's nothing wrong with marching to your own drumbeat. Where would I be if I hadn't done the exact same thing? But it can be a lonely road at times, yes?"

He seized Beatrice's hand and kissed it. She nodded. "I guess you and I have even more in common than I realized."

After a thoughtful pause, Tanner slapped his napkin down on the table and announced heartily, "Enough with the dreary analysis! We should be of good cheer on New Year's Day. So I have a happy mission for you. How would you like to help me choose the new dog of the manor? Gertrude's replacement?"

"Sounds like great fun." Then looking down at Ralph and Horatio, she added wistfully, "But maybe we should leave these guys here, to minimize the canine chaos."

*   *   *

After dumping their plates in the sink and suiting up for the cold weather, Beatrice and Tanner walked hand in hand toward the kennel. The biting wind instantly reddened their cheeks, but the snow had stopped and, at this altitude at least, the lemony sun was beating back the clouds.

Halfway to the kennel, Beatrice slipped her hand from Tanner's grasp and bent over the snow. She removed her gloves and stirred the flakes with her naked fingers.

"What are you doing, crazy lady?" Tanner asked. "You'll get frostbite!"

"No, no. It's the perfect consistency and depth!" she exclaimed, beaming up at him. Then she plopped none too gracefully in the snow, lay on her back, and began sweeping wide arcs with her arms and legs.

"What in God's name…?" gawped Tanner.

Beatrice stopped and looked up with playful innocence. "Haven't you ever made snow angels?" She gestured toward the snow-covered ground to her left.

"Apparently, I missed that course. Get up before you catch your death!"

Leaning forward, he extended his hand to help her to her feet. She grabbed his wrist, but instead of levering herself up, she jerked her arm downward and caught him off balance. He pitched into the snow beside her.

"Well, as long as you're down here…" she said impishly and then instructed him in the art of making snow wings.

Tanner complied, laughing in spite of himself. "Is that enough?" he asked after a few sweeps.

"I think so. Let's get up carefully to preserve our imprints."

Scrutinizing their work, Beatrice frowned like a disapproving art appraiser. "Oh phooey, I messed up my right wing. Probably because of favoring my knee. But yours, Tanner! That is one glorious angel! Probably the biggest freakin' snow angel I've ever seen."

"That, my dear, is no mere angel. That is a snow-archangel."

Laughing, she extended her right hand, "Congratulations, sir."

Her gesture was aborted when Tanner, grabbing her hand, ducked down and slung her over his right shoulder in a fireman's carry. "Turnabout is fair play," he chuckled.

"Jesus, don't drop me!" she squawked breathlessly.

"Furthest thing from my mind," he said, trudging toward the kennel. "I figure you're about ready to catch pneumonia with those wet clothes. So emergency measures are called for."

Beatrice was in no position, literally, to protest — or see his sly grin.

Opening a side door to the kennel, Tanner entered what appeared to be an office, equipped with desk, chair, and large leather sofa. As soon as he slipped Beatrice from his shoulder, he locked his lips on hers while zipping off his jacket then hers. Kissing, laughing, hyperventilating, and tearing at each other's clothing, the couple frog-marched toward the couch.

Placing a palm against Beatrice's sternum, Tanner shoved her down onto the cushions and then collapsed onto her. Odd articles of clothing still encumbered them but didn't slow the frenzied clip of passion.

An indeterminate amount of time later, Tanner kissed Beatrice's bare shoulder and whispered, "Rise and shine, *mo mhuirnin*. The shadows grow long, and someone will have my ass in a sling if I don't get her back home before Miss Clara arrives."

"Hmmpf," Beatrice murmured, burrowing more deeply into his embrace while tucking the sofa's ratty afghan under her chin.

"Wakey, wakey," he teased, swatting her rump.

"Must I?" she asked sleepily, as she pulled his arm around her waist. "Besides, I don't think I can walk. May never walk again."

"I didn't hear you complaining an hour or so ago."

"Who's complaining? I think maybe I was bragging." She rotated in his arms to look at his face. Beaming, she proclaimed, "Best New Year's ever! What a great year this will be!"

You hear that, Cosmic Chuckle?

TWENTY-NINE

A Cup of Sunshine

EVEN THOUGH IT WAS ALREADY SEVEN-THIRTY, the hollow that Ben Buckhalter called home was so starved for sunshine he needed to turn on the kitchen lights to locate the correct box of cereal. He didn't want to shake the wrong choice into his bowl: the cloyingly fruity and garishly colored rings favored by Virgil. Now that Amanda's godfather was a permanent member of the household, Froot Loops competed for space in the kitchen cabinet.

Having retrieved his boring but unobjectionable Cheerios, Ben paused by the kitchen window. He crouched down to scan the top of the east-facing hill in back of his doublewide and was rewarded by a cup of golden light emerging there. The remarkably level ridgeline of the low mountain spur on the opposite side of his home contained several small dips, roughly V-shaped. On winter mornings, before the rising sun cleared those hills and started burning off the fog, it would shine through one of those Vs. The light spilling through the notch wasn't enough to brighten Ben's hollow, but it worked its magic on the opposite summit. The brightly lit treetops, visible only from a certain angle inside the kitchen, and only on mornings that weren't too overcast, always cheered Ben. They offered hope that the day would be precipitation-free and not too cold—attributes important to a contractor who spent much of each day outside.

Despite his native pragmatism, Ben had developed a superstition about that small cup of sunshine. Seeing notch light before the sun topped the eastern hills presaged a good day.

On this Saturday morning, he had an added reason to hope his superstition would prove true. Mike was stopping by en route to a Marlboro County jobsite where the main contractor was offering time-and-a-half in an effort to finish a new townhouse development by March. Although he normally safeguarded his weekends, Mike was eager to escape Loretta's volcanic eruptions of morning sickness. He jumped at the contractor's plea for workers to show up on Saturdays. Because he could pick his own arrival time for his weekend labors and because he passed Ben's home during his southbound commute, Mike arranged for a breakfast get-together with his brother. He had called Ben the previous evening to announce good news but refused to provide any details.

The phone teaser piqued Ben's curiosity, even if he was skeptical about the positive nature of the information. The two brothers often diverged in their perceptions of things good and bad. Mike was inclined to seize on short-term benefits, while Ben absorbed the longer view, which often factored in dubious side-effects. It was not that Ben was a pessimist; he was just a mature adult, a realist.

Ben's optimism waned with every minute past the scheduled arrival time of seven-thirty. Too hungry to wait for Mike, he began slurping his Cheerios. He spooned them into his mouth as he stood over the sink. Occasionally, he dipped down to catch more of that golden light illuminating the hilltop.

Glad he had urged Amanda to sleep in, Ben was pouring his second cup of coffee when Mike's truck crackled on the driveway gravel. It was eight-ten. Virgil, who had already installed a new battery in his rusted, fifteen-year-old Ford Ranger that morning, arrived in the kitchen at the same time, ostensibly for a break. Clearly, he was curious about Mike's news, too.

Virgil and Ben had to wait another ten minutes until Mike glugged a glass of orange juice, shoveled two spoonfuls of sugar into his coffee, poured out his Cheerios, and chopped up a banana for the topping. Pulling up a chair at the kitchen table, he motioned for the other men to join him. Once all three were seated, Mike began.

"Well, I had me a little chat with the county's prosecuting attorney the other day. About Madsen. Looks like ol' Rodney is on the fast track to Beaver." He smiled at his companions and waited for their reactions.

"What does that mean?" asked Ben impatiently.

"It means he's about to start a ten-year sentence in the federal prison there."

"I didn't know Beaver had no prison," mused Virgil.

"Damn, I was hoping he'd end up a lot farther away," said Ben. "Once I heard the feds were involved, I figured he'd go way off in some other state."

"West Virginia has a lot of federal prisons, so it stands to reason Rodney would serve his time in state. But remember, Ben, if the feds didn't grab him, he could be doing time a lot closer to home. And I figure the feds will keep a tighter watch on him than the local Barney Fifes."

He continued, "C'mon, y'all! Stop worrying about *where* Rodney does time. Be glad he's doing time, sooner rather than later. And that's all because he copped a plea." Mike paused again, enjoying his role as street-smart commentator.

"Is that like copping a feel?" Virgil asked, giggling.

"Jeez, Virgil. Don't you watch any cop shows on TV? It means Rodney isn't demanding a trial. He's admitting he's guilty of cooking meth and selling it all over the place. Even out of state, to some big-time distributors."

"But, Mike, what about the other charges against him?" Ben interjected. "He planned to kidnap Clara. He attacked Beatrice. He was staking out her home and spying on Clara. Then there's what the pervert did to our girl a year ago—the whole reason we had to get her away from Charyce and find her a safe place to stay while you were working in Virginia."

"Lord have mercy," Virgil murmured, shaking his head.

"The state is dropping those charges, thanks to this deal." Seeing the confused look on Ben's face, Mike added hastily. "Just as well. J.R. Whelland would probably bungle the case anyway."

"Ain't that Earl Whelland's son?" Virgil asked. "I thought he become some big-shot lawyer up in Charleston?"

"That's just what his daddy said," Mike explained. "J.R. didn't do so hot in the capital. So he came back here with his tail tucked between his legs and decided his family ties might get him a cushy job with local government. He's the prosecuting attorney now. Don't you ever vote, Virgil? Sheesh!"

"How can someone commit crimes and never have to answer for them?" asked Ben.

"That's what plea bargaining is all about. The state saves itself a bundle by not holding a trial. And Rodney saves himself the risk of another coupla years tacked onto his drug sentence for what he did to Clara and that Desmond woman. The feds get Rodney to rat on his meth-head buddies.

And — most important — Clara never has to get on the stand. She's a tough kid, but testifying would be really scary for her."

"Yeah, I didn't much like the idea of that," Ben said. "Just think how awful it would be to have to tell the whole world about Rodney acting like a pervert. But I'm kinda surprised he would go so quietly. He's the whiny type who tries to justify whatever he does. Didn't he claim he was trying to 'save' Clara from sin? As if living with Beatrice is sinful but getting molested by a stepfather is perfectly normal."

"Ben, he was fried on meth when he said that. I guess once Rodney sobered up, he was smart enough to read the writing on the wall. The feds could have thrown him in a maximum-security prison. The slammer in Beaver is medium security, so he'll have more freedom there. But the clincher for Rodney was that the pervert charges would never make a splash. J.R. says guys who do things to kids get beaten up — and worse — in prison. He made sure Rodney knew that."

"Maybe Junior's smarter than we thought," Ben said. "And it was nice that he took the time to tell you what was going on."

"I guess he needed to make sure I wouldn't make a stink about dropping the charges involving Clara. J.R.'s coming up for reelection this year. He contacted the Desmond woman, too, and got her okay — but only after she talked about it with Clara. I talked to Clara, too."

"And how does she feel about all this?" Ben asked.

"She sounded relieved. She's been worried the kids at school'd find out about her link to Rodney. And make her life miserable. Teenagers can be little bastards."

"Lord have mercy," Virgil repeated.

Ben weighed all the hidden crimes that would never be punished against the crimes that were not only punished but showcased for all to see. He wasn't entirely comfortable with the priorities in the Madsen case. But he relished the immediacy of hiding a bad man away in a dark cell, regardless of which charges landed him there. So Ben raised his coffee mug. "A toast, boys. Here's to Rodney Madsen never seeing the light of day again."

"Amen, brother!" said Mike, clinking his mug against Ben's.

"Amen!" added Virgil.

THIRTY

Peep-Toed Makeover

AFTER CLOSING HER LAPTOP, Amanda caressed the smooth mahogany of her desk. She might not have a proper office for her labors on estimated taxes, but at least she had a lovely secretary tucked into a corner of her living room. She didn't pretend to know French Provincial from Colonial, but she recognized elegance when she saw it in a Virginia antique store. In a rare departure from her frugal ways, she handed over five hundred dollars to bring it home. It was far too small to handle all the paper generated by the business. But Amanda had no regrets. The desk made her feel special. It made her feel like she was going somewhere. Somewhere up in the world.

The roar of an engine jerked her gaze from the secretary's tasteful curves to the nearby window, where she saw a sedan in her driveway. The blue Ford was familiar, but it wasn't until she saw the legs emerging from the open driver's door that Amanda placed the vehicle. The legs were clad in dark stockings, visible from mid-thigh to ankle, where they were hidden by low-cut, high-heeled peep-toe boots—in faux snakeskin. The car belonged to Charyce Trask, her former sister-in-law.

Can I pretend to be out?

Her visitor, tottering up the walkway, ducked forward to peer into the living room window and spotted Amanda standing by her elegant desk. Charyce grinned broadly and waved a gloved hand enthusiastically. Sighing, Amanda raised a limp hand.

"How you doin', girl?" Charyce called out cheerfully as Amanda opened the door. Not waiting for an invitation, the visitor bustled inside, proclaiming, "It's colder than a witch's tit out there. S'ppose you could scare me up a nice hot cuppa coffee?"

Amanda responded, "I'm doing well, thank you." Her synapses were already on overload.

Why is Charyce in my living room? What's she up to now?

Amanda's synapses were also processing her guest's footwear.

Open toes? When there's snow on the ground?

When uncertain how to act, Amanda usually fell back on good manners. She beckoned Charyce into the kitchen and fed the coffee maker. A sharp observer of the world around her, Amanda had realized as a young woman that money and education weren't the only factors separating the classes. Good manners were equally essential for anyone aspiring to rise above her raising. The fact that she had learned proper etiquette relatively late in life infused a certain stiffness into Amanda's social skills. Nevertheless, she knew what to say when greeting a new client, which fork to use when eating salad, and what clothing to wear on any occasion. Her attire would never include peep-toe boots.

Playing the proper hostess, even if the woman in her kitchen was more intruder than guest, would clearly differentiate her from Charyce. The two might share a common background, but the well-mannered Amanda now stood head and shoulders above Charyce. She was determined to maintain that metaphoric height advantage.

She retrieved a sugar bowl from one cabinet and set it on the kitchen table. Peering inside the container, Charyce said, "Look at them cute little cubes. But, honey, a girl's gotta watch her figure. Ain't you got some Equal or Splenda?"

"Unfortunately, no."

"Damn, how do you keep so trim?" Charyce asked, eyeing her hostess up and down.

"I drink my coffee straight and I exercise," Amanda replied tightly.

"With a man like Ben, I guess I'd get me plenty of exercise, too." Charyce winked.

A beep from the coffee maker summoned Amanda to the kitchen counter, where she pinched her nose briefly, as if she had just smelled a foul odor. Returning with two full mugs, she said, "You've caught me in the middle of preparing quarterly taxes. So we won't be able to visit long. Was there something you needed?"

"I never could mess with all them figures. That's what men are for, seems to me. Why don't you go to the tax guy next to the Walmart?"

"We have an accountant, Charyce. But I'm still the business manager."

"Look at you! Got yourself a title and everything. I'm just a teeny bit jealous of how smart you are. And I guess that's why I'm here. I need advice from someone what's got her shit together. I need an itsy-bitsy favor, seeing as how you and me go way back."

Amanda did not for a moment believe her former sister-in-law was jealous of her. Charyce had always been inclined to mock her proper ways and quest for an education.

"What favor do you need?"

"Well, Amanda, you know I got no problem attracting the boys. But one of them boys is kinda tricky. Don't get me wrong. Clay is plenty interested. But I need the right kind of interest. That whole Rodney mess learned me that a girl needs a man who'll take care of her."

"I'm not sure how I could help you with that."

For the next fifteen minutes, Charyce spun out the tale of Claiborne Lightfoot, the distinguished gentleman who, several months earlier, had wandered into the karaoke bar where she worked. The owner of a Mercedes-Benz dealership in Roanoke, he was in the area to deliver, personally, an S550 sedan to a wealthy mine owner in Marlboro. Clay, and the employee who had convoyed out to West Virginia with him, wanted to celebrate the sale before heading home. Charyce was their waitress. Clay was a decade older, recently widowed, and lonely. He told her his troubles. She pegged him as a big tipper, so she listened attentively, and they chatted on, even after her shift ended. He left her fifty dollars. The next weekend he was back. She listened some more. He tipped her generously again. He became a regular, showing up almost every week to talk and flirt. Nothing more.

The Saturday when Rodney was arrested, Charyce missed her shift at the bar, because she had so many details to address. Clay asked for her and learned she had a family emergency. Alarmed, he tracked her down at her apartment. She told him how her husband had been arrested. She said Rodney had abused her. She cried on Clay's shoulder. They ended up in bed. "He might be fifty, but he can still cut the mustard," she assured Amanda.

"So, did he lose interest after that?"

Charyce narrowed her kohled eyes and said, "Men don't lose interest after spending a night with me, honey. But I got me some competition. The dead wife. Clay got that guilt thing going—like he's cheating on a ghost if another gal gets his engine revving. But I can handle that all right. I'll hold back for a while. No more sack time till I'm divorced from Rodney. Just a flash of titty now and then while I wait for good ol'-fashioned horniness to kick in." Charyce emphasized the point by cupping her left breast and leering at Amanda.

Amanda swallowed her revulsion and said, as evenly as she could manage, "Well, it sounds like you have everything in hand. So what do you need my help for?"

Cocking her head, Charyce said, "I ain't got my hands on nothing. Like I said, no more slap and tickle for a while." With a giggle, she added, "I even hinted maybe Clay took advantage of me, while I was so upset over Rodney. I gotta remind him I ain't easy. I'm just as good as that dead wife."

Charyce paused to take a gulp of coffee. "But it's like this, see. She come from one a them snooty Virginia families. The kind that thinks their shit don't stink. Clay talks about what a 'lady' she was. He describes these bang-up parties she used to throw. I guess the kind of shebangs where everyone stands around holding their drinks with their pinkies up in the air. Clay says she always wore just the right thing, knew the right things to say. And sometimes he gets this little smile on his face when I say something. He'll tell me—real nice, like—I used the wrong word and shoulda said such and so." Charyce tossed her head and continued. "He's got this funny idea of what a wife should be. So that's where you come in."

"You want me to play Henry Higgins to your Eliza Doolittle?" Amanda gasped.

"Oh, hon, I ain't talking about no threesome. Get a grip, Amanda! Nope, all's I want is for you to give me some ideas about how I can look like wife material. I figure Clay is my best chance of getting back on my feet, after losing the house and all."

Noting the stern look on Amanda's face, Charyce added, with feigned despair, "Elsewise, I'm gonna have to look to the Buckhalter boys. Mike, he owes me for giving him the daughter he always wanted. And I figure Ben does, too, since I gave him a goddaughter he's unnatural fond of. And what do I get? Nothing. No child support. No help."

Charyce sniffled and dug into her purse for a Kleenex. She peered out the corner of one eye to see if the implicit threat registered with her hostess.

It had. While her visitor twisted the Kleenex, Amanda processed the information flooding her brain. The prospect of helping Charyce reel in a better-heeled replacement for Rodney was repugnant. Sure, this Clay might be an egotistical jerk with a Pygmalion complex. Or he might simply be a fool, as so many men were around loose women. Then again, grief might have temporarily displaced his better judgment. In that case, he deserved compassion, not exploitation by a grifter like Charyce. But refusing to help class up her act in order to land the wealthy widower might have consequences close to home. Amanda could care less if Mike was somehow bamboozled into paying off his ex. But Ben would care. And that comment about Ben's "unnatural" fondness for Clara was as unsettling as it was preposterous.

Perhaps there's some way I can play along, without getting in too deep?

Finally, Amanda asked leadenly, "So will my help with a makeover be sufficient?"

A small smile of victory spread over Charyce's lips. "You know, I been thinkin' how you got that schoolmarm look down pat? A guy like Clay would probably see that as real ladylike. Acourse, he'd be thinkin' about what's under that buttoned sweater." She poked at Amanda's cardigan.

Amanda ignored the insult. "Okay," she sighed. "I suppose we could take a look at my closet. I could show you the kind of outfits I'd wear to certain occasions—like a fancy party, dinner at a nice restaurant, or even a family cookout. But I really couldn't lend you any of my clothes, because we're clearly not the same size." She glanced disapprovingly at Charyce's ample bust.

"You got that right, girl!" Charyce snickered. "I got me a woman's proper curves."

"But first," Amanda snapped, aborting the other woman's chuckles, "let's start with a critique of your current outfit." She managed a tight little smile.

Charyce glared menacingly but failed to intimidate her hostess, who shrugged and said, "Do you really think that getup would remotely fit

Clay's idea of how a wife should dress?"

Charyce's glare lost focus. She responded, with only mild petulance, "Why not?"

"For heaven's sake!" Amanda exclaimed. "Just look at those ridiculous boots!"

Raising one leg to rest the foot on an adjacent chair, Charyce earnestly regarded her boot—while also revealing more thigh than Amanda cared to see. "What's wrong with them?"

Charyce was not being defensive. She genuinely had no idea of the inappropriateness of her footwear. If it induced a man to look, that was a good thing, wasn't it?

"For starters, they're not very practical," Amanda said with exasperation. "Sometimes, Charyce, looking ladylike boils down to exercising a little common sense."

Charyce squinted in a mixture of confusion and concentration.

"Look, it's probably easier if I just show you the kind of shoes I'd wear if I were visiting you on a snowy winter's day." Amanda rose and headed for her bedroom.

Charyce followed clumsily. It was difficult to walk in peep-toe boots with four-inch heels while simultaneously looking down at them.

THIRTY-ONE

Not So Pretty in Pink

As she prepared dinner, Beatrice was not focused on the carrots she was chopping. Her thoughts drifted back to New Year's, to Tanner, to the baritone warmth of his voice, the tautness of his biceps, the exciting feel of his beard against her skin, the crazily pale blue of his eyes. Her reverie imploded with the slam of Clara's over-the-shoulder bag landing on the kitchen counter.

"Hey, easy on the Formica!"

"Sorry," the teenager grumbled. She poured a glass of milk and collapsed onto one of the kitchen chairs. She ripped down the zipper on her quilted parka and flung the jacket on an adjacent chair.

Still chopping, with her back to Clara, Beatrice winced. She didn't need to see the girl to absorb her radiating anger. "Is your father coming inside?"

"No."

"Okay, want to tell me what's going on?" Beatrice wiped her hands on a towel and joined Clara.

"Loretta's a bimbo."

"I believe we established that some time ago. I also trust you're smart enough not to share that perception with your father?"

"Duh!" Then Clara's face shifted from anger to supplication. "Do I really have to go to Daddy's wedding next week?"

Beatrice responded with a wooden stare and folded her arms over her chest. Groaning in exasperation, Clara rose and headed for the utility room. She returned with the garment bag she had dumped there, after Mike had dropped her off by the back door. Before Beatrice could pose a question, the girl raised an index finger and unzipped the bag.

Inside was a very pink dress made of some indeterminate synthetic fabric. The hem, at mid-calf length, was trimmed with rickrack the color of

162

Pepto Bismol, as were the puffy short sleeves. Appliquéd hearts festooned the high, boat-neck bodice.

Beatrice slapped a hand over her mouth and said, "Oh, my."

"Wait," Clara admonished, "I'm not finished." From the bottom of the bag, she extracted a pink plastic hairband, erupting with pink plastic hearts. Clara mashed the hairband onto her head. Holding the dress at arm's length with one hand, she dug the other hand into her hip, cocked her head defiantly, and glared at Beatrice.

Beatrice fell forward onto the table in paroxysms of laughter. Against her will, Clara joined in. She folded the dress over one of the chairs and sat down, still wearing the headpiece at a skewed angle.

Struggling to recover her composure, Beatrice wiped tears from her eyes. Zeroing in on the hairband, she got the giggles again. "Take that off, will you? Maybe there's something we can do." She reached for the band and examined it. "Oh, Christ it's hopeless. I could never remove those hearts without breaking the whole damn thing."

Reading the sudden dejection on Clara's face, Beatrice winked, and her lips widened in a grin. Holding the pink monstrosity in both hands, she stretched it, as if to try it on herself. She kept stretching, now at an upward angle. The band cracked in two. "Oops! So sorry, Clara," she said, fluttering her eyelashes innocently.

Clara's jaw dropped in admiration. "Here let me finish it off," she said, raising a fist.

"No! That's way too obvious. With a clean break, you have plausible denial. Wait until the wedding day next week, and when you get to the church, tell Loretta how sorry you are for the last-minute accident. Blame me for being ham-handed as I adjusted your hairdo. Jesus," Beatrice added, scrutinizing the two broken pieces. "What was Loretta thinking?"

"Suppose we can shred the dress, too?" Clara asked.

"No, but the appliqués are just tacked on. I can remove them without any problem. Maybe the god-awful rickrack, too. Chances are, Loretta will be so preoccupied with her own dress, she won't notice the changes in yours. Of course, even if she does, it'll be a done deal by then."

"But the dress is still ugly. And the color is just awful for my hair."

"I don't think I can do anything about that, kiddo. Even if I can find some decent fabric dye, it might make things worse, make the dress streaky."

"It couldn't get any worse."

"Well, maybe not, but there's a limit to how far you can push the bride and, more important, your father. It's one of the hard facts of life. Bridesmaid dresses always suck. Junior bridesmaid dresses suck even more. It's a plot to make sure the bride is the best-dressed woman in the wedding party."

"Did you make your bridesmaids wear ugly dresses at your wedding?"

"No, but I didn't go for the full regalia. It was a small, brief ceremony before a priest. No white gown. Only a few guests. Everyone just wore their own nice clothing—me, Kate, Arthur, Evie, Bart, the groom, his brothers." Beatrice chuckled over some private joke.

"What's so funny now?"

"I was just imagining Evie's reaction if I'd tried to get her to wear a monstrosity like that." Beatrice waved a hand in the direction of the dress-draped chair.

"Thanks," Clara grumped.

"Sorry. But look at it this way, how many of the wedding guests will you actually know?"

"Not many, I guess. I don't think Daddy bothered inviting many people. Maybe a few of the guys he's worked with. And Ben and Amanda, of course. I think Uncle Virgil bowed out. He's not real comfortable at parties. From what I've heard, most of the guests will be Loretta's family and friends."

"Okay. Of the people you know, how many do you really care about?"

Clara shot Beatrice a skeptical look but answered, "I guess just Daddy and Ben."

"Aha! And they're men. Men never notice anything a woman wears. Unless she's showing lots of skin. If you blindfolded them and asked them to describe your hair, they wouldn't know whether you had a pixie cut or a long ponytail. As for the other wedding guests, what do you care if they think your dress is hideous? Everyone knows bridesmaids' dresses reflect the taste of the bride, not the poor sap wearing the dress."

"Maybe I can catch a bad cold before next week," Clara mused glumly.

"Oh, no, you don't! You're not infecting me with a cold before knee surgery. But maybe you can take along another dress and change into it shortly after the reception begins. Tell Loretta you spilled something on the Pepto Abysmal dress."

Clara's expression brightened. "I think I really will spill something on it."

"Sounds like a plan. But speaking of the surgery, I'm going to need a lot of help from you when I come home from the hospital. With any luck, the recuperation won't take as long as it did last year for the broken leg. But it will be a few weeks before I can drive or get up and down the hill to the barn. So in addition to haying, graining, and watering the llamas, you'll have to shovel manure, too. Sorry. Before I go under the knife, I'll give the llamas their shots and trim their toenails, so we won't have to worry about that until after I get more mobile. And Evie will be here the first week after surgery. She'll handle the cooking, which she really likes to do. But remember, we can't overload her with chores, because she'll still be recuperating herself. So I'll need you to be my strong right hand from the get-go. Okay?"

"I did it before. I can do it again," Clara responded with self-important stoicism. Then her confident facial expression morphed into a worried frown. "But how are we gonna get stuff from the store when we need it?

"I'll do a huge shopping run to stock up before I go to the hospital. And I'll probably be able to drive in less than a month. But that still leaves a gap of a few weeks. Do you suppose we could ask one of your relatives for help? God, I really hate to ask for favors!"

"That stupid dress tells me they already think I'm a helpless five-year-old. So I'll play helpless and ask them for favors. The only problem is when Ben or Daddy or Eltie could get away from work. Amanda doesn't work full time, so maybe I could ask her. But…" Clara shuddered.

"Yeah, I know. Some people are harder than others to hit up for favors. I had planned to ask Tanner to lend a hand, but he's heading off for Europe and then Africa fairly soon. I see no point in telling him about the surgery before he leaves. He'll have enough on his plate. He doesn't need an added serving of guilt."

"He's gonna be mad at you when he comes back and finds out."

"Probably. But I don't want to be one of those whiny women who string their men along on guilt trips."

Clara sucked in her breath when she realized Beatrice thought of Tanner as her man. The teenager was just as glad Tanner would be out of the picture, so she could be the go-to person, so she could consolidate her position with Beatrice and safeguard her current living arrangement. It suddenly became crucial for Clara to solve the transportation problem.

"I've got it!" she announced triumphantly after a few minutes. "Vaughn! She doesn't work. She likes us. She's nice. Besides, you'll look awful after surgery. You wouldn't want certain people to see you that way, right? But you wouldn't feel embarrassed around someone like Vaughn."

Not until later that evening would Beatrice realize Clara meant Tanner when she mentioned "certain people" — and that the girl felt like she was competing with Tanner for Beatrice's affections. For now, however, she focused only on an obvious solution to the transportation crisis. "Hmmm," she said. "That's worth a shot."

Before Beatrice could have any second thoughts, Clara headed to the phone. "I'll call Vaughn right now," she said confidently.

THIRTY-TWO

Beyond the Fence

RALPH LACKED HUMAN POWERS OF ANALYSIS. But he was hardly devoid of analytical skills. Like other long-nosed, flop-eared, pendulously flewed dogs, he could parse olfactory data to a degree that would put to shame humankind's most experienced, hawk-nosed oenophile or perfume developer. If he suddenly lost the use of his eyes, for example, his nose would tell him he was currently in the company of three young humans: two female and one male.

One was Clara. Ralph now associated her smells and sounds with the noise people made when they said her name. When his primary human uttered, "Noise, noise, noise, Clara," Clara-smells infused the air, or soon would. They were good smells. She was a good pack member.

Although the young human male walking beside Ralph was not part of the pack, his smells were good, too. The setter did not yet know the boy was called "Lane" but knew enough to offer a courteous "hello." In other words, when Lane arrived, the dog would push his black nose into the boy's crotch.

Well-raised pups exchanged sniffs to the genitals to signal a lack of aggression and swap useful olfactory information. For reasons that eluded Ralph, humans missed that basic lesson in etiquette. Worse, they often reacted to a proper canine greeting with aggressive gestures and loud noises. At best, they briefly tolerated the intruding canine nose before gently moving it aside.

Lane was an exception. When Ralph sniffed hello, the boy scooted the dog between his knees, bent over the dog's lower back and gave it a brisk rub. Neither Ralph's nor Lane's nose was quite where it should be, from a canine perspective, but close enough to communicate friendliness.

The other young female — whose name, Leslie, he also hadn't yet learned — numbered among the humans who made loud noises when

Ralph greeted her with canine politeness. Startled, the dog would quickly abandon the social amenities, and the girl would settle down. And once he sat, she would make soft noises and stroke his head. As a result, he graciously overlooked her earlier rudeness.

So Ralph was cheerful in the presence of these three humans on this cold, windy day, all the more so because he was on a walk with them. He was now well beyond the Invisible Fence, that unseen barrier that emitted high-pitched beeps and stung his neck if he didn't retreat at the first squeal. His primary human had not walked him in a while. Being a dog, Ralph could not measure time. But he certainly remembered happy walks with Beatrice. So today, when Clara jingled his leash, Ralph wiggled with joy.

It was ecstasy to inhale all the new scents that lay beyond the Invisible Fence. Because the young humans often paused in their stroll to exchange happy sounds, Ralph had ample opportunity to sniff out chipmunk pee here, deer poop there, and make his own regular contributions to the olfactory mélange. Nose to ground, he suddenly began inhaling an intense level of llama odors. Those large beasts might dwell in the world beyond the beeping barrier, but his humans were awash in their scents. So the smell was very familiar. Looking up from the snow-dusted trail, the dog realized his two-legged companions had turned into the llamas' territory.

Ralph lowered his tail just a bit. Although the llamas were part of his extended pack and thus lay under his protection, he was not entirely comfortable in their presence. It was unnerving when their huge eyes locked onto his, especially when they snaked their gigantic heads down to his nose for a closer look. Instead of inhaling his scent, they would puff air into his nose—occasionally with startling force. So Ralph padded closely beside the three young humans as they entered the barn. He avoided eye contact with the llamas.

The youngsters were focused on the llamas' wool. Days earlier, Lane had eagerly agreed to the girls' plan for a joint 4-H project—harvesting the animals' fiber and producing some article of clothing from it, while providing exemplars of all the fiber-processing stages. He was happy for any excuse to spend time with Leslie.

Inside the barn, the teenagers discussed the division of labor. Ralph, bored, curled into a sleepy ball in the tack room. Clara would be the animal handler and shearer. All three would share the tedious washing, drying, picking, and carding tasks. Lane would take care of the spinning and knitting. And Leslie, the budding artist, would design the final product, a scarf, and figure out the most appealing color combination.

Clara already had six large bags of wool, sheared during the previous spring. Winter wouldn't get in the way of processing that fiber. But in the interest of harvesting at least one intact fleece for show-and-tell purposes, the teenagers would have to wait for warm temperatures, probably in early May. Meanwhile, Lane would attempt to perfect his technique on Beatrice's spinning wheel, and Leslie would research scarf patterns.

Happy to have hashed out some essential details of their project, Clara deemed it was time to get in out of the cold. "Beatrice made chicken parm this morning before she left to run errands in Marlboro," she told her friends. "And for dessert, I can defrost the chocolate chip cookies we made last week."

"Let's go. I'm starved," Lane said.

"Was that your stomach squealing and gurgling?" Leslie asked him.

"Not me. I think it's coming from that stall over there. See? Ralph's looking in that direction, too."

Ralph was sniffing toward the stall in question. Clara entered it but saw nothing amiss. As soon as the girl approached, Buck danced toward her and puffed a melon-scented greeting into her face. They were in the half of the barn housing the geldings and weanlings. Barn and pasture were still divided to ensure the full weaning of Dip and Buck.

"I dunno. I don't hear anything now," Clara said. "Would one of you grab Ralph's leash? We'll leave through the main pasture gate," she added, waving a hand forward. "Make sure you close each little gate after you."

The pair complied, with Ralph at Lane's side. Once in the pasture, they heard the gurgling noise again. Ralph reacted with a short bark. The sound came from Buck, currently prancing parallel to the temporary fence bisecting the llamas' feeding grounds.

"What the heck's he doing?" Lane asked.

"I dunno," Clara answered. "But he looks healthy enough." She noted the animal's high tail, forward ears, and friskiness.

The gurgling got much louder. To Clara, the noise sounded somewhat like the llamas' alarm call but not quite. Then several of the female llamas on the other side of the interior fence began clucking. One didn't need a course in camelid behavior to infer active disapproval.

Before they could exit the pasture, Clara and her friends needed to enter the territory occupied by the clucking females and then leave by the wide gate that led to the world outside. Unsettled by the herd's sudden restlessness, Clara opened the inner gate only a bit and beckoned Lane and Leslie through the narrow opening while she hung back, using her body to block access to any of the llamas. As she was about to close the barrier, Buck sprang toward her. She thought he was saying farewell. But as she reached out to pet him, he ducked under her arm and bolted into the forbidden land of the adult females.

"Nooooo!" Clara shouted.

Chaos reigned for the next fifteen minutes. Clara ordered her friends and Ralph out of the llamas' territory. Then while Leslie kept the dog under control, Lane reentered to help Clara corral Buck. Figuring the young llama was looking for his mother, they sped to Reine to thwart any nursing that would undo the weaning process. Reine showed little interest in her wayward son. Nor he in her. Buck's focus was on Barrie. And nursing was the last thing on his mind.

Barrie was at the far end of the divided pasture. She ran away from Buck, stopped abruptly, turned and shot a wad of spit square in his face. Stunned, he paused in his pursuit. With lower lip hanging, he tried to cough the vomit-like smell from his nose and mouth, while Barrie danced toward him and circled him provocatively.

Realizing that the gurgling was what Beatrice's llama books called "orgling"—the noise male llamas make when breeding—Clara dashed back to the barn to grab a halter and lead. When she returned, Barrie was kushed serenely, with the much smaller, madly orgling Buck straddling her lower back. Lane stood nearby, wide-eyed, grinning and shaking his head.

With less difficulty than anticipated, he and Clara slipped a halter on the preoccupied Buck. Next she clipped the lead onto the halter. Realizing it might be risky to attempt to pull the randy llama off Barrie, she waited, gripping the lead tightly. It was another fifteen minutes before Buck dismounted.

Barrie rose with ponderous dignity, walked a few yards away, and calmly began nibbling tufts of dead grass poking out of the light snow cover.

Taking advantage of Buck's temporary disorientation, Clara led him to the other side of the dividing fence. Lane closed the inner gate after them. Graf, the dominant gelding, walked heavily toward the errant weanling and stared down at him with menace. Still full of himself, Buck raised his head and broadened his chest. Graf flattened his large, banana-shaped ears and spat with expert aim. With that, the young llama's feistiness shriveled. Clara removed his halter cautiously, to minimize contact with the green slime speckling Buck's face. The weanling slinked off to the sidelines to make himself as inconspicuous as possible.

As soon as Clara and Lane rejoined Leslie outside the pasture, all three erupted in nervous laughter. Ralph wagged his tail expectantly. Clara reached down to pet him—and thereby steady her nerves—but her spit-slimed hand induced a sneezing jag in the dog. Lane and Leslie laughed again. Clara moaned, "Beatrice is gonna kill me."

THIRTY-THREE

Invasion of the Body-Snatchers

Dear Diary,

I don't get it. I figured Beatrice would go postal when I told her about Buck getting out and messing around with Barrie. She's always warning me about closing gates and paying attention when I work around the llamas. In fact, I considered keeping my mouth shut. I checked a couple of Beatrice's llama books and they said male llamas usually can't make babies until they're over a year old. So probably nothing will happen. But what if it does? And what if Barrie has trouble being pregnant, just like Reine did last year? So I figured Beatrice would be even angrier if the truth came out later. So I fessed up.

And you know what she said? "Spit happens." That's all. She understood it was an accident, that I wasn't acting irresponsible. She said she was glad we returned Buck to his side of the fence without anyone getting hurt. Phew! Was I relieved! She just said we'll have to keep a closer watch on Buck until he can get fixed. Eltie won't geld him until he's at least a year old. That's two months from now.

The only time Beatrice looked like she might get mad was when she talked about looking for signs of pregnancy in Barrie. Then she counted up the months and sighed, saying the baby if there is one would arrive at the worst possible time, in the middle of next winter. I guess it's hard to keep a winter baby healthy. Especially if the birth happens when no one's around to dry the little guy off. I didn't think of that. So I hope Barrie doesn't get pregnant, even though it would be cool to see another birth and have another fuzzy little llama romping around, giving nose kisses and looking adorable. Anyways, Beatrice might have acted worried for a while there, but she never got angry. She said Eltie could maybe do a blood test to look for pregnancy hormones. And then she shrugged and quoted a line from Scripture: "Sufficient unto the day is the trouble thereof." Huh? Since when does Beatrice quote from the Bible? And if I understand that line, it means not to worry about tomorrow. But Beatrice ALWAYS worries about tomorrow. And the day after that and the month after that.

I think alien invaders landed in Seneca County and possessed Beatrice. Just kidding, LOL! But she's sure been different lately. She laughs more. She's drinking less. I bet I know why. No, it's not space aliens. It's Tanner. She's got a real thing for him now. He's okay, I guess, but can be scary sarcastic. Beatrice said he's coming over tomorrow to help her trim the llamas' toenails. I don't know why I can't help her with that. But she said Vike and Graf can be tricky and if they act up, she'll need a stronger helper than me. I think that's just an excuse.

She told me Tanner will be going away on some big trip in a little while. It would be okay with me if he stayed away. We can handle the llamas just fine by ourselves.

In the meantime, Beatrice will get a few reminders of just how handy I can be. She's having knee surgery soon. Because she won't be able to drive for a few weeks, she couldn't figure out how we'd manage when we need stuff from the store or when she needs to go to physical therapy. So I'm the one who came up with the idea of asking Vaughn to help. Not only that, but I'm the one who called Vaughn. Beatrice gets uncomfortable asking people for favors. So I did it for her.

Vaughn was great. No surprise there, since she's a genuinely kind lady who never meanmouths anyone and helps out however she can. Last year, when I was first living here and Beatrice was laid up with the broken leg, Vaughn would visit me sometimes. I was awful lonely back then. Kind of scared, too. And Vaughn's visits made me feel better. Also she used to bring food. And, boy, can she cook! Especially desserts!

Vaughn said she'd be glad to help. She even offered to take Beatrice to the hospital all the way over in Charlottesville, in Virginia. That's three hours away! That's a lot of driving. Didn't I tell you Vaughn was nice?

Beatrice isn't the only one acting different, Dear Diary. Maybe space aliens have possessed Momma, too. Because she called me the other day. It's been ages since she called. Of course, I don't figure she was all that interested in how I was doing. :-(For one thing, she was looking for dirt about Daddy's wedding. She wanted to know what Loretta was wearing. Wanted to know if Loretta was showing yet. Wanted to know if Loretta was still "barfing her guts out." That made me laugh. Loretta sure does spend a lot of time looking green.

So then I told Momma about that ugly junior bridesmaid dress I have to wear. Boy, did she laugh. Years ago, she said, she got stuck wearing an awful dress at a girlfriend's wedding. Her dress was pink, too. And frilly. Momma hates pink. And she's not a frilly kind of girl, as she put it. Said she couldn't wait to take it off.

Then Momma told me she's dating some new dude. He's old, like 50. But he's "cute" anyhow. I bet he's richer than he is cute, though. He owns some business that sells fancy cars. Big deal. Rodney had a place that sold expensive tractors. It didn't make him any Prince Charming. But Momma says this new guy, Clay, isn't like anyone she's ever gone out with before. Clay is educated, she says, and comes from a good family. And he's not scared about marriage. He was happily married for a long time before his wife died last year. So he's sad and lonely now. He and Momma are taking things slow, doing things right, she says. She'd like me to meet him. I hesitated when she said that, but she told me not to worry. "Clay ain't Rodney." He has a daughter in college and is a "real gentleman." We'll see. But he does sound a whole bunch better than Momma's usual dates.

So a lot of stuff is going on. There's the 4-H project with Lane and Leslie. It's fun being around them so much. Even if Leslie is so different. Rich and refined and everything. Even if Lane hangs around only to be close to Leslie. But he sure was a big help when Buck escaped.

I think I could probably talk about stuff with Lane. Maybe even more than with Leslie, cause sometimes she makes fun of my "hick from the sticks" ways. She's just kidding, but it bothers me sometimes. But Lane is never snooty. I've never had a boy as a friend before. And yes, Dear Diary, that's TWO words: "boy" and "friend." Lane is definitely not my "boyfriend." I feel way older than him, even though he's months older than me. But that's nothing new. Back in middle school, I felt older than all the boys in my class. They were always sticking their hands in their armpits to make fart noises. Or bragging about how they'd just taken a major dump in the boys' room. Or joking about peeing their names in the snow. What is it about boys and bathroom jokes? They should have to shovel llama manure. Then maybe they'd stop thinking pee and poop were so hilarious. At least Lane isn't that much of a tool. He's pretty smart, too.

Sometimes I worry that I've never been attracted to any of the boys in school. Does that mean there's something wrong with me? But I'm not attracted to any of the girls, either. Honest. Well, sure, I pay attention to their clothes. Leslie's in particular. She has beautiful clothes. And I notice how the other girls fix their hair and make up their eyes. But that's only so I can figure out how I can make myself look sharp. Or at least how I can pass for normal.

I wonder if I'll ever feel normal.

It sure doesn't help living with someone who's so different. I wonder if Beatrice has ever fit in anywhere? Her brother Bart seems normal enough, though. He was so nice to me when we visited him last year. But Beatrice's best friend, Evie, is just as weird as she is. I have never heard a grown woman swear so much without being slutty. She even invents her own cusses. Some are pretty funny, I admit. Evie's a little scary, but she can be fun. She's visiting after Beatrice's operation. I may have a lot of work the week she's here, because Evie was sick recently. She spent Christmas in the hospital. Something about her heart. Not as bad as a heart attack, though, and she's supposed to be fine. But Beatrice warned me not to expect Evie to take care of the chores Beatrice would normally tackle if she could walk.

So I don't know how that week will be. But I can handle it. And Beatrice will see that I'm a lot more grown up than she realizes.

Now if I can just get through Daddy's wedding. Ugh. That dress! It's going to be a strain being nice to Loretta. And I'm not feeling all that sweet on Daddy, either. Did he have to hook up with another girlfriend so soon? Did he have to get her pregnant? It's embarrassing. When I told Leslie about it, she said, "Didn't your father ever take a sex-ed course? You'd think people his age would have more sense." I just wish he'd stop saying how much fun I'll have with a little brother or sister. Oh yeah, that will be lots of fun, won't it? Changing stinky diapers. Listening to a baby screaming its lungs off. I can hardly wait. Am I supposed to play babysitter when I spend summer vacation at Daddy's? Will there even be room for me there? Last year, it was just Daddy and me. This year it will be him, Loretta, the baby, and me. I don't think all of us can fit in that cabin. I hope I can keep staying with Beatrice.

I hope I can stay here forever. Or at least until I go to college.

THIRTY-FOUR

Heavy-Handedness

AT PRECISELY ELEVEN-THIRTY, Ralph announced the punctual arrival of Tanner's Hummer in the driveway. Beatrice peered into the oven to monitor the croustades she was toasting for lunch then dashed for the back door. Already in her utility room, Tanner was crouched in conversation with the adoring setter.

He gave Ralph's ears a final scrabble before rising to greet his hostess. She went up on tiptoe to kiss him, but just as he pulled her closer, the tinny kitchen timer went off. "Oh damn! Sorry, gotta get that or lunch will burn."

Tanner followed her. She removed the tray from the oven and set it on the counter. Raising an index finger, she said, "Lemme just stuff these and I'll be all yours."

Tanner loomed in back of her, his palms splayed on the countertop where she tended to her culinary tasks. As he pressed into her, his tongue etched a languid circle on the side of her neck. "Don't mind me," he teased. "I'm getting an appetite and need to nibble on a little something."

Holding her hands up by her shoulders to prevent contaminating Tanner with shredded ham and mozzarella, she turned to face him. They shared a lingering kiss.

When it ended, he tugged on the shoulder strap of her apron. "Where did you acquire this tasteless thing?" he asked, pointing to the apron's leering leprechaun, whose cartoon bubble read, "Kiss me, I'm Irish."

"Evie. In addition to all the nice things we've given each other over the years, we often play a little game of exchanging horrendously kitschy items. The stupider the better."

"Ms. Rudner's sense of humor escapes me."

"I'm just relieved she's recovered it. She had some heart trouble a few weeks back, and it scared the fun out of her for a while. She needed angioplasty, can you believe it?"

"Sounds like Evie wasn't the only one who got scared."

"Damn straight. So I'll need you to take good care of yourself during your upcoming travels." Beatrice bumped her forehead into Tanner's chest then turned back to the food.

"What smells so good?" he asked, digging his chin into her shoulder to eyeball her work.

"Sautéed garlic. Okay, one last roll to stuff and then I can stick everything in the fridge for a while, and I'll be good to go."

"Who knew you were such a domestic goddess?"

"I'm an excellent cook. About time I showed off a bit for you. Besides, you're gonna earn your lunch."

"I thought we were headed to the barn, not the bedroom," he said, grinning boyishly.

"Promises, promises," she quipped.

The llamas' toenails needed trimming every few months. Although some of the animals docilely accepted their pedicures, two of the males actively resisted. With them, four hands were needed. Eltie occasionally helped, if she was already at the farm for some other task. Otherwise Beatrice recruited Clara. But the girl's strength was insufficient if Graf or Vike got testy, so Beatrice had asked Tanner to help.

The already-haltered llamas were waiting in two stalls when Tanner and Beatrice arrived at the barn. Graf was the first one led into the chute. Following Beatrice's instructions, Tanner stayed about twenty feet away, lest his presence unnerve the big male. When the animal was secured, she signaled Tanner to approach. Revealing significantly more white than usual, Graf's right eye rolled rearward to monitor the stranger. The big gelding widened his stance and dug all four feet more firmly into the floor of the chute.

"Let's start with the front right," Beatrice said. "Crouch forward of the leg, grab the hock, and guide the elbow up and to the rear. Yeah, like that! Okay, hold it while I get into position."

Sitting on the ground, she reached under the side rail to snatch Graf's foot with her left hand. The animal tried to jerk away, but Tanner's grip was too strong. The llama grunted in annoyance but gradually relaxed. Beatrice had all the time she needed to clean out the dirt, get a good view of the foot, and snip away. Graf's resignation held to the last snip of the last toenail.

"Wow!" Beatrice said, as she stroked the gelding's neck while releasing it from the front V. "What a good boy! I guess you figured you'd met your match, huh?"

"If llamas are anything like horses, they probably just need to know who's boss," Tanner commented.

"I guess. But they can be such individuals. What works for one doesn't necessarily work for all."

Beatrice brought Reine out for the next pedicure. As she gently squeezed the front stanchions on either side of the llama's neck, she said, "This one, for example, doesn't need much muscle. She's a sweetheart about vetting. I'll tackle her by myself."

As Beatrice lowered herself to the ground again, Tanner approached and grabbed for Reine's right front hock. The leg rocketed leftward, completely eluding his grasp.

"No, Tanner. Let me do it. She's antsy about you."

"Don't be silly. You can't handle her alone if she's acting rebellious." He reached for the hock again.

Before Beatrice could protest, Reine bucked—to the extent the chute allowed—and bashed her head into the topmost horizontal cross-bar. Beatrice dived to the side, lest one of those flailing front feet connect with some portion of her anatomy.

"Please, Tanner, go to the far stall while I try and settle her down."

Tanner frowned but complied. Beatrice rose and walked to the front of the chute. It took a ten-minute neck massage and soothing words before Reine's flattened ears moved forward and her front legs stopped dancing.

The next attempt to address Reine's right front leg went better, but the animal made a halfhearted effort to jerk her foot out of Beatrice's fist. Tending to the second pair of toes was easier—some nervous shifts to evade human hands but no sudden movements. By the time Beatrice approached the fourth leg, Reine was fully cooperative.

From a distance, Tanner watched silently. When Beatrice returned to the stall to retrieve the next llama, he commented, "You spoil them, you softie."

"If I need a different technique for each llama, who cares? As long as the job gets done without anyone getting hurt. But with this guy, Vike, I'll welcome your muscle power again."

The remaining pedicures played out uneventfully. Tanner backed off when instructed and wielded a firm hand when asked.

As he and Beatrice returned to the house, she thanked him for his help. He assured her he was happy to be of service. He appeared to mean it, but his mood was pensive.

It lightened with a hearty welcome from Ralph. "You're so easy to please, Ralph," Tanner said affectionately, thumping the dog's wiggling rump. "You don't care how heavy or light the hand is. How skilled or clumsy. Everyone's a dog whisperer around you."

Looking up at Beatrice, Tanner added suddenly, "I miss Gertrude. I still want you to help me choose a likely replacement from among the kennel hounds."

"Maybe next time we'll actually get as far as the dog pens." She winked at him.

"No guarantees." Tanner smiled.

"Of course, there's no guarantee I won't want to bring the entire pack into your house."

"I told you, you're too soft."

Once inside, Beatrice washed her hands and focused on the final preparations for lunch, while Tanner, after a quick cleanup, sat down at the kitchen table. After she placed the sheet of stuffed croustades into the oven, she asked, "Have you heard the good news about Rodney?"

"Has he developed terminal cancer? Lost a body part? Preferably his prick?"

Settling into the chair opposite him, Beatrice snorted in appreciation. "Good news but not quite that cheerful. It seems Rodney has accepted a plea bargain. He's copping to all the drug counts. In return, the local charges will be dropped, the assault on me and the attempted kidnapping of Clara. So that means none of us has to testify. Most important, Clara doesn't have to go through that grief."

"And this is what you call good news?"

"Never having to see Rodney's flat face again sounds pretty uplifting to me. And he's looking at a long sentence. The main advantage for him, as I understand it, is that he doesn't land in prison with the label of child molester—a hard way to do time, I gather."

"But that's exactly what he is!" Tanner shouted. "His crazed attempt to snatch Clara was the logical consequence of his sexual obsession with her—something that disrupted the kid's whole life and placed her in a stranger's care. And now he doesn't have to answer for that evil?"

"He'll still be locked up for years," Beatrice reasoned. "She'll be an adult, probably far from here by the time he gets out. She'll be safe. And she won't have to tell how he jacked off in front of her. The local prosecutor said that detail would be important to establish a kidnapping motive—even if there wasn't enough evidence for a charge of sexual molestation, child endangerment, indecent exposure, or whatever they'd call it. But the sexual angle would come up in trial, nonetheless. And Clara would have to endure cross-examination by some idiot accusing her of lying or acting provocatively. So she's been spared that. And she's been spared explaining why she's living here and not with her mother. Clara won't have to relive her mother trying to pimp her out."

"Don't be ridiculous, Beatrice. Clara is reliving that trauma every day of her life. It's bad enough she doesn't matter to her mother. Now she finds out she doesn't matter to the state, either. Some pervert can turn her life upside down, and he doesn't have to pay for it."

"I'll make damn sure she knows she matters," Beatrice insisted. "Ben will, too. But now every kid in her class won't find out all the gory details and make her life miserable. I'm not sure Clara would be strong enough to take that on top of everything else."

Tanner snorted derisively and said, "So the Rodney Madsens and Rita Berrigans of this world can maintain their web of lies. Posture as responsible guardians. Good Christians. Or whatever other claptrap helps them sleep at night."

Beatrice shivered at the mention of the nutcase who had made Tanner's childhood a dark, twisted hell. Rarely did he mention either of his parents. It was only because of her work on his autobiography—including a long interview with his sympathetic ex-wife, Patty Scanlon—that Beatrice knew of the abuse Rita Berrigan had inflicted on her only child.

"You didn't want Rita's sins becoming a chapter in your book, any more than Clara would welcome Rodney's sins becoming the hot topic in her school cafeteria," Beatrice countered, as gently as possible.

"Write about it decades after Rita's death? What good would that do? Good God, woman, don't you see the difference? It's about having your day in court, facing down your tormentor. That's the only way to exorcise the demons. Did anyone ask Clara what she wanted?"

"Of course I did, Tanner. She cringed at the very idea."

"Did she, really? Or did she just respond to your guidance – to take the path of least resistance? Keep a low profile? Bury herself in the deep woods the way you have?"

A hot flash snaked from Beatrice's chest to her scalp. Looking down at the table, she responded tightly, "Tanner, I did what I thought was in Clara's best interest."

"And how many bourbons did it take to convince yourself of that?"

Beatrice fixed him with cold, gray eyes. "Get out," she said in a low, hoarse voice.

He snapped his head back, sniffed and said incredulously, "Come again?"

Beatrice stood up slowly. Her face was drained of color. She pulsed her fingertips on the back of the chair.

Quietly, she said, "You have the arrogance to lecture me. You have the temerity to accuse me of not protecting Clara's interests. And then you flat out insult me. In my own house. Get out! Now!"

As shocked as he was angry, Tanner rose. "Fine! I'm gone. And glad to go!"

He slammed the door when he left.

Beatrice waited until she heard the Hummer start up and rattle down the driveway. Then she dropped into her chair. And screamed out her rage, frustration, and hurt.

THIRTY-FIVE

Exchanging Smiles

RAISED A PRESBYTERIAN, Amanda Buckhalter had parted ways with her church two decades ago after a painful counseling session with her pastor. Back then, she was desperate for help in dealing with her abusive first husband. After several "falls" had sent her to the emergency room, she viewed divorce as her only option. But before she took such a drastic step, so at odds with her Calvinist upbringing, she wanted her church's blessing. Instead, the pastor directed her to submit to her husband. When the final beating killed her unborn child, Amanda left her marriage and her church. It took a family wedding or funeral to get her into any house of God these days — like the wedding of Mike Buckhalter and Loretta Lowther.

The occasion introduced Amanda to the inside of a Baptist church. Loretta was a Baptist. Mike was only a nominal Catholic, so he bowed to his bride's desire to walk down an aisle she had known since childhood.

Amanda might have jettisoned her allegiance to the Presbyterians, but their skepticism about other denominations continued to exert some influence on her. She considered Baptists to be one tiny step above snake charmers. She entered the Seneca Baptist Church and nervously scanned the interior for any clues that the congregation would suddenly break out in glossolalia or burst forth in raucous song, with palms waving toward Heaven. Far from seeing a choir the size of a swing band, however, she deduced the only source of music would be an upright piano, manned by a shriveled octogenarian with tightly curled white hair.

Amanda relaxed her vigilance and indulged in some discreet people-watching. She had been assigned to the groom's side of the aisle, of course. Even without that architectural divide, she would have been able to identify the bride's family and friends. On that side of the church, every female over the age of thirty was obese and moon-faced, with a short, upturned nose and large, vacuous blue eyes. The young ones had blonde

182

hair. The old ones had blue hair. All of the men over age thirty were bald or getting there. They were short, wiry, and bandy-legged. They, too, had tiny noses. Amanda, although hardly possessed of a Roman beak herself, wondered how the Lowthers coped when they had head colds.

Because Ben was the best man, he and Amanda had arrived early. Amanda sat in one of the front pews, hands folded in lap. She hoped to give the appearance of pious communion with her Maker, a pretext for not socializing. She heard quite a bit of chatter to the rear, as new arrivals spotted old friends and second cousins twice removed.

All that chattiness was not only annoying but also threatened to prolong the already tedious wait for the ceremony to begin. So Amanda was relieved when she saw Ben, Mike, and the pastor finally take up their positions at the front of the church. She had to admit Mike made a good-looking groom. His height served him well, as did the talents of a Marlboro County unisex stylist who managed to minimize Mike's tonsure point. Flatly refusing to rent an uncomfortable tux "and look like a doofus," the groom wore a conservative, dark-navy business suit and a handsome, striped silk tie. Suits were novelties enough in Seneca County. Amanda wondered where and when her brother-in-law had acquired his current apparel. It probably dated back a few years from the way Mike was fidgeting with the buttons to relieve the pressure on his middle. Before the ceremony was over he would open the suit jacket.

As dapper as Mike looked, he was overshadowed by his best man. Amanda cast an appraising eye on her husband. No, she wasn't merely prejudiced. He was the handsomest man in the room. He was tall (taller than Mike) and well proportioned (without any tug on the buttons of his jacket). He had a full head of hair, cut just as well as Mike's. And his suit was a work of art. That was Amanda's doing, of course. Before this wedding, Ben had just two dress-up options. One was a navy blazer with khaki trousers, selected by his wife. That attire served for the rare business meeting with a particularly upscale client or for the occasional celebration at a fancy Marlboro restaurant. Ben's one real suit, however, was more than a decade old and looked it. Amanda had insisted he buy a new one. He balked at traveling all the way to Roanoke to upgrade his wardrobe. He groused even more at the price tag. But he bought the suit she picked out and had it tailored to fit perfectly.

Amanda smiled into her lap as she savored her victory. Suddenly she felt Ben's gaze. When she looked up, he caught her eye and shot her an appreciative, sexy grin.

My husband isn't just the best-looking man in this room. He isn't just Mike's best man. He's the best man. Period.

In marriages that endure, the glue that binds two very different people comprises molecules such as these. When the wife bristles with resentment over her husband's inclination to take all her hard work for granted, the memory of a fleeting exchange of loving smiles can drain her anger more quickly than any bouquet of roses. The frustration roiling in a husband's gut over his wife's expectation that he read her mind dissolves in a flash with the recollection of how her gentle touch restored hope at a seemingly hopeless moment.

Immersed in the euphoric molecules of her matrimonial bond, Amanda felt a surge of generosity as she watched the bride and her attendants walk down the aisle. Loretta's short white dress was surprisingly attractive. Perhaps the sweetheart neckline revealed a tad too much bosom, but Amanda could forgive that. Pregnancy could render a perfectly fitted bodice too tight in just a few days. The bride's blonde hair was swept up in a fetching, classic style. The sweetheart rose pinned into one curl blended beautifully with her pink-and-white bouquet.

Loretta's sister, the matron of honor, had been assigned an attractive lilac-colored dress. Its cut created the illusion of a waistline and downplayed her saddlebags. Amanda assumed the matron of honor also benefited from some sturdy shapewear.

The two bridesmaids were similarly lucky in the dresses they wore, in plum. The women were significantly overweight. But the empire lines hid the belly bulges, while the hem length (slightly above mid-knee) and the tastefully tall sling-backs suggested longer, shapelier legs than either bridesmaid actually possessed.

Then there was Clara's dress. Its hideousness was all the more glaring because of the contrast it presented with Loretta's other attendants. Their dresses looked like they came from a halfway respectable bridal salon, probably La Femme in Marlboro's Old Town. The junior bridesmaid's costume, on the other hand, looked like it had been whipped up by Gamma Lowther on her pedal-powered Singer. Clara's apparel wasn't the regrettable choice of a wedding planner utterly lacking in taste. Her dress looked a lot like punishment from a vengeful bride.

Amanda couldn't imagine what Clara might have done to incur Loretta's enmity. The teenager could certainly be annoying at times—too boisterous, too quick to speak her mind, too much of a tomboy—but she was also cheerful, helpful, honest, and hard-working. She lacked the snotty condescension all too many girls manifested toward their elders. Nor had she shown any signs of flirting with the youthful crimes infiltrating even such a family-oriented place as Seneca County: drug abuse, underage drinking, shoplifting, vandalism.

Then Amanda, who had occasionally experienced her own jealous twinges over her husband's devotion to his goddaughter, speculated that a protective, nesting instinct had seized Loretta. Rivalry was often an unlovely aspect of the stepmother-stepdaughter dynamic. But when the stepmother is thrall to progesterone, she can get downright paranoid in her determination to carve out a secure niche for the life growing inside her belly. In that frame of mind, she might see any half-sibling as a threat to her unborn baby. The threat perception would almost certainly increase if the expectant mother was as lacking in overall confidence as Loretta.

You haven't done your daughter any favors in your choice of mates, Mike. First, the horror show known as Charyce. And now this immature girl who'd gladly throw Clara under the bus to seek an advantage for her own child.

The glum look on the teenager's face saddened Amanda. Clara would never be Amanda's favorite relative, but she was family nonetheless, and that merited loyalty and basic decency. So when the girl glanced forlornly at her aunt, Amanda stifled her first instinct to look away in embarrassment. Instead, she smiled and winked knowingly. She hoped to convey some sense of female solidarity, however weak. Surprise flashed across Clara's face. Then she smiled shyly. And winked back. Amanda couldn't help chuckling at the teenager's pluck. Seeing the unmistakable sympathy, Clara grinned broadly—and held her chin just a bit higher.

ALTHOUGH AN EXCELLENT DRIVER, especially behind the wheel of her nine-year-old but still zippy Miata, Vaughn Lankford was unnerved by road trips in excess of one hundred miles. But today she was glad that more than three hours lay between the University of Virginia Medical Center and home. Vaughn had much to process since dropping Beatrice off for knee surgery in Charlottesville.

Vaughn liked the fellow come-here. She admired Beatrice's combination of resourceful practicality and compassion. The latter quality was evident in her fostering of young Clara. Although a more maternal woman might be better suited to smoothing the sharp edges in the teenager's life, Beatrice was a stellar role model for the coping skills that would serve Clara well for years to come.

Right now, however, Beatrice didn't appear to be coping all that well herself.

Vaughn had looked forward to conversing with her driving companion. During visits with Clara, the occasional chat with Beatrice had been entertaining. The woman's perspective was refreshingly different. Highly articulate, she laced her anecdotes with humor, if occasionally darker than suited Vaughn. Beatrice was interesting, an attribute in all too short supply.

Vaughn had yet to establish any substantive friendships in Seneca County since she had taken up residence several years earlier. Her partnership with Eltie wasn't that much of an obstacle. Vaughn often mused how clueless her neighbors were about the nature of that relationship. If two unrelated forty-something men lived together, they would have attracted all sorts of gossip. But when it came to two women sharing a household, the typical Seneca County native was likely to assume they were Platonic friends, whose living arrangement was a matter of economic

186

expediency. Lacking menfolk, more than a few mountaineer women had come together over the centuries to share the load in a harsh landscape.

Other differences, however, posed larger obstacles to Vaughn's effort to make friends. First, she was not a native of Seneca County or even West Virginia. As a result, she sounded and looked alien.

Second, she was childless. With the exception of Eltie, almost every other female contemporary in the area was a mother. All—especially the single mothers—were frazzled by the challenges of making ends meet. Many worked outside the home in less-than-satisfying jobs, often involving long commutes. Not surprising, Vaughn's contemporaries appeared older than their years. Many simply had no time for friendship. If they did, they were often looking for emergency babysitters or sounding boards for parenting concerns. Vaughn didn't aspire to either role. She liked youngsters well enough but tired of the endless bragging about children's accomplishments and the endless complaining about children's shortcomings. She longed to talk with other women about the novels and music they enjoyed, about their beliefs or lack of same in an afterlife, about hopes and dreams that went beyond getting Junior through high school and marrying off Amber before she got pregnant.

Vaughn had joined the local Methodist church to fill the social void. But most of the other church ladies were much older. Their focus of conversation was grandchildren. Gallstones, the curse of a high-fat diet and super-hard water, seemed to rank a close second.

Her culinary talents afforded Vaughn some social stature, at least. Her dishes formed the centerpiece of many a church event. Her cakes and pies regularly raised money for the volunteer fire department. She happily distributed handwritten three-by-five index cards in response to requests for her recipes. But even an avid cook can grow weary of the ongoing controversy over the best shortening for biscuits.

Vaughn enjoyed the occasional, animated conversation with a fellow gardening enthusiast, of course. But such chats reminded her of her failed dream of launching a landscaping business. Seneca County residents loved flowers as much as anyone else. But they lacked the discretionary income to hire a gardening consultant. Nor did any local businesses feature grounds of sufficient size to warrant more than a park bench or the odd dogwood. Once, Vaughn had partnered with Eltie's cousin Ben on a satisfying project to landscape five acres surrounding a large pond he had built for a Washington client's elegant summer residence. But clients like that were few and far between. It was highly improbable she would ever put to use her master's degree in landscape architecture.

She reminded herself that acquiring knowledge was never in vain. And if she had not gone to Virginia Tech, where she had earned her degree, she would never have met Eltie, who was enrolled at Tech's College of Veterinary Medicine.

But a girl couldn't help wishing for a little intellectual stimulation from someone other than her partner. She couldn't help wishing for more opportunities to make meaningful connections with interesting people. Vaughn had jumped at the chance to do this favor for Beatrice.

What did I expect, for heaven's sake? The poor woman was probably terrified of her upcoming surgery!

The inhospitable hour of their departure—5 a.m.—certainly didn't help, either. Neither woman, as Vaughn learned, was an early riser. Perhaps if the trip had begun three hours later, the conversation would have flowed.

But Vaughn didn't really think so. People are often more talkative than ever when their nerves are jangling. She suspected pre-op nerves were not the primary reason for Beatrice's grim, lifeless demeanor in the Miata's passenger seat.

Motivated by equal measures of curiosity and compassion, Vaughn had tried to elicit some information from Beatrice. The responses provided few insights, at least at the time. Now, hours later, as she downshifted, and the Miata purred onto the second Lexington exit off I-64, with the goal of stopping for lunch, Vaughn focused on some telling snippets from that unsatisfying conversation.

When she had prodded Beatrice to air some of her fears about the knee replacement, on the theory that shared concerns are less ominous than worries festering in silence, only some of the terse responses were expected. Yes, Beatrice appeared worried about how successful the surgery would be and how long the recuperation would drag on. She mentioned the difficulty of tackling farm chores when she was not fully ambulatory. At one point, she alluded to insurance hassles. Those concerns were hardly surprising.

But the limited conversation also brought to light an issue that never would have occurred to Vaughn if she were the one en route to the operating room. The prospective patient expressed concern about her post-op appearance. She hated the idea of looking like some "ugly hag" hunched over her crutches. She dreaded the upcoming physical therapy sessions — not because they would be painful but because she would look so "clumsy" and "graceless."

Perhaps it was because Beatrice was more than a decade older. As she scanned the Lexington road signs, Vaughn wondered whether menopause's inevitable cosmetic insults made women of a certain age more sensitive than ever about their looks. Except Beatrice was probably less vain than anyone Vaughn knew — apart from Eltie.

As Vaughn merged onto Route 11's business lane, an insight blossomed in her brain. Beatrice wasn't obsessed by the reflection she saw in a mirror. She was focused on her reflection in someone else's eyes. In a man's eyes. A man had made her feel unattractive, unloved — unlovable. And being handicapped, however briefly, would deepen that negative self-image.

Shame on you, Mr. Fordyce!

Who else could it be? Vaughn didn't know exactly what had happened between Tanner and Beatrice. But her instincts told her a budding romance had hit a nasty patch. Sharp, hurtful words from a lover could quickly cut the self-worth out of a woman, at least temporarily. Especially if that woman was as hesitant as Beatrice to open herself to others.

Vaughn had heard enough anecdotes about the otherwise charming Tanner Fordyce to know he had a caustic wit. No doubt he was capable of verbally julienning a woman. But shortly before she was scheduled for surgery? When she would be particularly vulnerable?

Shame on you, Tanner Fordyce!

THIRTY-SEVEN

The Three Dwarfs

"HEY, EASY, GIRL!" EVIE SAID AS BEATRICE, wincing, made little hops alongside the kitchen countertop, balancing herself with right hand on the counter and a crutch tucked under her left armpit.

"I'm supposed to put some weight on it. But I guess it's too soon for just one crutch. Damn! I can't even get a freakin' drink for myself as long as I still need two crutches."

"Jesus H. Christ! You've only been home a few days! And I'm happy to play bartender. But you might want to slow it down. The Jack Daniel's factory isn't closing anytime soon."

Grunting with disgust, Beatrice gimped back to her seat at the kitchen table, leaned both crutches against her chair, and gingerly elevated her still-bandaged right leg onto an adjacent seat. Clara looked up from her homework while Evie poured a generous amount of bourbon into an ice-packed glass. Ralph, lying near Clara's feet, eyed the crutches nervously. The dog had learned those aluminum appendages could unexpectedly spring to life. A wag of his well-feathered tail was often all it took to animate the scary things and send them crashing to the floor.

"*Mazel tov!*" Evie placed the frosty glass in front of Beatrice.

"You're not joining me?"

"Those new meds I'm on make me tired and blotto enough. I'm not banned from drinking, but I gotta take it easy. Word to the wise," Evie added pointedly.

"Jack Black is my painkiller of choice. I hated how Vicodin made me feel. I stopped after just one pill. Besides, I abstained for a few weeks before surgery, so I'm entitled."

"Fine. You're marginally less grumpy soused."

An ill-humored silence hung over the room. After several minutes, it was broken by five sneezes from Clara.

"Jesus, what a bunch we are!" exclaimed Evie. "The halt, the blind, and the deaf. Or maybe that should be Grumpy, Sneezy, and Sleepy." She yawned inadvertently and then, surprised, stabbed an index finger at her sternum and added, "See what I mean?"

Beatrice snorted in appreciation. Clara, in the midst of blowing her nose, laughed and thereby triggered a high-pitched honk from her clogged sinuses. From the floor, Ralph yodeled quizzically. All three humans erupted in giggles, which got Clara coughing—and touched off another round of laughter.

*   *   *

After Evie had retrieved her old friend from the Charlottesville hospital, the mood at Beatrice's farmhouse pendulumed between conviviality and dolor. It didn't help that three of the inmates were processing the trauma of recent incarcerations: Evie and Beatrice at hospitals, Ralph at the Marlboro boarding kennel. The fourth resident was still morose about her father's wedding, her ghastly bridesmaid dress, and the head cold apparently inherited from Virgil.

While Beatrice was in the hospital and Mike was still on his honeymoon, Clara had stayed at Ben's. Those two days eased some of her post-wedding blues. She and Ben enjoyed a special Saturday in Marlboro's Old Town, where he indulged her entreaties to view a violent movie. It featured a refreshingly resourceful female lead, savvy enough to sling an AK-47 over her shoulder before investigating the moans echoing from a dark cave.

Then there was Uncle Virgil, sweet as usual. With childish delight, he showed Clara the cacophonous log-splitter he had liberated from the county dump's "nearly new" shed. And he happily engaged her in Scrabble, even though he was hopelessly outmatched.

The biggest surprise was Amanda. She actually seemed pleased to see Clara and treated her to a favorite dessert of peppermint ice cream pie with a homemade chocolate wafer crust that was overlaid with fudge sauce.

Still, Clara would be glad to return to the Desmond farm. An irrational part of her brain wondered if knee surgery was some ruse, designed so Beatrice could flee her foster-care responsibilities. A scarier form of abandonment also occurred to the girl. What if Beatrice didn't wake up from anesthesia? What if she lost too much blood during the procedure? Her first evening at Ben's, Clara shared those fears with Amanda, who tracked down the patient-information number at the hospital and insisted the teenager inquire for herself about Beatrice's progress. Relief washed over Clara when she learned the patient had already been transferred to a regular room, and her condition was stable.

Two days later, after bailing a joyous Ralph out of the kennel, Ben drove Clara back home minutes before Evie's Subaru rolled up Beatrice's long drive. Ben restrained the ebullient dog, while Ralph's mistress laboriously extracted herself from the SUV. Clara knew exactly how Ralph felt. She, too, wanted to hurl herself at Beatrice in celebration of the homecoming but held back until the woman beckoned. With crutches wedged under both armpits, the patient cautiously extended one arm and then wrapped it around Clara in a wobbly but warm embrace.

Beatrice's return did not restore normalcy, however. She withdrew, for the most part, into the darkly quiet state of the previous winter, after she had broken her leg.

Evie occasionally succeeded in lightening the atmosphere. One evening, for example, she tuned to a worthy Bette Davis vehicle on satellite TV's classic movie channel. Clara, initially dismayed at the black-and-white format, quickly became entranced by *All This and Heaven, Too*. She was fascinated with its themes of forbidden (but unconsummated) love, betrayal, shame, and stoic female grit, as the wrung-out heroine journeyed from scandal in France to redemption in the New World. The teenager also enjoyed the sideshow, as Evie and Beatrice launched into joint recitations of Bette's lines. The two women would high-five each other at each accurate recital. Then they would offer up some skewed psychoanalysis of various characters. At times, their laugh-laced chatter drowned out the on-screen dialogue. Clara didn't mind too much. It was fun to see her housemates shedding a few years and cares.

*   *   *

Evie had several moments when she questioned her choice of Beatrice's farm for a time-out from a hectic lifestyle. It was unsettling to see her friend — no longer an energetic twenty-four-year-old with a merrily perverse sense of humor — weighed down by every one of her fifty-six years. Beatrice's bourbon intake was worrisome, too, as were her gray complexion and mood.

Evie took some comfort from the pluck Beatrice exhibited negotiating her way around the first floor, with the living room serving as makeshift bedroom, as well as the sang-froid evident when Beatrice changed bandages. Evie admired her friend's resolve in doing the prescribed exercises, despite the attendant pain. That mindset augured well for the professional PT sessions that would begin in another week, after a visiting nurse yanked the zipper-like staples closing the front of Beatrice's swollen knee.

Evie's caretaking tasks at the farmhouse were limited. They consisted of fetching the occasional item to spare her hostess some extra steps and serving as resident chef. She was proud of her culinary skills and enjoyed having an appreciative audience.

Nevertheless, she was happy to retreat to Beatrice's office. At night, she slept on the Spartan day bed in the cabin's tiny back room. She also withdrew to that sanctuary for several hours every afternoon. Sometimes she would nap. Sometimes she would take a long walk around Beatrice's acreage. Sometimes she would sit and think. Although no fan of introspection, Evie used this opportunity to ponder her future. Regardless of the mood at the farmhouse, she needed time to think. And think some more.

On her last full day with Beatrice and Clara, Evie decided her pondering was done. She had reached that conclusion while walking Ralph. The activity featured nothing tailor-made for epiphanies. The sky was as gray as she had come to expect from a winter's day in Appalachia. The ground, at least, was snow-free except for the brushy areas. And the temperature had shinnied all the way up to the high forties, with less wind than usual. Somewhat wistfully, Evie imagined the thermometer back home reading ten degrees higher. She wondered how tall her daffodils were now and when they would bloom. Such musings came and went, carelessly, as she walked on, stopping regularly so Ralph could soak up all the tantalizing scents. A bundle of happiness, he was an invigorating companion.

For whatever reason, this dog-walk had a clarifying effect on Evie's mind. Here she was, doing nothing that would earn her money or prestige. There was no one to impress. There were no business intrigues to analyze, no reputations to burnish. Yet she was content.

Suddenly, retirement didn't look all that bad.

Selling her PR business in Northern Virginia and moving to Massachusetts were almost certainly prerequisites for marrying Bart. Although he had offered to move instead, Evie knew that leaving his lovely home in Dover would break his heart. Selling her McLean townhouse, on the other hand, would not be so wrenching. More than likely, it would be enormously profitable. The sales of townhouse and business could underwrite many creature comforts, perhaps including a sun-kissed second home offering a respite from New England winters.

Maybe in Charleston?

Evie certainly didn't mean the capital of West Virginia.

And so she realized she *would* marry Bart in just a few months. The prospect of losing him—as she surely would if she broke their engagement—was enormously sad. He was fun. He was kind. He had a calming effect on her. She liked the person she was when he was around. And a cuddly physical intimacy had developed between them, which filled a need Evie hadn't known existed.

Bart inspired no lust in her. Evie doubted her libido was revivable; nor did she care. She had experienced enough fires of passion in years gone by. Even then, she had been wise enough to understand the men who kindled those flames—for her, at least—would have been disastrous long-term partners. Bart was refreshingly different. Maybe she should have reeled him in years earlier. No, she wasn't ready before. She was now.

She wanted to share her epiphany with Beatrice. But in the interest of holding on to her current lighthearted, clear-headed feelings, Evie reconsidered. She would wait a few weeks and hope her friend's funk would dissipate by then.

THIRTY-EIGHT

Ladies Who Lunch

BEFORE STARTING THE DISHWASHER, Clara cocked an ear toward the living room, where Beatrice had relocated after dinner. The girl sighed when she heard no television, no music from the CD player, no cooing to Ralph. She was just able to make out the light clatter of fingertips on a keyboard. "Dang," Clara murmured, "she's working again."

Office chores consumed a greater portion of Beatrice's day than usual lately. She could now manage the short drive from house to office, but more and more she was bringing work back home in the evening, too. Clara found it depressing to compete with the laptop for attention. Yet she wasn't sure she wanted the attention of her increasingly dour housemate.

Well, who wouldn't be grumpy on crutches?

Of course, Clara feared another reason for Beatrice's ill humor. Maybe she was tired of playing caretaker to an unrelated fourteen-year-old?

No, she needs me more than ever, since the operation, since Evie left.

Further analysis would have to wait. Right now, Clara needed to revisit, one last time, a painful subject with Beatrice. Squaring her shoulders, the girl walked toward the living room. She did an about-face as she passed the half-gallon of Jack Daniel's on the kitchen counter. Grabbing a rocks glass from a cabinet, she half-filled it with bourbon and tossed in a handful of ice cubes. Maybe a drink would improve the conversational atmospherics.

As she walked, Clara pulled the kitchen towel from her left shoulder to contain the sloshing from the glass in her hand. She wearily took note of the tightness in Beatrice's shoulders, hunched over the computer. "You haven't had a drink in a while, and I thought maybe you'd like one," the teenager said, a bit too forcefully.

Beatrice looked up over the top of her reading glasses, first at the drink, then at Clara. She narrowed her eyes and arched a brow. Clearly, the sight of the frosty bourbon had no jollying effect. "Did I ask you for booze, Clara? Dump it in the sink." Shaking her head in disgust, Beatrice resumed her tapping on the keyboard.

As she turned back, Clara pouted, "Yeah, well, sometimes you like it when I fix you a drink." In a softer voice, inaudible in the living room, she added, "And sometimes I like you better when you're drinking."

Clara didn't know why Beatrice hadn't been drinking much lately. Nor did she know if less bourbon contributed to the blues. Was this awful mood wholly unrelated to alcohol, the surgery, or the crutches? Clara fretted anew about her status in the Desmond household.

After washing the rocks glass, she headed back to the living room with heavy steps. There was nothing to do but plunge ahead. She noisily slumped into the sofa opposite Beatrice, who didn't look up from her labors. Taking a deep breath, Clara began, "Any chance you've changed your mind about Momma picking me up? I mean, inside? She can't figure how to explain things to that Clay guy. So she's pushing me to..." Clara let the sentence hang, in the hope that her obvious martyrdom would inspire second thoughts in Beatrice.

"Look, Clara, I'm not trying to complicate your life," Beatrice said, closing the laptop. "You have every right to a relationship with your mother, as long as your get-togethers have safe venues. You have my permission to go to lunch with her tomorrow. But I won't have Charyce in my house. Period."

Clara hung her head. She hadn't really expected any change in the house rules, instituted after her mother's last visit nearly one year ago. Back then Charyce was desperate for Rodney to make good on his potentially lucrative marriage proposal, but he was waffling after Clara had moved out of her mother's apartment. So Charyce paid a visit to the Desmond farm to browbeat the girl into moving back — and acquiescing to Rodney's perversion. Beatrice, returning from her office that day, interrupted the confrontation and struck the infuriated Charyce to prevent her from hitting Clara.

Since then, Charyce was persona non grata at the farmhouse. The rule for any maternal visit was for mother to pick up daughter in Beatrice's driveway without ever leaving her car. Another permitted option was a reunion at one of the Buckhalters' homes, with some trusted relative seeing to the girl's transportation.

Charyce had shown little interest in visiting her offspring. The reason for the upcoming contact was Charyce's latest boyfriend. Clay Lightfoot wanted to learn more about his new love interest and her family. His own daughter would be in the general area to compete, for her college equestrian team, in a hunter/jumper show at the Virginia Horse Center in Lexington. So he proposed bringing everyone together for lunch at his Roanoke country club. Charyce saw the gathering as an opportunity to showcase her maternal side and gain points with this well-heeled, fatherly Virginian.

The inclusion of Clay's daughter eased Clara's mind somewhat. She welcomed any buffer between herself and one of her mother's beaux. Charyce could insist all she wanted that her new boyfriend was nothing like Rodney, but the teenager was wary.

Wary or not, Clara was also curious. In addition, the luncheon offered respite from the heavy atmosphere at home. But this temporary escape would hardly be a lark. In addition to watching for signs of creepiness in her momma's new boyfriend, Clara would be on full alert for whatever Charyce's latest Plan B might entail.

Maternal scheming had already triggered several uncomfortable conversations with Beatrice. According to Charyce, the gentlemanly Clay insisted on doing all the driving. He would head west and pick up first his date and then Clara before motoring back to Roanoke. Under that plan, of course, the new beau would wonder why the Desmond house was off-limits. So Charyce pressed her daughter to effect a change in Beatrice's stern rule.

Clara didn't care for that task. Nor did she look forward to relaying Beatrice's refusal. With a fatalistic shrug, the teen rose from the sofa and left Beatrice to her labors.

I tried, Momma. You'll just have to think up some excuse for driving your own car to Roanoke.

*   *   *

The next morning, a Saturday, found the teen standing by the (closed) front gate to Beatrice's farm. Hopping from one foot to the other to stay warm, she regretted her decision to wear a dress. She also rued her punctuality. Just because Charyce had set a nine o'clock rendezvous time hardly meant she would actually arrive at the appointed hour. Indeed, it was nine-twenty before the familiar Ford econobox rolled into view.

During the eastbound drive, mother informed daughter of how she had revised her story with Clay. In the new version, Clara had overnighted at her father's cabin in northern Seneca County. Because Mike's home was considerably out of the way, Charyce could logically point to the expediency of driving herself and Clara to Roanoke. Charyce had also fictionalized her daughter's living arrangement at the Desmond farm as purely a matter of proximity to the Marlboro Academy.

Clara grudgingly admired her mother's talent for tailoring lies so they skirted the truth and thus acquired a sheen of credibility — so much so that Charyce at times appeared to believe her own tall tales. At one point during the drive, she teared up when "remembering" her terror of the violent Rodney and how his temper had once landed her in the emergency room. Reasonably sure the pervert had never roughed up any adult, Clara realized this revised history borrowed elements from Amanda's first marriage. And Amanda's influence didn't stop there.

After arriving at the Roanoke Country Club, Clara noticed a surprising change of style in her mother's attire. Charyce shed her inexpensive quilted coat to reveal a pale gray, boiled-wool suit. The skirt extended all the way to an inch above the knee. Clara suddenly recalled the almost identically cut outfit Amanda had worn at the recent wedding. Admittedly, her aunt's boiled-wool suit was pale blue and accompanied by a navy blouse, while Charyce had chosen a black, scooped-neck top, revealing only a bit of cleavage. Nevertheless, the luncheon outfit was far more representative of Amanda's style than Charyce's.

"You look real nice, Momma. That suit looks great. Where'd you get it?"

Charyce smiled as she straightened the jacket. "Oh, I just found it on sale at the Marlboro Dress Barn. I figured I should change things up some for my new guy. New honey, new clothes."

Clara was shocked her momma would even enter a store she had once dismissed for catering to "dried-up old biddies." Clearly, Charyce was intent on a makeover. Amazingly, she was pulling it off.

Fifteen minutes after meeting Clay, Clara relaxed. He was definitely no Rodney. For one thing, he was older. Momma had said he was fifty, but he looked a lot older than Tanner Fordyce. Maybe it was because of his eyes, which turned down at the outer corners. He was still wearing his grief as a widower, Clara thought. Feeling the need to cheer him up, she smiled more brightly than usual in response to his questions about school. And she showed more appreciation for his corny jokes than they deserved.

At the same time, she avoided flinching over her mother's conversational gaffes. Charyce was deploying an unusual number of four-syllable words, not always appropriately. She was making a Herculean effort to match subjects and verbs in number and person. A few sentences with "you was" and "she don't" slipped out nonetheless.

Charyce did a worthy imitation of rapt listening whenever her boyfriend held forth. Knowing her mother, Clara doubted much of Clay's side of the conversation was actually being absorbed. As he spoke, Charyce impatiently jiggled her right foot under the table—even as she wore her prettiest smile.

The atmosphere became decidedly less comfortable when Clay's daughter arrived. He had explained that Britt was driving down from Lexington and might be late. She would need to change from her riding gear. His sad eyes drew downward even more when she finally appeared in sweat-stained jodhpurs. But he sprang from his chair, bussed her cheek, and made gracious introductions. Britt's eyes darkened as they took aim at her father's woman friend.

Describing the morning's horse show, Britt shared anecdotes about the "hopeless West Virginia competitor" whose mare couldn't master even the low hurdles. She speculated that the rider was one of the college's "charity cases," owing her spot on the equestrian team to some "backwoods quota." Gently chiding his daughter, Clay said West Virginia had some excellent horse farms and horsewomen, regardless of this competitor's performance. Britt sighed and said, "If you say so, Daddy, but it's hard to believe anything respectable could come out of West Virginia." Ever so slightly, she cocked her head toward Charyce then Clara.

Clara shot Britt a cow-faced stare. But Charyce smiled sweetly through all the insults, although the tempo of her ankle-rocking accelerated. Under other circumstances, Britt would have found her pasta-filled plate upended on her jodhpurs.

Although Clara had moral reservations about her mother's efforts to ensnare Clay, who seemed like a nice man, the teenager was beginning to imagine some benefits if those efforts succeeded. Marriage to someone like that might have a calming effect on Charyce and make her less likely to cause trouble for Clara and the rest of the Buckhalters.

By the time lunch was over, she was hoping her mother would indeed marry Clay — not least of all because the contemptuous Britt was so obviously opposed to any such turn of events. As the four dining companions left the restaurant, Clara couldn't help smirking at the older girl's morose, almost tearful demeanor. Then Britt's expression turned angry when her father gave Charyce a chaste parting kiss on the lips and chucked the woman's chin affectionately.

For the entire trip back to West Virginia, curses caromed inside the little sedan. For a change, none was aimed at Clara, who did some venting of her own but couldn't match her mother's creativity in denouncing that "frump-assed, skinny cunt whose horse face would shrivel the balls off any boy with eyes in his head." When Charyce mused that horse flanks would be the only body parts ever to get between Britt's legs, Clara dropped her jaw — but then guffawed. Charyce swatted her daughter's thigh appreciatively. "That's the freakin' truth, girl!" she laughed. "And I'll tell you what. You and me was the only ladies at that table. And Clay saw it. He coulda just eaten you up with a spoon, you was so smart and nice. You done me a solid, honey, and I ain't gonna forget it. No, ma'am, I ain't."

Clara well knew her mother's sense of indebtedness would have a short expiration date. But she basked in the maternal praise anyway.

THIRTY-NINE

Spreading Cheer

SIGHING, RALPH TRIED TO EXHALE DAYS OF FRUSTRATION, boredom, loneliness, and worry. Something was broken in his pack leader. She didn't walk him anymore. She rarely petted him. And it had been a long time since he had heard her say "good dog." Being a dog, Ralph had no idea whether an hour or a month had passed since those two words were uttered, but he craved the reassurance they provided.

When Beatrice was angry, she made loud noises. She fixed him in the eye until he averted his gaze and lowered his muzzle. But there had been no scary eye contact. There had been almost no eye contact at all.

His human walked like a wounded animal. Except his sensitive snout did not detect any of the diverse scents of disease. Her breath smelled the way it always had, featuring a bizarre combination of delectable food aromas, the repellant sharpness of the liquid she often drank in the evening, and the cloying sweetness of items she applied every morning at the bathroom sink.

Days (weeks?) earlier, he had briefly smelled blood and some harsh chemical from her knee. But it smelled normal now. And Beatrice's gait had improved. Less frequently did those frightening aluminum appendages sprout from her armpits. Instead, she wielded a long wooden stick. It was not the good kind, however. Instinctively, Ralph understood he should not try to fetch it.

So her wound was clearly healing. And she did not appear to be infested with worms or suffering from distemper, at least not the kind Ralph was inoculated against. But something was still wrong with her.

It did not help that they were, yet again, in the Boring Building. Even when his human was in high spirits, she spent an unfortunate amount of time inside this structure. If she was there, he had to be there, too. It was his job to provide companionship, to keep her safe from bears, and chase off nuisances like the squirrels chittering raucously from the trees.

Every morning, when it was time to relocate from home to the Boring Building, Ralph danced with happy anticipation. Any trip, no matter how short, could be exciting, after all. Just think of the scents he could inhale along the way! Imagine the sights he might see. Chee-ing hawks wheeling overhead. Small birds rattling dried stalks in their quest for seeds and survival. Rodents scuttling through duff. And maybe, just maybe, this would be the day when the trip did not end at the large table that was not for food, the table where his human sat, clicking her fingertips on the surface and rustling papers. Alas, today was not that happy day.

In sunnier times, the monotony of the Boring Building would be interrupted by back rubs and ear scrabbles. Beatrice would sometimes take Ralph outside and toss a ball his way. She would clap her hands when he caught the toy. She would laugh when he missed. Pretty much anything Ralph did with the tossed object seemed to delight her. At least it used to.

Ralph got the notion of trying to delight his human once again. Searching for the ball, he sniffed it high, high up on a shelf. He stared pointedly at it and then at Beatrice. And then at the ball. She was oblivious to his focused effort. So he charged through the dog panel in the office door to search for a substitute outside. He found just the right stick for a game of catch, long enough but not too long for reentry through the dog panel, sturdy enough to withstand rough landings but moist enough to telegraph tantalizing scents about its history. Eagerly, the setter plopped the spit-slimed stick into Beatrice's lap. She picked it up, looked at it briefly, and then wordlessly deposited it in one of those containers off limits to good dogs.

Defeated, Ralph settled onto the pillow next to the desk, circled three times, scratched up all the Ralph smells, and collapsed. With one last sigh, he curled into a ball and invited sleep to transport him to jollier places.

After some time, he awakened to cheerful sounds. They came from his young human, a rarity at the Boring Building. Yet here she was. Salvation, jiggling his leash! As she exchanged some noises with the woman, Ralph heard "walk" several times. Wagging his tail, he looked expectantly from Clara to Beatrice. When it became clear that a walk was indeed imminent, he bounced so much that Clara had difficulty draping the chain collar over his head.

"You enjoyed that, didn't you, boy?" Clara asked at the conclusion of the walk. Standing in the utility room of the main house, she stripped the choker off Ralph's neck and replaced the Invisible Fence collar. With both hands, she cradled his silken head. He met her eyes worshipfully. "What a good dog," she cooed. Ralph slurped her palm gratefully.

Clara settled on the living room floor, her back braced against the couch. With one hand, she aimed the remote at the television. With the other, she beckoned to Ralph, who ambled over, conferred one polite lick on her cheek, and then lay down, his long head draped over her thigh. Focused on the television screen, Clara absent-mindedly stroked his flank from time to time.

When her program of choice ended, she stood up and turned on the lamp by the couch. Ralph padded closely behind, in hope that dinner might come early. Instead, Clara walked to the utility room to retrieve her backpack. She brought it into the kitchen, pulled out a textbook, and laid it on the kitchen table. Monitoring her every move, Ralph sat close to her chair. Clara felt his gaze and, turning from her homework, accepted his proffered paw.

"Yeah, I know, Ralph, things aren't much fun lately, huh?" She scratched behind a furry ear. Ralph raised his other paw then launched his upper body into Clara's lap. Only briefly caught off guard, she laughed and hugged the dog, while his tail thumped against a table leg.

"It's a good thing I've got you. I hope you're glad to have me, too, 'cause we sure don't have Beatrice, do we?"

Now stroking the dog's head slowly, Clara sighed. "I dunno what's wrong, Ralph. S'ppose she's just hurting from her knee? Except she seems so sad. And maybe mad, too. No, I don't think either one of us did anything wrong. How could a sweet dog like you make anyone sad or mad? She's a lot like she was last winter. Remember? Back then, I guess she was still thinking of that friend of hers who died. And then I got dumped on her, and she wasn't real thrilled about that for a while. But I did come in handy, didn't I, boy? Especially after she broke her leg. You and me both, Ralph. We helped her out. Yes, we did!

"And Tanner helped out, too. Remember how he loaned us his driver so we could get to the store and stuff? But now Tanner's off on the other side of the world. Funny. I don't think Beatrice has heard from him. I guess he might have emailed her. But she would have said something about what he was doing, dontcha think? I mean, they seemed awful lovey-dovey just a few weeks ago. I couldn't figure out why she didn't want him to know about her knee operation. If I'da gone to the hospital, I'da wanted every one of my friends and family to know. Hmmm. You think maybe I should let Tanner know? He can be a pain, but hearing from him might cheer her up. Whatcha think, boy? I could probably find out from Evie how to contact him. Think that's a good idea, Ralph?"

The dog panted, which Clara took to mean agreement. She hugged him again, saying, "Anything would be better than the way things are now. It's so depressing in this house. I feel sad all the time. And you're looking right grumpy yourself."

Clara rested her chin on top of the setter's head. Dog and girl maintained their connection for a few seconds, until Ralph started at some noise. He extricated himself from the embrace gently, to avoid hurting Clara. Once free, he dashed to the utility room.

"Hey? I'm home early!" Beatrice called from that room, as she shed jacket and boots. Snapping her head in the woman's direction, Clara was surprised by the almost hearty notes in Beatrice's voice.

"Let's get Ralph fed and start dinner for ourselves!" she said, with forced cheer. Ralph didn't care whether the tone was sincere or not. He wiggled around Beatrice's knees and then skidded across the kitchen floor in the direction of his dinner bowl.

Clara just stared at Beatrice, as the latter shook kibble into Ralph's dish. Ostensibly focused on enforcing the dog's sit-stay before releasing him to chow down, Beatrice turned her head from the teenager's gaze. She was afraid she wouldn't be able to quash the tears that were an instant away from blurring her vision. She had arrived in the utility room in time to hear the end of Clara's conversation with Ralph. Did Clara really feel sad all the time? And was Ralph suffering from the overall funk, too?

Well, aren't you just the life of the party, Desmond? Spreading cheer wherever you go. Pull it together, girl, before you lose what few friends you have left in this world.

FORTY

Mad Germans, Parasites, and Intrigue

"So, LET ME GET THIS STRAIGHT. Fordyce misses the interviews we set up for him with the *Frankfurter Allgemeine* and ZDF. And nobody thinks of telling me? Who fucking dropped that ball? And just as *Fortune's Byway* is about to hit the European market. Son of a bitch!" Evie ended her tirade by slamming both palms on her desk and glaring at a quivering subordinate.

"I guess Adriana lost track of the dates," stammered the administrative assistant for Evie's youngest account executive. "Mr. Fordyce was originally supposed to do the interviews before he went to Africa, but then the German TV people asked for a postponement. So then everything was put off until after he got back from Rwanda. Except he didn't get back. And … well … Adriana got mixed up and thought the interviews were a done deal in late January."

"And just where is Adriana?"

"Ummm, the ladies' room? Want me to track her down?"

"Goddamned right! I've got a bunch of pissed off Krauts ready to start World War Three. And she can bloody well put out that fire! Bring her to me the second you find her. And on your way out, ask Shirley to come into my office."

The girl fled. A few minutes later, Shirley appeared.

"No sense taking it out on the assistant, Boss."

"Jesus! I have a little heart surgery. I take a little break in West Virginia. And the whole fucking business goes down the crapper!"

"Well, first of all, your business is hardly dependent on a relatively minor project like *Fortune's Byway*," Shirley suggested, referring to Tanner's autobiography. Evie's firm was promoting the book as a favor to her fiancé, who was, in turn, helping out a publisher friend.

"Second of all," Shirley continued, "shouldn't you be focused on ferreting out the missing author? Which, of course, is precisely what I've done." Shirley smiled slyly and slid a fax across Evie's desk.

Evie stared at the paper. And then looked up at her secretary. "Tanner's in a German hospital? In Würzburg?"

Shirley touched index finger to nose. "Bingo. Or at least he was at the Missionsärztliche Klinik. It's big on tropical diseases, like the corker afflicting our MIA."

"I'm gonna take a big guess here and assume 'malaria' means the same thing in German as in English?" Evie said, looking down at the fax. "I didn't think that was a big deal anymore with the right meds. Surely he would have been on them before he left home?"

"It is a big deal when it affects the brain. The parasites can reduce cerebral blood flow and cause all sorts of nastiness like ataxia, seizures, coma, and death."

"Well, aren't you just an encyclopedia of gloom. You gathered all this information in the last half-hour?"

"Of course not. The hospital spokesman just shared the diagnosis of cerebral malaria with me. But I knew what that entailed. Poor Mr. Fordyce."

"Let me guess. You were Walter Reed in a previous life." Evie alluded to her secretary's penchant for reminiscing about her colorful incarnations. No one knew whether Shirley's karmic anecdotes were serious or related with tongue firmly planted in cheek.

"Regrettably, Dr. Reed does not number among my personae. But not all that long ago, malaria was endemic to much of the South. My Uncle Beaufort — from the Louisiana branch of the McClintocks? — nearly died of cerebral malaria in the late 1940s. Poor Beaufort had a weakness for sorghum whiskey, so when he started staggering, the family thought he was just tipsy, until he had a conniption fit and fell into a coma. He was out for two weeks. My Aunt Cordelia picked out a lovely black dress, in taffeta. She put a down payment on a fine mahogany coffin, too. And then wouldn't you know? Beaufort woke up, asking for his breakfast grits. Just like nothing had happened, bless his heart."

Evie stared hard at Shirley then blinked and shook her head. "Hallelujah. Beaufort escaped the Grim Reaper. But what about Tanner?"

"Oh, he'll be fine, too, I expect. He never reached the coma stage. As it turns out, he's had malaria before, the prosaic kind that presents like the flu. He started feeling poorly when he was in custody in South Sudan. The officials there detained him for a few days on suspicion of conspiring with a nearly extinct rebel group. All he was doing was visiting an organization that rehabilitates former child soldiers, for heaven's sake. The officials knew that. They were just angling for a bigger bribe. Anyway, he missed taking his weekly chloroquine pill when he was in custody. Maybe that lapse gave the upper hand to the nasty buggers lying dormant in his liver from an earlier infestation. Or maybe his immune system was flagging for some other reason. His doctors are quite sure, however, the cerebral malaria didn't result from a recent mosquito bite. The timing would be all wrong.

"Initially, he wasn't too concerned about the fever and chills. He figured he could finish his business, and the symptoms would recede like they always did. So he went on to Rwanda. But on his return flight to Europe, he was doing a passing imitation of a derelict in withdrawal. Fortunately, he had it together enough to tell a flight attendant he had malaria and would need to get to a hospital ASAP. An ambulance was waiting for him when he landed at Frankfurt."

"Jesus. So what now?" Evie asked.

"He checked out of the hospital two days ago and rented some villa in Provence to recuperate for a few weeks. I have an address and a phone number. But first I thought I'd try emailing him to minimize the risk of disturbing his rest. The villa is fully wired, so maybe we can sort things out with him directly."

"You found out all this information in thirty minutes?"

"I chatted with a charming young man at the Würzburg hospital," Shirley replied, smiling. "He couldn't have been more helpful."

"You were lucky you found one who spoke English."

"Who said he spoke English?"

"Shirley," Evie sighed, "you're a treasure."

"Why, I'm just a resourceful Georgia country girl." She winked then turned to reopen the office door. "I'll let you know if I get a hit on Mr. Fordyce's email. If not, I'll place a call to Provence myself. I wonder what the weather is like there right now?" She tottered off in her stiletto heels.

Evie shook her head in awe at the twists and turns in the past twenty-four hours, starting with a surprising call the previous evening from

Beatrice's young charge, Clara. Phoning from her bedroom and speaking in a low voice, the girl said she hoped to arrange a surprise and needed to know how to contact Tanner without cluing in Beatrice. Evie figured she was hearing only part of the story but couldn't see anything wrong with helping Clara track down the world traveler. So she promised to do some research and email Clara.

Evie had already planned to call Beatrice that morning to update her on wedding plans and find out how the physical therapy was going — while also eliciting clues about her old friend's frame of mind. Now she would have another reason to call. Had Beatrice known about Tanner's troubles, she surely would have alerted Evie by now. Clearly she didn't know — further evidence that something had gone amiss since their New Year's Eve date.

While visiting in West Virginia, Evie was unable to extract details about that momentous event. She surmised something sexual had indeed happened. How could it not, with Beatrice staying overnight at the lodge? At first Evie thought her friend was being respectful toward Tanner by opting not to kiss and tell. In addition, post-op pain could render anyone less chatty than usual. But it now looked like the love affair must have crashed and burned shortly after that first bedding — reason enough for the heavy mood at the farmhouse. Such developments were painful for anyone; they would devastate a woman like Beatrice.

For a moment, girlfriend solidarity made Evie glad of Tanner's brush with death.

Serves him right, the prick!

Then she realized Beatrice would be a challenge for any man, even the best intended. Who knew how the breakup played out?

However it happened, Beatrice had the right to know what was going on with Tanner. So Evie would make that call, after dressing down Adriana and waiting to see if Shirley turned up more information. Meanwhile, Clara needed a discreet email update.

I'm gonna miss all this subterfuge when I'm retired.

But somehow, Evie suspected, life's intrigues would continue to fascinate her whether she was married or single, retired or running a business, sixty-something or ninety-something. The thought pleased her.

FORTY-ONE

Fantasies

"WHAT GODDAMNED MISERABLE SADIST thought up this exercise?" Beatrice gasped as she lay on her back, atop the bedcovers, with butt and sock-clad soles pressed against the wall. Slowly, she slid her right foot down in an effort to improve knee flexion. The theory was to get an assist from gravity. In practice, however, the swelling inside the knee joint would at some point make a mockery of gravity. By then, the patient's hamstrings and abdominals were supposed to contract heroically and force the traumatized leg to bend at a sharper angle. Sweat beaded on Beatrice's forehead as she willed her right foot another inch lower. Her right knee screamed in protest. She maintained the god-awful position for a count of thirty before her left foot reacted in panic to nudge her right heel back upward.

It was then that the phone rang, triggering a litany of curses from the patient. She struggled to flip onto her side and lever her torso into a vertical position.

Beatrice panted a hello.

"You sound rode hard and put away wet," a familiar voice snickered on the other end of the line. "Should I be envious?" Evie asked.

"Only if you're into S and M. Physical therapy is hardly an erotic adventure."

"Well, I knew Tanner couldn't be the one giving you a workout. But I was hoping you'd found some buff therapist to get you all hot and sweaty."

Beatrice's response was a loud raspberry.

"What are you, fifty-six going on four?" Evie teased. "Oh, Christ! I just realized I forgot all about your birthday. Damn! I'm so sorry. It's awfully lame to wish you a happy birthday almost two months after the fact. So I'll wish you a happy new natal year, instead."

"Thanks. And don't worry about it. On that momentous day, you were still clearing the cobwebs out of your head from your own hospital stay. What a pair we are, huh?"

"Why didn't your crummy brother remind me?" Evie complained. "I'll kick him in the shins next time I see him."

"Bart called me and wished me well. But he was pretty preoccupied himself, fretting about your health. And probably wondering whether his engagement was still on. So, is it? You never told me whether you'd reached any conclusion during your Seneca County walkabout a few weeks ago."

Evie was annoyed at derailing herself from the course she had charted for the call. She had planned to lead with the information about Tanner, hence her opening reference to him. When presented with a good-news/bad-news scenario, Beatrice always wanted to hear the negative first. In this instance, Evie preferred that order, too. She wanted to close on a light note—the happy news about her wedding to Bart.

At least Evie assumed the news about Tanner would be difficult to hear. If Beatrice still had feelings for the man, she would be troubled by his brush with death. Even if she now hated him, the news would remind her of the painful reasons why—whatever they were.

But between two good friends, conversation takes its own spontaneous direction. Right now, the subject was the wedding. So Evie described the walk she took with Ralph around Beatrice's farm, when she suddenly experienced complete certainty. Of course, she would marry Bart. To do otherwise was unthinkable.

"I'm glad for both of you," Beatrice said when Evie finished. "You make each other happy. You complement each other. And for me, it's all gravy. My closest friend becomes my sister-in-law. And I'll probably see a lot more of Bart as a result."

"Thanks. I figured I'd have your blessing, but it's nice to know for sure. And that means I don't have to stick another person with the matron-of-honor chores."

"I'll eviscerate you if you even consider anyone else," Beatrice laughed. "Oh, but wait! Maybe you want to ask Darleen? It sounded like you two sisters bonded some at the hospital."

"Oh, puhleeze, Beatrice! We're still as different as night and day. She's hardly the one I'd want talking me down if I get the last-minute jitters.

One robust swear from me and Darleen would probably faint. But I've come up with a brilliant way of having my cake and eating it, too. It's all about clever casting."

"You've lost me."

Evie shared her personnel list for the wedding. Darleen would officiate — as clergy. Since neither Evie nor Bart, agnostic Jew and lapsed Catholic, had any strong religious preferences, a Unitarian service struck both as a happy compromise. It would also honor a family member without necessitating much face-time between her and the bride. The couple crafted an equally felicitous way of handling another difficult relative. Bart's daughter, Martha, would be the best man. That role would involve minimal interaction with Evie and thus lessen the potential for conflict. Worried about her filial inheritance, Martha had initially opposed her father's courtship. That changed when she learned her prospective stepmother had an impressive financial portfolio of her own.

"But I haven't told you the best part," Evie continued. "The bride will wear crimson."

"Ever the scarlet woman. Even at the altar."

"I'm certainly not going to wear virginal white," Evie snorted. "And I won't be caught dead in menopausal beige. For a while I thought of just trotting on down in business clothes to the nearest courthouse and getting hitched by a JP. I don't need a bunch of ritual to marry Bart. Then it occurred to me there's really only one good reason to have the whole foofaraw. A wedding gives the bride an excuse to try on a different persona for a couple of hours and make everyone dress up in fantasy costumes they'll never wear anyplace else. Kinda like Halloween, except with flowers instead of Jack-o'-Lanterns. For my dress-up fantasy, I've decided to borrow from Hindu attire, with the bride donning the celebratory color of red.

"Uh-oh."

Evie detailed the dress code. Although Bart had laughed "his ass off" at the idea of suiting up in a white Nehru jacket, like a proper Hindu groom, he eventually agreed to an off-white, Western suit, on the condition they keep to the original venue, his Dover garden.

"It will be a memorable event, Evie. I wouldn't expect anything less from you. But can you pull it off by early May?"

"Piece of cake. Which reminds me…"

Evie then discussed her plans for the wedding cake, rings, and myriad other details. A half-hour passed before she realized she had yet to inform Beatrice about Tanner's illness.

"I'm sorry," she said suddenly.

"For what?" Beatrice asked, puzzled.

"Well, here I am babbling about wedding plans at a time when you aren't doing so hot in the romance department. I gather things went south between you and Tanner? You never provided any details during my visit. But I had the distinct impression the knee surgery wasn't the only thing weighing down your spirits. I would have expected at least one tantalizing tidbit about New Year's Eve. But you clammed up as soon as I mentioned the subject. And that's just not normal. Not between you and me. So clearly something bad happened. On New Year's Eve? Or after?"

"I'm the one who should be apologizing. Surgery or no surgery, I was a lousy host a few weeks ago. And you're right. A big part of it was Tanner. I let myself think we might have some kind of future together. When that proved wrong, I started spiraling into the abyss — until I got fed up with myself and began climbing out of the hole I'd dug all by my onesies. And I'm better. Really."

"Wait. Back up. I've got soooo many questions. What the hell happened?"

Beatrice sighed. "Big fight, about a week before he left for Europe. Too tedious to go into. He said some pretty hurtful things. And I told him to get out."

"Good for you!" Evie exclaimed then added, less exultantly, "I'm really sorry. Christ, I thought one of the good things about getting older was leaving behind all that angst about sex and love. But here we are. Me going through a bout of cold feet over marrying a sweet guy like Bart and you getting your heart stomped by Fordyce. The bastard."

Evie paused then added, "And now I'm afraid of adding fuel to the fire by sharing what I just found out about him."

Inadvertently, Beatrice sucked in her breath as she waited for her friend to continue. Evie related the whole story: the detention in Juba, the missed interviews in Germany, the hospitalization in Würzburg, the recuperation in Provence. She finished with some speculation. "He might still be a bastard, of course. But what if, after he left Europe for Africa, he had second thoughts about how he treated you? Except then the shit hit the fan, and he wouldn't have had any chance to contact you and make amends. Or am I just fantasizing?"

"I honestly don't know," Beatrice said, shaking her head. "He can be so ... caring one minute. And then he turns into Mr. Hyde."

"Just for the sake of argument, if he *did* reach out to you and apologize, would it make a difference?"

"I don't know. I don't *want* it to make a difference. I don't want to get hurt again."

"Oh, Beatrice, no one does. But we only stop hurting when we're dead."

"I hate it when you get philosophical."

After a cough of skepticism, Evie said, "Let's face it. Every single one of us is fucked as soon as we emerge from the womb. We might as well celebrate when and where we can. So start practicing your sari-wrapping, sister, 'cause some serious partying lies ahead."

Beatrice laughed. Now she was more confused than ever about her feelings for Tanner, and she worried about submerging back into the gloom she was trying so hard to escape. Nevertheless, the image of Evie whirling down the garden path in a crimson sari brought a smile to her face. That was one party she wouldn't miss for all the tea in Darjeeling.

FORTY-TWO

The Jokester Gods of Weather

THE HEAVY CLOUD COVER DIMMING THE DESMOND FARM was white, not the usual gray. Factoring in the complete absence of wind and the mackerel sky of the previous evening, Beatrice could almost smell snow in the air. A lot of it. Anyone raised in Boston can recognize a snow sky.

The weatherman disagreed — to the extent any forecaster paid attention to Seneca County at all. The National Weather Service showed little interest in sparsely populated areas of the southern Appalachians. The region's self-reliant residents were unlikely to lobby for federal aid after catastrophic storms. Instead, they would fire up their chainsaws, strap on their tool belts, and rebuild by themselves. Figuring out the next day's temperature was thus a matter of triangulating from the forecasts for Pittsburgh, Charleston, and Roanoke. The current hunch was the winter storm system blowing in from the west would train harmlessly up the Alleghenies and not dump its load until Pennsylvania. The county's sole radio station (a low-wattage outpost unheard by a third of local residents) cheerfully predicted this particular Saturday would be overcast, with only a ten-percent chance of precipitation.

Beatrice was skeptical. When her bionic knee started signaling distress the previous afternoon, she suggested that Clara and her 4-H partners reschedule their plans to attack the next stage of their fiber-work at the farm. The girl protested that a deadline with her 4-H adviser loomed. Already behind schedule, she and Lane and Leslie needed to produce evidence of their efforts. This was the weekend to push ahead. The weather would have to cooperate.

Detouring only slightly north of her community-college class in business accounting, Mary Beth Vanderlick deposited her daughter and Lane on Beatrice's doorstep promptly at nine-thirty. Lane's father would ferry both youngsters back to Marlboro County in late afternoon. Beatrice

214

appreciated those two chauffeurs, because she had only just resumed driving and was uncertain how her right leg would perform in any situation requiring emergency braking.

By eleven o'clock, the ten-percent chance of precipitation materialized as snow flurries. Engrossed in sorting llama wool on a newspapered floor, the three teens briefly took cognizance of the swirling flakes before returning to their labors.

The flurries remained haphazard through lunch. Nevertheless, Beatrice offered to help with the picking and carding to speed up the work in hope of facilitating an earlier departure. The youngsters happily accepted her offer. In this convivial, focused company, even Beatrice forgot about the weather.

It wasn't until a snow-encrusted Ralph bounded in through the dog panel that all of the wool-workers realized the flaws in the local forecast. Beatrice's driveway was covered with three inches of the white stuff. Meanwhile the snowflakes that had been pirouetting in the still air began driving into the windowpanes.

Lane assured everyone his daddy was a seasoned snow driver, who always carried chains in his truck cab. At three o'clock, however, Mr. Utterback called with the news that his truck had slid into the ditch off his driveway. His property, sitting on a west-facing slope, had twice as much snow as the six inches now shrouding Beatrice's farm. Although he confidently predicted freeing his truck with a come-along "by and by," Beatrice urged him to stay put and stay safe. She would keep the youngsters overnight, and Mr. Utterback could retrieve Lane and Leslie the next day after the storm had ended and the road crews had plowed and sanded.

Leslie called home to relay the change of plans, and the youthful trio focused anew on their clouds of fiber, while Beatrice pulled two large chicken breasts from the freezer to steam. Next she built a pile of blankets, sleeping bags, pillows, and towels in the living room and assembled flashlights, matches, candles, and a gas lantern in the kitchen. Then she began stockpiling water, filling the upstairs bathtub, the utility sink, and numerous pots and buckets in preparation for losing power to the well pump. Her kitchen counter permanently housed a five-gallon container of potable water. But she knew how quickly four people would go through five, ten, twenty gallons for drinking, washing hands, rinsing dishes, and flushing toilets.

After those chores were done, Beatrice asked the youngsters to pack the barn's wall racks with hay and return with armfuls of firewood from the nearby shed. Meanwhile, she started coaxing warmth from the kindling already stacked inside the woodstove.

By the time she had piled on the extra wood, the overhead lights flickered out. The hour was not yet six, but the farmhouse was already submerged in a bluish gloom. The teens shivered gleefully over the adventure and began lighting candles. Beatrice, less charmed by the power outage, silently gave thanks for her propane-fired kitchen range. Working by lantern light, she boiled water for linguine, recruited Lane to chop vegetables, and asked the girls to set the table and pour glasses of iced tea and soda.

The entrée, chicken with sesame noodles, was a hit. Sufficiently exotic to appeal to Leslie's sophisticated palate, it intrigued the budding chef in Lane. The chunky peanut butter in the homemade sesame sauce was probably the main reason for the dish's success. Beatrice had been exposed to enough adolescents over the years to know that kids would pretty much eat anything containing peanut butter.

For dessert, she applied the "use it or lose it" maxim and opted for ice cream, lest a prolonged power outage reduce the tub in her freezer to soup. She trisected the ice cream and poured her own preferred dessert choice into an ice-jammed rocks glass.

Beatrice recognized that her common sense and planning, and a well-stocked larder, were now serving her well. Nevertheless, since early childhood, she had always grasped just how much could go wrong. She knew an ice-laden tree could crash, schooling her in the illusory nature of her cozy shelter. She envisioned a snapped power line or upended candle turning that shelter into an inferno. She pictured a bone-shattering misstep in the snow. And she knew that, for any of those developments, help could be a long time coming. She had yet to hear a plow on the county road, and her nearest neighbor was one treacherous mile away. So she needed some distilled calm, in the form of one stiff drink, to ease the grip all that knowledge was exerting on her brain.

As the quartet relocated to the den to toast their limbs by the woodstove, while freezing their GI tracts with dessert, Lane asked suddenly, "Ooh, is that bourbon, Miz Desmond? Do you suppose I could have a sip?"

"Yes, it's bourbon, and you may indeed have a sip—when you're twenty-one."

"Could I maybe just smell it, then?" he asked, unperturbed by the rejection.

Amused, Beatrice passed the glass to the boy, who swirled the liquid under his substantial nose and inhaled deeply. He smiled with delight as he did. "I thought so!" he said triumphantly, returning the drink to its owner.

By this time, all three females were peering at Lane curiously. He explained, "See, Dad and me have this competition. He's big on grilling spare ribs, chicken—just about anything out back. We keep trying different recipes for barbecue sauce. I read once how some folks add bourbon to their cookpot. Always wanted to try it, but Daddy never has hard liquor around, only beer and wine. But just by smelling your bourbon, I can tell it would be the winning ingredient for my sauce. It smells sweet and sour and maybe a touch smoky. Perfect! And maybe the alcohol would make the meat more tender?"

"I dunno," Beatrice said. "It usually takes a while for marinades to break down the fibers in meat. And aren't most barbecue sauces slathered on shortly before cooking?"

"That's how we usually do it. But I expect we could always experiment some."

Leslie gave a little laugh. "You have such a weird way of phrasing things, Lane. You always 'expect' instead of 'think' or 'believe.'"

"Seems like a perfectly good word to me," Clara countered, as Lane began fidgeting with one cuff of his sweatshirt.

"It sounds so countrified. And I was merely making an intellectual observation," Leslie said primly, as she tucked her legs under her on the floor.

"Earth to Leslie," Clara wisecracked from her perch on the beanbag pillow, "You're in the country, now. 'Countrified' is normal. Get used to it." Clara's eyes shot a challenge at her friend, who dropped her head sheepishly.

Seeing Leslie's discomfort, Lane affected an exaggerated drawl. "Aw, Clara, I expect we'uns do speak a whole 'nother language from them folks way up thar in New Yawk. Ain't that right, city girl?" Bumping Leslie's shoulder with his, he added, "I'd be happy to tutor you in the local language."

Leslie smiled. Lane stuck out his tongue at Clara. Clara responded with a loud raspberry then laughed.

Beatrice observed the interplay and resisted the urge to intervene to smooth the social ripples. The conversation promptly turned to safer topics, like the fiber project. The subject matter then bifurcated half a dozen times before branching off into things ghostly—inevitable, given the howling winds, the power outage, and three active adolescent imaginations, two of them well steeped in haint-filled folklore.

People who grow up in rural areas understand that logic doesn't always prevail in the natural world. Sometimes, the paranormal offers the best explanation why one truck skids off an icy road and plunges down a five-hundred-foot slope to explode in a fireball, while another pickup, in similar circumstances, inexplicably rolls to a gentle stop just before the precipice. Perhaps some demonic entity, prowling that stretch of road, gave the first vehicle the fatal shove. Or, in the second case, a protective spirit—perhaps the victim of an earlier accident on the same road—got between the truck and disaster.

By ten o'clock, three pairs of pupils were fully dilated, more from an overload of spooky anecdotes than from the dim candlelight. Beatrice had already decided the youngsters would all bed down in the living room, one on the sofa, two in sleeping bags on the floor. They would benefit from the woodstove in the adjoining den. From observing the teenagers, she doubted sexual experimentation was likely. Besides, there was safety in the number three. And now, after two hours of ghost stories, it would be unkind to split up the shivering trio.

Letting the teenagers decide for themselves who got the couch and who got the floor, Beatrice shooed a reluctant Ralph out the dog panel to do his business for the night, while she rebuilt the woodstove fire, extinguished the candles and gas lantern, switched on a battery-powered lamp in the living room, and distributed one flashlight to each youngster. Once Ralph returned, shaking snow from his fur, Beatrice—cane in one hand, flashlight in the other — slowly climbed the stairs to her chilly bedroom, the setter padding behind her. In the living room, the soft chatter continued. Beatrice interpreted it as noise to keep ghosts away. She knew no ghosts would trouble *her* sleep, however. She wasn't so sure about the jokester gods of wind and weather.

FORTY-THREE

Blizzard

AT TWO O CLOCK, CLARA CREPT UPSTAIRS, made a pit stop, and was flushing the toilet with water from the bathtub when a gentle rap sounded on the door. Beatrice asked softly, "You okay in there?"

"Yeah," Clara said, opening the door. "My stomach was feeling funny, and I thought this bathroom would be best. More flush water available."

"How's the gut now?"

"Fine. False alarm. But since I'm already up here, I think I'll sleep in my own bed. I'm afraid I'll disturb Lane and Leslie if I go back downstairs."

"Suit yourself. Grab an extra blanket from the closet. It's cold up here."

Clara took the suggestion and was soon buried under heavy bedcovers. She was glad Beatrice hadn't questioned the fibs. There was never any stomach trouble. Nor was the girl worried about waking her friends. Both were dead to the world when she had quietly vacated the living room. Clara's relocation had other motivations. She badly needed to think. In private.

She was troubled by an uncomfortable conversation with Leslie. Not long after Beatrice's exit, Lane was overtaken by sleep. But Leslie, lying on the couch, and Clara, nestled in her sleeping bag just below her friend, continued chatting. After a competition to see which girl had experienced the worse blizzard, Leslie blurted out, "I'm sorry if I made you or Lane feel bad earlier."

Clara replied, "And I guess I shouldn't have gotten pissy. But I really don't think Lane sounds like that much of a hick. And everybody has some kind of accent, after all."

"I don't!" Leslie protested.

"You say 'becoss' instead of 'because,'" Clara insisted.

"That's the way you're supposed to say it!"

"Yeah, right. You sound like you're from New York. I sound like I'm from West Virginia. Big deal. Who cares?"

After a pause, Leslie whispered, "Oh, it's just that I'm so tired of everything sounding—and being—so different from how I always thought things were."

"You mean since your parents got divorced and you had to move here?" Clara asked.

"That's not the half of it. My mother is so different from the witty, upbeat woman she used to be. Now she's just sad. She bursts into tears. She's drinking a lot. And now … now I find out my father isn't who he once appeared to be."

"Whaddya mean?" Clara asked, sitting up in her sleeping bag to hear better.

Leslie then related a shocking conversation she'd had with her mother a month earlier, when she learned her beloved, charming father faced criminal charges on both sides of the Atlantic. He had done some really bad things like destroying one of the family businesses and making deals with mobsters. Then he looted family assets to finance his life as a fugitive. Leslie didn't know if she'd ever see him again—or whether she wanted to. Because of his misdeeds, she and her mother were dependent on the charity of her "dull West Virginia grandparents, whom I always considered an embarrassment," Leslie added, shaking her head in disbelief. "If it weren't for them, I don't know where Mother and I would be now."

With Leslie sounding so down, Clara wanted to show solidarity. So she shared some similar secrets. She revealed that sometimes her "great aunt" drank excessively and got scarily depressed, too. Immediately after saying that, Clara felt disloyal. And nervous. To establish an emotional bond with her new friend, had she just jeopardized her link to Beatrice?

"But you haven't been dumped into a completely different culture, like I have," Leslie complained.

"Yeah, I have," Clara said quietly. And then, suddenly, it all spilled out. She revealed how she had come to live with Beatrice, a come-here who was not her great aunt at all. She talked about Rodney's pedophilia. She described Charyce's maternal betrayal. She said her father had essentially abandoned her. She talked about being bounced from Ben's doublewide to Eltie's house before ending up with Beatrice. She even related Rodney's kidnapping attempt and his subsequent arrest as a major drug dealer.

When she was finished, the only sounds were Lane's rhythmic breathing and the ticking of Beatrice's grandfather clock. Clara instantly regretted her recitation of such mortifying personal history.

Finally, Leslie said, even more softly than before, "Wow. No wonder we hit it off. We have so much in common. My father and your stepfather are criminals. We've both been uprooted. And our lives aren't really what they seem to be on the surface."

I have a lot in common with Leslie, a rich New Yorker?

Clara was stunned by the realization that she felt far more kinship with the alien Leslie than with a fellow mountaineer like Randy "Wilma" Carver. But could she count on her new friend?

"Please don't tell anyone else what I told you, Leslie. Not even Lane."

"I won't," Leslie promised. "But you don't have to worry about him. He has his own family secrets. Of course, he shared them with me in confidence, so I can't tell you."

If Leslie could keep Lane's secret, whatever it was, she could probably be trusted with the Buckhalters' dirty laundry. Nevertheless, Clara's sense of overexposure had made her long for privacy. So she withdrew upstairs. And fretted until sleep finally came.

✳   ✳   ✳

Beatrice arose much earlier than normal. She had set her battery-powered alarm clock for six-thirty but beat it to the punch. Thanks to the storm, the guests, and the power outage, a mountain of chores awaited her. A peek out the window told her the storm was over but had left maybe eighteen inches of snow. Digging out would not be easy, even with three youngsters manning shovels. Her truck wouldn't be able to negotiate the long driveway without the help of a plow. Who knew when that could be arranged?

But first things first. With the help of her blackthorn cane, Beatrice eased down the frigid stairs and headed for the kitchen stove, which she set at three-fifty to warm the downstairs. Discerning no signs of life in the living room, she decided to tend the woodstove later. Instead, she focused on Ralph, whose nose was poking through the back door's dog panel, as he reconsidered how badly he needed to pee. With a little encouragement, he finally exited and dolphined through the snow. Meanwhile, Beatrice fired up the teakettle and debated where to do her physical therapy. The usual venue, her bedroom, was prohibitively cold. Looking around the kitchen, she noted a respectable amount of floor space affording some privacy, thanks to the L-shaped counter. So after preempting the teakettle's shriek, she began her tedious drill.

Beatrice saved the worst part for last: sliding her foot down the wall to improve knee flexion. As she lay on the floor and began the excruciating exercise, she realized she had an audience. A rumpled Lane was quietly watching from the kitchen doorway.

"That looks awful," he groaned.

"It is." Beatrice paused to see if the boy would leave. But he remained, apparently fascinated. So she soldiered on. When she finished, she realized that getting down on the floor was a lot easier than getting up. Before she could weigh her options, Lane grasped her right forearm near the elbow, told her to do likewise with his arm, and then, once she maneuvered her left leg close to her butt, he leaned back and levered her up. Beatrice didn't outweigh Lane, so it wasn't a heroic move, but it was deftly executed.

"Thanks. Where'd you learn that trick?" Beatrice asked.

"From my mom's physical therapists. She often has trouble getting up."

Beatrice had assumed Lane's mother was dead. After an awkward pause, she thought of a safe way of eliciting information. "Where does she go for physical therapy?"

"She doesn't exactly go anywhere. She's already there. She lives at a kind of nursing home. Up in Charleston. She has Huntington's Disease. It's pretty bad now."

"Oh, Lane, I'm so sorry." Beatrice had heard enough about that neurodegenerative disease to know that its victims withered away, some suffering major dementia before death. Worse, the victims' children had a fifty-percent chance of developing Huntington's themselves.

"Mom got the first symptoms early. She's only forty, but the disease is pretty far along. That's why we can't take care of her at home anymore."

"It must be hard driving all the way to Charleston to visit her."

"Yeah. But I see her a couple of times a month. I used to go more often, but she doesn't always recognize me now. It's pretty frustrating."

"I can imagine. Well, no, I can't. That's a heavy load for a kid to bear."

"It's a lot heavier for her," Lane said softly.

"You're a good person, Lane."

The boy shrugged, but a shy grin telegraphed his appreciation for the compliment.

The refrigerator's compressor suddenly shuddered itself awake. "Hallelujah," Beatrice breathed softly, "the power's back on."

She poured Lane a glass of orange juice and inquired about his appetite. They agreed to wait for breakfast until the others stirred. For the next hour, Lane and Beatrice shared a pot of tea at the kitchen table. Sleepiness caused some conversational lapses, but the chatter moved along with surprising ease, largely because of Lane's curiosity about everything, including her PT regimen. At one point, when she griped that limping made for a stiff back, he stood to demonstrate a Qigong stretch that often helped his mother's rigid muscles. The boy was executing a kind of football stadium wave, creating lateral flow in the spine, when Leslie appeared. Beatrice braced for the sneering comment a teenager might make about Lane's performance, but the girl merely sat down on the floor to watch with quiet interest.

The only mockery came fifteen minutes later when Clara arrived. "Hey, you're making us mountaineers look bad, like we're too wimpy to sleep on the floor," Lane chided. Leslie laughed, "She probably couldn't take the sound of your snoring, Lane." Clara's defense was to rub her tummy plaintively and puff out her cheeks. "You got sick? Don't get near me!" Lane gasped in mock terror.

The banter continued through breakfast preparations. As Beatrice blotted the cooked bacon on paper towels, Ralph bellowed and bolted out the back door. A moment later, the humans heard what had startled him: the roar of heavy machinery. Clara dashed to the living room windows and announced, "It's a plow! Coming up our driveway. Hey, I think it's Uncle Virgil! Looks like he borrowed the Aldermans' big tractor to dig us out."

"God love him!" Beatrice exclaimed gratefully. In a few minutes, she would fret about how to prioritize breakfast and Virgil's unexpected arrival. For now, however, she was processing the happy shock of finding herself in the midst of this slapdash assembly of kindly, wounded souls. No longer as a distant bystander.

FORTY-FOUR

Dysfunctional Family Snapshots

THE MARLBORO ACADEMY APPEARED TO HAVE a personality disorder, as it simultaneously embraced New England preppiness and Old South grandeur. Neo-gothic and neoclassical buildings stood uncomfortably side by side. In another month, the campus's many bulb gardens would soften the jarring contrasts. For now, the manicured boxwood hedges coexisted uneasily with the ponderously drooping hemlocks.

After parking in the visitors' lot, Beatrice felt grateful for the unusually balmy weather on this March day. She had a long walk to the headmistress's office. Relying on her cane more than usual to negotiate the bumpy brick walkways, she reflected on the pretention implicit in the school's staffing. It had both a principal and a headmistress. Apparently, the former was a hands-on administrator, while the latter functioned as the academy's PR director, interfacing with community leaders and affluent alumnae. Beatrice's destination was thus proof of the high honor being accorded Clara. The Marlboro Academy clearly considered its annual Emily Dickinson Poetry Award sufficiently prestigious to merit the headmistress's involvement.

Clara had not told Beatrice of her plans to enter the Dickinson contest, which required multiple submissions on a common theme. Beatrice certainly knew of the girl's interest in and aptitude for writing, whether diary entries, class essays, or school newspaper items. But her fondness for poetry was a surprise. Weeks after the fact, Clara finally revealed she had entered the competition — and won. She had initially feared that her lyrical talents would attract mockery from her contemporaries, perhaps even family members. But after a jury of English teachers (including one published poet) found her work worthy, Clara was eager to share her victory with Beatrice. The latter was impressed by her young charge's submissions: vignettes of life on the farm featuring Ralph, the llamas, and all the wild creatures sharing turf with the human residents. Beatrice particularly admired the economy of language. Ably channeling the belle of Amherst, Clara avoided the overblown rhetoric and contrived phrasings that often curdled youthful poetry. The poems were plainspoken and insightful, much like Clara herself. Beatrice savored a swell of pride as she climbed the stairs to the administration building.

The headmistress's substantial office was the designated venue for the award ceremony, involving some faculty members, a few of Clara's friends and relatives, a photographer, a reporter from the *Marlboro County Recorder*, and a local bank official. The poetry award included a check for one hundred dollars, donated by the bank.

When she entered, Beatrice scanned the room for familiar faces. Clara, looking ill at ease as she answered the reporter's questions, waggled her fingers at Beatrice and nodded toward the folding chairs set up for guests. Leslie jumped up from one of those seats to greet the new arrival. As she and Beatrice chatted, another guest entered the room. Beatrice didn't recognize Mike Buckhalter at first. He had gained weight in the months since she had last seen him. The kinship with his brother was unmistakable, nonetheless. Like Ben, Mike was tall, blue-eyed, and cleft-chinned. But he lacked Ben's open, friendly demeanor and looked profoundly uncomfortable, pulling at his starched collar.

Beatrice walked toward him, extended her hand, smiled and said, "It's good to see you again, Mike. You must be so proud of Clara."

Mike retracted his fingers quickly from the handshake. "Hi," he nodded in a low voice, without eye contact. The headmistress freed him from further conversational challenges by rapping on her mahogany desk with her fingertips. Then she theatrically swept her hand toward the folding chairs. The guests dutifully sat down, while Miss Pendergast, as she identified herself, came out from behind the mahogany fortress to make her presentation.

It was a lengthy one, delivered in a reedy drawl suggesting the Virginia piedmont rather than the West Virginia mountains. Although Miss Pendergast had effusive praise for the young poet, her kind words were undercut by evident surprise that Seneca County could produce such artistic sensibilities. Beatrice narrowed her eyes. Mike fidgeted in his seat.

Then the headmistress beckoned Clara to the fore and said, "Our award-winner will give us an example of her Dickinsonian powers of observation. I understand she has chosen a haiku on the interplay of light and dark." She unfurled a palm toward a slightly puzzled Clara.

The teenager took a deep breath and then looked down at the paper shaking in her hand. As she began to read, a quaver forced her to clear her throat. Starting over, in a somewhat stronger voice, Clara announced the title, "The Shades of January." Then she read, clearly:

"Black seed husks on snow:

The black-capped chickadee signs winter's white canvas."

"Seventeen syllables, yes indeed," Miss Pendergast affirmed, nodding and clapping. After a few seconds, the guests joined in the applause. Headmistress and poet shook hands, while the photographer worked the shutter. Then, on cue, the banker stepped up, pulled a check from his breast pocket, handed it to Clara, and also shook her hand. More photographs.

An announcement came next. "I'd be remiss if I didn't introduce Miss Buckhalter's proud family. Would her father and great aunt please come up here and be recognized?"

Uh-oh. Beatrice knew the paperwork submitted to the academy clearly identified the family members responsible for handling emergencies. She was not among them. Mike, as the custodial parent, was listed first, followed by Ben. Beatrice was merely the contact point for quotidian communications—about snow days, for example. But the headmistress (precisely because she did not tend to the school's daily affairs) must have overheard chatter about Clara living with a Seneca County great aunt. The teenager's fib clearly enjoyed broad acceptance.

As both "relatives" walked across the room, Beatrice could hear Mike's teeth grinding. Miss Pendergast clasped Beatrice's hand firmly and smiled broadly. Next she turned to Mike, who suffered a longer handshake and overblown comments about his parenting skills. The photographer took more shots of the celebrants. The headmistress ordered Beatrice and Mike to pose with Clara, and Mike whispered, "Mighty glad you could join us, Auntie Beatrice."

Beatrice just stared ahead, smiling weakly for the camera, but Clara was unable to stifle a soft moan. As the headmistress hailed various faculty members, the key celebrants stood together awkwardly. During the wait,

Mike tweaked Beatrice anew. "Funny, I always thought Aunt Rose was the baby among Ma's sisters. My memory must be faulty, huh?"

Clara winced and lowered her head. Beatrice placed a steadying right hand on the girl's shoulder and flashed her broadest, falsest smile at Mike. "Mikey, you always were such a jokester. Ever since we finally got you out of diapers." With her left hand, she reached over behind Clara and chucked the cleft on Mike's chin.

The photographer captured the moment: Beatrice smiling, making this maternal gesture; Mike, looking like a deer in the headlights; and Clara giggling. The framed photograph would later occupy a conspicuous position on Beatrice's living room wall.

Because the ceremony took place in late afternoon when classes were out, Beatrice and Clara planned to drive to a Marlboro restaurant to celebrate. But first the girl wanted to say goodbye to her father and thank him for coming.

"You wanna blow this popsicle stand and grab some pizza?" Mike asked her.

"Oh, gee, Daddy," Clara stammered. "Beatrice and I have reservations at the Valley Inn. I wasn't sure you'd be able to break away from work to be here. But you could come, too. Please?"

"Reservations! Ain't you the fancy one?" Then, seeing his daughter's face crumple, Mike added gently, "Naw, I can't wait to get out of this scratchy shirt. Besides, I probably should pick up some Big Macs for dinner anyway. Loretta isn't much on cooking these days. You have yourself a good time." He kissed the top of Clara's head. "I'm proud of you, honey."

Beatrice, buttonholed by an English teacher, caught the father-daughter tableau from the corner of her eye and breathed a deep sigh of relief. When she finally joined Clara, she apologized. "I'm sorry if I made your father angry, Clara."

"It's not your fault TenderAss thought you were my great aunt. I'm glad you said what you did—and shut Daddy up before he outed me for fibbing. It was actually pretty funny."

Beatrice squeezed the girl's shoulder affectionately and headed for the front door. In the foyer, Clara paused, craning her neck left, then right. After a shrug, she skipped to catch up with Beatrice.

"Forget something?" she asked.

"Oh, I just thought Lane might have arrived too late for the ceremony and was hanging around the entrance. Something must have come up at his school." Clara's tone was nonchalant, but Beatrice read disappointment in her eyes, now scanning the campus.

As each discreetly processed the significance of Lane's absence, the conversation lapsed until the pair reached the truck. Beatrice cranked the starter and broke the silence. "So, how you gonna spend that hundred-dollar check?"

"I can't decide. I'd really like an ebook reader. That way I could download library books without worrying about how to get there and back. And it would be nice to be able to buy an ebook now and then. It's not like there's a bookstore around here."

"All valid points. But?" Beatrice prodded.

"Well, I'd also like to buy some DVDs. Online I found this awesome series on Japanese culture. Cool stuff about history, art, religion. Even an introduction to the Japanese language. But it costs close to a hundred bucks. And anyway it might be too advanced for me."

"Where'd this fascination with things Japanese come from?" Beatrice asked.

"I think it started with the beautiful Japanese print my grandmother had—with flowers and birds. When I'd visit her as a little kid, I'd stare and stare at it. I don't know why."

"It spoke to you," Beatrice said decisively. "Doesn't matter why. How about you buy the ebook reader with your award money, and I'll buy you the Japanese DVD."

"Really?"

"Really. Consider it my way of apologizing for being in such a funk for the past month. I got awfully down about winter, the surgery … other stuff. I know I wasn't much fun to be around. And speaking of fun, how would you like to come up to Massachusetts with me for Evie's wedding? You could be my navigator. Unless being around us old folks would be boring."

"Boring? Evie's hilarious and I really like Bart. And just think of all the new states I could check off!"

Chuckling at Clara's zeal for adding states to her life list, Beatrice stepped on the gas. "One road trip coming up."

FORTY-FIVE

Harbingers

THE DREAM HADN'T HAD MUCH OF A PLOT. Beatrice was just wandering through an unknown house. But, oh, how that house made her feel: protected, hopeful, joyous, and exactly where she belonged. While still half asleep, she tried to resurrect the minute details. Didn't the living room bring to mind her beloved fixer-upper in Purcellville? And the kitchen had some kinship with hers in Seneca County but was somehow different, better. There was even a secret room — not scary but a place of light and wonder. Yet the more she tried to recreate the house's precise layout, the faster each room took to the ether, like a kite to the wind. And suddenly, the kite became as real as the house had been. She reached up, unsure if her arm was actually moving from beneath the bedcovers, and ripped off the kite-tail just before the frail, beautiful frame wafted into the stratosphere. She clutched the tail of a dream fragment to her breast and re-experienced the bliss of awed wandering through those inviting rooms.

Moments later, with one hand closed tightly over her chest, she knew she held no kite tail. Fully awake now, she retained just an echo of the dream's original euphoria. In earlier decades, after a similarly enchanting vision, Beatrice would try to dissect it. Did it manifest some happy event from the previous day? Some happy plan for the day to come? Inevitably, the answer would be no, and she would suddenly feel sad. So Beatrice no longer indulged that form of buzz kill. Although far removed from enlightenment, she knew enough to savor the ephemeral bliss that dreams sometimes conferred. It mattered not whether the good feelings resulted from angelic intercession or fluctuations in brain chemistry.

There were no obvious signs the dream presaged some blissful turn of events. Beatrice awoke to pleasant but unremarkable weather for Seneca County in mid-March. Despite a new dusting of snow, the green pockmarks advancing on the pasture attested to the sun's growing vigor.

By nine o'clock, the thermometer read forty, encouraging Beatrice to take Ralph for a brisk walk before burying herself in her office.

Unless the footing was treacherous, dog-walks were now almost daily occurrences, albeit still requiring a cane. In the earlier phase of Beatrice's recuperation, an expedition in the fresh air all too often resulted in a swollen knee. Lately, however, strolls on level ground, like the border of the pasture, actually seemed to strengthen the traumatized joint. The exercise had clear mental health benefits from Ralph, too. His buoyant cheer was infectious.

The vigilance required for scanning chuck holes and slippery patches absorbed only a minor portion of Beatrice's brainpower and did not impinge on the walk's olfactory joys. She delighted in smelling humidity again for the first time in months. Ralph, loping ahead, off-lead, would occasionally crush wild-onion sprouts, and his tail would fan the fragrance backward for Beatrice to enjoy.

Just before taking the curve leading to the creek path, Ralph halted abruptly. He lowered his head so that crown, shoulders, and tail were perfectly aligned. He lifted his right front leg and curled the paw toward his elbow. Beatrice sped up as best she could to discover what had put the setter on point. She feared a mad canine dash after geese and into the frigid water.

The dog stayed frozen, as Beatrice drew alongside and scooped up his leash. Now she, too, could see what had riveted Ralph's attention: a convention of turkeys. Several waddled prudently into the deep brush on the mountain side of the path. Others flapped their large wings and only just managed to reach low branches in the trees growing along the creek bank. Some, once they found that low roost, took to the air again, only to plop back down on the path and scuttle, heads craned forward, in search of a better hidey-hole—even though that quest put them closer to their potential predators. In their indecision, several of the tall, bottom-heavy birds nearly collided. Beatrice spat out her laughter. In the next instant, she had to jerk on Ralph's leash, because the dog took her eruption as a green light for chasing the perplexed turkeys. The laughter further agitated the large birds, which finally opted en masse for the deep brush, upslope from dog and human.

Beatrice recalled some anecdote about certain Indian tribes designating the turkey as a totem of abundance. Because turkey had dominated the groaning board at the first Thanksgiving, that interpretation wasn't much of a stretch. Clearly, her property overflowed with such abundance, for which she was grateful. Aware that few Americans would ever witness the spectacle of twenty befuddled wild turkeys, she felt blessed. Ralph, however, felt frustrated. But after several appreciative thumps to his flanks, the tension drained out of his muscles, and the thwarted birddog resumed his scent-sniffing, scent-marking patrol.

As woman and dog approached within a hundred feet of the house, Beatrice spotted an SUV heading down her driveway toward the road. The yellow light on the roof identified the vehicle as belonging to the mail carrier. Although Beatrice's mailbox was at roadside, the postman would often deliver oversized parcels up the long driveway. Sure enough, there was one of them, leaning against her back door.

It was too big to handle with Ralph in tow. Changing his collar and shucking her jacket, she wondered if Clara had ordered something and forgotten to tell her. That was highly unlikely, however, given the girl's native frugality and inclination to agonize over any withdrawal from the meager PayPal account her father had set up for her. Then Beatrice remembered that Clara's fifteenth birthday was less than a month away. Perhaps the unwieldy package was an early gift ordered by one of the Buckhalters.

It wasn't until Beatrice deposited the large, rectangular package on the kitchen counter that she read her name, not Clara's, on the label. Next she spotted the odd stamps. The denomination was euros, not dollars. Only then did she notice "Eire" as the point of origin. Since three of her grandparents had been born in Eire, she wondered if some long-lost relative could be looking her up. But surely the first contact would be a letter, not a package.

She ripped into the parcel's multiple layers of protection. Once stripped down, it revealed a crude frame: two long horizontal wood stretchers affixed to three verticals, one of them in the middle. Lying in between the stretchers was an envelope with "Beatrice" penned on the front.

She put the envelope aside, as she flipped the frame to see what those pieces of wood were stretching. A canvas. An oil painting.

What the hell?

Bent over the counter, Beatrice briefly thought she was looking into her own face from twenty years earlier. Except she had never worn her hair that way. The woman in the oil painting had shoulder-length dark hair—precisely Beatrice's color—with a forties-era comb securing one side. The subject of the portrait was lovely, if not conventionally beautiful. Beatrice was certain she herself had never looked that good. Yet she shared many features with the face in the painting: arched eyebrows, high forehead, gray eyes, strong chin, and wide, full mouth. Perhaps it was the woman's expression that made her so striking—defiant, free-spirited, and vulnerable all at once.

The artist had painted his subject (Beatrice had little doubt the painter was male) with her hands resting on a stone wall overlooking a turbulent sea. The wind ruffled her hair and long woolen scarf. Although the woman's body faced the water, her head was turned back toward the observer. The expression was unmistakable. *Just what do you think you're looking at?*

Beatrice had difficulty shifting her eyes from the woman's challenging gaze. But finally, she focused on the envelope. Inside was a sheet of stationery fully occupied by angular scribbling and bearing the stamp of "The Hag's Head Inn." Scanning to the bottom of the page, she read Tanner's signature.

He began with a reference from Irish mythology. *Much as King Cu Chulainn had difficulty escaping from the mad witch Mal, for whom Hag's Head, County Clare, is unchivalrously named, I have had trouble shaking thoughts of you. At first, I blamed those discomforting thoughts on the manner of our parting. But then I actually felt your glare as I walked down a street overlooking the waters of Malbay. It took me a while to locate the source. An insignificant art gallery. And there you were—glowering down from one wall.*

Tanner described how he promptly purchased the painting and then chatted up the proprietress. Did she know the subject of the portrait? Perhaps the artist? No, to each question. As far as the gallery owner knew, both were long dead. But the artist's granddaughter lived in the next town. After charming the granddaughter's address out of the proprietress, Tanner tracked down "Ann Sheehan." She turned out to be the descendant, one generation removed, of an affair between the married painter and the much younger woman in the portrait, Julia Forestall.

Beatrice sucked in her breath. There was a Julia Forestall in her family tree, a maternal great aunt. Julia's older brother Dennis had left Ireland in the 1920s to seek a more prosperous future in Boston. There he met and married a local girl and fathered Hanorah Desmond, Beatrice's mother. Dennis was the only member of the Forestall clan to cross the pond. Julia, who stayed behind, probably would have been in her early thirties during World War Two—just like the woman in the portrait.

Tanner wrote about the rest of his conversation with Mrs. Sheehan. She knew of no Desmonds in the family but added that her great uncle, Dennis Forestall, had emigrated to Boston sometime in the early twentieth century. Little was heard from him after he left. But perhaps he or his issue eventually met up with some American Desmonds.

It would appear I've found your long-lost cousin—as well as you, in an earlier scandalous incarnation. Scandal becomes you, Hillwilla.

And that was it, except for the bold signature. There was no explanation why her estranged lover would suddenly send her such a uniquely personal gift. His note contained no apology for his hurtful insinuations. The Irish gallery had sent the painting—by the cheapest, slowest method possible—in late January, ten days after Tanner uttered those hurtful words. He probably bought it during the week he spent stalking Connemara woodcock before jetting off to his African troubles. Was this a peace offering? Or was it merely a polite gesture from someone returning a lost article to its owner?

Since learning of his illness, Beatrice had debated emailing him if only to wish him a full recovery. But pride and confusion got in the way. And now she was more confused than ever.

"I don't know, maybe it will all make more sense in a day or so," she said, tucking the portrait with its packaging into the hall closet.

FORTY-SIX

Humbling Experiences

JULIA FORESTALL STARED DEFIANTLY AT CLARA, who gaped back, thunderstruck, at the painting, which Beatrice had temporarily perched on two screws on the living room wall late the previous night. "Wow, you used to be pretty, Beatrice!" the girl shouted toward the kitchen.

"There are just so many ways to take that observation," Beatrice laughed, walking to the kitchen entranceway. "But it's not me. Apparently, she's my long dead Irish great aunt. Tanner just happened to stumble upon her portrait when he was in Ireland weeks ago."

"Tanner?" Clara asked with interest. "He's back? Is he healthy?" Both Evie and Beatrice had informed her about Tanner's illness. As a result, she promptly dropped her plan to tell him about the knee replacement and recuperation. The whole idea of that plan was to get him to shake Beatrice out of her funk. If he was half dead himself, that didn't seem likely.

"I don't know what his current status is. The painting was sent back in January. It just took forever to get here."

"Oh," Clara said, obviously disappointed. Then an idea occurred to her. "But you'll probably find out what's going on when you send him a thank-you email, right?" The youngster knew Beatrice was a stickler about manners.

"I sent off a thank-you to his Gmail address yesterday after the package arrived. But who can say if he'll get the message. He could be traveling. He might still be in Provence. For all I know he's right here in Seneca County."

"Without letting you know?" Clara asked, wide-eyed.

"Things weren't so great when he left."

Beatrice returned to her breakfast, while Clara, with one last look at Julia, shrugged into her backpack and, waving farewell, headed out the door to catch her carpool to school.

Beatrice was up and about earlier than usual because she was expecting

Eltie at nine to geld Buck. As that hour approached, she headed to the barn to halter Buck and separate him from the rest of the herd. She did so while reflecting on the situation with Tanner. She had spent a ridiculous amount of time gearing up to write that email. She finally opted for the most cautious approach. Her expression of gratitude for the painting and her wishes for a speedy recovery sounded formal—as if she were addressing a distant colleague.

Well, that's how we started out, as colleagues working on his autobiography.

Nevertheless, she felt cowardly for avoiding the elephant in the room. Of course, the note Tanner had included with the painting was less than direct, too.

Smirking, Beatrice thought of an alternative email she had drafted in her head:

What the fuck is that painting supposed to mean? You act like a total asshole, leave the country without a word of farewell, nearly die and fail to let anyone know? Damn near two months go by since I've laid eyes on you. And suddenly, this incredibly personal gift appears out of nowhere? Thanks, I think. Talk about mixed messages!

Psychiatrists claim any relationship worth having requires honest communication. Beatrice wasn't so sure. She knew long-married couples who opted for politeness (and peace) instead of full revelations. And they seemed fairly happy. Did the wife really need to know that her husband found her anecdotes tedious? Did the husband really need to know that his wife was repulsed by his weight gain?

The appearance of Eltie's truck in the driveway gave Beatrice a welcome respite from analyzing relationship pitfalls. She turned her attention to Buck, whom she haltered, hugged, and tucked into a stall. After shooing the other llamas into the pasture, she waved her cane to catch Eltie's attention.

Moments later, the vet entered the barn, and Beatrice greeted her cheerfully, adding, "The weather's cooperating for a change."

Eltie nodded. "Yeah, it was snowing when I gelded a horse last week. So I had to do it in the barn instead of the field." She leaned forward to exchange puffs of breath with Buck.

"You want to do this surgery in the paddock then?" Beatrice asked.

"Yup, I'll take clean grass over a barn floor any day of the week."

Beatrice led Buck out of the barn and into the paddock end farthest away from the main pasture where the other, barred, members of the herd jostled one another for a better look at the tall stranger. Eltie temporarily tied Buck to a fence post. Then she went down on her haunches to sort through her kit. She filled a syringe and promptly tucked it into her pocket. When she rose, she scrabbled Buck's lower back with her left hand, while her right jabbed the hidden needle into the muscle high up on one of his hind legs. "Okay," Eltie directed, "untie him quickly and lead him over to that nice grassy spot. It will take a few minutes for the sedative to kick in, but we want him in the right place before it does."

Buck soon kushed but held his head high. Eventually, the bleary llama could no longer maintain that posture and stretched his long neck on the ground. After flicking his eyelashes to assess his level of sedation, the vet draped a towel over his eyes then busied herself at his other end. As Eltie snipped, Beatrice, stroking Buck's reddish-brown head, rattled off a series of questions about post-op care.

In response to one of them, Eltie said, "If there's any personality change, it will only be for the better. As young as he is, he probably hasn't gotten ornery, even though he's already tried to breed one of your girls. Llamas are a lot more laid-back than stallions anyhow, but you never know. Rising testosterone levels can do a real number on some males."

"And not just the four footed ones," Beatrice added.

"You got that right! I can think of a few guys who'd do the world a big favor if they had their nuts cut out. Like Rodney Madsen. And there was this one miserable professor at Tech. There, all done," Eltie announced, rising and wiping her hands on a towel. "You got any nominations?"

"For gelding?"

"I got the impression your pal Fordyce can be a major jerkwad at times."

Beatrice snorted with good humor at Eltie's clumsy elicitation effort and promptly shifted the focus by commenting, "I can think of a few women who might benefit from neutering, too."

While monitoring the rate at which Buck's sides bellowed in and out, Eltie chuckled in agreement. "Dang right. The mating frenzy has fried a lot of female brains. And turned other women into scheming shrews. That piece of trailer trash Charyce comes to mind. That's one gal needs to have her raging hormones dialed waaay down."

"No argument here."

Several minutes later, Buck levered his neck more or less erect. Gradually coaxing him to his feet with the lead, Eltie explained that moving around sooner than later could prevent various side effects. The llama lurched a few uncertain steps forward, as the vet nodded her approval. She unclipped the lead and gave Beatrice a rough timetable for the healing process. She was interrupted by a stertorous comment from the patient. A dazed Buck raised his throat in a protracted orgle, the mating cry. Both women laughed.

"What's that all about?" Beatrice asked.

"Good drugs. He's high as a kite. Probably hallucinating about romping with the ladies. Dream all you want, boy. Those days are history." She patted the orgling llama's flank.

*   *   *

Well after the vet's departure, Eltie's confident professionalism continued to have an empowering influence on Beatrice. She was relieved that Buck had tolerated the surgery well and was now moving about normally, even grazing. All eight llamas could be reunited shortly with no fear of an unwanted breeding. Even the jokes about neutering disagreeable humans had a grounding effect on Beatrice by trivializing the gravity of endlessly complex romantic relationships.

With such a propitious start to her day, Beatrice was ready to tackle the assignments waiting in her office — even the dicey task of editing one of Wolfgang's more notorious divas, a man who knew everything about the Nuclear Nonproliferation Treaty but was dreadful about communicating his expertise coherently. He was equally dreadful about having his tortuous articles altered in any way. Wolfgang had promised to prepare the author for extensive revisions. He had also promised to send Beatrice an email detailing certain pitfalls to avoid in her upcoming communications with the diva.

Her email inbox showed nothing yet from Wolfgang. But it did contain a message from Tanner. Beatrice took a deep breath before opening it.

He began by expressing relief that the package had finally arrived from

Ireland. He hoped the painting had some meaning for Beatrice. Then:

You were probably taken aback by the gift, since I was in full snarl when last you saw me. Truth be told, I was still in a pet in Ireland. As angry as I was, however, I just couldn't overlook that fragment of your family history. Besides, I thought there might be some witchery at work and I would be in deep trouble if I ignored Julia and failed to forward her to you.

As you know, I ended up in trouble anyway. My entire adult life, Beatrice, I've been physically strong. When a man is confident he can take care of himself, whether facing down adversaries or pushing a car out of a ditch, he acquires a sense of invulnerability. That translates into mental toughness, too. But after leaving Africa, when I was 35,000 feet above the Mediterranean, I felt as weak as the proverbial kitten. The weakness soon became prostration. I didn't like feeling vulnerable—just as I did in childhood. Well, you already know that tediously sordid story.

For the first time in eons, I couldn't muscle, cogitate, or buy my way out of trouble. I had to depend on other people for my every need, while I simply waited for my body to heal or die. That humbling experience offered some insights into the struggles other people face—how they must husband their resources, pick and choose their battles, save their strength for those slugfests that absolutely must be fought. Which is precisely the approach you took on Clara's behalf regarding Madsen. I was so wrong to accuse you of cowardice, of being anything less than Clara's staunch champion. That girl has no idea how lucky she is that you entered her life. I hope you'll accept my apology.

Beatrice couldn't completely track Tanner's logic. Then again, she had never felt invulnerable. Nor had she ever had a near-death experience. But she had no doubt about the sincerity of Tanner's apology. Certainly she would accept it. She was less certain, however, about where things should go from there.

FORTY-SEVEN

A Hectic and Thankful April

EVEN IN SENECA COUNTY, where frost warnings linger through May, life speeds up as spring advances. After months of stasis, each day brings new sensory input. The phoebe rasps its claim to nest sites, while the robin's syrinx reworks long-dormant, complex melodies. As each wildflower species, in turn, celebrates its day in the sun, the colors intensify. With March come the brown stripes of skunk cabbage, hugging the snowy ground. In April, trillium's white splotches dapple otherwise dark hillsides. In May, entire fields morph from green to brilliant yellow, as legions of wild mustards bloom.

So, too, the pace of life accelerates in Appalachia's domesticated patches. The Desmond llamas take breaks from greedily ripping at juicy wild-onion tufts to prong round and round the pasture. They're celebrating the disappearance of both the snowcap and the interior fencing that limited their freedom.

This particular spring has increased the human traffic to and from the Desmond farm. Twice a week, Lane, Leslie, and Clara collaborate on their fiber project, as their 4-H deadline approaches. The days grow longer, and Ben sometimes drops by after work to take a walk with his goddaughter. Virgil, whose back has much improved since his surgery the previous June, is resuming his handyman functions at the Desmond homestead and often takes time out to joke with Clara. Vaughn occasionally arrives with a freshly baked pie and lingers at the kitchen table for a chat.

Other communication is on the upswing, too. Almost daily, Evie and Beatrice share phone consultations about the early May wedding in Massachusetts. Beatrice's telecommuted translations and editing assignments are also proliferating, after the winter lull. And for several weeks, emails between her and Tanner, still in Europe, have shuttled across the Atlantic.

Flipping the kitchen calendar to April, three days after the month began, Beatrice fretted about her suddenly hectic schedule. Too many priorities were competing for her attention. Clara's birthday, a special event being organized by Amanda Buckhalter, a road trip to Evie in Northern Virginia, and—perhaps—her first face-to-face meeting with Tanner since their dustup.

Today was Clara's birthday, but circumstances prevented Beatrice from celebrating the occasion. The previous evening she had given the almost-fifteen-year-old her presents (a digital camera, a coffee mug labeled "Barn Goddess") and made the teen's favorite dinner (homemade calzone and homemade cannoli). Clara would spend her actual birthday and the following four days at her godfather's house, which was to be the venue for a multipurpose party. The participants would pay homage to the girl's birthday as well as celebrate her mother's recent engagement to Clay Lightfoot.

On the guest list were Ben, Amanda, Virgil, Clara, Eltie, Vaughn, Clay, Charyce, and one of Charyce's gal pals from the karaoke bar. Mike, loath to attend any event featuring his ex-wife, would wait a day before honoring his daughter by taking her to a Lady Antebellum concert in Roanoke. Eltie had initially turned down Amanda's invitation because of her animosity toward Charyce, but Vaughn induced a change of heart by arguing that they owed it to Clara to attend. Curiosity was also a factor. After hearing how different Clay was from Charyce's usual fare, both Vaughn and Eltie wanted to case out the new beau.

Beatrice had not been invited. The Buckhalters were well aware of her hostility toward Charyce and knew that, unlike them, Beatrice was unencumbered by the family ties that, by Seneca County standards, required tolerance of even the most noxious in-law. Of course, she would have declined an invitation anyway, because matron-of-honor duties required her presence in McLean, Virginia.

Beatrice gave a last look around the farmhouse to make sure everything was secure. She clipped the leash to Ralph's collar and called upstairs, "C'mon, Clara! You told Amanda you'd be there by noon. We're gonna be late unless you get a move on."

The first order of business was driving the teen to Ben's house. He planned to take her out to lunch in Marlboro Old Town before the birthday/engagement party so uncle and niece could have some one-on-one time.

The next chore was to deliver Ralph to the boarding kennel, just off I-64, the first high-speed link on the five-hour drive to Northern Virginia. Because any delay would increase the odds of bogging down in the Washington Beltway's rush-hour morass, Beatrice was having difficulty mastering her impatience. "You alive up there?" she called again.

"Yeah, yeah, I'm coming," Clara groused, bumping her carryon down the stairs.

*   *   *

As Beatrice's truck turned onto the main county road, she asked her passenger, "So, what's with the sudden friendship between your mother and Amanda?"

"No way they're friends. But something changed after Momma decided she needed tips on how to act around someone as classy as Clay. Amanda suggested she tone down her clothing. And Momma did. You should have seen the nice suit she wore to that lunch we went to in Roanoke."

"You're kidding! I don't know which is more surprising, that your mother would alter her … umm … flamboyant style or Amanda would act as her fashion adviser."

"Maybe Amanda was flattered that Momma considered her a model of good taste?"

"That doesn't ring true. Your aunt's no dummy."

Clara shrugged. "Maybe Amanda really wants Momma and Clay to get married. Why else host an engagement party?"

"Hmmm," Beatrice mused. "S'ppose Amanda considers the guy a good influence?"

"My guess is that Amanda and Ben and Daddy like the idea of Momma leaving the state. If she marries Clay, she'll have to move to Roanoke, won't she?"

"You'd think so. But how will *you* feel about your mother being two hours away?"

Clara chewed on a thumbnail. "It's not like I see her much anyhow. And if she was all the way over in Roanoke, well, I guess she'd be less likely to cause trouble for Daddy or … anyone. But I'm not so sure there ever *will* be a marriage. No date's been set, even though Momma gets her divorce in June. In fact, I'm not convinced she actually *is* engaged. When I talked with Momma the other day, I got the impression Clay hasn't really asked her to marry him. She bragged about putting the words in his mouth before he knew what was happening."

"Yikes," Beatrice said. "Does Clay realize he's about to attend his own engagement party?"

"I dunno. For all the bragging, Momma sounded nervous on the phone. I think she sees this party as a way of pushing Clay toward marriage. Like he'd be too much of a gentleman to back out after Momma told everyone she was engaged."

"Good manners are one thing. Stupidity's another," Beatrice said, shaking her head.

"And then there's Clay's daughter. She hates Momma and was really snotty at that luncheon. Her father seemed disappointed in her, but they're still awfully close. No surprise that Britt—that's the daughter—won't be at tonight's party. Supposedly she had an exam and couldn't leave college. But I think she wouldn't be caught dead in the same room with Momma ever again. Okay by me. Things will be squirrely enough without her—what with Amanda, Eltie, and Momma all in the same house together."

"Should be interesting. Just keep out of the line of fire."

Clara scrunched up her face and shuddered. "Sure you don't want to come?"

Beatrice swatted the girl's thigh and laughed.

*   *   *

The Chevy truck pulled up to Ben's house, and Ben and Virgil came outside. Virgil hugged Clara, grabbed her bag, and took it inside. Ben shrugged down to kiss her on the cheek. "Happy birthday, godkid," he said. Then he addressed Beatrice, "Hi. Thanks for dropping off the birthday girl. Wanna come inside for a cup of coffee?"

"Thanks, but I don't have time. I've got to drop off Ralph and head east pronto, so I make D.C. before rush hour kicks in. Gotta try on a bridesmaid dress."

Ben cupped his hands over Clara's ears and said, grinning, "Hope it looks better than *hers* did."

Clara yanked Ben's hands away. "Jeez, I gotta go pee," she said abruptly, speeding for the house. Then she screeched to a halt, ran back, hugged Beatrice and said, "See ya in a few days. Say 'hey' to Evie for me." She dashed inside before Beatrice could say a proper farewell.

"I don't even remember what it was like to have that much energy," she said to Ben.

"You want to see energy? You should check out Amanda, cleaning, dusting, cooking, and generally stressing out over the big event. You'd think she was getting ready for Prince What's-His-Face and Kate, instead of her former sister-in-law."

"I didn't realize Amanda and Charyce were friends," Beatrice said with false innocence.

"They're not. But Amanda seems to think this Clay could solve a lot of problems for the family. He sounds like a decent guy. And he's rich. So maybe Charyce will have some incentive to get her act together. At least we can hope." Ben crossed both index fingers.

"At very least, her act will be a hundred miles away," Beatrice said with wry humor.

"Ya got that right. I guess I shouldn't be happy about it, since Clara hasn't stopped caring for her mother. But I'll be glad to see all those miles between them."

Nodding in agreement, Beatrice added, "And they can always get together now and then for chaperoned occasions like this party."

"It will be well chaperoned. You can count on it." Ben sighed heavily. "If it was up to me, Clara would be living with us permanently. But Amanda thinks we have to put Virgil's interests first, what with him being so down on his luck. According to her, there's just not enough room here for him *and* Clara. And there certainly isn't room for Clara to stay at Mike's cabin, now that he's married and expecting a baby. I confess I didn't see that twist coming. I get the feeling Clara's none too happy about becoming a big sister?"

Beatrice fanned out her hands and said, "Ben, what can you expect? She hasn't had much face time with her father, as is. He'll have even less time for her once the baby arrives."

Ben clicked his tongue against his front teeth. "My kid brother hasn't brought a smile to many faces in the past year. I'm disappointed in Mike, and that's a fact. But, truth be told, I'm kinda disappointed in myself, too." He hugged his arms to his chest.

"You may not be Clara's father, Ben, but you've always been a bright beacon for her, even when things were otherwise pretty dark in her young life."

Ben tucked chin to chest and shook his head doubtfully. "I shoulda done more. I shoulda kept her here, regardless of Amanda's worries about Virgil." Then, looking up, he said solemnly, "You'll never hear this from Mike. But this is one Buckhalter who's mighty grateful you stepped up for Clara. Sorry I haven't said it outright before. Thank you, Beatrice."

Ben extended his hand. Beatrice, fully grasping the difficult nature of such an admission from a proud mountaineer, gripped his hand tightly. No further words were necessary. With that firm shake, come-here and born-here bridged an ocean of difference.

FORTY-EIGHT

The Crux of the Matter

AFTER GRIPING about the Washington area's perennially abysmal traffic, Evie and Beatrice — each with full wine glass in hand — collapsed into the sofa. In unison, each woman slipped off her shoes and propped her feet on the simple, hand-hewn chestnut coffin that served as Evie's unique coffee table.

"It never gets old seeing that thing," Beatrice said. "It's a wonder the four of us didn't get hernias carting it in here."

They both laughed, recalling the day nearly two decades earlier when they, along with Kate and Arthur Stuart, had returned victorious from an antiquing expedition in the Blue Ridge Mountains. Evie had scored the century-old but pristine coffin for a ridiculously low price, because its presence in the antique store unnerved the proprietor. The coffee table was one of the few items that saved Evie's living room from being yet another sterile, minimalist design statement.

Every part of the McLean townhouse contained at least one Rudneresque touch, like the wrought-iron menorah that dominated the cherry buffet in the dining room or the delicate hamesh hand that adorned an otherwise bare foyer wall. Both of those items were Sephardic artifacts inherited from an archeologist cousin who had brought them back from Spain, probably illegally. Evie salved her conscience by bequeathing them in her will to a Granada museum, the Palace of the Forgotten. For Beatrice, the highly personal and/or offbeat accent pieces were precisely what made the otherwise chic townhouse feel welcoming, albeit in an often quirky way. The aroma wafting from the kitchen didn't hurt, either.

Evie apologized that the source of the current aroma was "only" a pork stew with marinara sauce, something she had whipped up the previous weekend and frozen. She promised to "do better" tomorrow, a Saturday.

"Too bad you couldn't schlep Clara along on this trip, but I guess school got in the way?"

"She's playing hooky today, because it's her birthday. No, don't worry. We celebrated last night. Today she's the guest of honor at Ben and Amanda's."

"Actually, it's just as well you're solo," Evie said. "We have some serious dishing to do. I don't have many weekends left as a swinging single. God, remember that awful term? I hope it's gone out of vogue by now."

"You're asking the wrong person," Beatrice laughed. "So, is your swinging-single self bracing for some kind of adjustment period, as two longtime singletons merge their lifestyles? And their stuff? Is this coffee table, for example, heading north to Massachusetts?"

"Bart said he'll tolerate a coffin in his living room, as long as I bury him in it if he kicks off before me. I told him, 'Sure, why not?' 'I'll just get a replacement antique table wherever I shop for a replacement antique husband.' He reminded me that antique stores are not exactly prime hunting grounds for future spouses. Your brother's sense of humor is about as warped as mine. But not quite as dark as yours."

"Says the woman resting her heels on a casket."

Ignoring the dig, Evie continued, "My main worry about merging lifestyles concerned the bedroom. And I am pleased to report…"

"LA, LA, LA, LA, LA!" Beatrice interrupted, shouting the off-tune notes and covering her ears. "TMI!"

"Oh, for Christ's sake! I wasn't going to offer up graphic details. I was merely referring to the prospect of sleeping—as in the dreaming, snoring kind of sleeping—with anyone. Even a cat. I've come to like the solitude and was dreading its loss and the attendant decline in sleep quality. But Bart has this sweet, snuggly mojo going that makes sharing a bed with him actually appealing. And maybe, once every six months or so, we can remember some other appealing things to do between the sheets." Evie winked as her guest squirmed.

"I'm glad for both of you, but sure as hell hope you're done with the bedroom revelations. It was one thing when you were dating that seriously studly lawyer a decade ago. For months, I lived vicariously off the recitation of your exploits. But now that your intended is my brother, even 'snuggly' sounds racy to my tender ears."

"I'm quite finished. But now it's your turn. The studly Mr. Fordyce is no brother of mine. So spill, awreddy! Have you finally taken pity on his ailing self and forgiven him for whatever it was he did? You never did tell me what the fight was all about. Since it happened shortly after New Year's Eve—when I assume you finally got laid—I gotta wonder if the first event caused the second. Does he keep a bullwhip under his pillow or something? You know I have a lively imagination. Ya gotta give me something, or I'll keep asking more and more embarrassing questions."

"Oh, all right," Beatrice sighed. "Yes, we had sex. And he was pretty damn great. And a few weeks later, when we had that fight he was pretty damn nasty. And no, it had nothing to do with sex. Tanner accused me of botching my guardianship of Clara, of not standing up for her in the whole Rodney Madsen mess. Essentially, he implied I was a shiftless, drunken coward."

"He actually used those words?" Evie gasped.

"No, but that was the intent. He accused me of burying myself in solitude and anesthetizing myself to the kid's pain. He may truly believe Clara would be better served by openly denouncing Madsen as a child molester. Maybe that's understandable, given Tanner's background of abuse. But he wasn't arguing his case so much as exploiting my vulnerabilities, to find the most sensitive spot to sink the knife in."

"Shit! What a prick! Well, now I'm doubly glad you kicked him to the curb, at least temporarily. I'll bet no one's shown Mr. Moneybags the door since he earned his first million. And then he gets slammed by cerebral malaria. Talk about karma!"

"I thought you didn't believe in karma?" Beatrice teased.

"I don't, unless the comeuppance is richly deserved—by anyone except Yours Truly, of course." Evie paused, sipped wine, and added thoughtfully, "But I wonder whether his intent was to hurt you or whether he launched a preemptive strike merely to safeguard his own sensitive spots. Clara's troubles with Rodney must have stirred some memories of his charming Mommie Dearest. Maybe he feels cowardly that he never made her pay."

"I suppose that's possible. In fact, in mid-argument, he mentioned how his mother had gotten away with her sins."

"There you go."

"But does that earn him a get-out-of-jail-free card? Sure, we all bring baggage to every new relationship. But that doesn't make it okay to go nuclear anytime the scar tissue starts twitching."

"Hmmm." Evie tapped a manicured fingernail against an incisor. "Verbal abuse isn't exactly Armageddon, Beatrice. The fact that you see it as such suggests your own scars are doing a little twitching."

"Maybe so. But I didn't react by throwing more hurtful words at him. I just told him to leave. And thereby ended the round before it got any nastier. I didn't tell him I never wanted to see him again. No threats. No ultimatums. I didn't call him any names. Hell, I didn't even yell. Jesus, I'm getting pissed all over again!"

"Does that mean you got *un*-pissed at some point? Did your Catholic guilt kick in because Tanner went belly up in Africa? It isn't like you hired the tsetse fly to bite him on the ass."

Beatrice recapped recent developments, including the gift of the painting, the email apology, and the subsequent exchanges of friendly messages.

"All by email?" Evie interrupted. "Why no phone calls?"

"I suspect we're both scared of stepping on land mines. With email you can edit out possible trigger words."

"It's a wonder you two ever got together in the first place! But isn't it about time you tested the limits? Otherwise, you're never gonna get laid again, girl. I can see both of you, in your nineties, sitting on your separate Seneca County porches, eight miles apart, texting each other until the arthritis gets too bad to punch the little keys."

"Well, Tanner did suggest we get together when I'm up here. He's flying into Dulles tomorrow. He had a minor relapse of malarial symptoms, which sent him back to that German hospital. That's why he's been in Europe all this time. Anyway, during the second hospitalization, he learned about some American research to develop a vaccine for malaria. He decided to help out. So he'll be checking into NIH where some experts will study him a bit," Beatrice said, referring to the National Institutes of Health, headquartered in the D.C. suburb of Bethesda.

"Finally! We come to the crux of the matter," Evie said with exasperation. "You absolutely have to see him before he plays guinea pig. When does he check into NIH?"

"They want him there the day after tomorrow to get him all prepped for whatever is scheduled bright and early Monday morning."

"Then meet him at the airport tomorrow, dummy! Our dress appointment isn't written in stone. You'll be here a few days. We can work around things. Do you have any idea what time he's coming in?"

"Yeah, he told me ten o'clock."

"Then get your ass in gear and drive to Dulles tomorrow morning! We've got a three-thirty appointment right here in McLean. If you can make it after you see Tanner, fine. If not, we'll reschedule."

"But the whole reason for me being up here is to help you out with wedding plans."

"And you *will* help—on Sunday, Monday, and Tuesday. Meanwhile, I'll go batshit with curiosity if I don't find out what's going on with you and Fordyce. And, unlike you, I will expect graphic details." Evie leered gleefully.

FORTY-NINE

Enlightenment

BEATRICE PROBABLY ATTRACTED SCRUTINY from undercover air marshals mingling with the crowd outside the arrival gates at Dulles International Airport. She paced back and forth. When standing, she would jiggle one leg or drum her fingers against one thigh. She wasn't gearing up to detonate C-4 packets in her purse. The prospect of seeing Tanner had triggered the jitters.

Beatrice was suddenly, painfully aware of the largely superficial nature of her recent email exchanges with him. What would they talk about now, in a crowded airport? Wouldn't their meeting feel strained? And where in heaven's name would they go from here?

Taking several deep breaths, she reminded herself that she hadn't done such a bad job of living her life without Tanner all these years. Perhaps this meeting would clarify some of the confusion regarding their relationship. As sad as it might be to learn they were hopelessly mismatched, knowing was always better than not knowing. She had not jettisoned her reliably logical brain, after all, just because she was involved with Tanner Fordyce.

Then she saw him, and the logical part of her brain dissolved into pablum. She was slammed by an undertow of emotion so forceful she leaned into her cane to maintain her physical balance. Despite walking perfectly well without the blackthorn stick for two weeks, she had brought it along as a precaution lest her knee protest after the road trip to Northern Virginia. She was now glad for that precaution. She welcomed whatever added, spiritual support she might absorb through the cane's dark, scarred wood from the Connaught ancestors whose hands had gripped it.

Because of his height, Tanner was easy to spot in a crowd, while she blended invisibly into the hoi polloi. As a result, she was able to observe him anonymously for a full minute, as he moved slowly through the sea of people.

She thought perhaps she was looking at Will Berrigan, Tanner's alter ego. He was not wearing the ubiquitous blazer and slacks of the business traveler but boots, jeans, black T-shirt, and army jacket, as if he'd just punched off the clock from Conley Terminal on the South Boston docks. The jacket concealed the weight loss otherwise evident in his face. Despite a new trim beard, hollows lurked beneath his cheekbones. But there was nothing weak about the pale blue eyes scanning the throng.

Seeing those intelligent, calculating eyes, Beatrice felt a fierce sense of ownership that overrode all the other emotions vying for her attention.

Mine. That man is mine.

Finally, he spotted her. She stretched her arm as high as she could and smiled broadly. The best adjective to describe his expression was "determined," as he elbowed his way forward. When he reached her, he dropped his bags with a thud and wrapped her in a wordless embrace so tight she was unable to take a deep breath. Maintaining the hug, he raised her a few inches off the floor. When he let her down, he buried his face in the curve of her neck. Only gradually did he ease his lock on her. After a few seconds, he stepped back, holding both her hands, and looked her up and down. A crooked grin spread across his lips.

"I figured the odds were you wouldn't show," Tanner said at last. "But here you are, looking even better than I remembered. God is good, His mercy is everlasting…"

"His truth endureth to all generations," Beatrice interrupted, finishing the line from Psalm 100. She reached up and touched Tanner's beard with the fingertips of one hand. "I like it," she said.

He snatched her hand, flipped it over, and kissed the palm quickly. "Let's get out of here before we get crushed." He hoisted one bag to each shoulder. When Beatrice grabbed for the remaining, rolling carryon, he swatted her hand away. "Take me to your truck. I've had quite enough of airports."

As they walked to the short-term parking lot, Tanner suddenly focused on the cane. "Is your knee acting up again? You seem to be walking spritely enough."

Beatrice told him how she had scheduled the partial knee replacement after Rodney's violent visit exacerbated her patellar woes and sharply reduced the number of limp-free days. Tanner interrupted her recap.

"Bloody hell! Another repercussion from that pervert! And if I hadn't behaved so boorishly back in January, you actually might have told me, and I might have been able to help out." He shook his head ruefully.

"Water under the bridge," she said. "And most days I no longer need the cane."

"From its calluses, I assume that's a family relic? Churning out black-thorn sticks must have been one of Ireland's few lucrative industries in the nineteenth century. Is there a family of Boston bog-trotters that doesn't have a blackthorn among the attic clutter? Yours looks much like the one my old man was wielding after his hip surgery last year."

Within a few feet of her truck, Beatrice stopped short in surprise. "I thought your folks were long dead."

"Only Rita, thanks be to God," Tanner replied, as he positioned a stabilizer bar to secure his luggage in the truck bed. "She had a massive heart attack twenty-five years ago. With her gone, I was eventually able to have some kind of relationship with my father. A few years ago, I stashed him in an assisted living facility on the Cape. I visit infrequently. He's harmless enough. When I'm up there, we pass the time avoiding the elephant in the room. Usually playing chess. One of the few useful things he taught me. He still plays a good game."

As they clicked their seatbelts, Beatrice silently reflected on some of the painful parallels in her and Tanner's early years. He prodded, "Penny for your thoughts?"

"Just wondering if there's any such thing as a healthy family. But yes, the cane is a relic. The last one to use it was my father when he was weak from congestive heart failure."

"So, in addition to crackpot mothers, we share faulty heart genes?'

"We put the fun in dysfunctional," Beatrice chuckled, starting the engine. "Care to tell me where we're going?"

"We're going to have the best deli food south of the fortieth parallel. Just get on eastbound 66. But first…" He pulled a smartphone from a pocket and entered a number. "And a hearty good morning to you, as well, Raj," Tanner said, with touch screen to one ear. "Yes, it's Fordyce. The prodigal has returned. Better, thank you. But my favorite lunch spot can speed my recovery. Yes, that's exactly why I'm calling. Let's go with the Number Three, the Number Four, the Number Ten. Good man. I'll be there in an hour to settle up."

After returning the phone to his pocket, Tanner slid his seat back as far as it would go and sighed. "It's good to be back in the U.S. of A., land of the open road, social mobility, and second chances." As he uttered the last two words, he turned and smiled at Beatrice.

*   *   *

Tanner's directions led them into a parking garage at the Watergate complex. A few minutes later, driver and passenger stood in a lobby where Tanner waved at a slender young man behind the front desk. From the latter's sing-song greeting, Beatrice deduced he was Raj. Her hunch was confirmed when he ducked behind the desk and surfaced with a white paper bag. Lunch. Tanner shook Raj's hand and, in the process, passed him some bills. Beatrice took custody of the bag.

During the wait for the elevator, she looked around at the posh décor. "Deli joints have sure gotten more upscale since the last time I ate in one. I gather this is your home away from home? I didn't realize your D.C. condo was in the infamous Watergate."

"Yup. It has its charms. And it projects an appropriate image for business meetings."

"For other meetings, too, I expect," Beatrice muttered as they entered the elevator.

"Relax. I'm not bringing you up here to view my etchings. Nor do I expect one pastrami on rye to send you into a swoon."

"I dunno. Given the aromas coming from this bag, you shouldn't underestimate the seductive powers of deli fare."

"Seriously?" Tanner teased as they arrived at his floor.

"No," Beatrice laughed.

"It was ever thus," Tanner said, opening the door to his condo. "Of course, even if you were willing, I'm hardly up to the challenge in my current state. If any swooning takes place, it's likely to be me, passing out from post-malarial jet lag."

"Tough flight in first class?" Beatrice mocked, as he led her to the kitchen.

"First class, schmirst class, you're still trapped in a flying tin can."

He pulled two beers from the refrigerator then opened the door to a balcony overlooking the Potomac River. They settled at a wrought-iron trestle table, with both chairs facing the water. Spreading out the bag's contents, Tanner pointed at each wrapped sandwich and said, "You have your choice of a Reuben, pastrami on rye, or a concoction of roast beef, beef tongue, Bermuda onion, and chopped liver on pumpernickel."

"Ooh! That last one!" Beatrice grabbed for it.

Tanner clinked his bottle of Foster's against hers and took a swig, while Beatrice began devouring her sandwich.

"Oh, wow!" she exclaimed. "You were wrong. This is up to northern standards. I haven't had chopped liver in ages. Not since Meyers Deli in Fields Corner."

"I remember it well. Wicked good food."

She snorted appreciatively at his reversion to Boston-speak. He grinned at the gusto with which she attacked her sandwich. She was so focused on her food that she was temporarily unaware of his gaze. When she finally met his eyes, she blushed, blotted her mouth with a paper napkin, and asked, "What? Am I dribbling chopped liver?"

"No. I was just thinking how natural all this feels. How I've missed being around you. How depressing it was to think I might have lost you." He took another swig of beer.

Beatrice said softly, "Nice to know I had company. I went into a major funk after our fight. It wouldn't have been so bad if I could have just concluded I was done with you. But…"

"But here you are," Tanner interrupted. "What that means, however, is less than clear."

"For me, too," Beatrice said, shaking off a shiver. "Obviously, I want you in my life. But how? We have such different lifestyles. I'm hardly suited to your jet-setting ways."

"Who said you had to traipse around the world after me? And why do I get the feeling we're talking about something more than plane travel?"

"Because we are," Beatrice groaned.

"Is this about Ilse Kohut again? I thought I'd made it clear she's exclusively a business contact." Tanner looked puzzled.

Beatrice tilted her head back in exasperation. "It's not about Ilse. It's about boinking all those other women. Christ, Tanner, I ghosted your autobiography! I know more than I care to about your romantic history, even during your marriage to Patty. I just couldn't handle that."

Tanner winced then asked incredulously, "Boinking?" He erupted in laughter.

"I was being polite," Beatrice said tightly. "But that particular verb aptly conveys the casual aspect I find abhorrent. Sex isn't casual for me. It's about trust and intimacy and…"

Tanner stopped her with a light touch to her forearm. "You're not telling me anything I didn't already know. But what you don't seem to know is that people change — even if I still find the 'boinking' verb as hilarious as I would have in my twenties."

"You're saying you've changed?" Beatrice asked, somewhat doubtfully.

"Well, I'd like to think I've grown up some over the years. That there's something more to maturity than reduced hormone levels." Tanner shifted his gaze toward the river. "For me, some realizations kicked in after Tim died. I ached for the light my incredibly golden son gave off. I wanted to nurture some of Tim's light inside myself. And you can't do that around trivial people, in trivial relationships. So, for the last few years — Jesus, it's six already — I've spent quite a lot of time alone, fanning a dim little flame. It gets brighter when I'm around you."

"Wow," she whispered.

"So it stands to reason I'd want to be around you permanently."

"I don't know what that means."

Tanner groaned. "Of course you do. You're just too scared to go there. Marriage, Hillwilla. Marriage is on my mind."

Beatrice choked, literally. She grabbed for the Foster's and took a deep swallow.

"Not quite the reaction I was going for," he laughed.

"Tanner!" Beatrice exclaimed. "You didn't think the M-word would catch me by surprise? Only a few days ago, I thought I'd never see you again." She flipped a palm upward in frustration.

"But here we are together." He drummed his fingers on the table as he collected his thoughts. "Beatrice, whatever success I've achieved in my life has been based on decisiveness. I've never had difficulty identifying what

I want. And going after it. Why should I hesitate now, especially about something this important?"

"Boldness defines you. But it also puts you leagues ahead of me." Hugging her chest, she hunched, deep in thought, over the table.

"Okay, I get that this requires a leap of faith. And faith isn't a quality you have in abundance."

Tanner wearily moved his uneaten sandwich aside, leaned back in his chair, stretched his legs beneath the table, and frowned at the river flowing by. Beatrice grabbed his hand and squeezed it. Squeezing back, hard enough to make her wince, he turned toward her and said solemnly, "Just don't take too long to catch up.".

FIFTY

Alien Travels

NOW FIFTEEN YEARS AND ONE MONTH OLD, Clara was fixated on getting her learner's permit. While waiting for her father to produce the written consent required by the DMV, the permitless teen scrutinized Beatrice's every move when they were on the road together.

They had been driving for nine hours, heading northeast for Evie's wedding in Massachusetts. Beatrice would have preferred breaking up the long trek with a motel stopover, but Clara was loath to miss more than two days of school, because she faced a math exam the following Monday. She would be returning home ahead of Beatrice by train. Evie's secretary, Shirley, abhorred air travel and had round-trip reservations on Amtrak's Boston-Washington route. She volunteered to shepherd Clara through Washington's Union Station and see her off on the westbound train to White Sulphur Springs. From there, the girl would be in Ben's custody until Beatrice returned.

The arrangement would leave Beatrice free to housesit for her brother and his new bride while they honeymooned. She would also take care of Bart's aged dog, Addie, who would be spared a week in a kennel—unlike poor Ralph.

Despite the endurance trials of the seven-hundred-fifty-mile trek, Beatrice savored the freedom of the open road—especially after two winters of impaired mobility. Behind the wheel of her Chevy, she saw life reduced to manageable priorities, mainly keeping her truck between the parallel lines. With that simple effort, mileposts were passed and goals achieved. And her mind was free to wander without guilt.

But not without interruptions from Clara. The girl's enthusiasm for the journey was so infectious that Beatrice didn't begrudge the constant questions. "Why are you pressing down on the clutch pedal?" (Downshifting for the toll plaza.) "How come I don't see any New York skyscrapers if we're crossing the Hudson River?" (Tappan Zee Bridge is well north of the city.) "What happens when a toll collector needs to pee, and there are fifty cars lined up at his gate? (Good question.)

The long ride also offered insights into Buckhalter family dynamics. Although Clara had already described the tensions evident at the April birthday/engagement party, she now shared some additional anecdotes. When Vaughn inquired about the wedding date, for example, Clay said they'd need to take things slowly, for the sake of his daughter. Charyce snapped that Britt should "wake up and drink the coffee." Clay looked sad the rest of the evening.

"And Momma still doesn't have an engagement ring. Scheduling problems, she says, since Clay's been real busy at work."

"That's odd," said Beatrice noncommittally, while gloating inwardly.

The road trip was also conducive to philosophical musings, with Clara inquiring about the ups and downs of social mobility. This stemmed from a growing interest in attending college out of state. She was worried about feeling like an outcast, a hick from West Virginia.

Shortly after entering Connecticut, she asked suddenly, "Did you feel homesick after you left Massachusetts?"

"Sure I did. Every time I dropped an R, I'd see the most perplexed look on the faces of the Virginians around me. They genuinely didn't understand what I was saying. So eventually, I stopped dropping them."

"But you still talk a little funny."

"And now I sound weird to people up north, too." Beatrice laughingly recalled the confusion of a Boston gas station attendant a decade earlier, when she asked him to check one of her tires. Realizing after the fact that she had pronounced the word in Southern-speak, as "tarrr," she reverted to Beantown patois, adding a syllable and dropping the R: "tie-yuh."

"That must feel creepy to be treated like an alien in your home state," Clara mused.

"Nah," Beatrice said. "Massachusetts hasn't felt like home for a long time. Besides, there are worse things than being a stranger around other people. Like being a stranger to yourself."

"Huh?"

"Sometimes people don't really choose what they do in life. For a lot of folks, it's absolutely the right thing to stay in their hometown or follow in their parents' footsteps by becoming a doctor, a farmer, whatever. But there are other people who know in their gut they're not suited for the job their father had — or for the career their parents have picked out for them. Sometimes a country kid yearns for the hustle of a big city. Sometimes a city kid wants to get her hands dirty making plants grow. It's always scary breaking out of the mold. Lonely, too. But the rewards are worth it."

Clara looked skeptical. "Do you feel at home anywhere? Do you feel like you belong in West Virginia?"

"Not sure. I do know my life in West Virginia is a lot more comfortable than it was just a few years ago. But what about you? Do you feel at home at the farm?"

After a pause, Clara replied, "Not completely. But I think I belong there more than I do at Daddy's cabin. Even at Ben's, I feel kinda out of place. And then there's school. I'm the Seneca County hillbilly, the oddball, even though I'm doing well. Of course, I'd be miserable at Seneca County High School."

"Why?"

"I'd be bored by the classwork. And I'd probably stick out there, too. I ran into Joanie Boggs at the post office the other day when you had me buy stamps. We went to middle school together. She claimed your snobbiness was rubbing off on me. I used the word 'ludicrous' to describe one stupid game we both hated in our old gym class. So because she's too dumb to know what the word means, I'm a snob. Gimme a break!" Clara folded her arms over her chest.

"Clara. The hillbilly with airs."

The teenager laughed. "You should talk! Isn't that what Tanner means when he calls you 'Hillwilla'?"

Beatrice grimaced. "That annoying name! But yeah, I guess a 'Hillwilla' is too countrified for the stylish set and too uppity for Seneca County."

"So we don't fit in anywhere?"

Receiving only a shrug in response, Clara continued, "After talking to Joanie Boggs, I'm not all that sure I *want* to fit in with Seneca girls anymore. Not if they think acting dumb is cool."

Beatrice nodded sympathetically. "When I was your age, I watched a sad transformation in a girlfriend when we hit high school. Sherry was smart, a good student. But her mother was always bugging her about not having a boyfriend. At some point, Sherry decided boys didn't like intelligent girls. So she dumbed down the way she spoke, and she blew off her schoolwork. Went from straight As to Cs."

"What happened to her?"

"She graduated from high school, just barely, and got married that July. Her mother was so proud of her — and of the grandchild that arrived six months later. Last I heard, Sherry was divorced and playing with grandchildren of her own. It seems like she walked down a path someone else had chosen for her. But, hey, she probably fits into her surroundings a lot more than I do. For all I know, she feels more contented."

"You just gave me an idea for the English paper due next week on *Hamlet*. Maybe I'll write about what Polonius says to his son: 'To thine own self be true.'"

"Maybe I'll get us matching T-shirts with those words on them."

"Joanie Boggs would be appalled," Clara giggled.

"More likely, she'd just be confused," Beatrice commented archly.

Clara slapped her thigh appreciatively. "Sounds exactly like something a snobby Hillwilla would say. Maybe our matching T-shirts should read 'Hillwilla.'"

"I've created a monster," Beatrice chuckled.

*   *   *

Somewhere in eastern Connecticut, Clara inquired about Beatrice's hometown. "I saw where you went to college when we visited Bart last year. But I never saw where you grew up. Is that anywhere close to where Bart lives now?"

"Mile-wise, not all that far. But slogging through traffic would make it hard to fit in while we're busy with wedding stuff. If you're really interested, we can take a detour now."

Clara wholeheartedly endorsed the idea. She was enthusiastic about the new entry for her travel log. Before their departure, she had charted their route and listed all the highpoints to check off: state lines, bridges, rivers, historic landmarks, toll booths, city limits. Now she added "Beatrice's house."

A few hours later, they were on the Southeast Expressway, where traveling at sixty miles per hour (five miles above the posted limit) meant being passed by Bostonians left, right, and even from the breakdown lane. Both passenger and driver were relieved to exit the expressway before entering the Massachusetts capital. Clara happily checked off two items on her list, as they crossed into Boston and bridged the Neponset River. Although disappointed by that lackluster waterway, the girl was enchanted by the hum the truck's tires made on the ancient span. Within a few minutes, the Chevy turned onto a street lined with three-deckers. After some confusion, Beatrice figured out which of the buildings had once housed the Desmonds.

Finding a parking spot only one door down, she stopped curbside and turned off the engine. Clara made a quick check to verify that the doors were locked. Beatrice assured her, "This neighborhood looks okay to me. In fact, there's some gentrification going on, even if our old three-decker looks down at the pasterns."

"Yeah, but that guy walking down the sidewalk creeps me out."

Beatrice saw a skinny teenager wearing low riders, an oversized T-shirt, a shaved head, and tattoos on one arm. "The kid looks harmless enough."

"If you say so. Is that dark brown house with the flat roof yours? It's weirdly narrow, but it's big. I thought you said you were poor."

"Three families lived there. The Hanrahans, who owned the house, lived on the second floor. The Sweeneys lived in the basement. We rented the top floor. Had a great view of the Southeast Expressway from the porch."

"What's that stink?"

Beatrice looked confused then sniffed deeply. "Oh, the marshes. Must be low tide. I always kinda liked that salty, sulfurous smell. It was natural, at least."

"Yuck." Clara looked around at the neighborhood: the potholed pavement; the faded paint on the older, wood-shingled sidings; the polyresin shrines to the Virgin Mary; the paucity of trees; the chain-link fences cordoning off tiny patches of lawn with tinier flower beds. She eyed the ubiquitous GoSox! bumper stickers, as well as the odd decal proudly declaring the driver a Masshole.

She scribbled some observations into her notebook. When she finished, she asked if Dorchester was anywhere near Tanner Fordyce's childhood home.

"He's from Revere, maybe thirty minutes north. Unlike Dorchester, Revere's not part of Boston. It's a separate, smaller city. But he grew up in a three-decker, too. So I imagine his neighborhood didn't look much different from mine."

"I wonder how many kids who grow up in places like this end up traveling all over the world like Tanner."

Beatrice, staring at her childhood residence, merely shrugged.

"Hey, I just realized—wasn't Tanner supposed to be home by now?" Clara asked suddenly.

"He returned to the States a month ago. But he had some medical tests to take in Washington. Then he went off on a book tour—speaking engagements to promote his autobiography. He'll probably be back in West Virginia by the time we return."

Losing interest in Tanner, Clara focused anew on her trip log. "How much longer to Bart's?"

"Less than an hour, I guess," Beatrice answered, before turning back to the brown three-decker. "Hard to believe this was ever home," she murmured.

"Is it weird to be back?"

"Yeah, but not in a bad way. I'm neither nostalgic nor repelled. It just feels alien. Like part of someone else's life."

"I wonder if Seneca County will feel alien to me one day? That would be scary."

"I guess it depends on the depth of your connection—and on what road you take when you grow up."

"Speaking of roads, can we get on the one that takes us to Bart and outta here?" Clara shivered.

Laughing, Beatrice cranked the engine. "Hold on! As the locals say, I gotta bang a uey." Burning rubber with Beantown bravado, she wheeled the truck around and headed back to the organized chaos that was the Southeast Expressway.

FIFTY-ONE

Pairings

CHAOS REIGNED IN BART DESMOND'S LARGE HOUSE on the first Saturday in May, his wedding day. Although bride, groom, and matron of honor were highly organized individuals who had done their homework, some of the people they hired turned out to be Type Bs. The caterer unilaterally made allergy-inducing, last-minute menu changes. The florist included much-hated gladioli in key arrangements, despite express instructions to the contrary. The furniture rental company didn't deliver enough chairs. The bartender called in sick.

The bustling noises filling the house as its occupants scrambled for alternative solutions peaked as the bride neared meltdown. A litany of curses suddenly reverberated from the kitchen. Only some were coherent. Beatrice, supervising the placement of a neighbor's folding chairs, dashed toward the noise. "What now?" she asked breathlessly.

Hunched over a cup of coffee and her Android cellphone, Evie looked up miserably. "It's official. The owner of the catering company is a certified moron! Jesus, why didn't we just trot down to the Dover Town House and do the deed there?"

Before Beatrice could offer any soothing words, the Android and the doorbell rang simultaneously. While Evie snapped, "Rudner," into the phone, Beatrice ran to the front hall.

Returning to the kitchen, she announced, "The cavalry has arrived. It's dumping its bags in my room."

Moments later, Shirley McClintock—iPad in one hand, notebook in the other, Bluetooth phone attachment curled around one ear—sat down beside Evie who immediately briefed her on all the snafus. At the conclusion, Shirley pronounced confidently, "Honey, I can sweet-talk most of those problems away. As for the others, I'll just knock a few heads together. Now isn't it time you beautified yourself, Boss? You go take a nice soak in the tub. Scoot, now." She flicked her fingers in a reverse wave at Evie.

*   *   *

Ninety minutes later, Beatrice entered the master suite, which Bart had ceded to his bride-to-be for the day. She knocked on the bathroom door. "Have you drowned?"

Evie opened the door. She was wearing a bathrobe and wielding a mascara wand. "Just putting my face on. Any new disasters? Any tornadoes headed this way?"

"A tornado wouldn't dare get within one mile of Shirley. Talk about a force of nature! That woman figured out some non-allergenic menu substitutions—from available ingredients, yet! She recruited a grad student down the block to play bartender. She charmed another neighbor into offering up his driveway for overflow parking. Then she fixed Bart a bloody mary to keep him from stressing out. So all we have to do now is figure out how to wind ourselves into our saris."

*   *   *

After another ninety minutes, a lone guitarist played Bach's "Air on a G String," and the wedding guests took their seats inside the great room. Bart looked dapper in a cream-colored, vested suit, as he waited by the French doors opening onto his glorious iris beds. Standing beside him was his daughter Martha, acting as best man and dressed in a cream-colored silk pantsuit with black cummerbund. On his other side stood Darleen in a navy dress.

As the guitarist switched to Mozart's "March of the Priests," all eyes turned to Addie the Labrador retriever, wearing a hot-pink neck ribbon from which hung the box holding the wedding rings. With long-distance coaxing from the groom, the dog walked down the red runner bisecting the great room. Wagging her tail, she paused to sniff a guest or two and give them the opportunity to admire her crimson bindi, painted on her black forehead with nail polish. Next to sashay down the makeshift aisle was Shirley, wearing a rose sari, pink bindi, and red stilettos. She was followed by Beatrice in a lilac sari, lilac bindi, and purple pumps. Then Evie appeared—defiantly unescorted. She was a vision in scarlet: bindi, sari, high heels, bouquet.

Bride and groom kept to traditional vows, thanks to Bart's horror of trendy personal revelations at the altar. As a result, just ten minutes passed before Darleen declared the couple married. Bart and Evie kissed and then high-fived each other. Addie woofed her approval.

The newlyweds posed for photographs in the iris garden, and their guests gradually drifted outside into the bright, airy wedding tent. There the guitarist regrouped with three other musicians to sweeten the atmosphere with the mellow notes of contemporary jazz. While servers circulated with hors d'oeuvres, the grad student showed off his mixology skills at a pace that should have triggered carpal tunnel syndrome and tennis elbow.

Beatrice soon exhausted her cocktail party repertoire. Eventually reprieve came with the sit-down luncheon, where she could count on Clara to be a convivial partner in conversation. She had arranged to have the girl join the members of the wedding party at the head table. With the teenager on her left, Beatrice could minimize the time spent conversing with Martha on her right. Relations between the two had been prickly ever since Beatrice failed to surrender her share of a modest family inheritance to her only niece.

But she couldn't ignore Martha entirely, especially when she noticed her sniffling quietly into a Kleenex. "You okay?" Beatrice asked.

"Oh, it's just that I feel like I'm losing Daddy," the younger woman whimpered.

"It's not like Bart's disappearing. He and Evie are staying right here in Dover. For most of the year, he'll still be only a few miles away. Sure, they're thinking about getting a winter home down south someplace, because Evie hates cold weather. But look at it this way. You'll have a nice place to visit in the gloom of January."

A sharp inhale ended Martha's sniffles. "A second home?" she asked. "I guess my new stepmother is bringing more assets to the marriage than I figured. Do you know whether she's already lined up buyers for her business and her house in Virginia?"

"Dunno," Beatrice mumbled into her salad plate.

Martha's financial queries persisted. After several unproductive responses from her aunt, she shifted her elicitation effort to Shirley. The latter responded with cheerful evasions, while Beatrice and Clara resumed their chatter, laughing about the mini-disasters earlier in the day.

The guests advanced to more serious partying as the dance floor/lawn opened for business. Beatrice stifled a groan, even though waltzing and fox-trotting figured in her skill set. Decades earlier, she and Evie had enrolled in a ballroom-dancing course. Both single and working in the Washington area at the time, they saw the lessons as a way of meeting eligible men. Unfortunately, that didn't happen. But at least the two girlfriends became competent dancers. That competence did nothing to overcome Beatrice's current queasiness, however, since she was one of the few attendees to lack a plus-one.

The effervescent Shirley, another single female, was quickly approached by someone twenty years her junior. Clara was next to acquire a dance partner—one of Bart's avuncular friends whose wife was in a wheelchair. Eventually, the only people on the sidelines were Beatrice, the wheelchair-bound spouse, and several octogenarians.

A few jazz selections later, Bart's college roommate took pity on Beatrice. She didn't spend much time with her gallant partner, however, because Evie decided to liven things up. Pirouetting Bollywood-style, she corralled all of the wedding's female principals for an impromptu hora. Beatrice spun off briefly to bring Clara into the circle. Then all six split into alternating pairs to whirl around like giddy children, laughing and panting (and in three cases trying to keep from tripping over their saris) while the rest of the guests applauded.

The spectacle was silly and exuberant. It overcame self-consciousness—and family tensions. Beatrice enjoyed even her twirl with Martha, and the two Rudner sisters appeared in high spirits as they shared a dance. Eventually, the six wheezed, laughing, onto the sidelines.

Beatrice had little time to catch her breath, however, because Bart soon grabbed her hands and danced her into the center of the tent. "Glad to see you enjoying yourself, BB," he said leaning in to peck her on the cheek. "How's the knee holding up?"

"The knee's just fine. And right back at you. It's goddamn wonderful to see you so happy. You and Evie make a great team. Can I take credit as matchmaker?"

"As I recall, you were just looking for a place to crash when you and your Washington gal pal stopped here en route to some vacation in Maine.

If matchmaking was on your mind, you sure let a lot of years go by after making the initial introduction."

"Hey, is it my fault you guys were so slow to figure out what was best for you?"

Beatrice paired up with two more dance partners before begging off, pleading a sore knee. In reality, her knee was fine. She was merely retreating from trivial conversation with men she barely knew. Inevitably, her thoughts turned to Tanner. Evie had invited him, but at last report, his book tour would keep him far from New England on the appointed day.

Beatrice knew she had little time for self-pity. As the festivities wound down, a new set of responsibilities would begin. First, she had to make sure Clara was properly packed in time to catch a taxi with Shirley to the Dedham train station. Sometime after that, Beatrice would see off the bride and groom, who were driving to an inn on the coast of Maine. Then she'd distribute the tips Bart had left for the catering help and musicians, while she supervised the final cleanup and generally made sure her brother's house was in order. That obligation would not end until Monday, when the wedding tent was dismantled and hauled away, and the rented furniture went back to its point of origin.

By the time the other members of the wedding party left, the sun was growing fat in the western sky, and a decidedly un-spring-like chill was setting in. After saying goodbye to the last, listless guests, Beatrice dashed upstairs and changed into a sweater and jeans, practical attire for after-party cleanup.

It was well into evening before the hired help cleared out. Exhausted, Beatrice slumped on a folding chair in the great room, now illuminated only by the light fixture on the deck. Absorbing the melancholy emptiness of the big house, she had nothing to distract her from her loneliness—apart from Addie lying nearby on the floor. One month had passed since her reunion with Tanner. For all the subsequent emails and phone calls, Beatrice ached to see him, smell him, touch him, make sure he was real.

She marveled anew at the apparent ease with which her old friend had shed decades of defiantly happy singleton status. What's more, the driven, edgy, unconventional Evie had chosen a highly unlikely mate in the well-grounded Bart.

If two such different people could be happy together, is it possible for me and Tanner as well?

Beatrice knew it would take courage to merge her life with Tanner's. Right now she certainly didn't feel very courageous, only tired and sad. "Just like you, old girl, right?" she asked Addie, who had waddled closer. Stroking the lab's black head, Beatrice added, "And both of us are missing our men."

FIFTY-TWO

Blue Hills, Blue Rocks

BEATRICE HAD FINISHED FOUR DAILY CROSSWORD PUZZLES from Bart's stack of Boston Globes. They helped distract her from the nerve-jangling booms and ripping noises in the backyard, where Rocco and Jake were striking the wedding tent and stacking the banquet tables and chairs. The Dover cul-de-sac's peace had been under assault since eight o'clock. Beatrice considered cooking up her usual oatmeal but fretted about being interrupted. Rocco had already popped into the kitchen twice, once in search of the bathroom and once, thanks to a depleted cellphone battery, to use the land line to berate a no-show worker. Beatrice opted for another cup of tea.

Addie wearily lifted her graying muzzle off the kitchen dog pillow, where she was resting from her job of supervising the workmen. The sounds of food preparation overcame her fatigue. She padded toward her new human and buffeted Beatrice's knee with a substantial black tail.

"Sorry, old girl, nothing interesting. Just tea." Beatrice displayed her empty palms to confirm the sad truth then peered at the cup of water circling inside the microwave.

When the timer beeped, Addie yodeled and trotted, more speedily than usual, toward the kitchen door. Hearing footsteps behind her, Beatrice mumbled, "Great timing." In an audible tone, she called out, "I'll be with you in a sec. Just let me fix my tea."

"You got a Phillips head I could borrow, lady?" a Beantown-nuanced voice asked.

Annoyed that Rocco wouldn't have such a basic tool, Beatrice raised an index finger to acknowledge the query, as she dunked the teabag several times and covered the cup with a saucer. Then she riffled through several counter drawers and said, "I'm sure Bart has one here, if I can just remember where he keeps the household tools."

A snort registered from behind her. Dander up, Beatrice wheeled around to glare at the rude interloper. Sun was flooding the entranceway, so she couldn't immediately identify the backlit figure slouched against the door frame. It wasn't until he chuckled that Beatrice realized she wasn't looking at Rocco.

"Close your mouth or you'll swallow a fly," Tanner said.

"Get in here right now," Beatrice ordered, opening her arms wide.

The embrace lasted a full minute before Addie interrupted with a short woof, demanding attention. Laughing, Tanner said, "There always seems to be a territorial dog around when I want to take you in my arms."

"Get used to it, boyo," Beatrice replied, beckoning him to join her at the kitchen table. "Now, fill me in. Are you just breezing by, or can you stay a while?"

Tanner said he'd finished his book tour, albeit not in time to make Evie's wedding. He had extricated himself a day early from a publicity event in Philadelphia in hope of spending time with Beatrice before heading off to another appointment.

"During a pre-wedding email exchange with the bride, I learned you'd be up here all week house sitting. So I figured strike while the iron is hot," he explained. "Tomorrow afternoon, I'm meeting with a biotech entrepreneur in town. I heard about his startup when I was getting poked and prodded at NIH. Sounds like a worthy enterprise to invest in, even if it will probably take forever to make any money. Might be a fun association, though."

"It's nice to see someone enthusiastic about his work."

"If work isn't fun, what's the point?"

"Well, there's money."

"Ever the practical one," Tanner teased. "It's just that my mind is focused on enjoyment right now. I have the next thirty hours free. I have a Sybaritic suite at the Copley. Why don't you join me? We can take a grand tour of our hometown."

Pointing at the large black dog head draped over her foot, Beatrice said, "No can do. I can't abandon Addie. But maybe you could ditch the Copley reservation? And stay here?"

"Happily." He smiled broadly. "But in the meantime, I need a replacement for my urban highlights plan." He bent over to scratch Addie's head. Then he sat up abruptly and said, "I've got it! You must have some finger food left over from the wedding, right?"

"Sure, lots."

"Then pack it up. As soon as Frick and Frack are done," he said, nodding toward the backyard, "you, me, and Addie are off to a picnic. I know just the spot."

*   *   *

Nearly two hours passed before Frick, Frack, and the wedding tent disappeared. Soon after, Tanner's rental SUV headed east. As they pulled into a small parking lot, Beatrice exclaimed, "Wow, the Blue Hills! I haven't been here in decades. Lots of happy memories."

"Me, too. My Boy Scout troop of urban delinquents went on some camping expeditions here. We might as well have been in the Amazon jungle. It was so different from home."

"Hard to believe this chunk of wilderness could be right next to a major city like Boston."

"You're forgetting Central Park."

"Well, sure, that's smack dab inside a teeming city. But the Blue Hills Reservation dwarfs that. This place sprawls over thousands of acres, if memory serves."

Watching Beatrice clip the lead on Addie's collar, Tanner asked, "Can your knee manage with her in tow?" He retrieved the packed cooler and cautioned, "It's a bit of a hike to the picnic area by the overlook."

Beatrice nodded happily. She and Addie hurried ahead through the sun-dappled understory. Occasionally, the pair stopped to inspect some particular tree or shrub that caught their fancy. "S'ppose there are still timber rattlers?" she called back at one point. "My father saw one in these woods. Bears, too. Hope they're still here."

Catching up, Tanner said, "I'll bet they are. It's amazing how clean the air smells, despite being so close to Route 128."

"Too bad it's not blueberry season," Beatrice mused.

"Don't let Ranger Rick hear you. We Scouts got regular lectures about not disturbing the vegetation."

"Never stopped my father and me. On some of his better days, he took me blueberry picking here. He knew a couple of patches off the beaten path. It's a good thing no one ever spotted us. They would have had us dead to rights. We were usually weighed down with two kitchen pots each, filled with berries."

"I'll bet you cooked up some awesome pies afterward."

"Damn straight," Beatrice replied.

"And how old was the budding chef at the time?"

"I dunno. Maybe ten."

"Jesus." Tanner shook his head.

They finally reached a high clearing, dotted with picnic tables and signs warning the reader to leash all pets, refrain from littering, keep hands off the flora, leave the fauna in peace, and not even think of the word "fire." Another sign, celebrating this "scenic overlook," reported the elevation as five hundred feet.

Setting the cooler on one of the tables, Tanner took in the view. Then he turned to Beatrice, frowning.

"Huh," she said noncommittally.

"Underwhelming, isn't it?" he asked.

"Is it because our memory is faulty?"

"What basis of comparison did two city kids have back then?" Tanner mused. "All these years later, we know what a mountain view looks like. This," he swept his right hand in an arc, "is not that view."

Beatrice nodded. "And you've spent so much time in the Hindu Kush. Talk about a basis of comparison!"

"No, I wasn't thinking of the Himalayas at all. Too different. Apples and oranges. I'm thinking of the lush wildness of West Virginia. Suddenly, I miss it."

Noticing a family walking toward an adjacent table, Beatrice said, "Let's relocate. How about over there, far removed from the 'view'? It will be more private, and we'll have pretty trees to look at. We can park comfortably on the pine needles."

"Good idea."

*   *   *

Once they had devoured the last of the wedding hors d'oeuvres, Tanner leaned back against a tree and sighed.

"You look sad," Beatrice observed with concern. "Bad memories?"

"I was just recalling the very first time I camped in the Blue Hills. I damn near jumped out the bus window on the way back to Revere. God, how I dreaded going home! I'd just spent a tranquil few days in a lovely natural setting. In a way, it's easier to tolerate ugliness when you've never experienced beauty. But once you have…"

"I'm sorry. I wish I could make those painful memories disappear."

"Don't be silly. The pain I felt on that bus trip home was powerful motivation to change my life for the better. And did I ever! I've packed lifetimes of learning into my brain. I've done a few things I'm proud of. I've made a boatload of money. I live awash in beauty. I'm one lucky bastard." He beckoned Beatrice to snuggle beside him, which she did.

"You're never down for long, are you? I envy your resilience."

"Stick with me, kid," Tanner laughed. "And right now I've more reasons than usual to be in good spirits. For the first time in months, I feel well and strong. It's a beautiful spring day. And I have you at my side." He stroked her shoulder.

"Damn, I almost forgot!" she said, easing out of his embrace and reaching across the sleeping Addie for her tote bag. "I've been keeping something for months now. When I heard there was a slight chance you might be at Evie's wedding, I brought it along, just in case." From the bag, she produced a small, velvet-covered box.

Tanner snapped his head back then chuckled, "Shouldn't I be the one giving the ring?"

"Just open it, smartass," she ordered, plopping the box into his lap. She nervously scanned his face as he picked it up.

"What the…?" he murmured as he extracted a polished triangular stone, affixed to a long deerskin loop. "Jesus, it's fossil coral! And what a specimen! Where'd you get it?"

"By my creek. I found it last fall during a dog-walk. And instantly thought of you. That light-blue color. Exactly like your eyes. So I had a jeweler polish it, drill a hole in it. He suggested the leather. I hesitated. I've rarely seen you wear jewelry. But if you don't like it around your neck, you could tuck it in your pocket or use it as a keychain fob. I thought of it as a touchstone. A little piece of West Virginia to take along on your travels.

A compass to guide your way back home. I had planned to give it to you before you left for Africa, but..."

Tanner interrupted her staccato recitation. "It's stunning." Slipping the leather loop over his head, he continued to scrutinize the stone, still in his hand. "I once had a geologist friend troop around my property to scope out likely spots for fossil coral. According to him, I have the perfect environment for *lithostrotionella*. For years I've looked. Never found anything. And now, this million-year-old gem just lands in my hands. It's a lovely gift, Beatrice."

"I'm pleased — and relieved — you like it."

"It's also unnecessary."

"After everything you've done for Clara and me? For a change, I wanted to give something to you, something meaningful."

"That's not what I meant," he said, fingering the stone. "I don't need a compass. I'll always find my way back to you."

Beatrice roughly brushed away a tear and lowered her head.

Tanner watched her thoughtfully and added, "But I do need something from you. A commitment. Or is this stone your roundabout way of giving me your pledge?"

Tears streamed down Beatrice's face when she looked up. "Oh, Tanner, I want to!" she gulped. "You don't know how much. But we're so different. Would it work? I couldn't take it if it didn't. Failing would break me. And losing you if I don't try? It might kill me. There's so much at stake. And I'm ... I'm just so..."

"Terrified?" Tanner shook his head sadly. "Don't you know I have courage enough for both of us?" With one arm, he pulled her against his chest. "Ah, *mo mhuirnin*, what will it take?"

With his free hand, he burnished the fossil coral. And sighed.

FIFTY-THREE

Homecoming

BUCK WAS PRONGING ABOUT THE FRONT PADDOCK in joyous appreciation of the warm mid-May weather. Matching him leap for leap was Dip, who had just celebrated her first birthday. Buck's mother, Reine, hummed with fretful protectiveness, urging the older geldings to tolerate her bouncing baby boy. Old Tess, Dip's mother, continued to graze. For a decade and a half, she had weathered the ups and downs of herd dynamics and knew youngsters sometimes needed to be schooled by their elders and betters. They usually ended up properly socialized adults.

From the way Vike was pinning back his long ears and raising his head every time the yearlings caromed too close, Buck and Dip would soon be schooled. Tess merely ripped at more orchard grass, although one of her long-lashed brown eyes monitored events — to be ready to dodge the volleys of spit herself.

Beatrice was also watching the unfolding drama from the safety of her deck, as she sat drinking a cup of tea. She winced when the inevitable happened. Vike sprayed a mouthful in the general direction of the offending youngsters. That was enough to chastise Dip, who pranced far away and only briefly shook her wooly gray head. Buck was too full of himself to surrender. Instead of backing off, he flattened his ears and raised his head. Unimpressed, Vike pointed his nose to the heavens, expanded his impressive chest and coaxed a fat bolus of semi-digested grass up his neck as he radiated sheer menace. Then he whipped his head forward like a timber rattler, firing one, two, three shots directly at the young upstart's nose. The contest was over without Buck ever deploying his own biological weapon.

Beatrice thought of someone who shared Vike's gravitas and self-confidence, someone else who could be menacing. But, oh, what an ally Tanner could be in a harsh world. A strong partner for her. A sturdy protector for Clara.

Is it possible?

The interplay in the pasture got her thinking about relationships. They didn't have to be devastating. Although llamas were perfectly capable of doing damage to one another, especially with the help of the male's Transylvanian fighting teeth, confrontations rarely got beyond the spitting stage. The victor experienced a measure of grief himself, of course. It was hardly pleasant for Vike to smell and taste the contents of one of his stomachs. Not surprising, llamas threatened fire a lot more often than they actually fired. Having shot off his missiles, Vike was now coughing and shaking his head with disgust. His target, however, was a living metaphor for shame, standing ostracized by his herdmates, with head lolling low, draining miserably.

While pondering the functionality of llama society, Beatrice reviewed her own recent interactions with members of the human species. She willed her thoughts away from Tanner and toward others who had come into her life in the past year or so. As a result, her farm was no longer an isolated outpost. It was now the occasional gathering ground for a happy mix of natives and outlanders.

Just yesterday, she had an unexpected visit from Vaughn. As usual, the woman didn't come empty-handed. Her coffee cake provided a delicious pretext for spending some time with a fellow transplant. As devoted as Vaughn was to Eltie, as willing as she had been to relocate to her partner's home turf, she occasionally needed to touch base with values and interests that extended beyond West Virginia. Sometimes she needed to vent about aspects of Appalachian life that still felt alien. Beatrice was a safe and welcoming sounding board.

Beatrice sipped her tea and chided herself for failing to establish any true friendship with a native West Virginian. The number of pleasant encounters, with Ben and Eltie, for example, was on the upswing, but the potential for cultural misunderstanding still loomed over every conversation. Draining her cup, Beatrice suddenly realized the flaw in her perception. Of course she had made a profound connection with a Seneca County native—with Clara.

Despite the rocky start to their relationship, despite her own self-protective attempt to keep the girl at arm's length, Beatrice had become hopelessly smitten. Clara had essentially become her daughter. Beatrice felt strongly protective of her, worried about her, exulted in her triumphs, and ached over her trials. By letting the girl in, the woman had given Clara the power to hurt her. It had been a risk well worth taking.

If I can take that risk, why not take another?

With a start, Beatrice realized why Clara just didn't seem representative of local society. It wasn't because sheer proximity to a Northern urban transplant had somehow infused the girl with come-here traits. Rather, like Beatrice, Clara was plying her own road, which would have diverged from the Seneca County norm in any event.

As Beatrice pondered this, Clara dashed up the stairs to the deck. "I think we're ready for you. Can you come down to the barn and supervise?"

The "we" referred not only to the llamas but also to Lane and Leslie. This was shearing day, when the animals would lose their heavy wool coats to prepare for the summer heat. Today was when the three teenagers would attempt to harvest at least one intact fleece to showcase for their joint project. It was ironic that the shearing, normally the first stage in fiber's journey from barn to fashion runway, would be the final stage in the youngsters' collaboration.

"You got everyone haltered?" Beatrice asked.

"Yup, and all the equipment's ready. I'll handle the shears while you keep the llamas settled down. Lane will take care of the bagging. He also volunteered to clip toenails. He's pretty good with his hands, so I think we can trust him. And Leslie will be documenting everything by taking notes and snapping photographs."

"Sounds like a well-organized plan. Let's go."

Clara nodded and walked toward the stairs. Suddenly she stopped and turned around. "This is bizarre," she said.

"What's bizarre?" Beatrice asked.

"A year ago, if you woulda told me my best friend would be a rich girl from New York City, I'da said you were crazy. If you woulda told me weird old Lane would be my next closest friend, I'da said 'no way.'"

"Those sound like positive developments, no?"

"Sure, but who'da thunk?"

"You can't always predict what's lying around the corner, in the shadows,"

Beatrice said. "And even though some nasty stuff has happened to you, you've made things turn out pretty damn shiny."

"*I've* made things turn out?" Clara sounded confused. "What do you mean?"

"Sure, you were thrust into dark situations not of your own making. But if you weren't who you are, you wouldn't have attracted such bright friends as Lane and Leslie. If you weren't who you are, you wouldn't be doing so well at your new school. And if you weren't who you are, I would have been in a world of hurt after knee surgery."

Clara looked thoughtful. After a moment, she said, "What about you?"

"What *about* me?"

"Well, a lot of unplanned stuff happened to you, too. I bet you never thought you'd be living with a teenager."

"No. But it's worked out well, hasn't it?"

"And I bet you never thought you'd have a rich boyfriend like Tanner."

"No. Truth be told, I never thought I'd be involved with another man ever again, rich or poor."

"But that's good, too, isn't it? I mean, you seem happy when he's around, right?"

Beatrice smiled and gave Clara's cheek a light pat. "It *is* good. I guess all of this proves that sometimes the surprises Fate throws at us can be serendipitous. Maybe we just need to be open to them. Easier said than done sometimes. You think?"

"Not for tough cookies like us." Clara elbowed Beatrice's side before skipping down the stairs.

"Who'da thunk?" Beatrice repeated fondly as she watched the teenager run into the barn. Her face brightened. She surveyed the healthy animals, the lush pasture, and the eager young people enlivening her Appalachian farmstead. Reflecting on all the dark detours in her life, Beatrice wondered if the long, crooked road she had traveled was finally leading her home.